AN UNOFFICIAL GRAPHIC NOVEL
FOR MINECRAFTERS

REDSTONE JUNIOR HIGH

WHEN ENDERMEN ATTACK

BOOK 4

CARA J. STEVENS

ART BY WALKER MELBY

SKY PONY PRESS
NEW YORK

Sky Pony Press books may be purchased in bulk at special discounts for sales promotion, corporate gifts, fund-raising, or educational purposes. Special editions can also be created to specifications. For details, contact the Special Sales Department, Sky Pony Press, 307 West 36th Street, 11th Floor, New York, NY 10018 or info@ skyhorsepublishing.com.

Sky Pony® is a registered trademark of Skyhorse Publishing, Inc.®, a Delaware corporation.

Minecraft® is a registered trademark of Notch Development AB.
The Minecraft game is copyright © Mojang AB.

Visit our website at www.skyponypress.com.

10 9 8 7 6 5 4 3

Library of Congress Cataloging-in- Publication Data is available on file.

Cover design by Brian Peterson
Cover and interior art by Walker Melby

Print ISBN: 978-1-5107-3798-3

Ebook ISBN: 978-1-5107-3801-0

Printed in China

Designer and Production Manager: Joshua Barnaby

REDSTONE JUNIOR HIGH

MEET THE

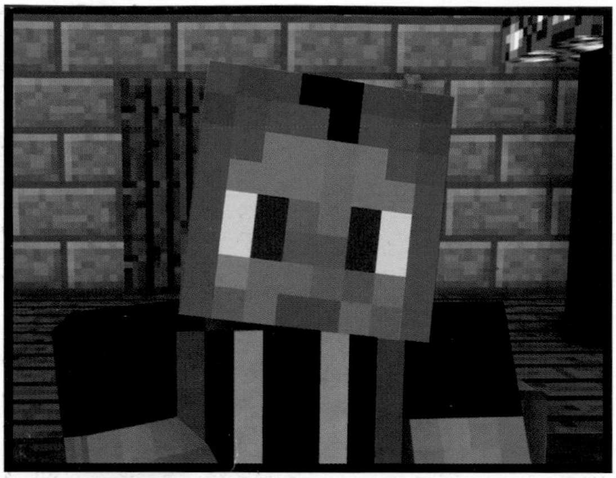

PIXEL: A girl with an unusual way with animals and other creatures.

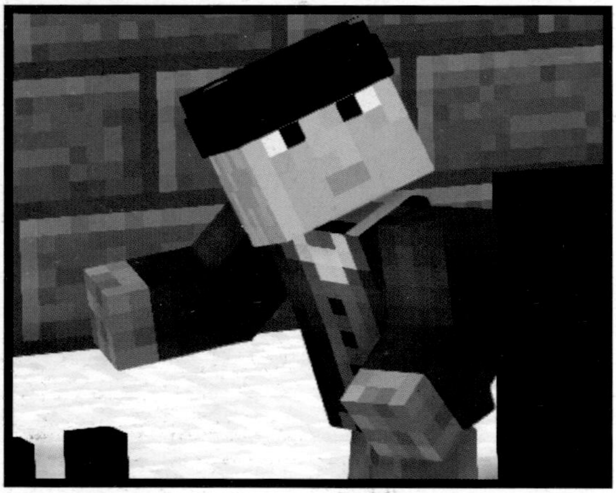

SKY: A redstone expert who is also one of Pixel's best friends at school.

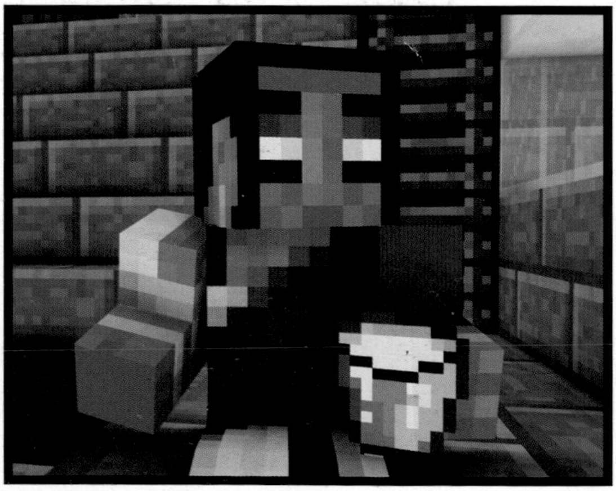

UMA: A fellow student at Redstone Junior High who can sense how people and mobs are feeling.

CHARACTERS

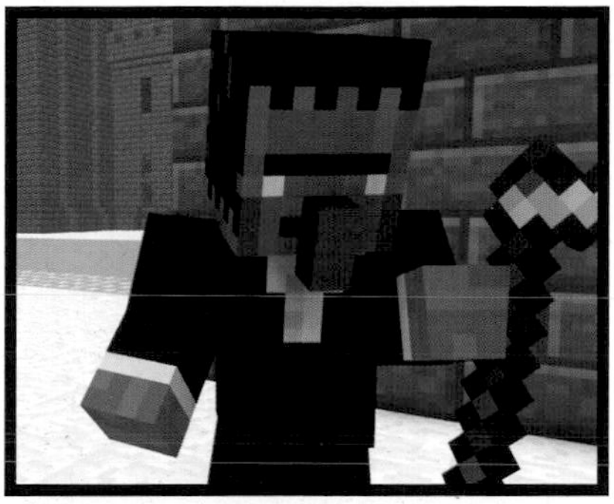

MR. Z: A teacher with a dark past.

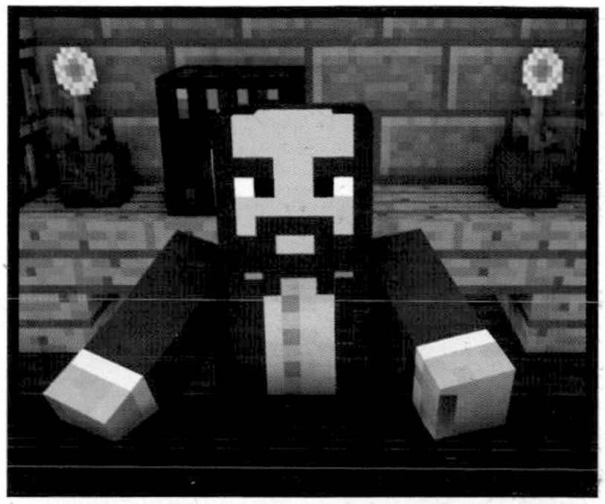

PRINCIPAL REDSTONE: The head of Redstone Junior High.

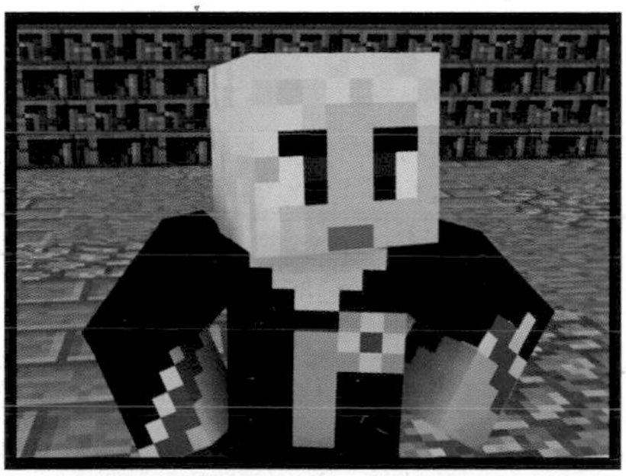

TINA: Pixel's nemesis.

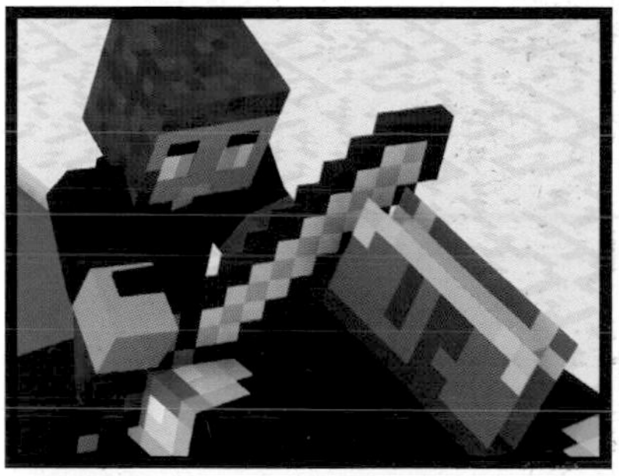

VIOLET: A student with amazing enchantment and conjuring skills.

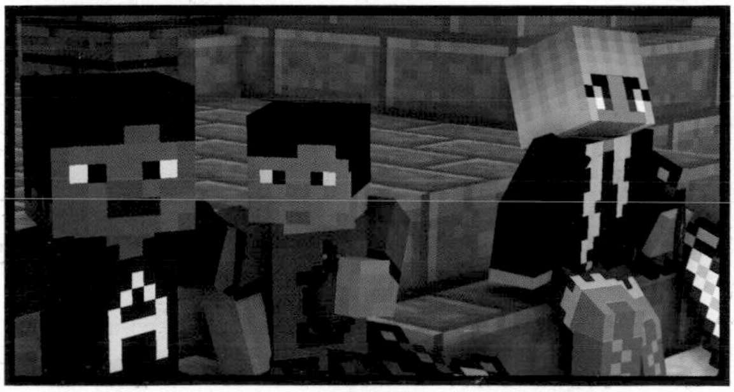
A

ALPHA, ZEB, AND DEBBIE: Tina's battle-ready friends from Combat School.

INTRODUCTION

If you have played Minecraft, then you know all about Minecraft worlds. They're made of blocks you can mine, creatures you can interact with, and lands you can visit.

Deep in the heart of one of these worlds is an extraordinary school with students who have been handpicked from across the landscape for their unique abilities.

The school is Redstone Junior High. Winter has come to Redstone Junior High, and Pixel and her friends are ready for some fun in the snow. Unfortunately, Tina has returned from Combat School, and she has brought a few battle-hungry companions with her. Tina and her gang are determined to take down Pixel and her friends, pitting her combat skills against their mystical powers. When the students resort to griefing, it turns into an all-out war.

To make matters worse, strange blocks start to appear throughout the school, making everyone, even the teachers, uneasy. It's clear that the principal knows the cause, and the kids believe his secret may be putting the kids and the entire school in danger. To discover the source of the danger and save the school, the students may have to face their most difficult challenge yet: learning to work together.

Will they figure out the source of the danger before war breaks out on campus, or will their school be taken down once and for all by an enemy so powerful, it makes other hostile mobs tremble in fear?

CHAPTER 1

TINA'S BACK

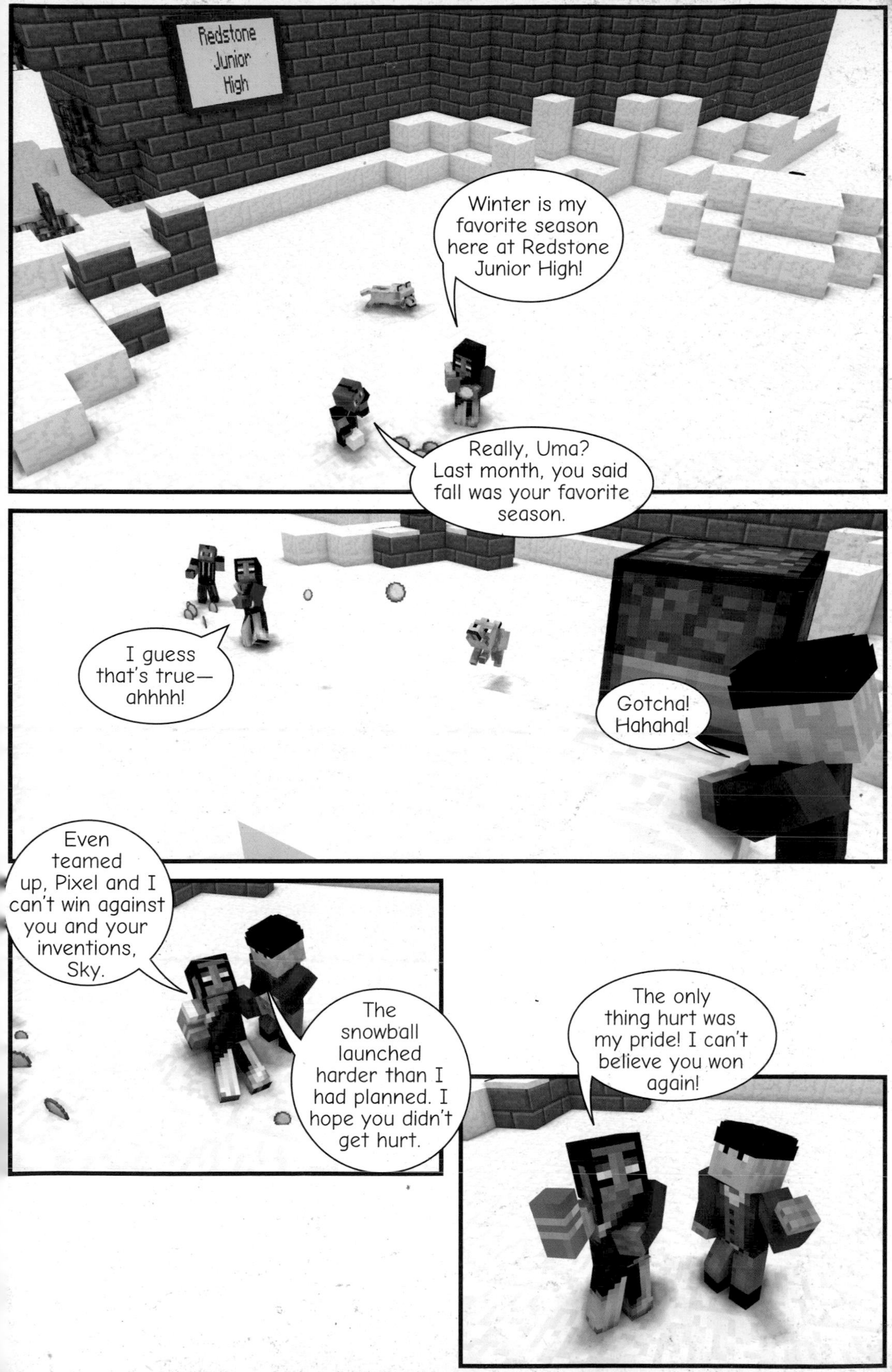
Redstone Junior High
Winter is my favorite season here at Redstone Junior High!
Really, Uma? Last month, you said fall was your favorite season.
I guess that's true—ahhhh!
Gotcha! Hahaha!
Even teamed up, Pixel and I can't win against you and your inventions, Sky.
The snowball launched harder than I had planned. I hope you didn't get hurt.
The only thing hurt was my pride! I can't believe you won again!

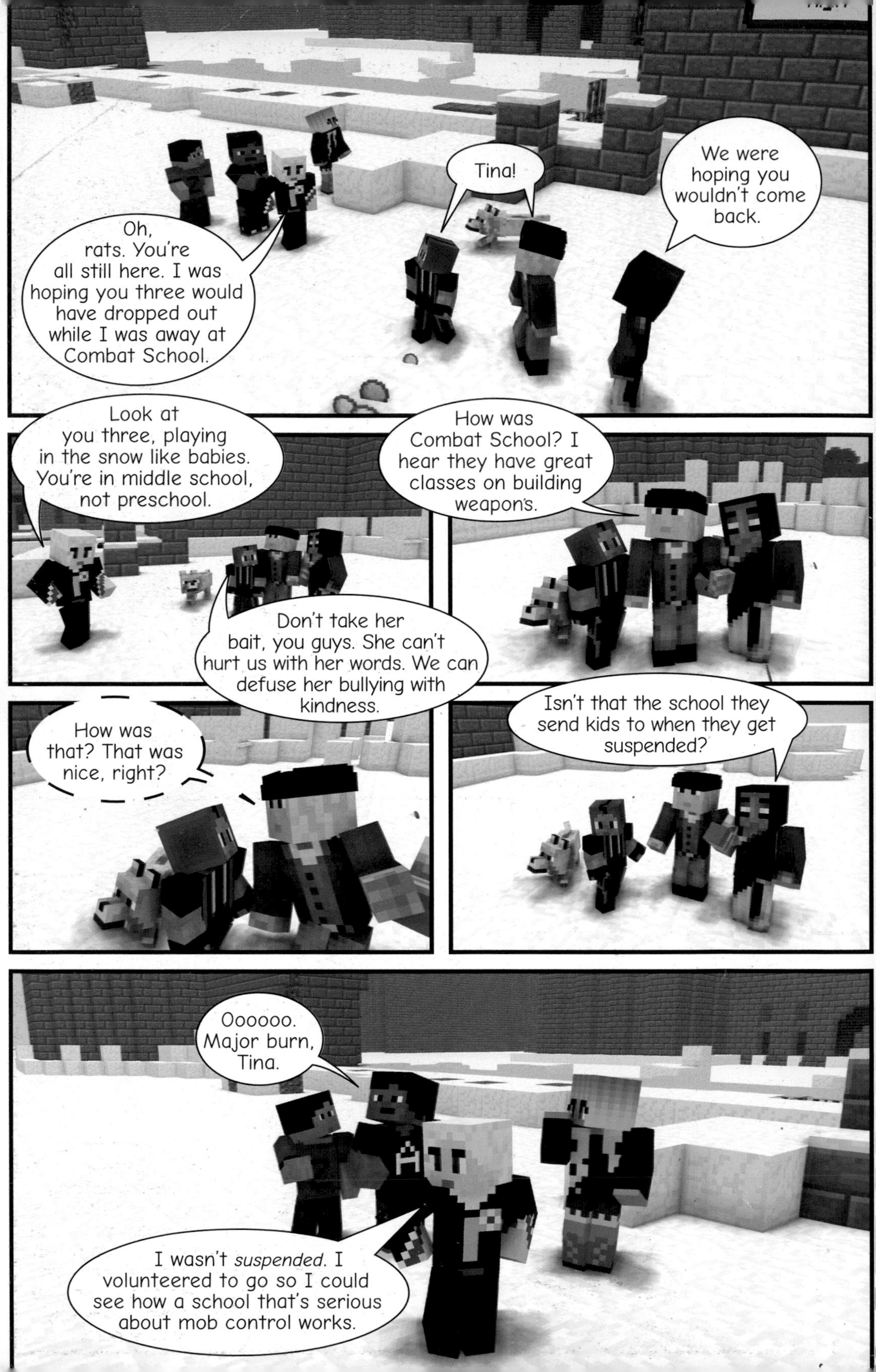
Tina!
We were hoping you wouldn't come back.
Oh, rats. You're all still here. I was hoping you three would have dropped out while I was away at Combat School.
Look at you three, playing in the snow like babies. You're in middle school, not preschool.
How was Combat School? I hear they have great classes on building weapons.
Don't take her bait, you guys. She can't hurt us with her words. We can defuse her bullying with kindness.
How was that? That was nice, right?
Isn't that the school they send kids to when they get suspended?
Oooooo. Major burn, Tina.
I wasn't *suspended*. I volunteered to go so I could see how a school that's serious about mob control works.

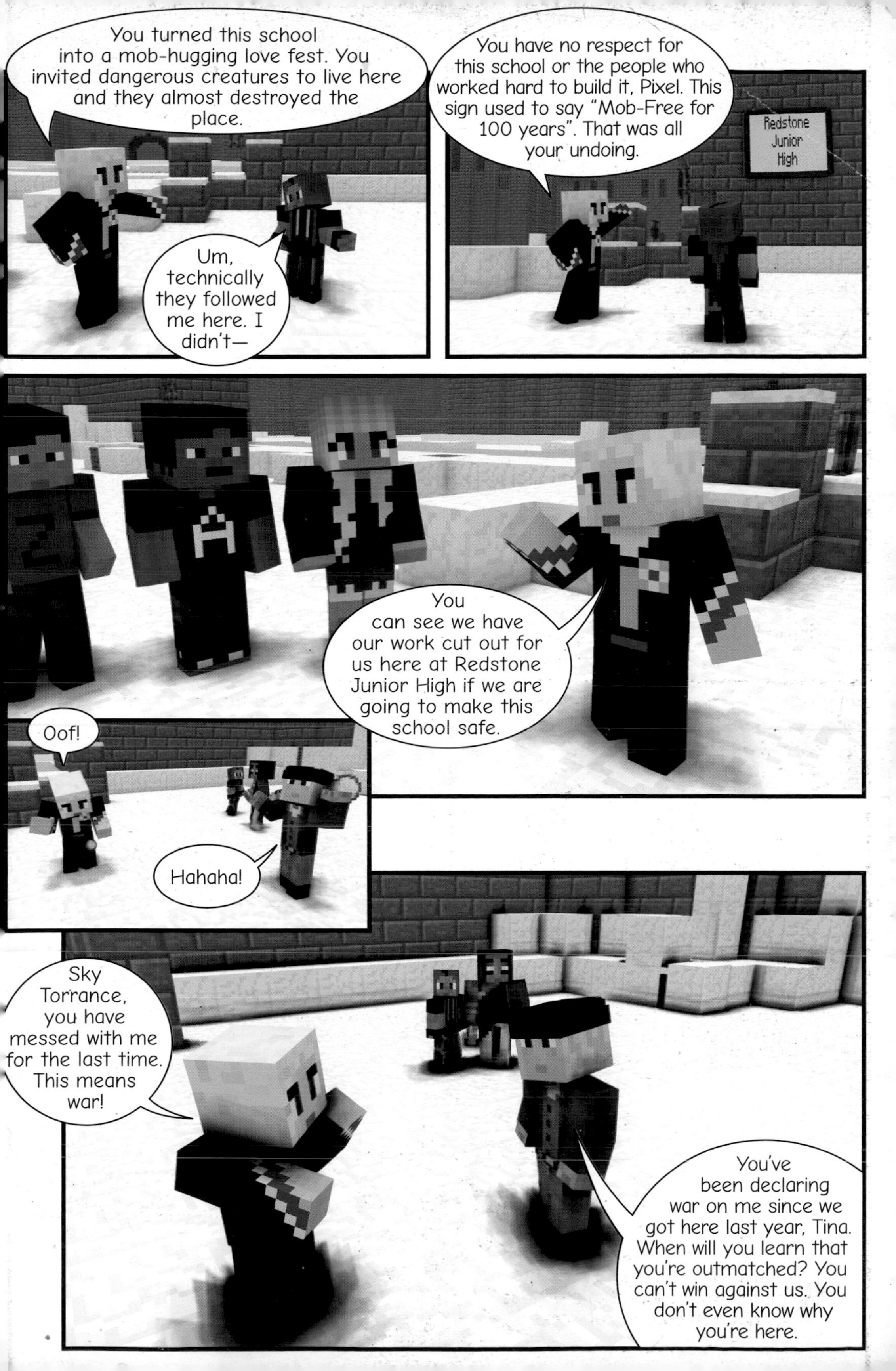
You turned this school into a mob-hugging love fest. You invited dangerous creatures to live here and they almost destroyed the place.
Um, technically they followed me here. I didn't—
You have no respect for this school or the people who worked hard to build it, Pixel. This sign used to say "Mob-Free for 100 years". That was all your undoing.
Redstone Junior High
You can see we have our work cut out for us here at Redstone Junior High if we are going to make this school safe.
Oof!
Hahaha!
Sky Torrance, you have messed with me for the last time. This means war!
You've been declaring war on me since we got here last year, Tina. When will you learn that you're outmatched? You can't win against us. You don't even know why you're here.

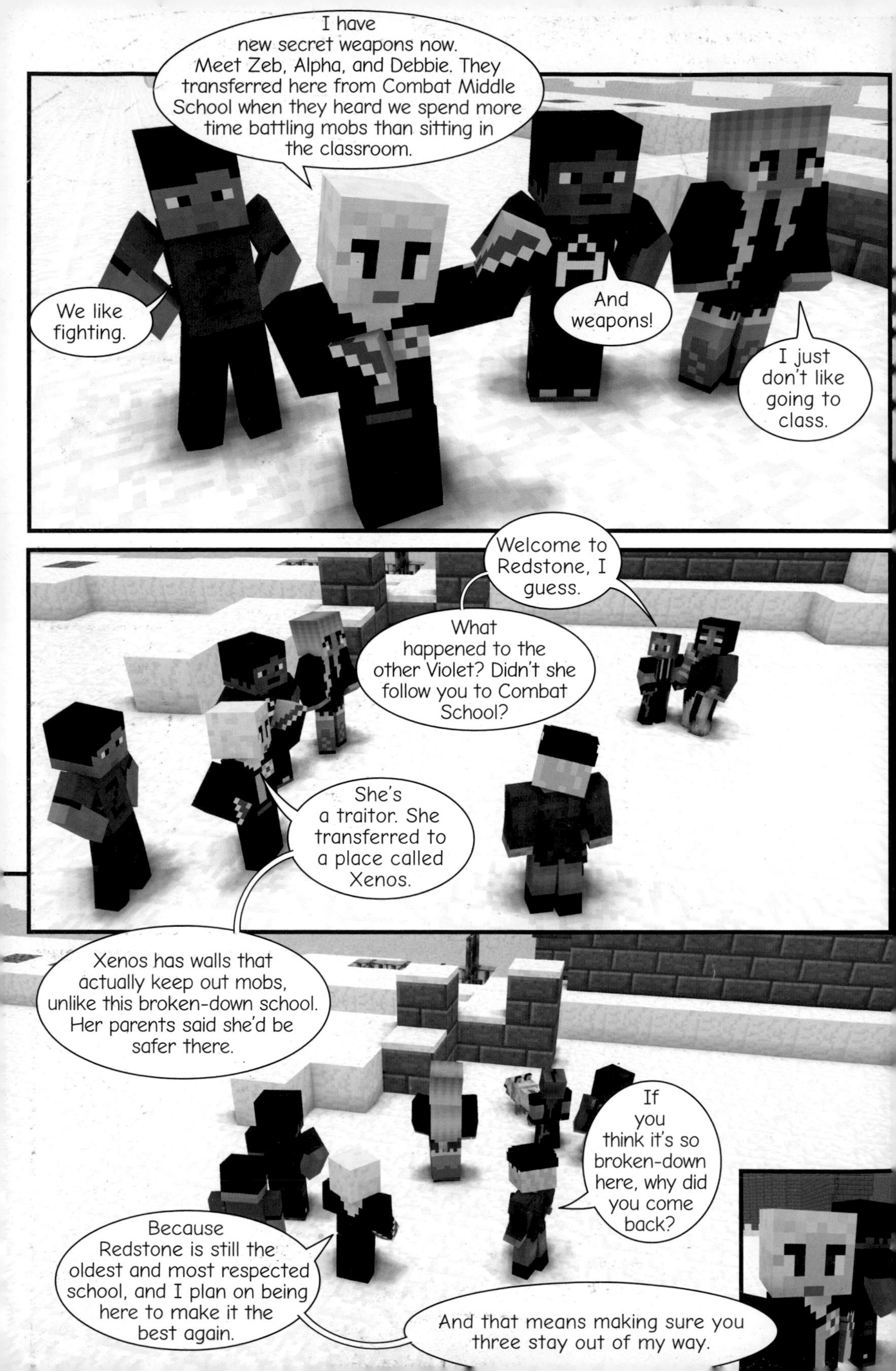
I have new secret weapons now. Meet Zeb, Alpha, and Debbie. They transferred here from Combat Middle School when they heard we spend more time battling mobs than sitting in the classroom.
We like fighting.
And weapons!
I just don't like going to class.
Welcome to Redstone, I guess.
What happened to the other Violet? Didn't she follow you to Combat School?
She's a traitor. She transferred to a place called Xenos.
Xenos has walls that actually keep out mobs, unlike this broken-down school. Her parents said she'd be safer there.
If you think it's so broken-down here, why did you come back?
Because Redstone is still the oldest and most respected school, and I plan on being here to make it the best again.
And that means making sure you three stay out of my way.

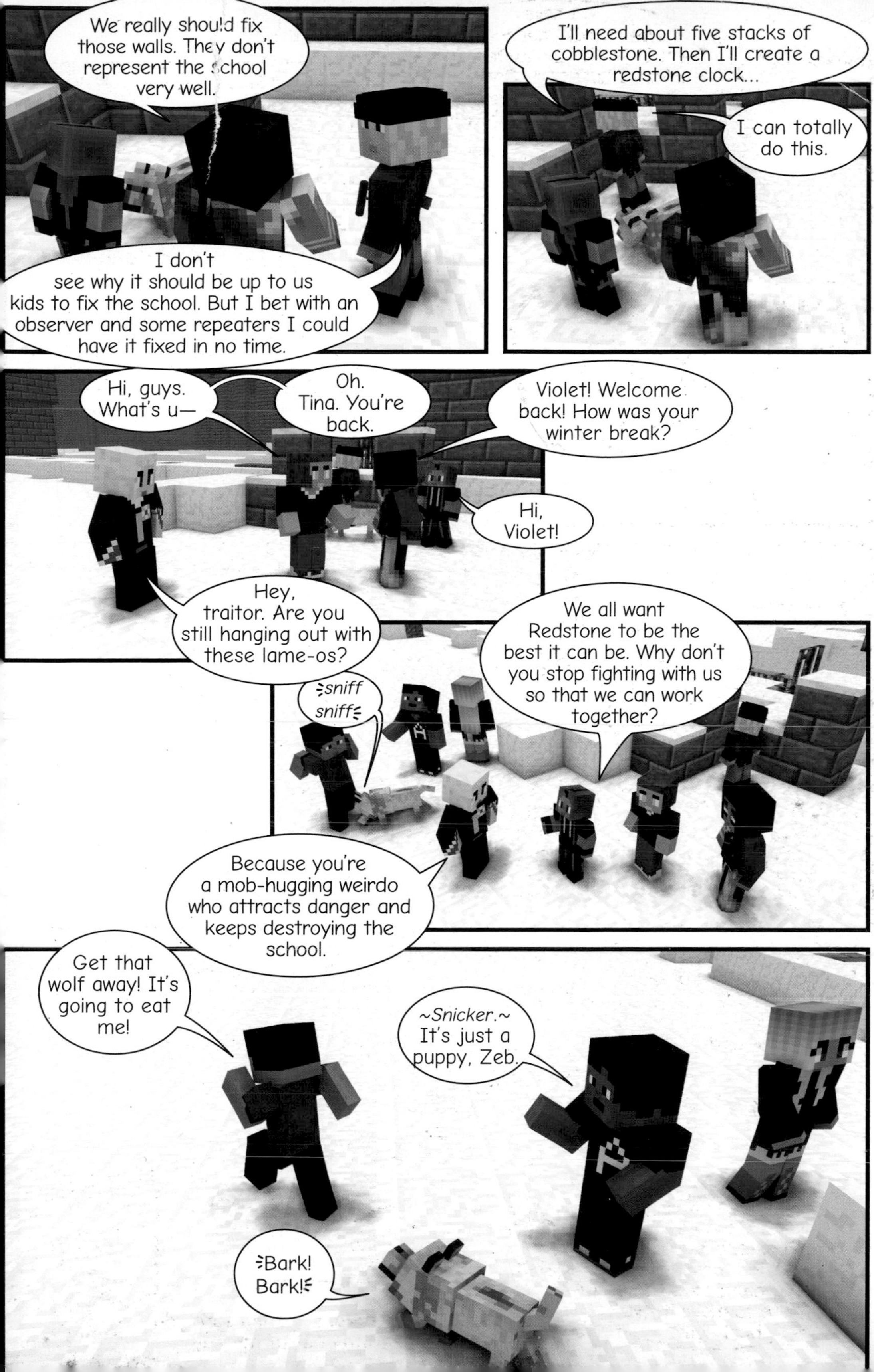
We really should fix those walls. They don't represent the school very well.
I don't see why it should be up to us kids to fix the school. But I bet with an observer and some repeaters I could have it fixed in no time.
I'll need about five stacks of cobblestone. Then I'll create a redstone clock...
I can totally do this.
Hi, guys. What's u—
Oh. Tina. You're back.
Violet! Welcome back! How was your winter break?
Hi, Violet!
Hey, traitor. Are you still hanging out with these lame-os?
We all want Redstone to be the best it can be. Why don't you stop fighting with us so that we can work together?
sniff sniff
Because you're a mob-hugging weirdo who attracts danger and keeps destroying the school.
Get that wolf away! It's going to eat me!
~Snicker.~ It's just a puppy, Zeb.
Bark! Bark!

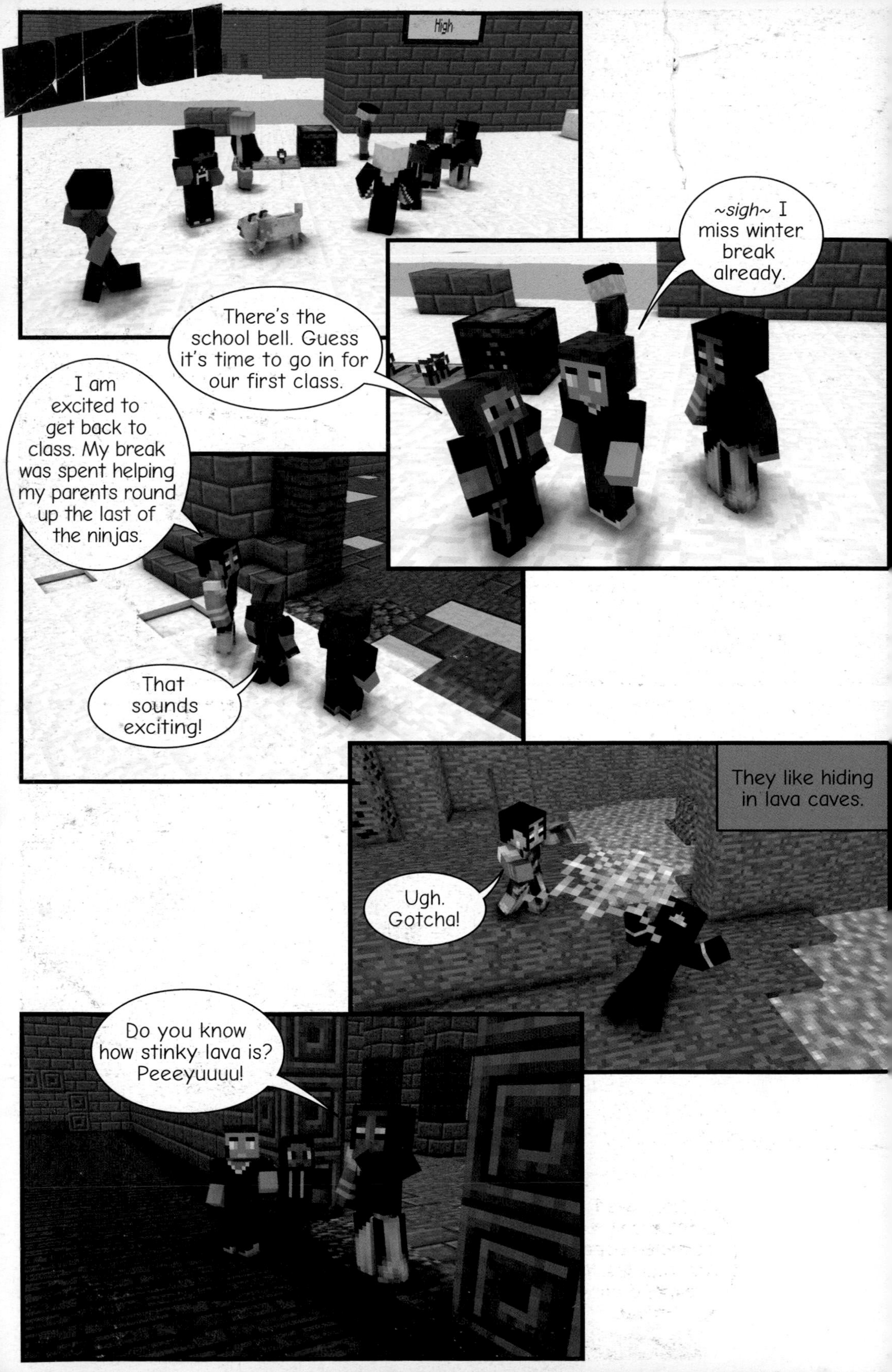
High
~sigh~ I miss winter break already.
There's the school bell. Guess it's time to go in for our first class.
I am excited to get back to class. My break was spent helping my parents round up the last of the ninjas.
That sounds exciting!
They like hiding in lava caves.
Ugh. Gotcha!
Do you know how stinky lava is? Peeeyuuuu!

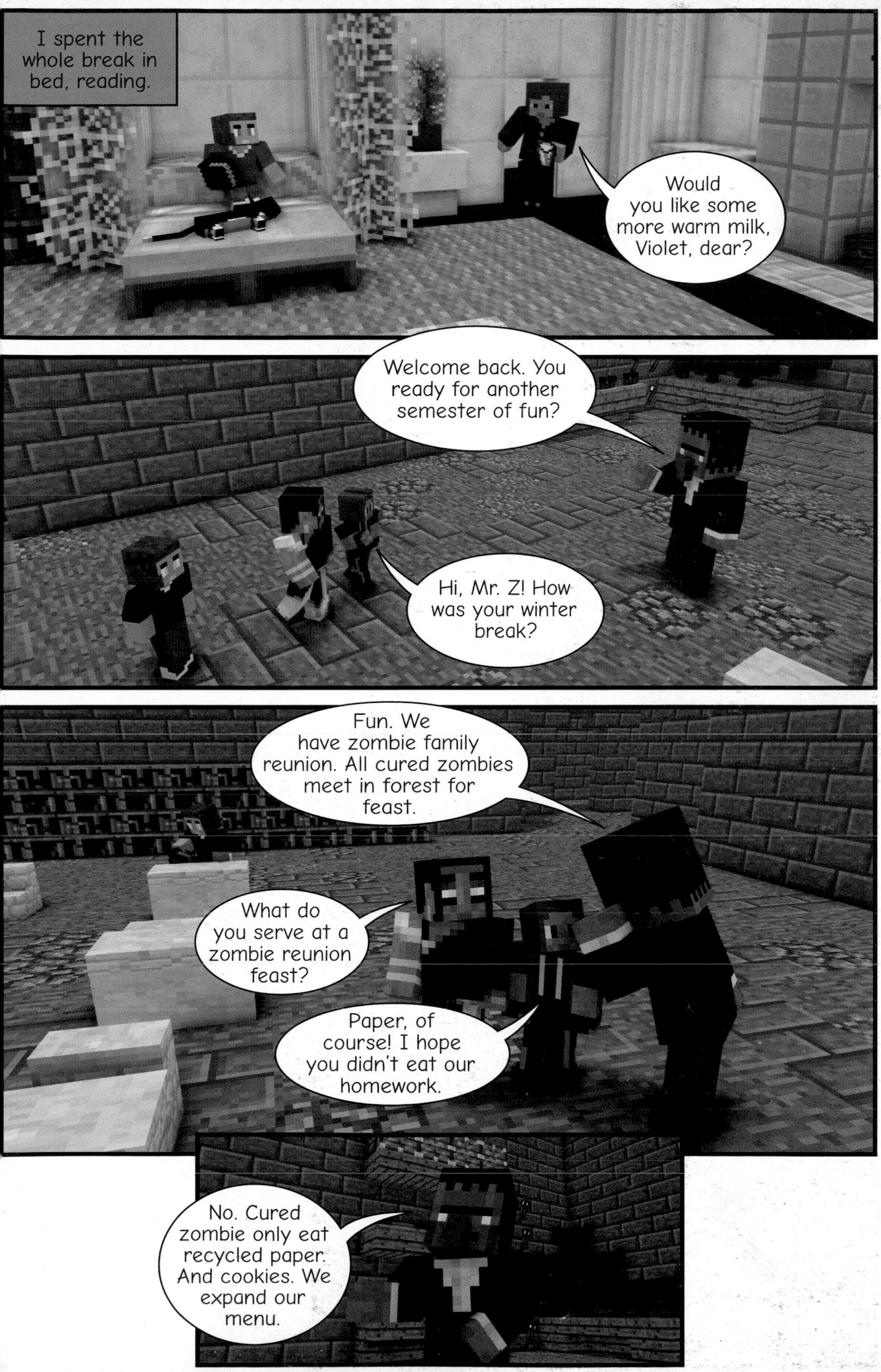

I spent the whole break in bed, reading.
Would you like some more warm milk, Violet, dear?
Welcome back. You ready for another semester of fun?
Hi, Mr. Z! How was your winter break?
Fun. We have zombie family reunion. All cured zombies meet in forest for feast.
What do you serve at a zombie reunion feast?
Paper, of course! I hope you didn't eat our homework.
No. Cured zombie only eat recycled paper. And cookies. We expand our menu.

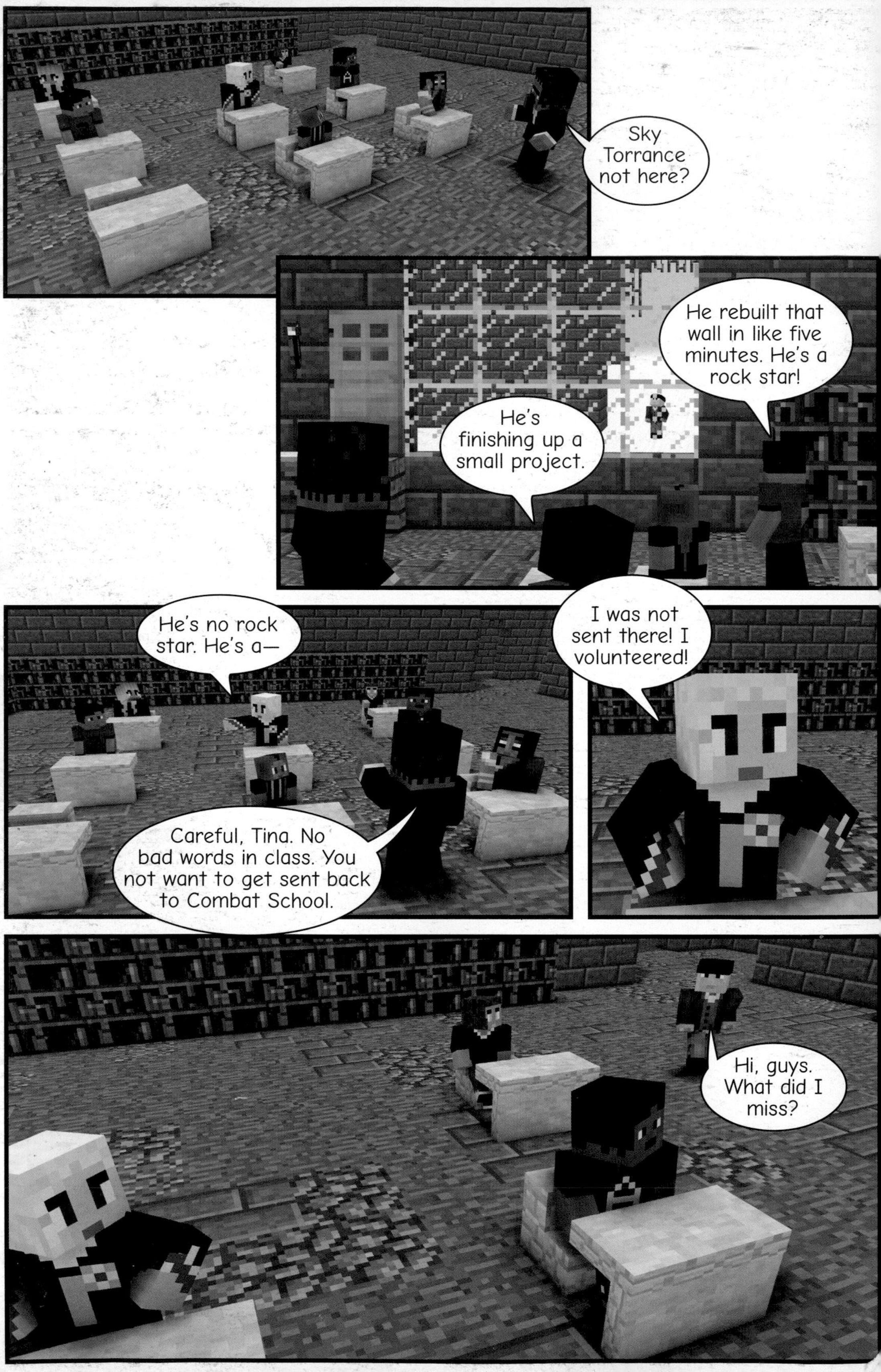
Sky Torrance not here?
He rebuilt that wall in like five minutes. He's a rock star!
He's finishing up a small project.
He's no rock star. He's a—
Careful, Tina. No bad words in class. You not want to get sent back to Combat School.
I was not sent there! I volunteered!
Hi, guys. What did I miss?

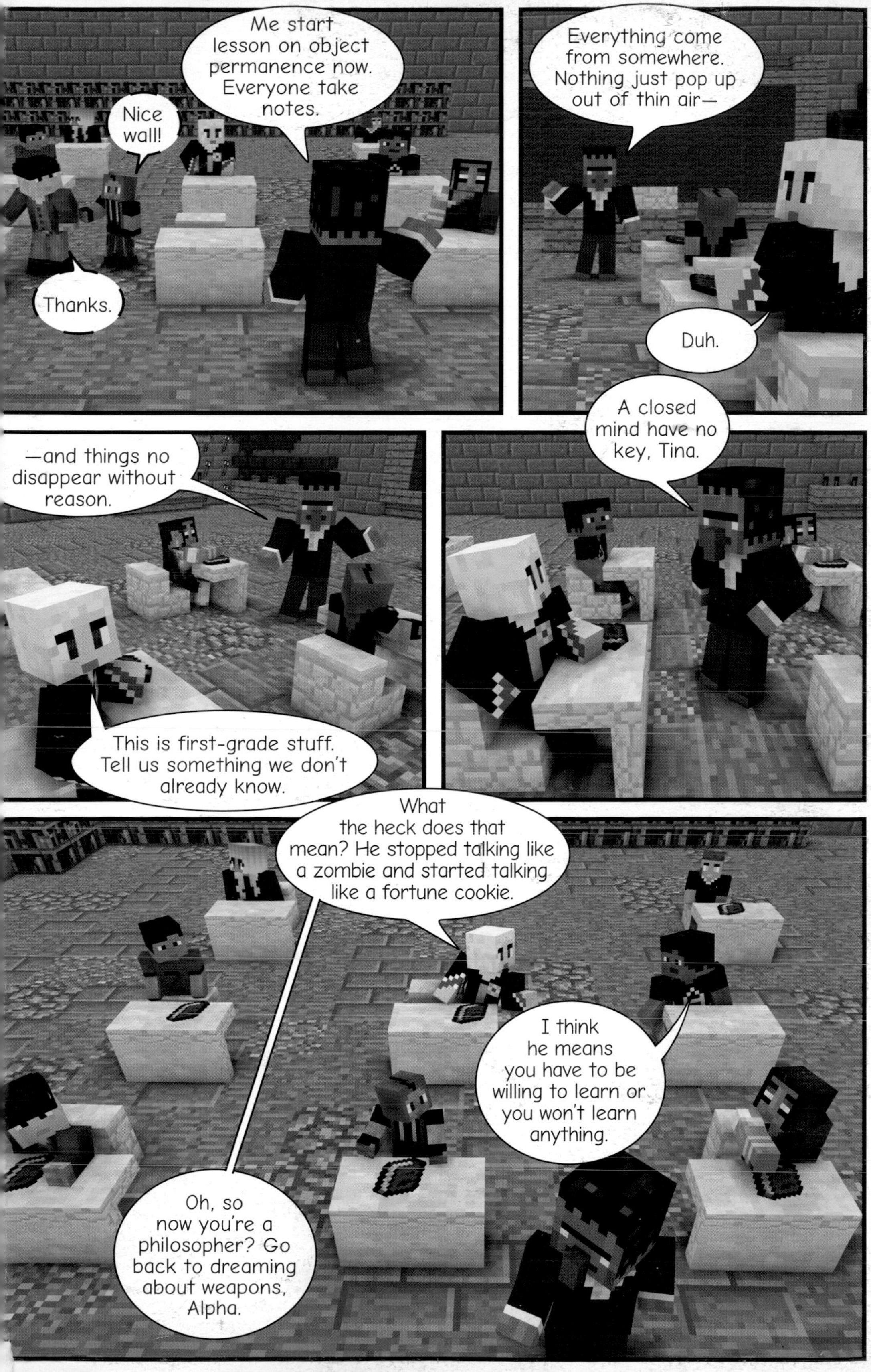
Me start lesson on object permanence now. Everyone take notes.
Nice wall!
Thanks.
Everything come from somewhere. Nothing just pop up out of thin air—
Duh.
—and things no disappear without reason.
This is first-grade stuff. Tell us something we don't already know.
A closed mind have no key, Tina.
What the heck does that mean? He stopped talking like a zombie and started talking like a fortune cookie.
I think he means you have to be willing to learn or you won't learn anything.
Oh, so now you're a philosopher? Go back to dreaming about weapons, Alpha.

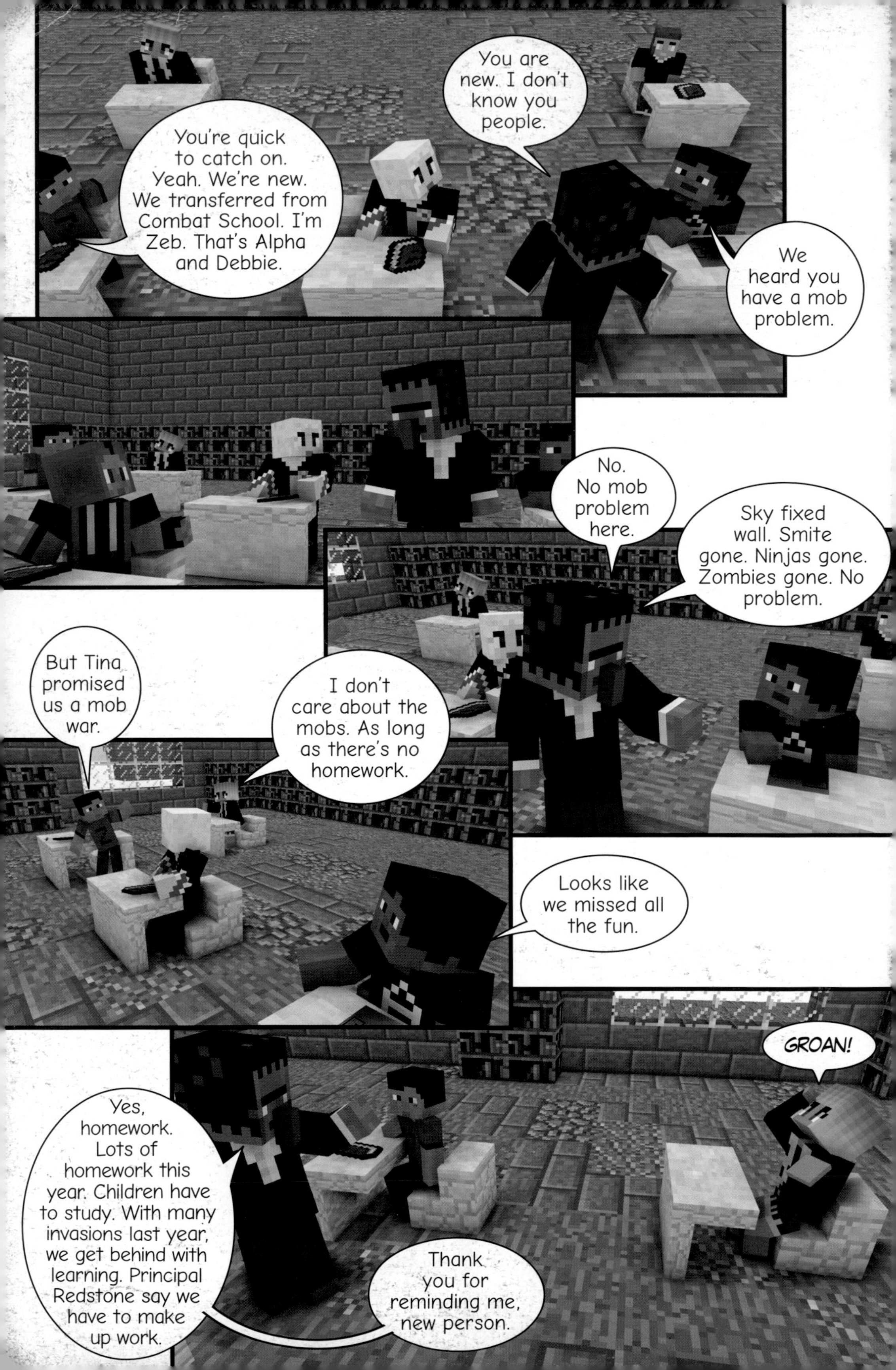
You're quick to catch on. Yeah. We're new. We transferred from Combat School. I'm Zeb. That's Alpha and Debbie.
You are new. I don't know you people.
We heard you have a mob problem.
No. No mob problem here.
Sky fixed wall. Smite gone. Ninjas gone. Zombies gone. No problem.
But Tina promised us a mob war.
I don't care about the mobs. As long as there's no homework.
Looks like we missed all the fun.
Yes, homework. Lots of homework this year. Children have to study. With many invasions last year, we get behind with learning. Principal Redstone say we have to make up work.
Thank you for reminding me, new person.
GROAN!

CHAPTER 2

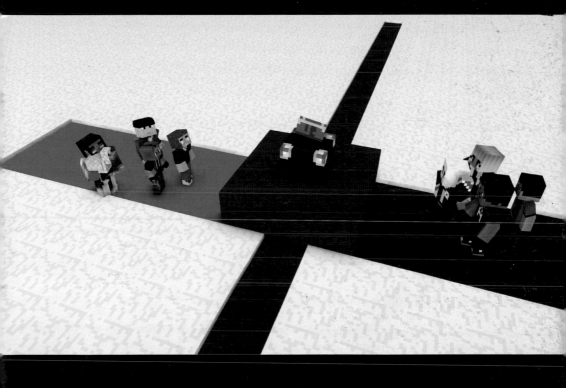

BATTLE SIEGE

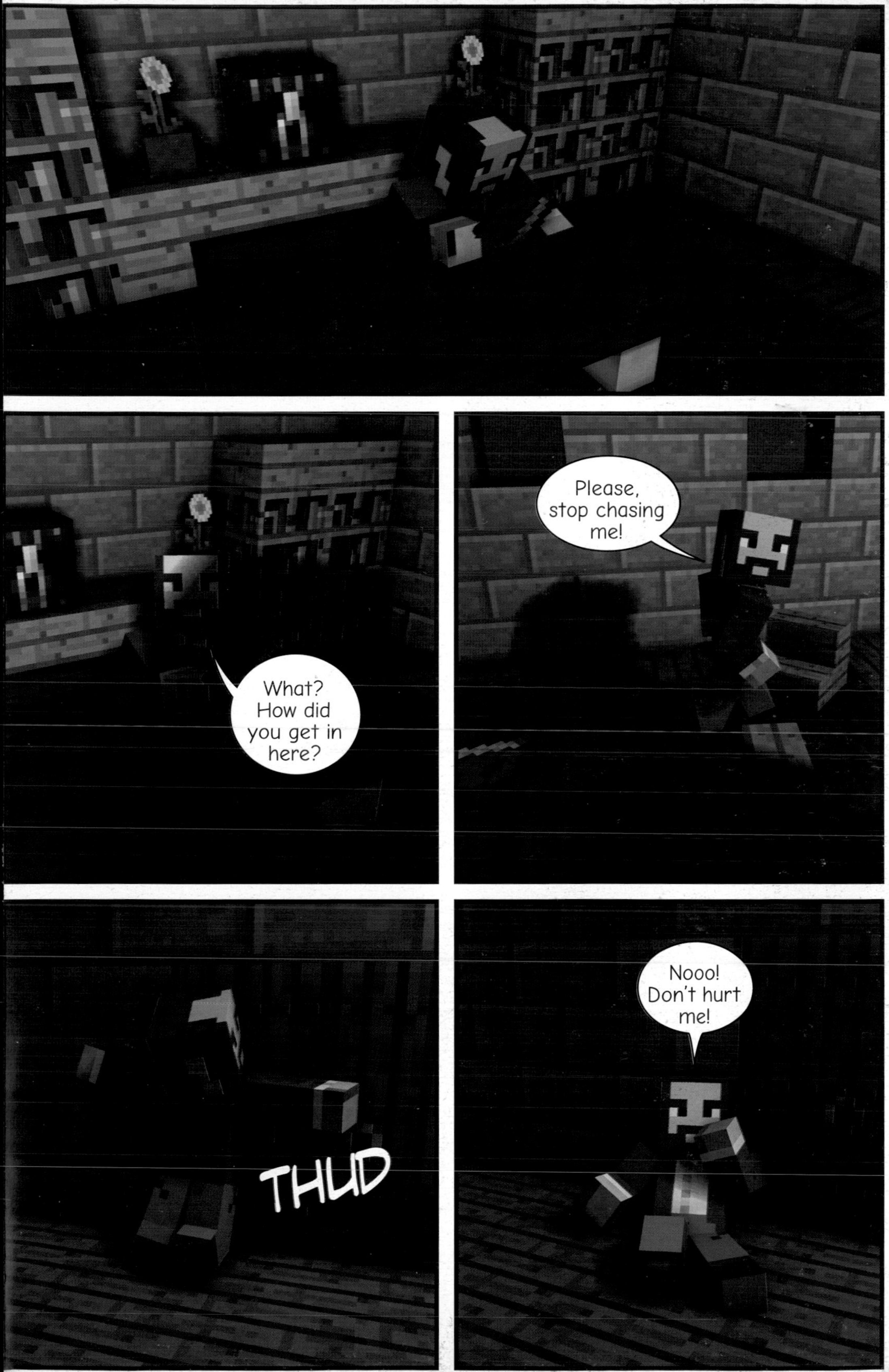
What? How did you get in here?
Please, stop chasing me!
THUD
Nooo! Don't hurt me!

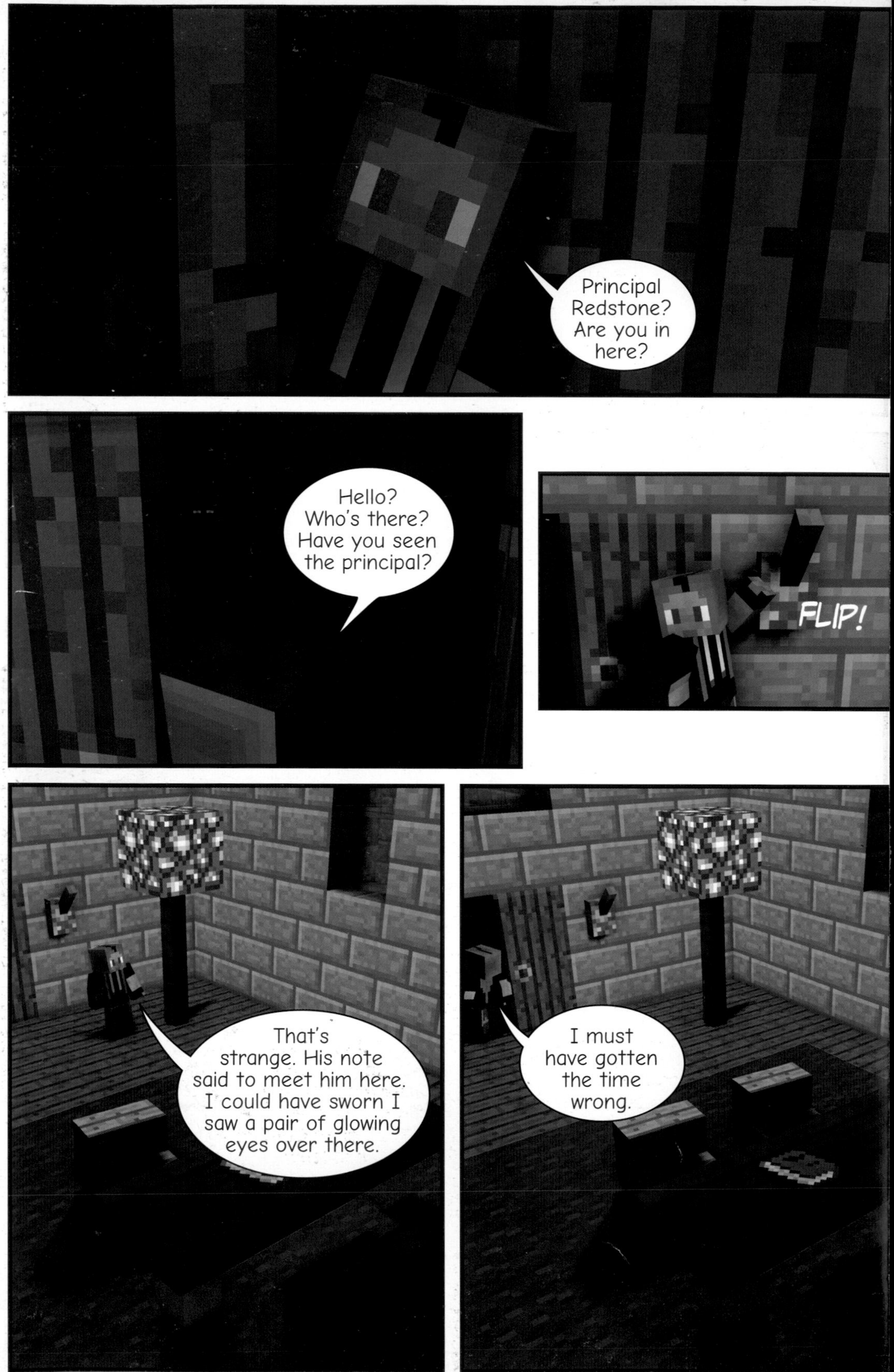
Principal Redstone? Are you in here?
Hello? Who's there? Have you seen the principal?
FLIP!
That's strange. His note said to meet him here. I could have sworn I saw a pair of glowing eyes over there.
I must have gotten the time wrong.

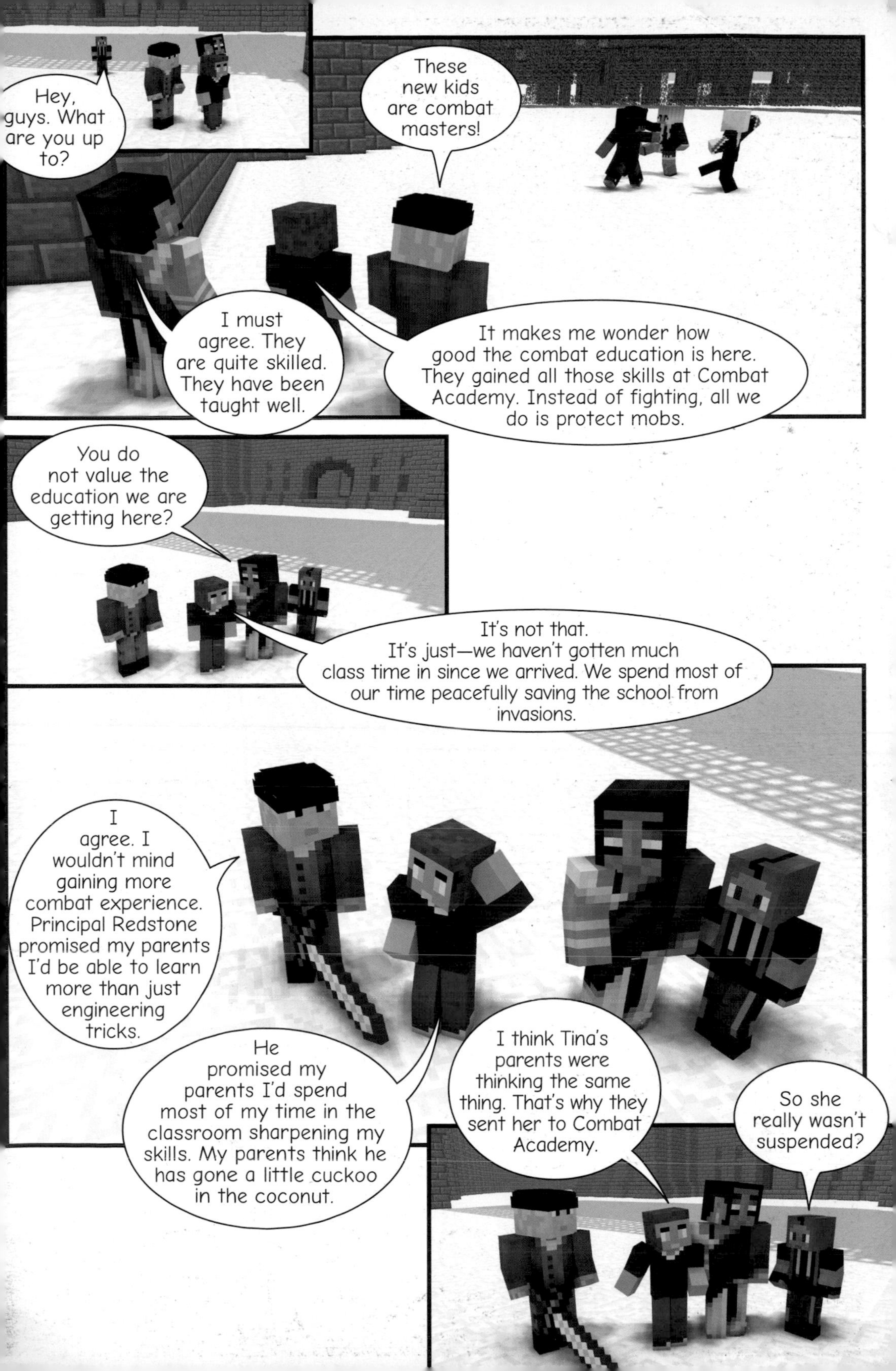
Hey, guys. What are you up to?
These new kids are combat masters!
I must agree. They are quite skilled. They have been taught well.
It makes me wonder how good the combat education is here. They gained all those skills at Combat Academy. Instead of fighting, all we do is protect mobs.
You do not value the education we are getting here?
It's not that. It's just—we haven't gotten much class time in since we arrived. We spend most of our time peacefully saving the school from invasions.
I agree. I wouldn't mind gaining more combat experience. Principal Redstone promised my parents I'd be able to learn more than just engineering tricks.
He promised my parents I'd spend most of my time in the classroom sharpening my skills. My parents think he has gone a little cuckoo in the coconut.
I think Tina's parents were thinking the same thing. That's why they sent her to Combat Academy.
So she really wasn't suspended?

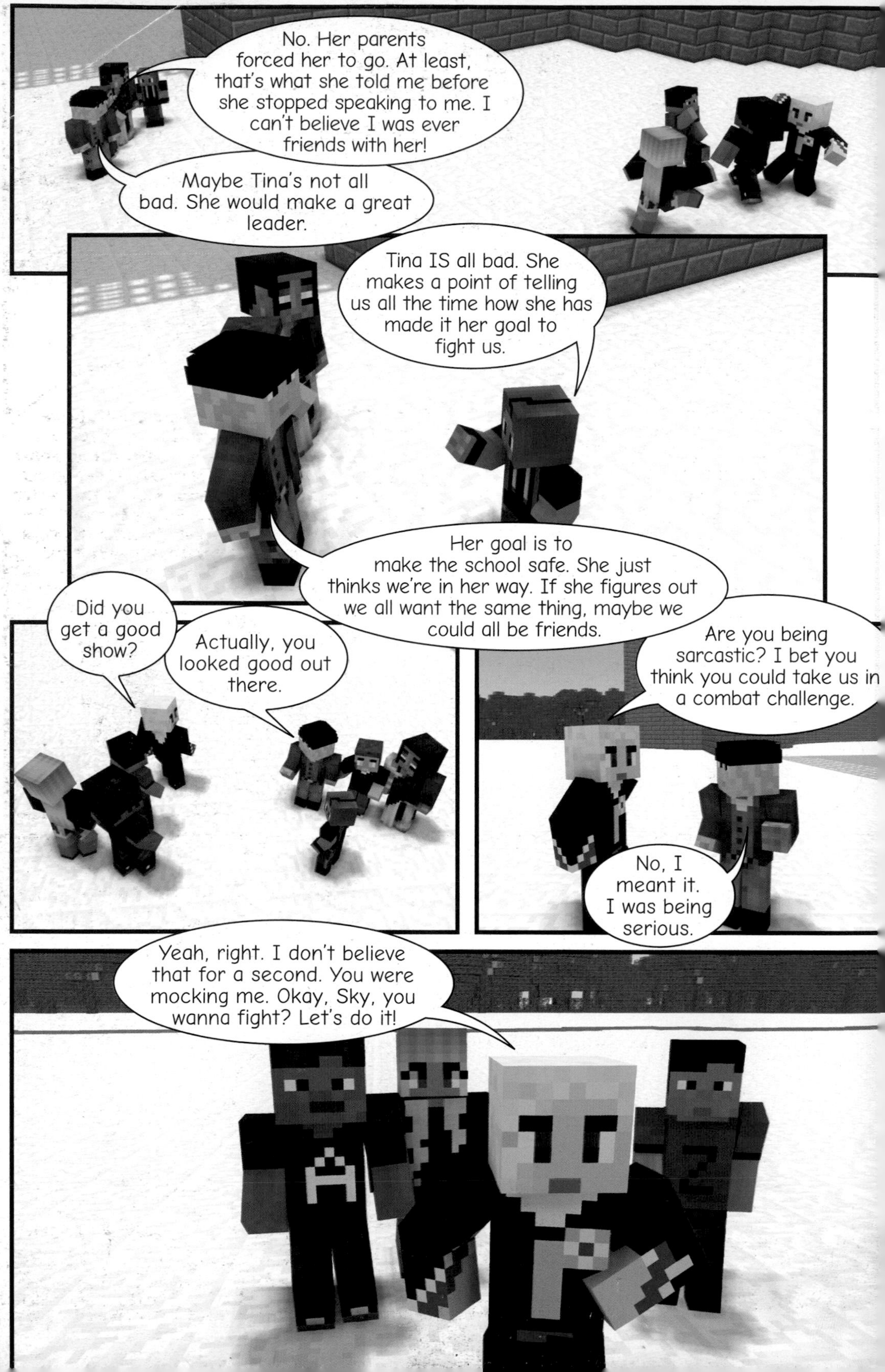
No. Her parents forced her to go. At least, that's what she told me before she stopped speaking to me. I can't believe I was ever friends with her!
Maybe Tina's not all bad. She would make a great leader.
Tina IS all bad. She makes a point of telling us all the time how she has made it her goal to fight us.
Her goal is to make the school safe. She just thinks we're in her way. If she figures out we all want the same thing, maybe we could all be friends.
Did you get a good show?
Actually, you looked good out there.
Are you being sarcastic? I bet you think you could take us in a combat challenge.
No, I meant it. I was being serious.
Yeah, right. I don't believe that for a second. You were mocking me. Okay, Sky, you wanna fight? Let's do it!

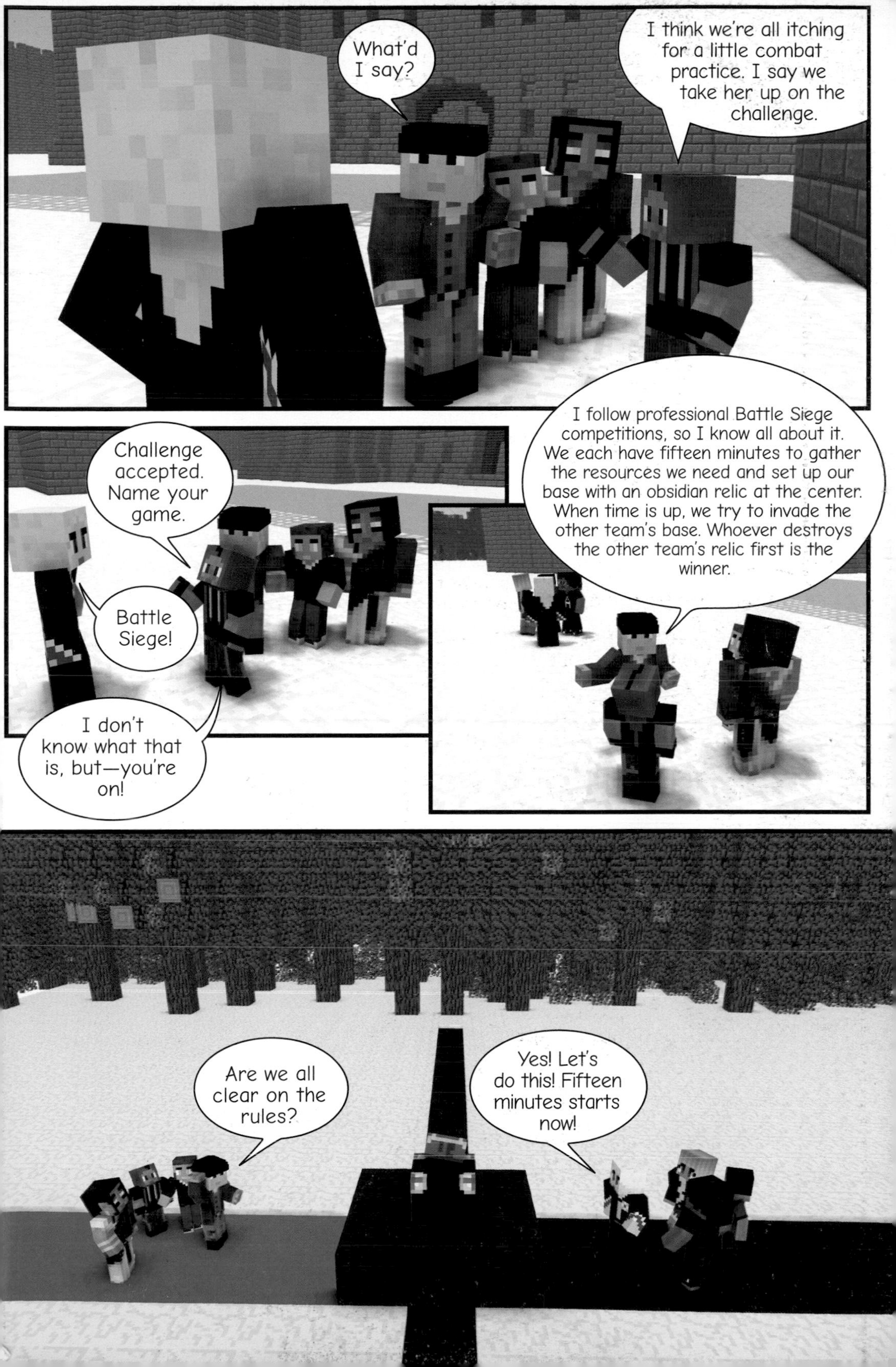
What'd I say?
I think we're all itching for a little combat practice. I say we take her up on the challenge.
Challenge accepted. Name your game.
Battle Siege!
I don't know what that is, but—you're on!
I follow professional Battle Siege competitions, so I know all about it. We each have fifteen minutes to gather the resources we need and set up our base with an obsidian relic at the center. When time is up, we try to invade the other team's base. Whoever destroys the other team's relic first is the winner.
Are we all clear on the rules?
Yes! Let's do this! Fifteen minutes starts now!

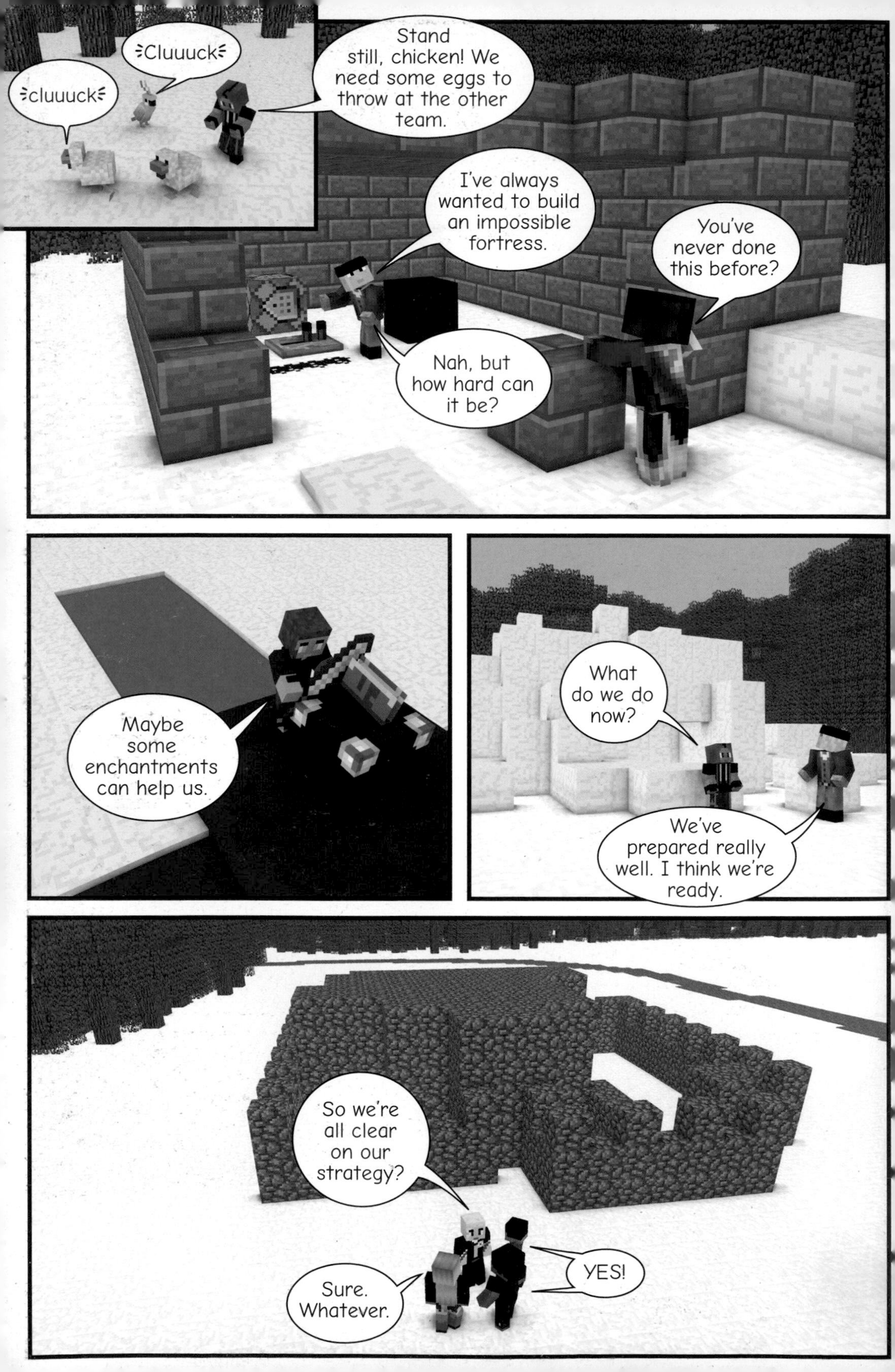

cluuuck
Cluuuck
Stand still, chicken! We need some eggs to throw at the other team.
I've always wanted to build an impossible fortress.
You've never done this before?
Nah, but how hard can it be?
Maybe some enchantments can help us.
What do we do now?
We've prepared really well. I think we're ready.
So we're all clear on our strategy?
Sure. Whatever.
YES!

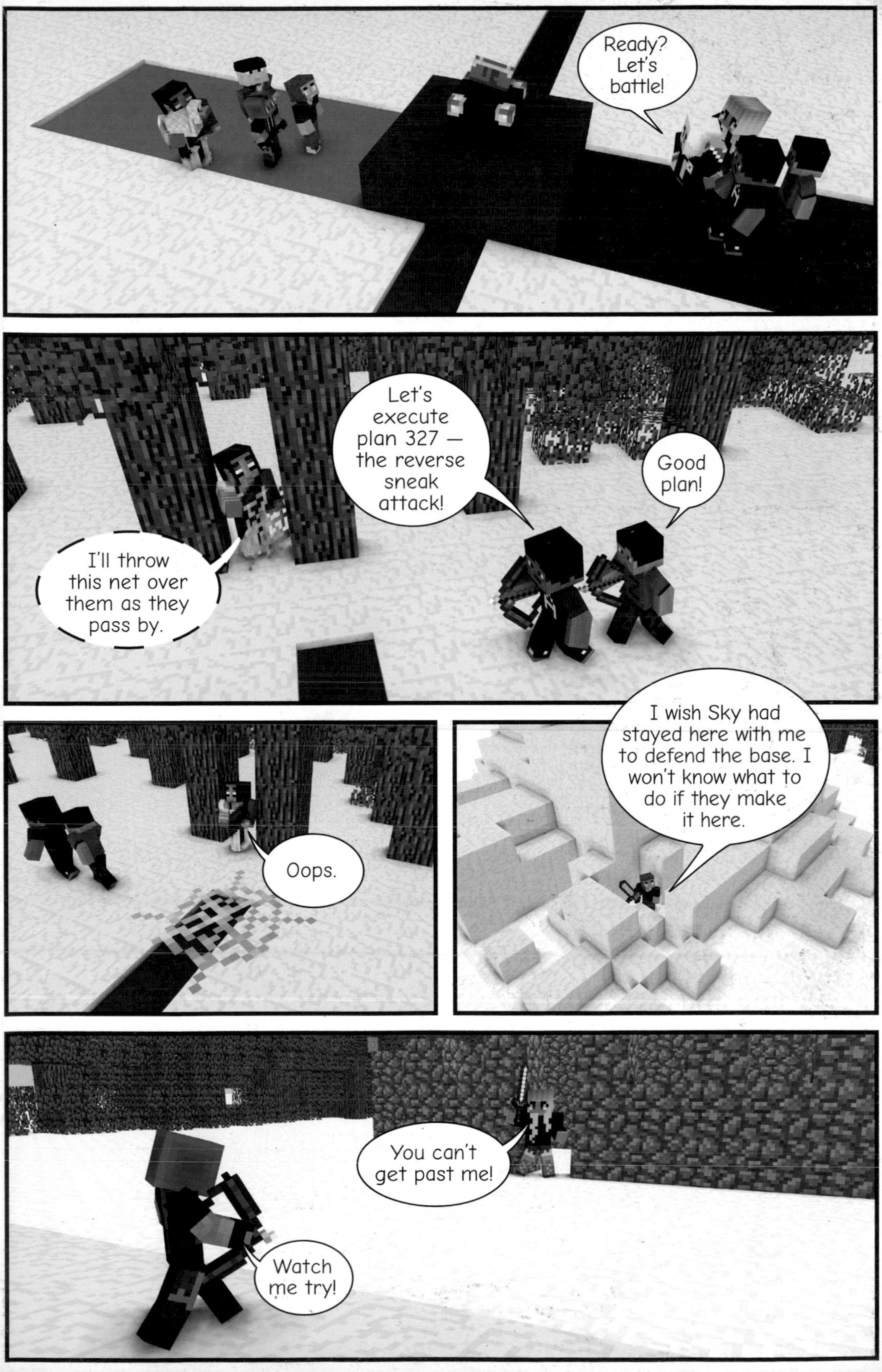

Ready? Let's battle!
Let's execute plan 327 — the reverse sneak attack!
Good plan!
I'll throw this net over them as they pass by.
Oops.
I wish Sky had stayed here with me to defend the base. I won't know what to do if they make it here.
You can't get past me!
Watch me try!

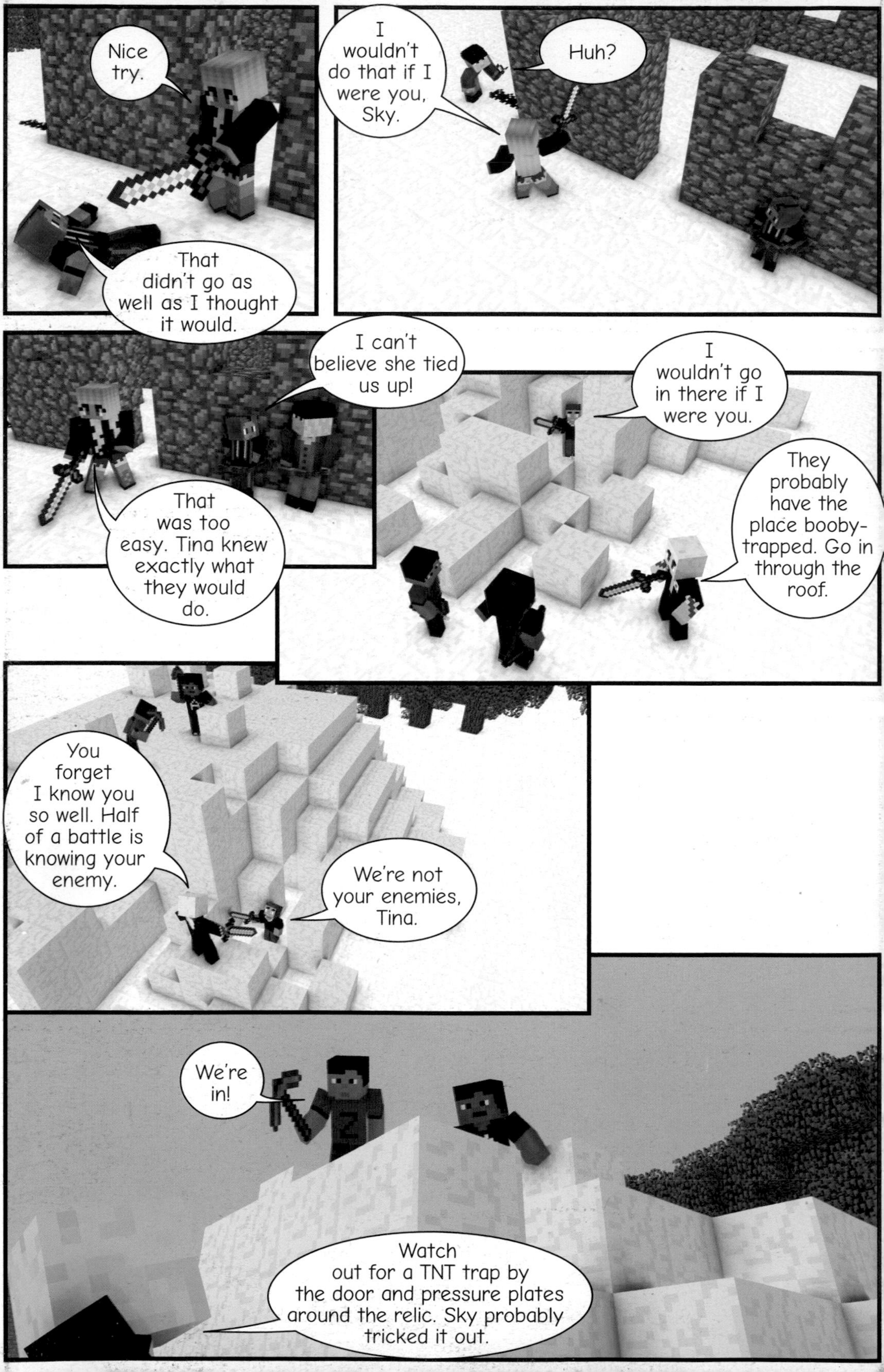

Nice try.
That didn't go as well as I thought it would.
I wouldn't do that if I were you, Sky.
Huh?
I can't believe she tied us up!
That was too easy. Tina knew exactly what they would do.
I wouldn't go in there if I were you.
They probably have the place booby-trapped. Go in through the roof.
You forget I know you so well. Half of a battle is knowing your enemy.
We're not your enemies, Tina.
We're in!
Watch out for a TNT trap by the door and pressure plates around the relic. Sky probably tricked it out.

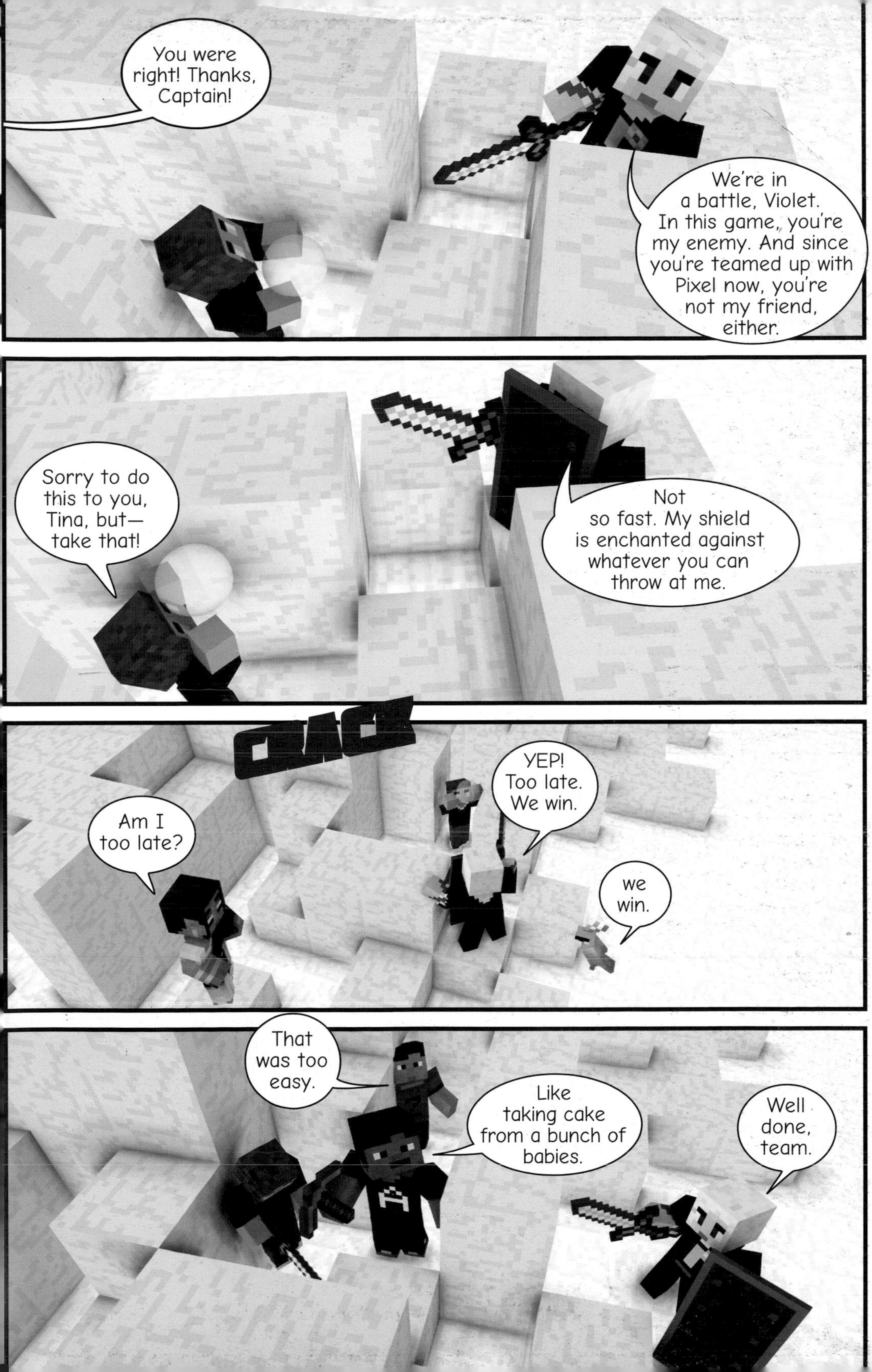
You were right! Thanks, Captain!
We're in a battle, Violet. In this game, you're my enemy. And since you're teamed up with Pixel now, you're not my friend, either.
Sorry to do this to you, Tina, but—take that!
Not so fast. My shield is enchanted against whatever you can throw at me.
CRACK
Am I too late?
YEP! Too late. We win.
we win.
That was too easy.
Like taking cake from a bunch of babies.
Well done, team.

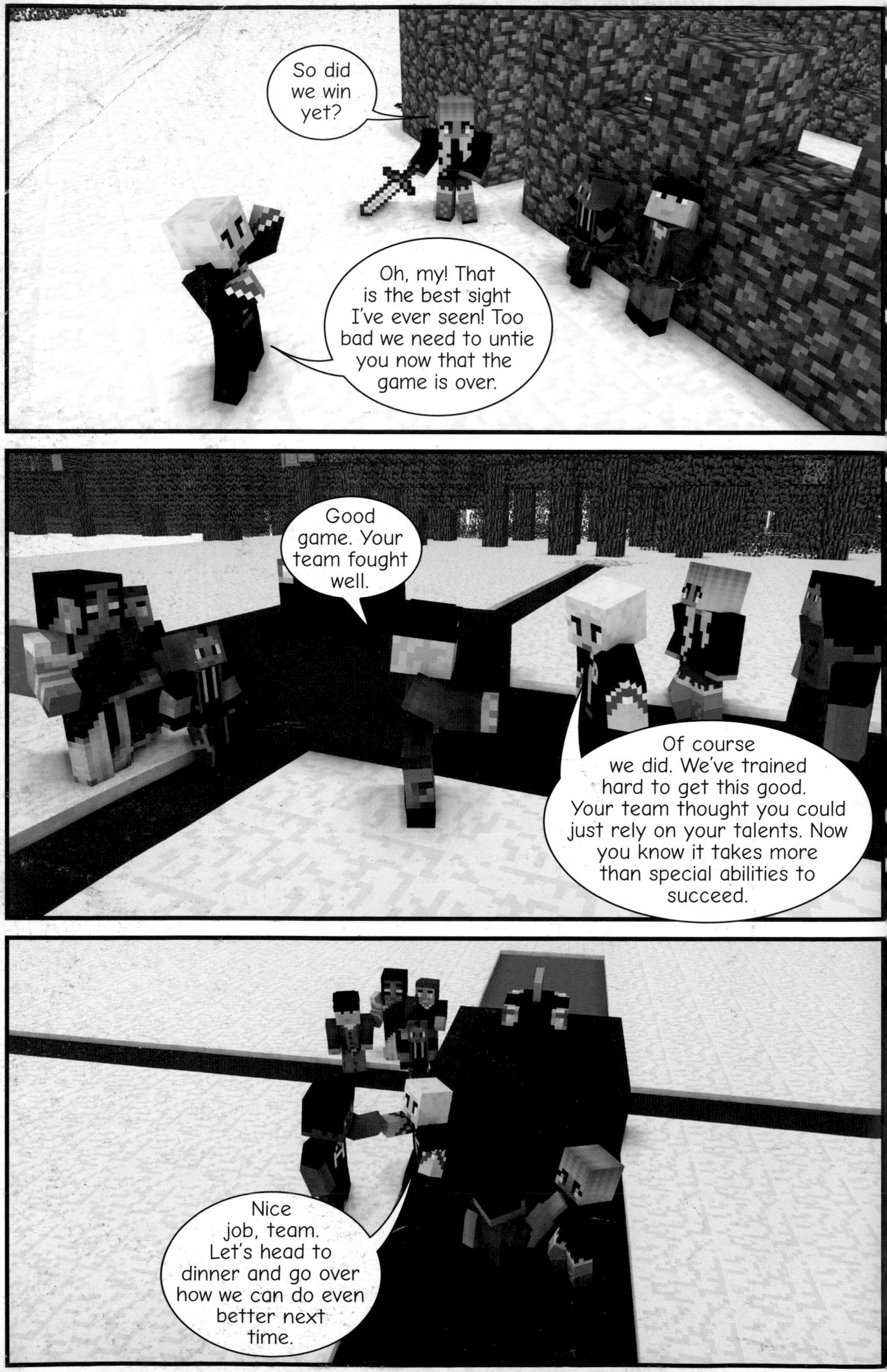
So did we win yet?
Oh, my! That is the best sight I've ever seen! Too bad we need to untie you now that the game is over.
Good game. Your team fought well.
Of course we did. We've trained hard to get this good. Your team thought you could just rely on your talents. Now you know it takes more than special abilities to succeed.
Nice job, team. Let's head to dinner and go over how we can do even better next time.

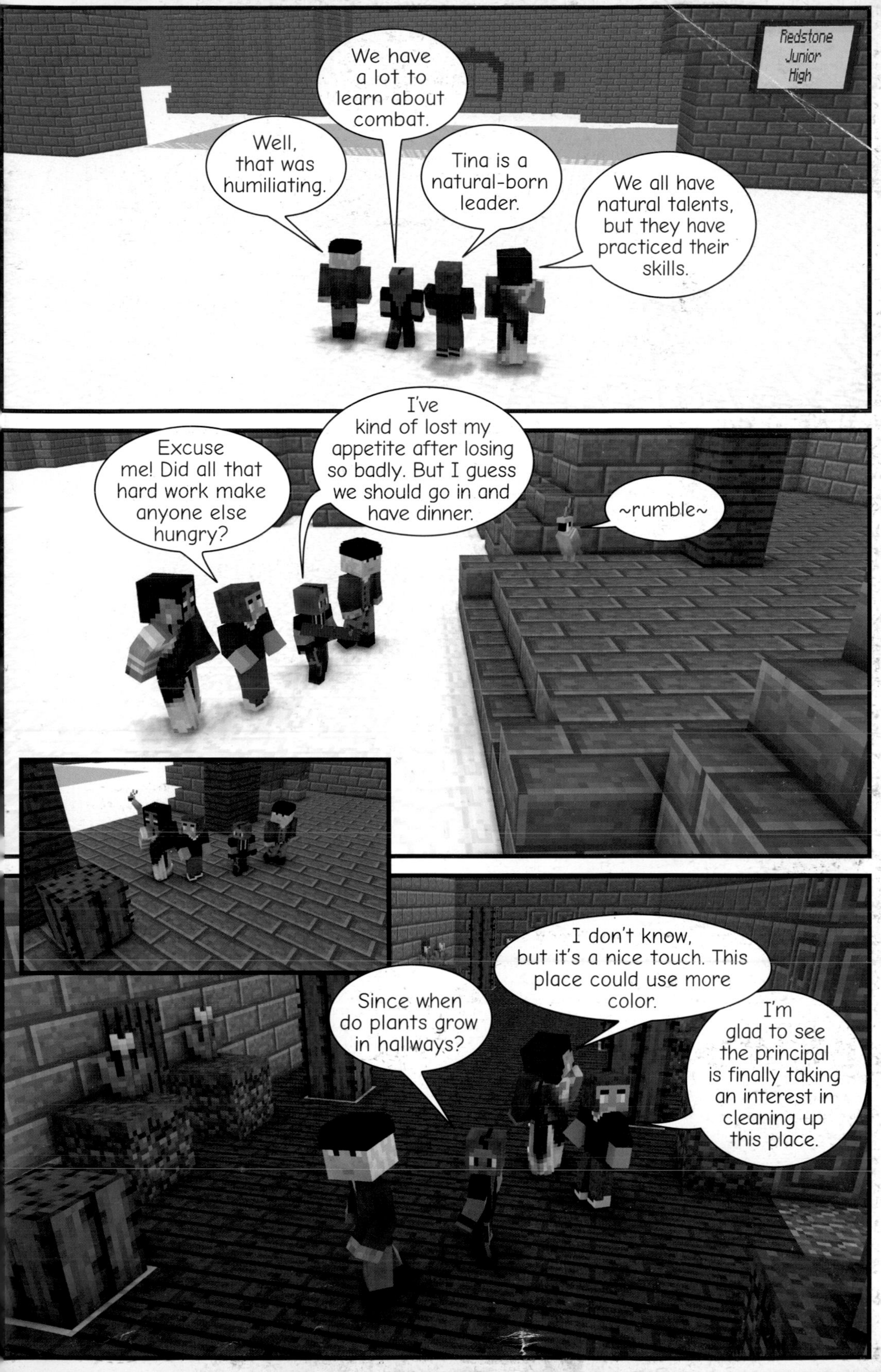
Redstone Junior High
Well, that was humiliating.
We have a lot to learn about combat.
Tina is a natural-born leader.
We all have natural talents, but they have practiced their skills.
Excuse me! Did all that hard work make anyone else hungry?
I've kind of lost my appetite after losing so badly. But I guess we should go in and have dinner.
~rumble~
Since when do plants grow in hallways?
I don't know, but it's a nice touch. This place could use more color.
I'm glad to see the principal is finally taking an interest in cleaning up this place.

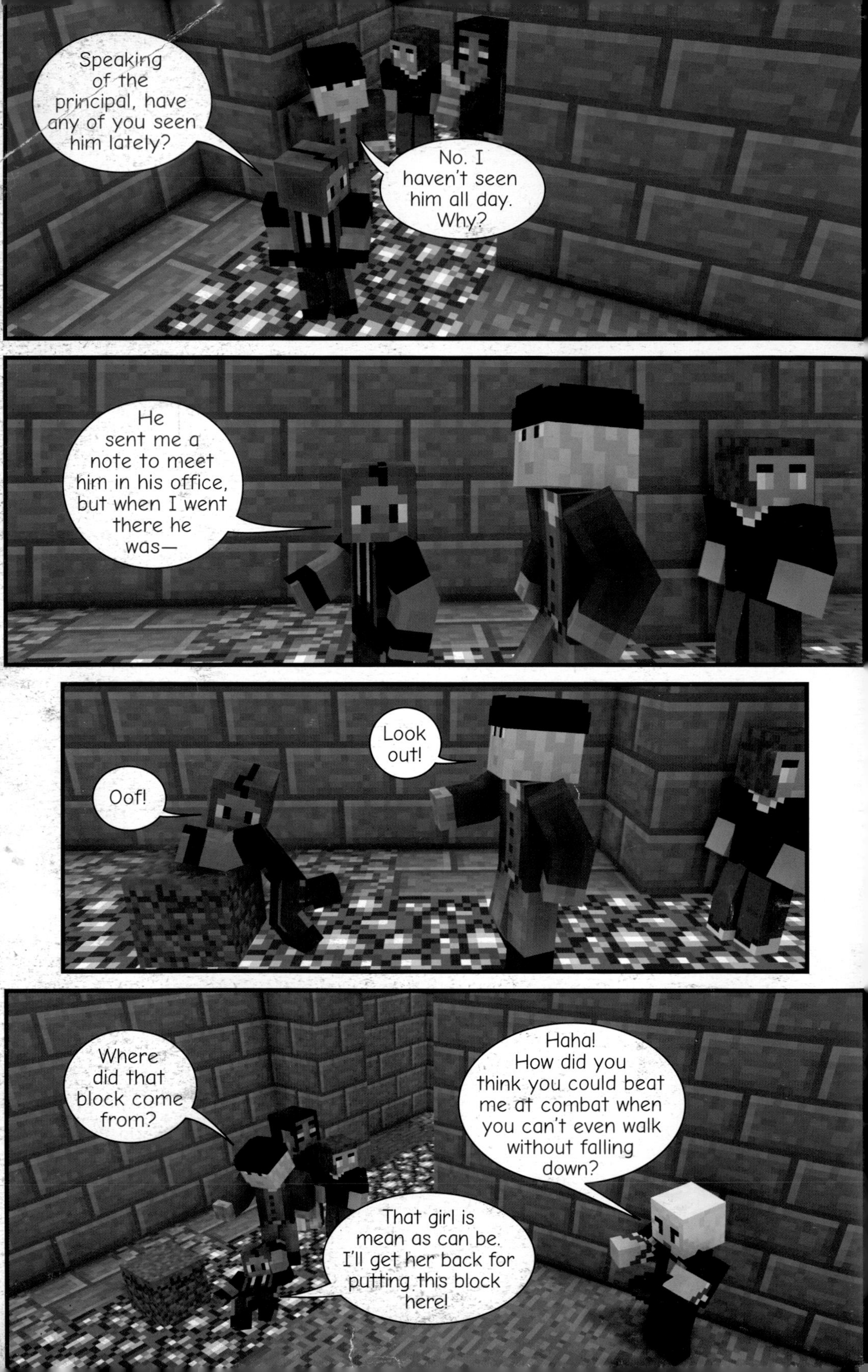
Speaking of the principal, have any of you seen him lately?
No. I haven't seen him all day. Why?
He sent me a note to meet him in his office, but when I went there he was—
Look out!
Oof!
Where did that block come from?
Haha! How did you think you could beat me at combat when you can't even walk without falling down?
That girl is mean as can be. I'll get her back for putting this block here!

CHAPTER 3

ZOMBIE OUT

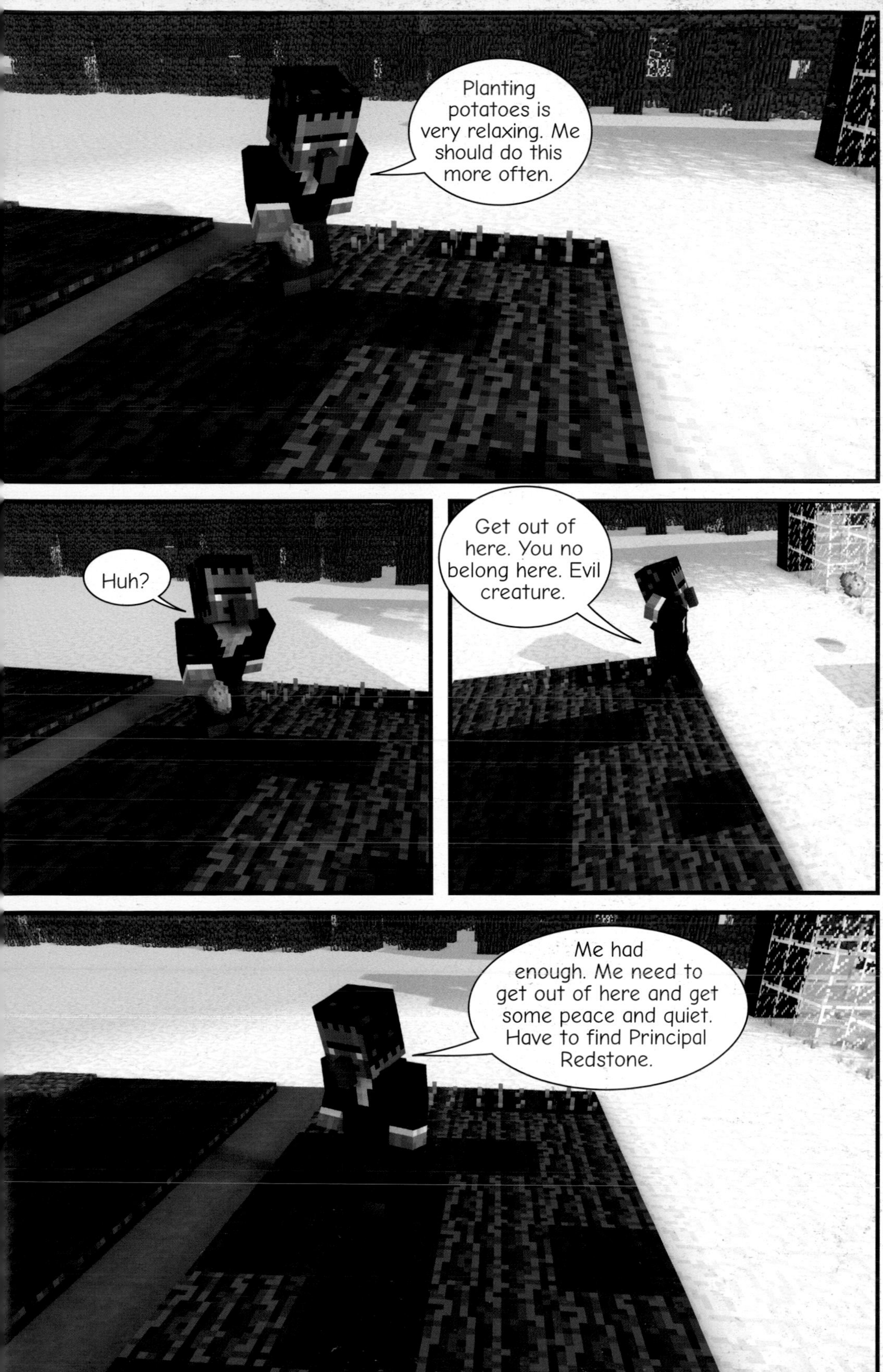
Planting potatoes is very relaxing. Me should do this more often.
Huh?
Get out of here. You no belong here. Evil creature.
Me had enough. Me need to get out of here and get some peace and quiet. Have to find Principal Redstone.

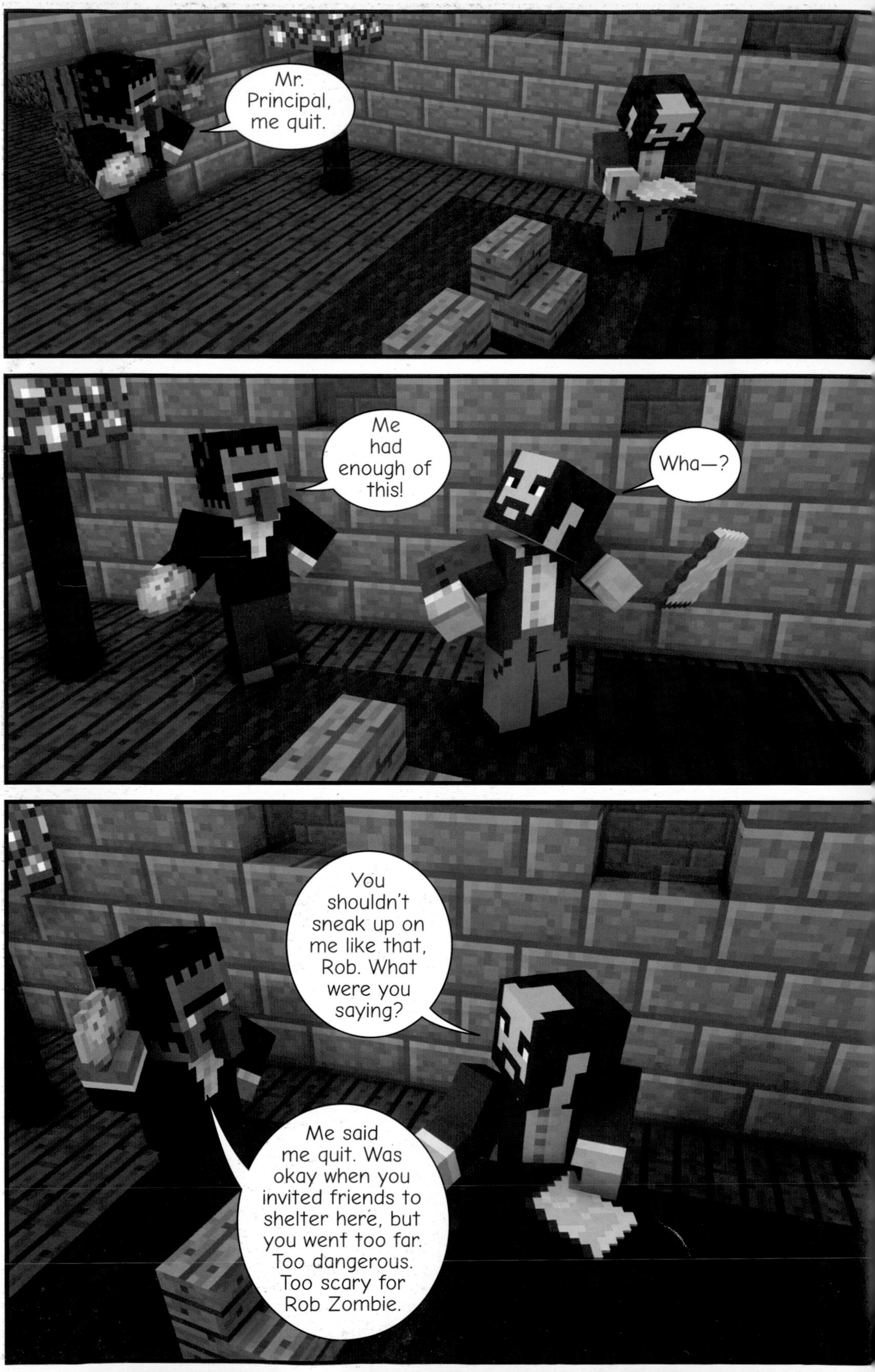
Mr. Principal, me quit.
Me had enough of this!
Wha—?
You shouldn't sneak up on me like that, Rob. What were you saying?
Me said me quit. Was okay when you invited friends to shelter here, but you went too far. Too dangerous. Too scary for Rob Zombie.

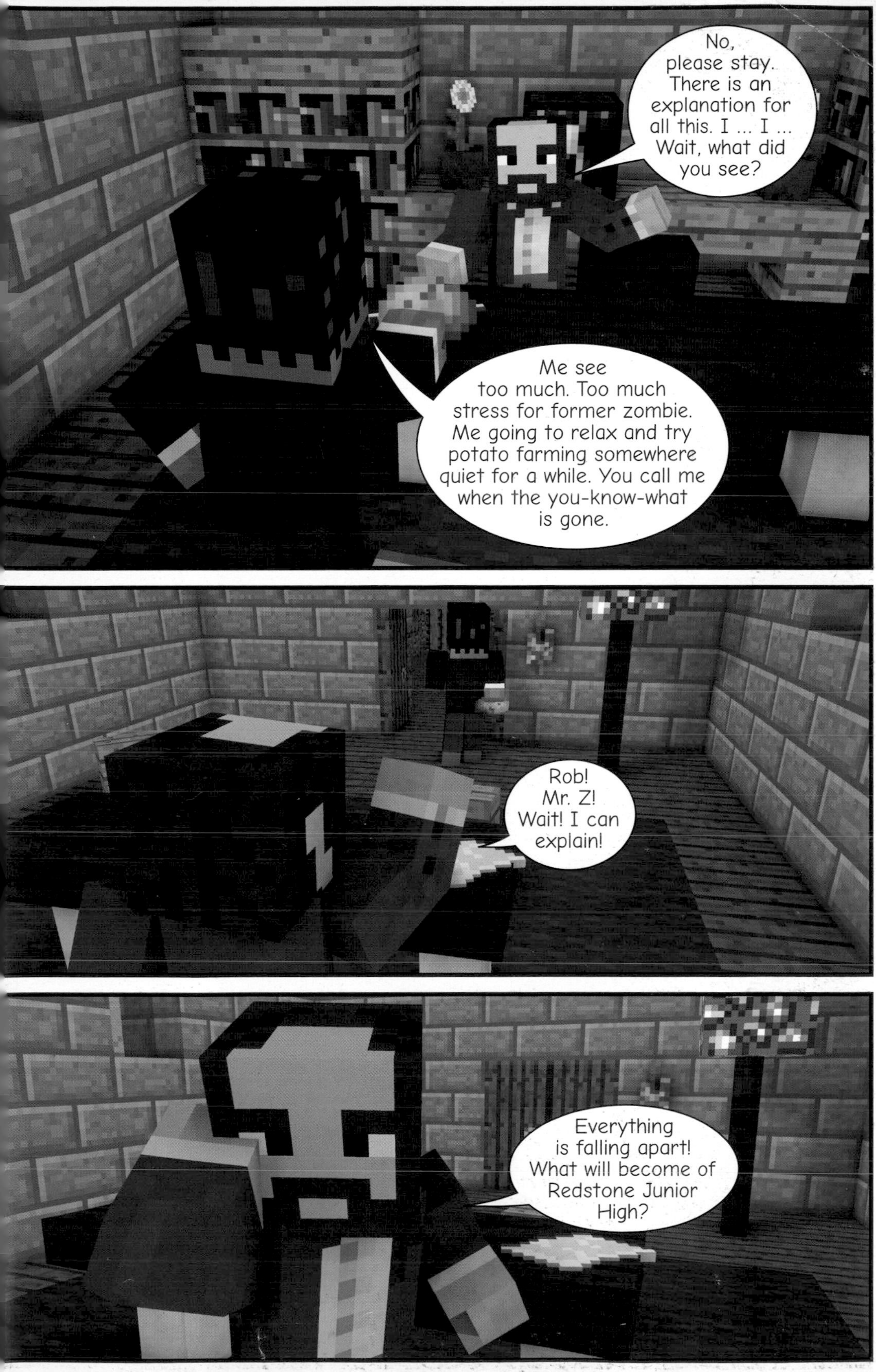
No, please stay. There is an explanation for all this. I ... I ... Wait, what did you see?
Me see too much. Too much stress for former zombie. Me going to relax and try potato farming somewhere quiet for a while. You call me when the you-know-what is gone.
Rob! Mr. Z! Wait! I can explain!
Everything is falling apart! What will become of Redstone Junior High?

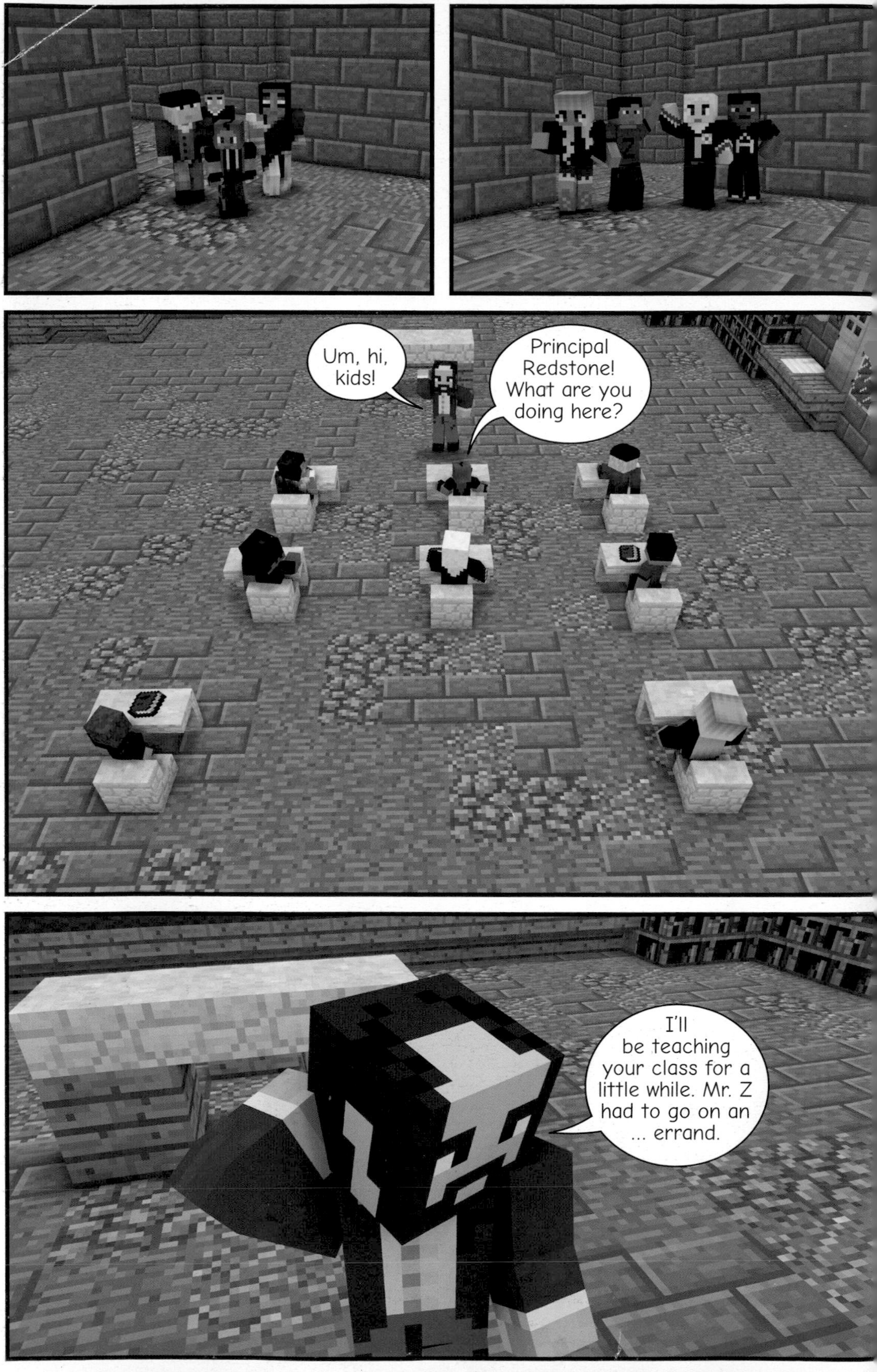
Um, hi, kids!
Principal Redstone! What are you doing here?
I'll be teaching your class for a little while. Mr. Z had to go on an ... errand.

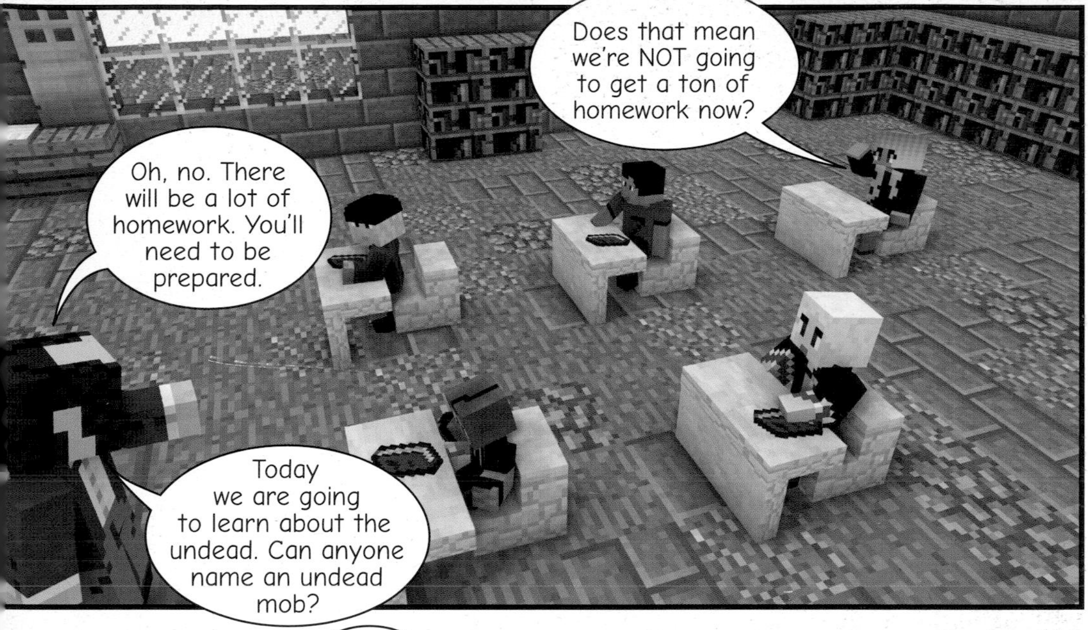
Does that mean we're NOT going to get a ton of homework now?
Oh, no. There will be a lot of homework. You'll need to be prepared.
Today we are going to learn about the undead. Can anyone name an undead mob?

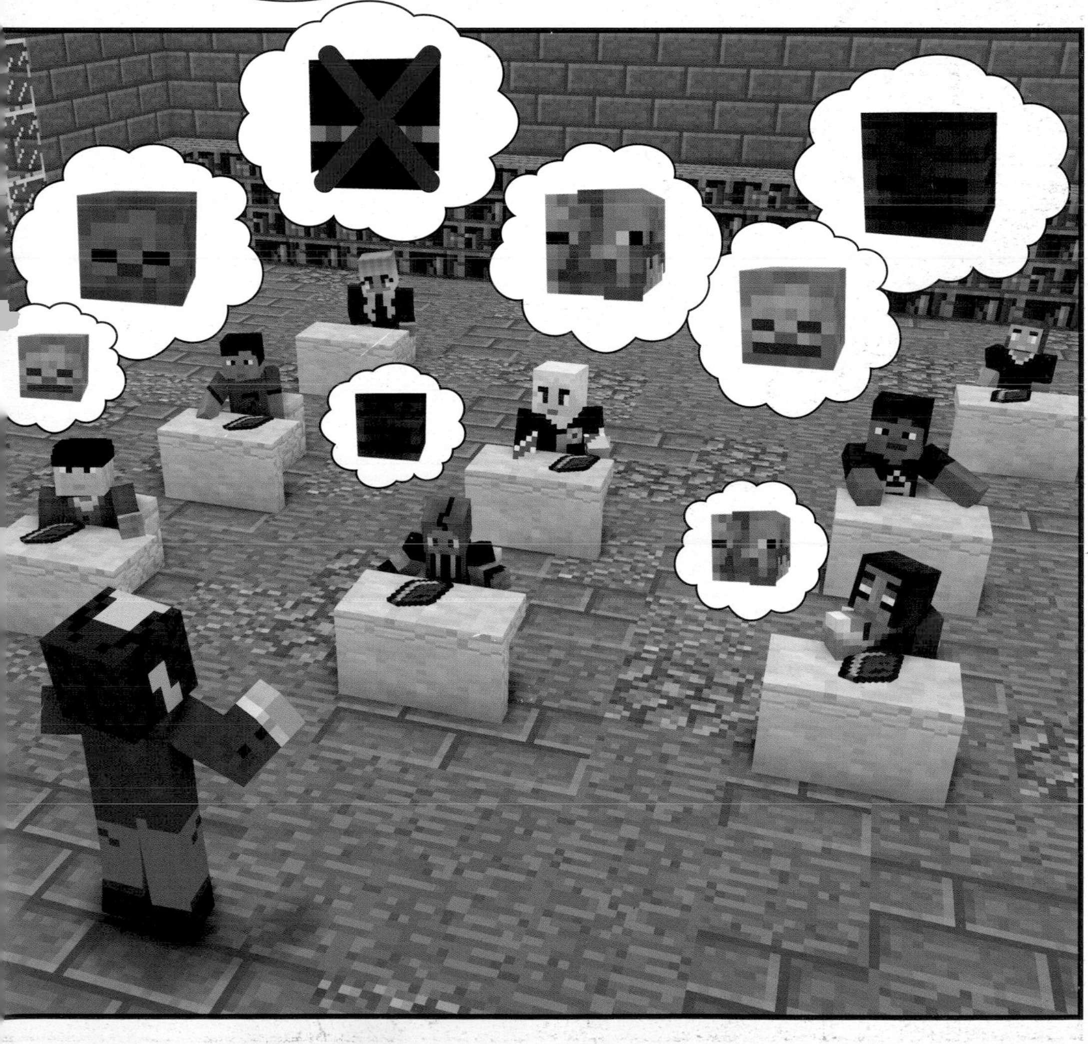

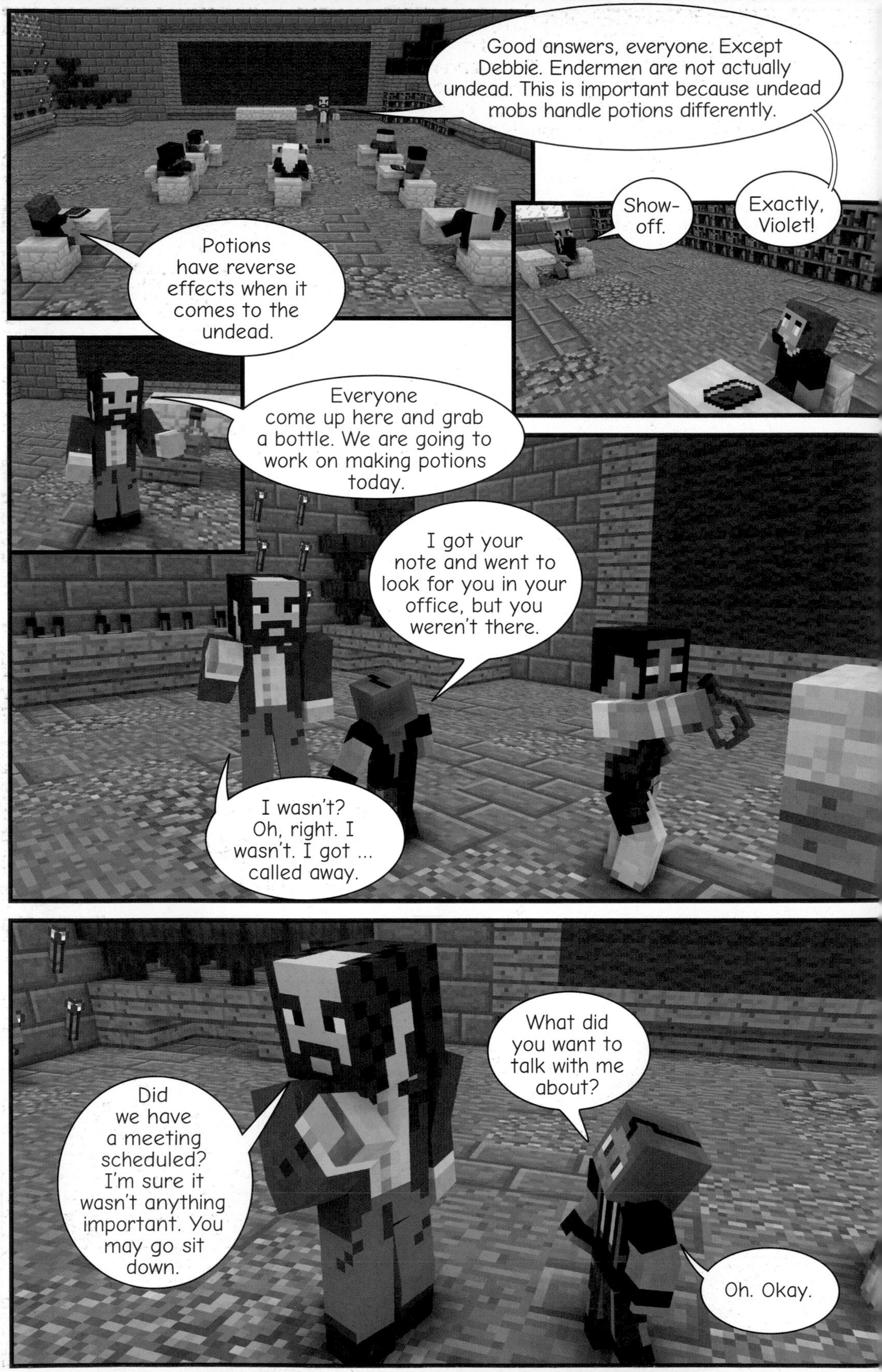
Good answers, everyone. Except Debbie. Endermen are not actually undead. This is important because undead mobs handle potions differently.
Potions have reverse effects when it comes to the undead.
Show-off.
Exactly, Violet!
Everyone come up here and grab a bottle. We are going to work on making potions today.
I got your note and went to look for you in your office, but you weren't there.
I wasn't? Oh, right. I wasn't. I got ... called away.
What did you want to talk with me about?
Did we have a meeting scheduled? I'm sure it wasn't anything important. You may go sit down.
Oh. Okay.

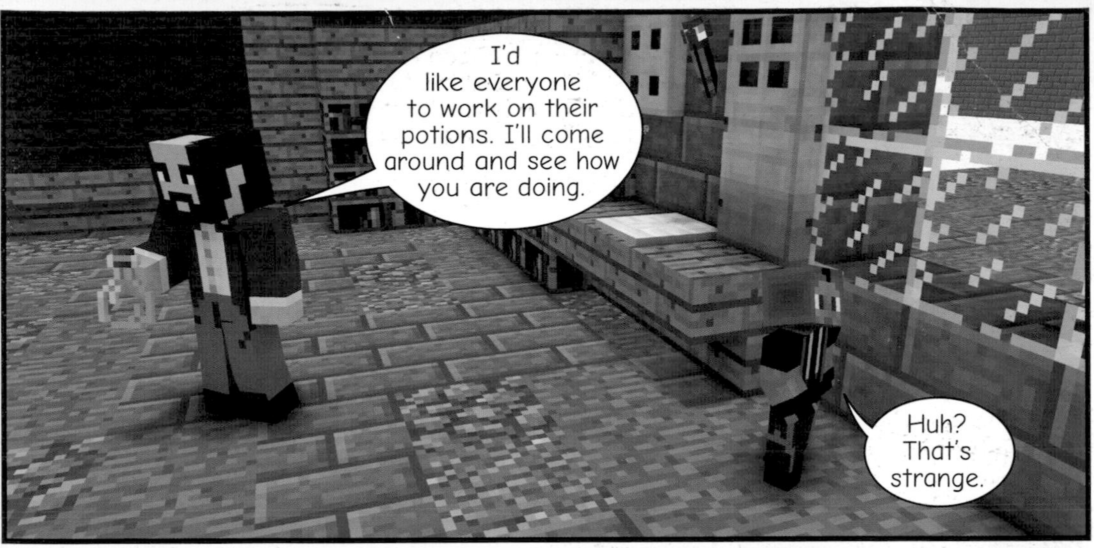
I'd like everyone to work on their potions. I'll come around and see how you are doing.
Huh? That's strange.
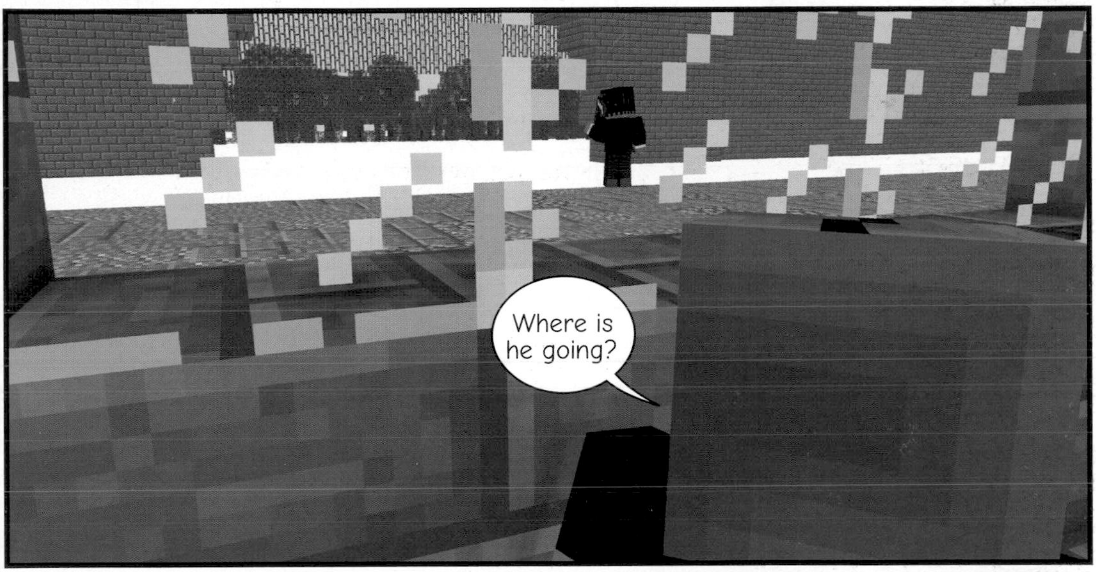
Where is he going?
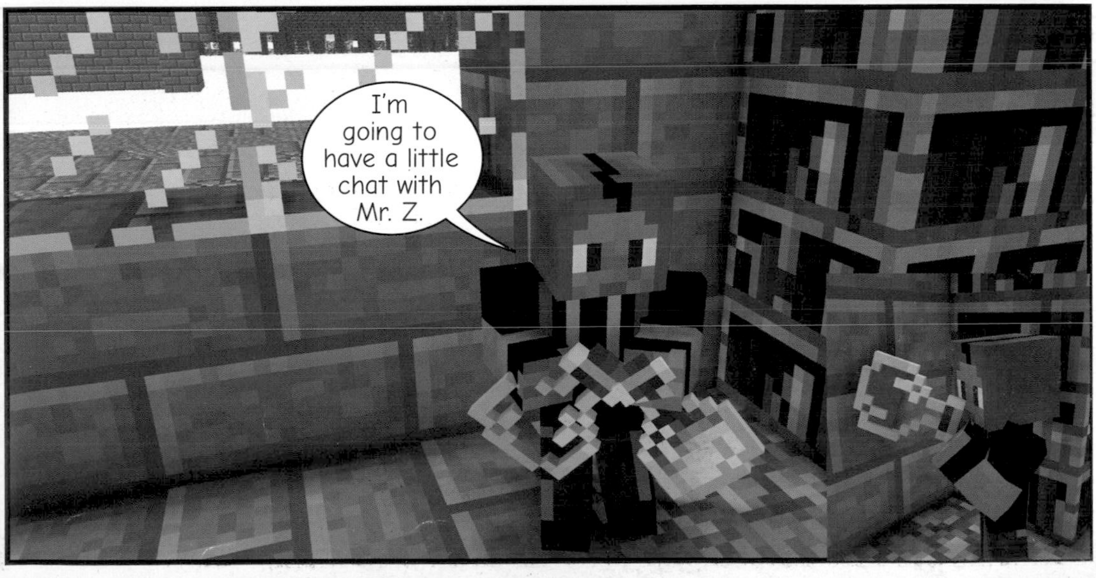
I'm going to have a little chat with Mr. Z.

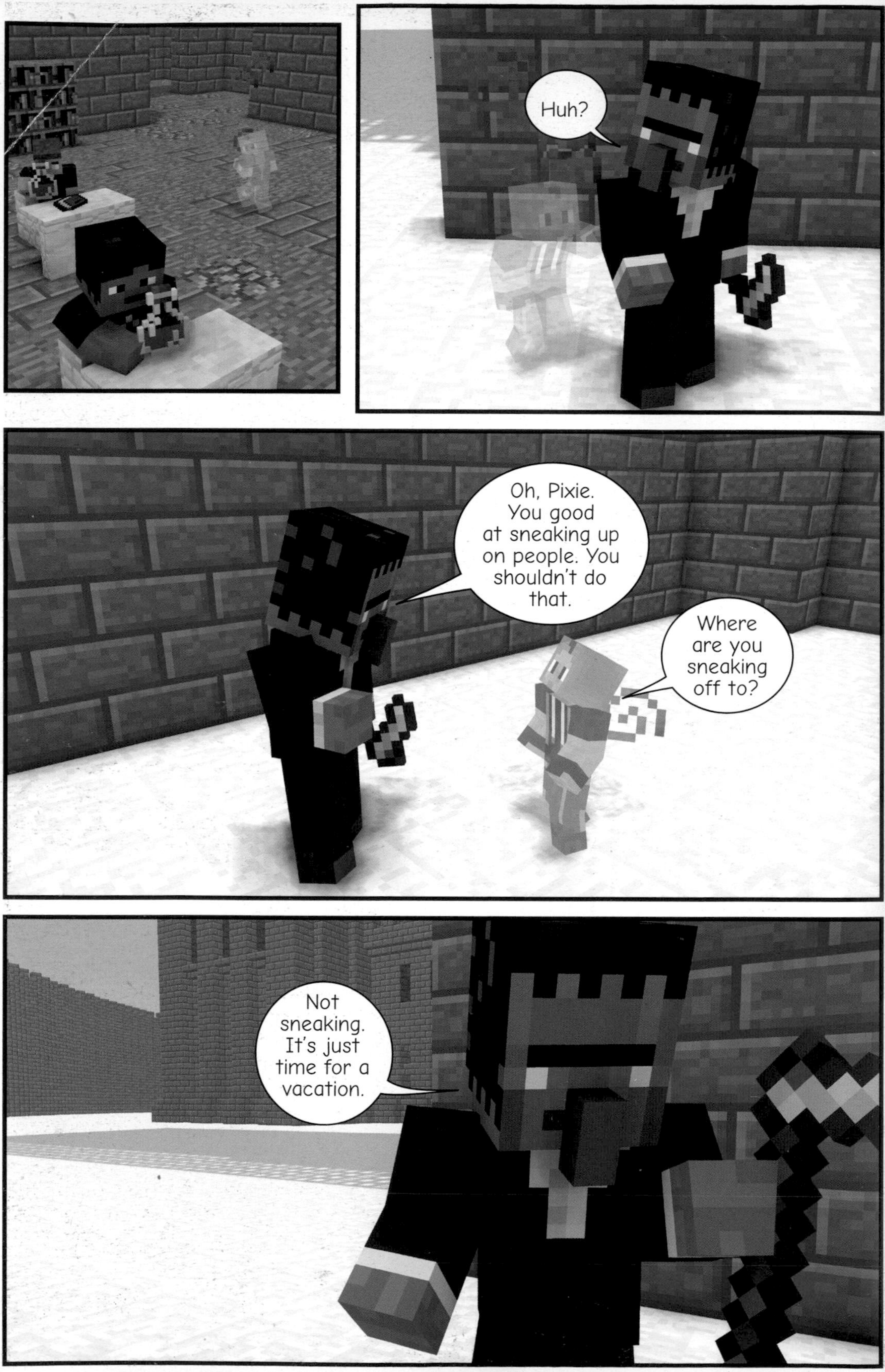
Huh?
Oh, Pixie. You good at sneaking up on people. You shouldn't do that.
Where are you sneaking off to?
Not sneaking. It's just time for a vacation.

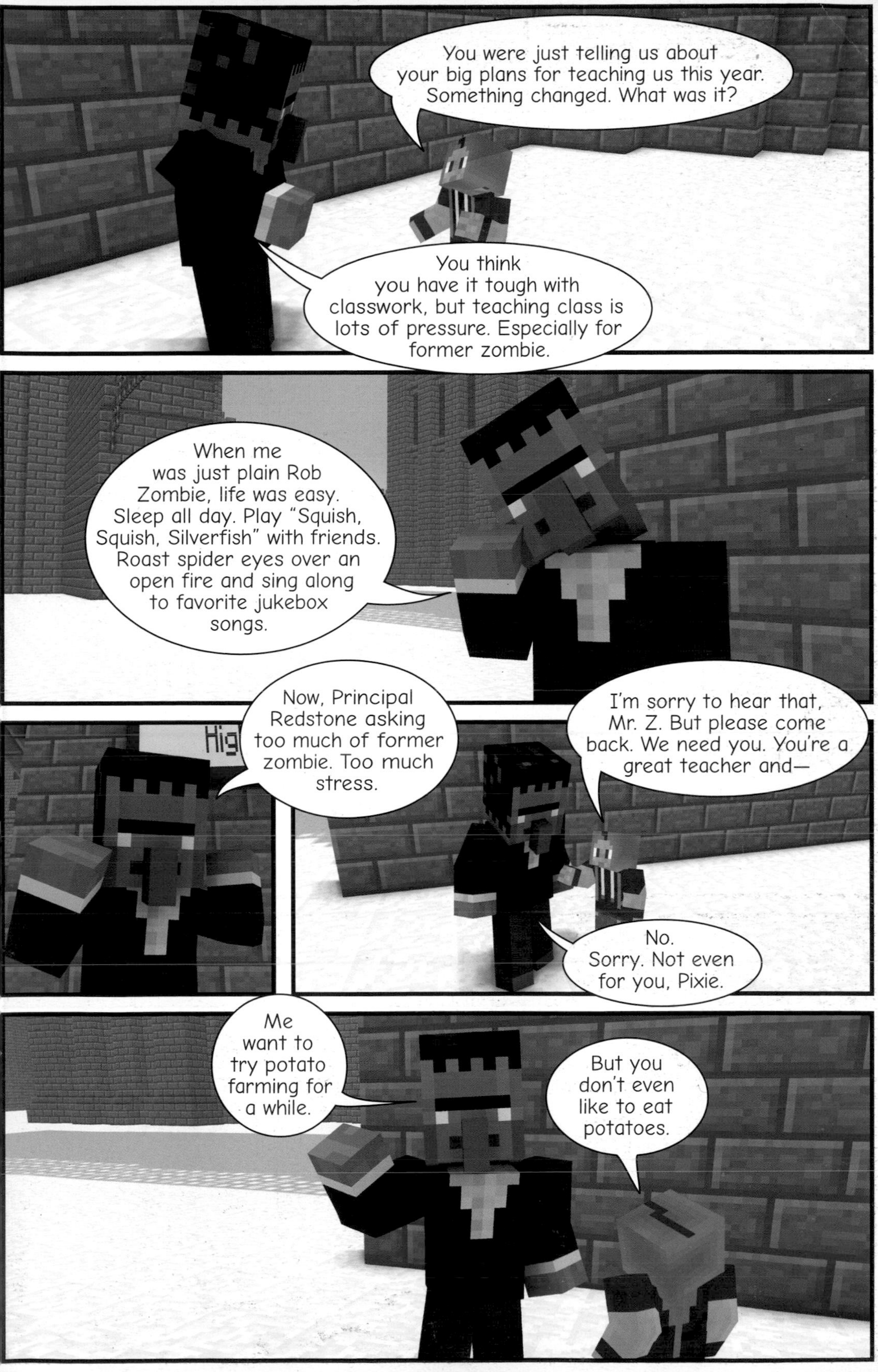
You were just telling us about your big plans for teaching us this year. Something changed. What was it?
You think you have it tough with classwork, but teaching class is lots of pressure. Especially for former zombie.
When me was just plain Rob Zombie, life was easy. Sleep all day. Play "Squish, Squish, Silverfish" with friends. Roast spider eyes over an open fire and sing along to favorite jukebox songs.
Hig
Now, Principal Redstone asking too much of former zombie. Too much stress.
I'm sorry to hear that, Mr. Z. But please come back. We need you. You're a great teacher and—
No. Sorry. Not even for you, Pixie.
Me want to try potato farming for a while.
But you don't even like to eat potatoes.

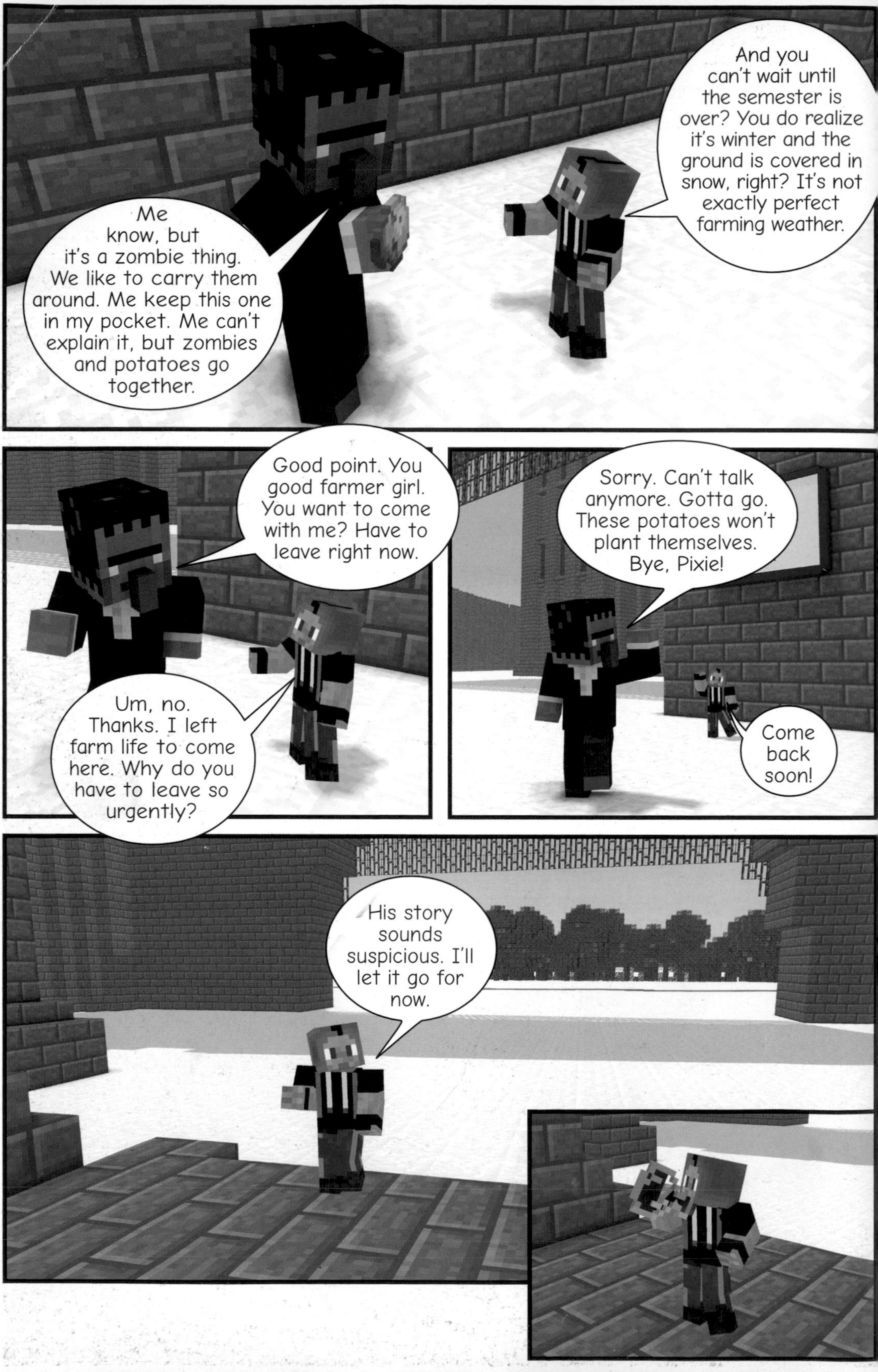
Me know, but it's a zombie thing. We like to carry them around. Me keep this one in my pocket. Me can't explain it, but zombies and potatoes go together.
And you can't wait until the semester is over? You do realize it's winter and the ground is covered in snow, right? It's not exactly perfect farming weather.
Good point. You good farmer girl. You want to come with me? Have to leave right now.
Um, no. Thanks. I left farm life to come here. Why do you have to leave so urgently?
Sorry. Can't talk anymore. Gotta go. These potatoes won't plant themselves. Bye, Pixie!
Come back soon!
His story sounds suspicious. I'll let it go for now.

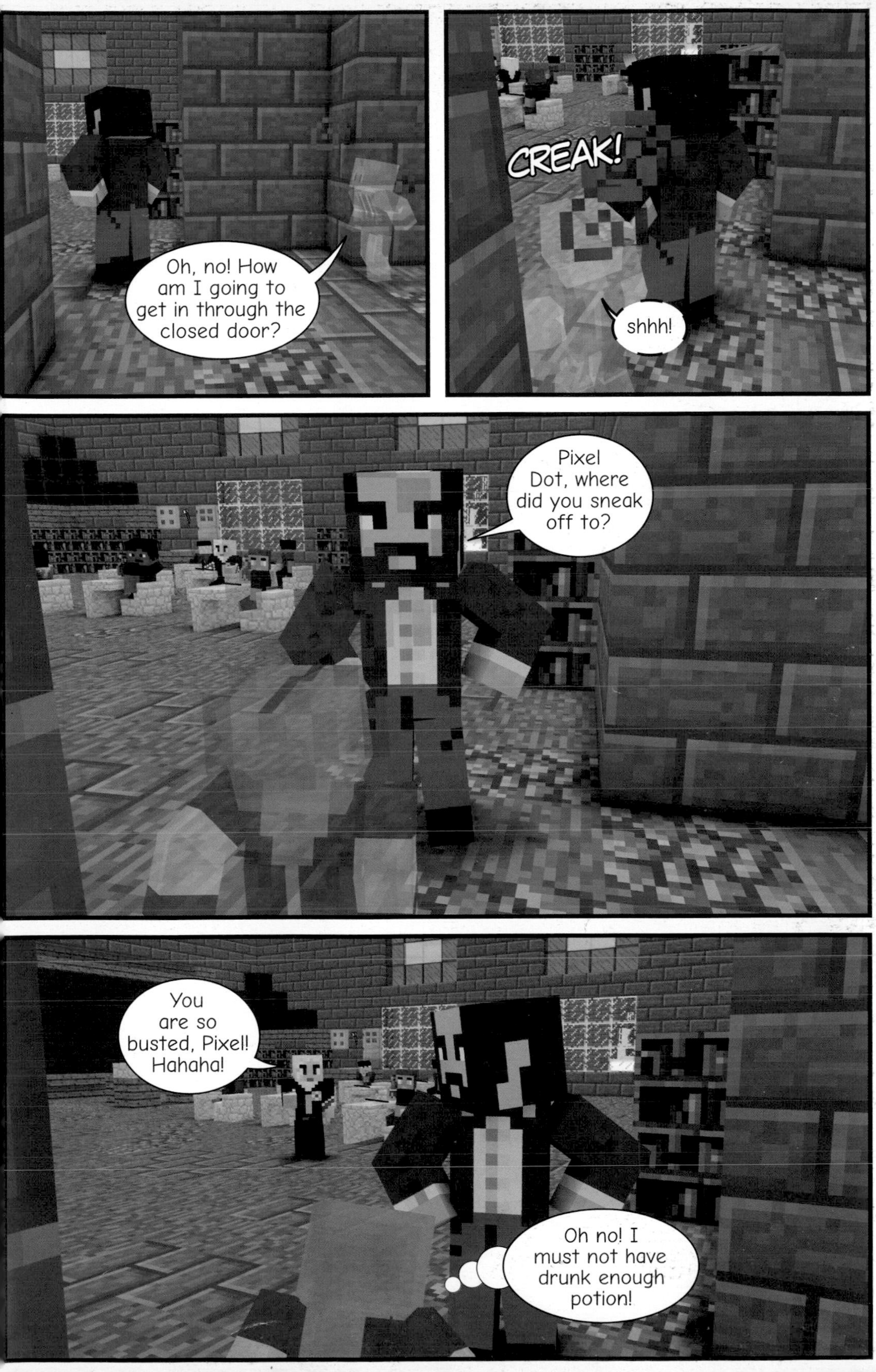
Oh, no! How am I going to get in through the closed door?
CREAK!
shhh!
Pixel Dot, where did you sneak off to?
You are so busted, Pixel! Hahaha!
Oh no! I must not have drunk enough potion!

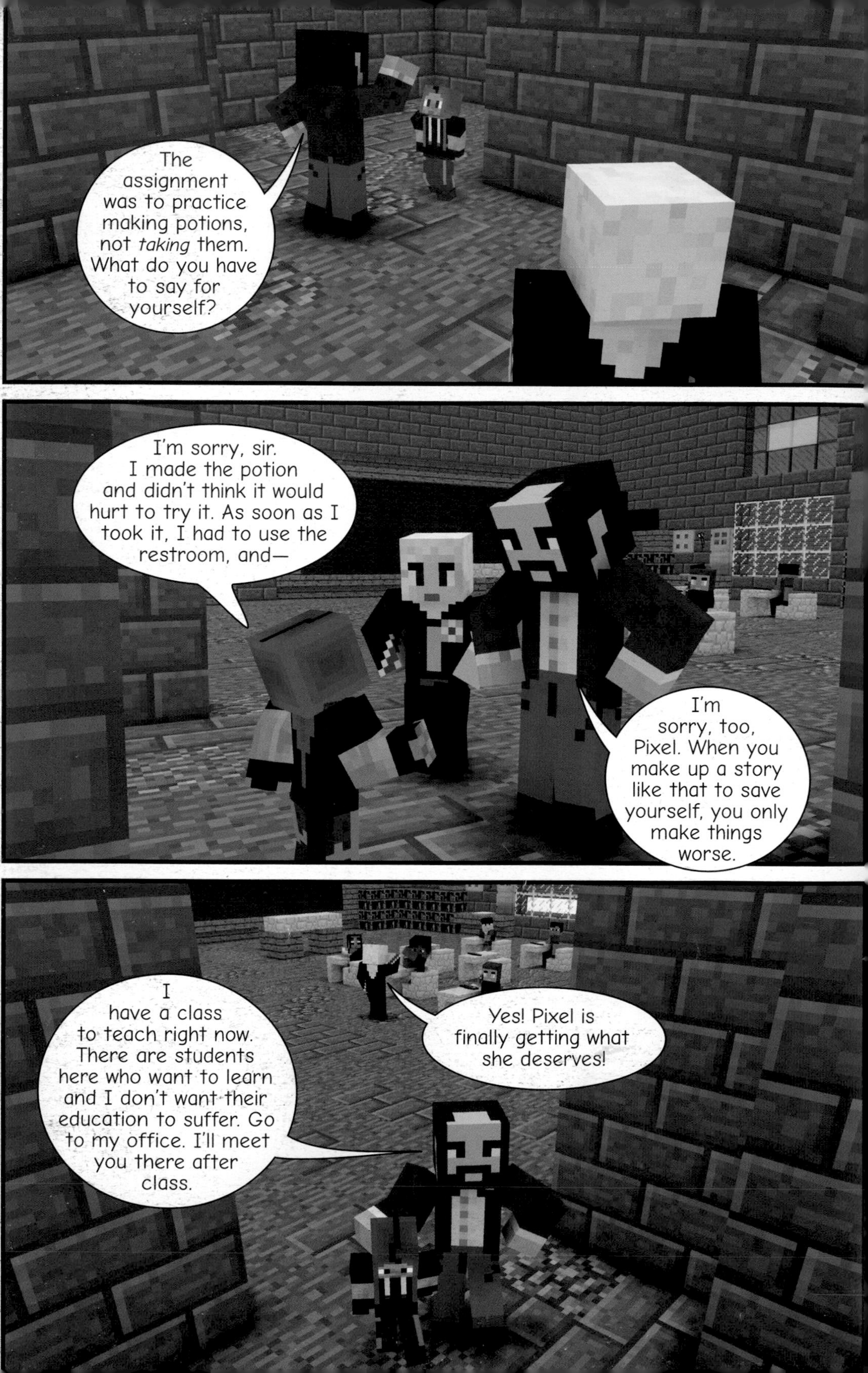
The assignment was to practice making potions, not *taking* them. What do you have to say for yourself?
I'm sorry, sir. I made the potion and didn't think it would hurt to try it. As soon as I took it, I had to use the restroom, and—
I'm sorry, too, Pixel. When you make up a story like that to save yourself, you only make things worse.
I have a class to teach right now. There are students here who want to learn and I don't want their education to suffer. Go to my office. I'll meet you there after class.
Yes! Pixel is finally getting what she deserves!

CHAPTER 4

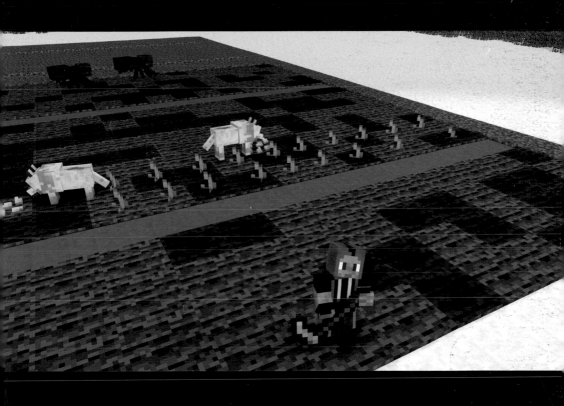

DETENTION

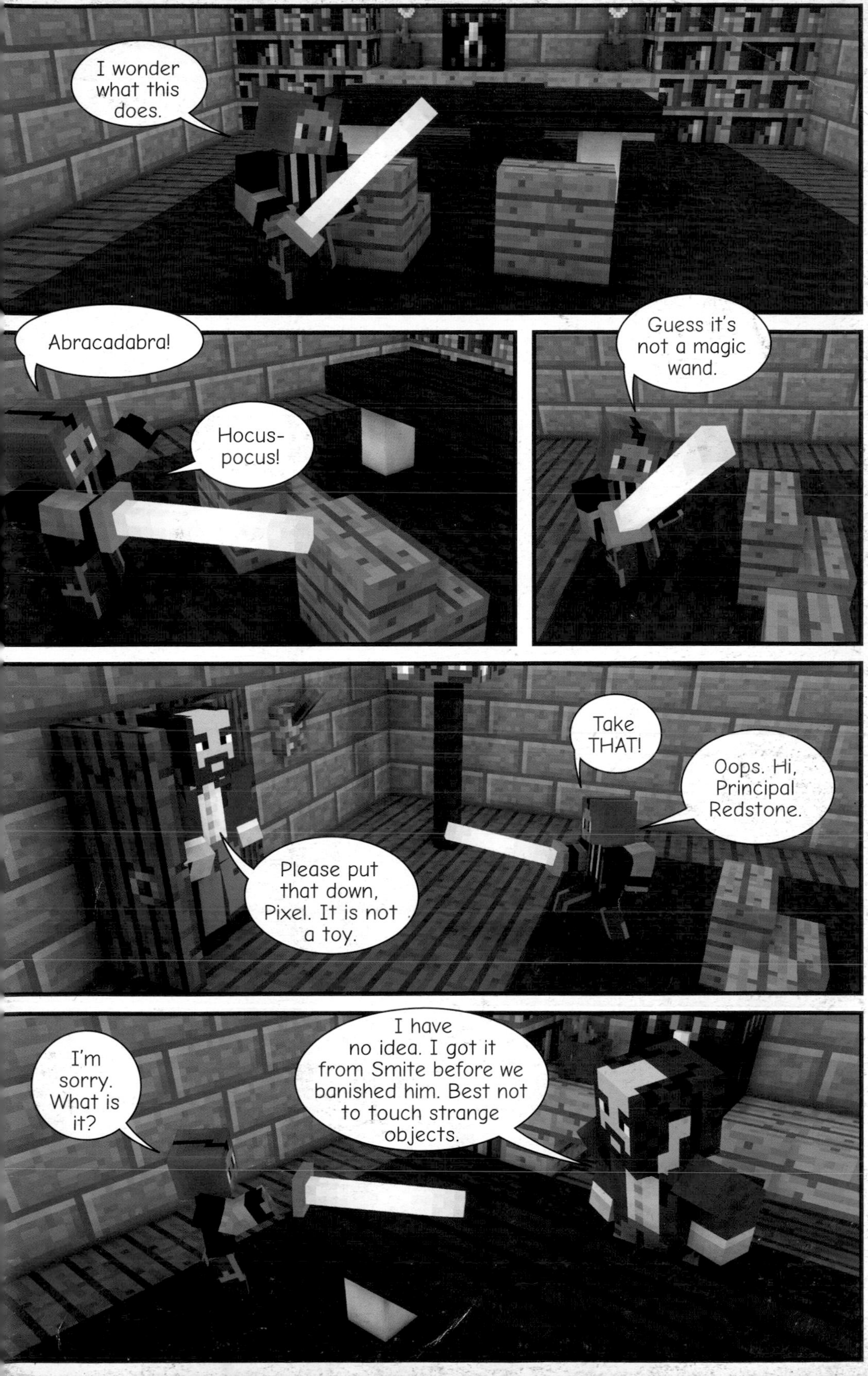

I wonder what this does.
Abracadabra!
Hocus-pocus!
Guess it's not a magic wand.
Take THAT!
Oops. Hi, Principal Redstone.
Please put that down, Pixel. It is not a toy.
I'm sorry. What is it?
I have no idea. I got it from Smite before we banished him. Best not to touch strange objects.

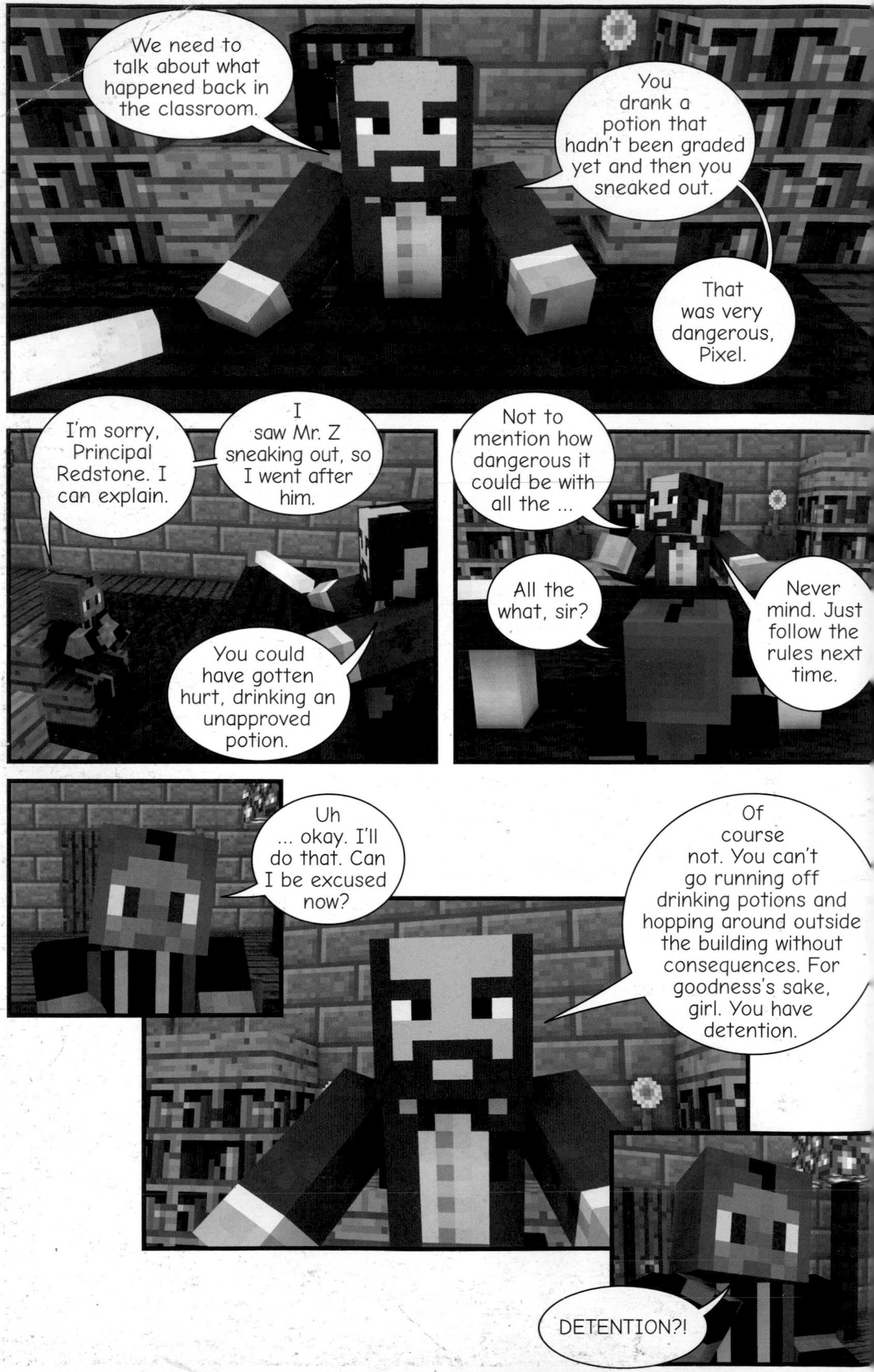
We need to talk about what happened back in the classroom.
You drank a potion that hadn't been graded yet and then you sneaked out.
That was very dangerous, Pixel.
I'm sorry, Principal Redstone. I can explain.
I saw Mr. Z sneaking out, so I went after him.
You could have gotten hurt, drinking an unapproved potion.
Not to mention how dangerous it could be with all the ...
All the what, sir?
Never mind. Just follow the rules next time.
Uh ... okay. I'll do that. Can I be excused now?
Of course not. You can't go running off drinking potions and hopping around outside the building without consequences. For goodness's sake, girl. You have detention.
DETENTION?!

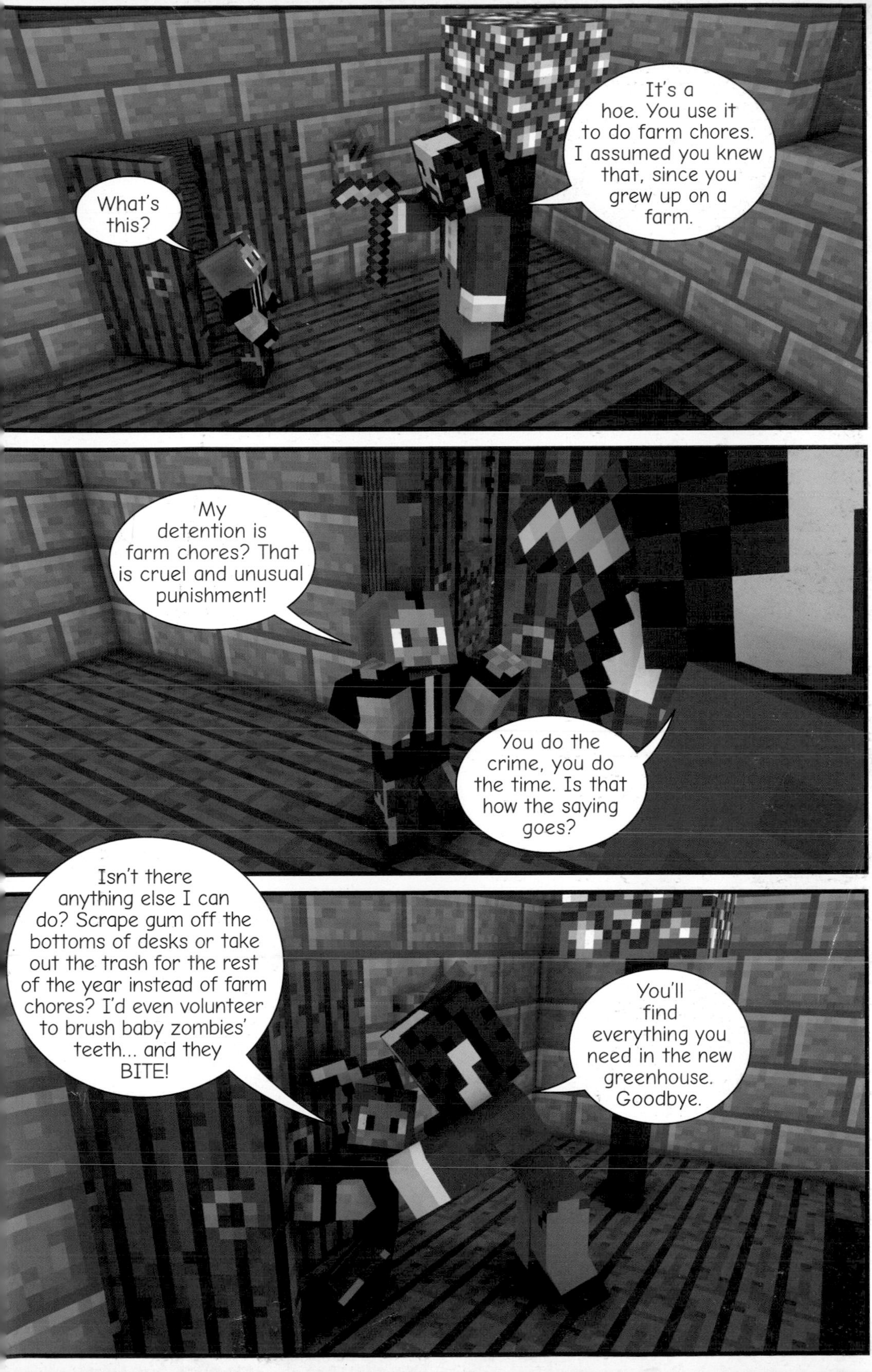
What's this?
It's a hoe. You use it to do farm chores. I assumed you knew that, since you grew up on a farm.
My detention is farm chores? That is cruel and unusual punishment!
You do the crime, you do the time. Is that how the saying goes?
Isn't there anything else I can do? Scrape gum off the bottoms of desks or take out the trash for the rest of the year instead of farm chores? I'd even volunteer to brush baby zombies' teeth... and they BITE!
You'll find everything you need in the new greenhouse. Goodbye.

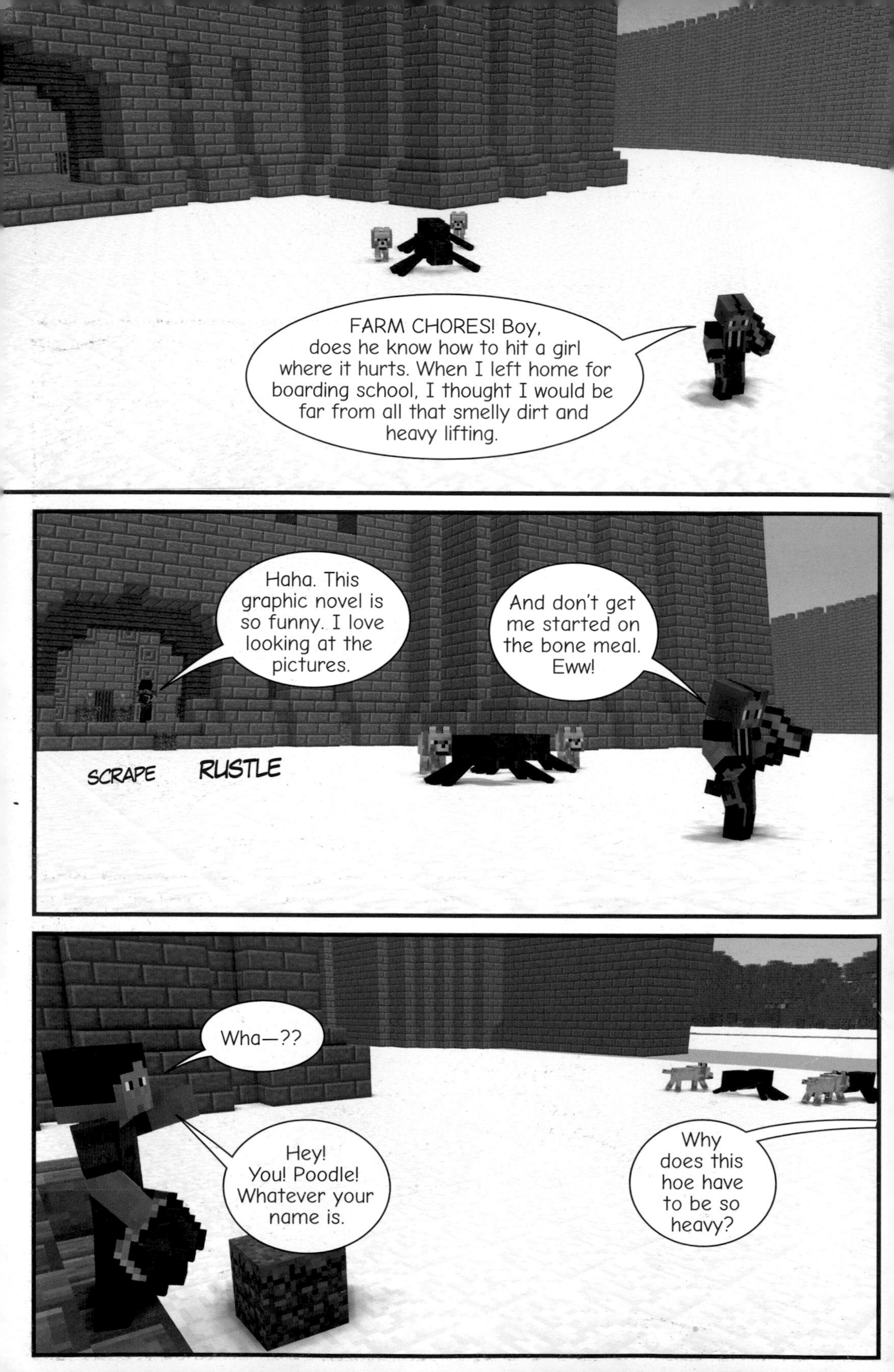
FARM CHORES! Boy, does he know how to hit a girl where it hurts. When I left home for boarding school, I thought I would be far from all that smelly dirt and heavy lifting.
Haha. This graphic novel is so funny. I love looking at the pictures.
And don't get me started on the bone meal. Eww!
SCRAPE
RUSTLE
Wha—??
Hey! You! Poodle! Whatever your name is.
Why does this hoe have to be so heavy?

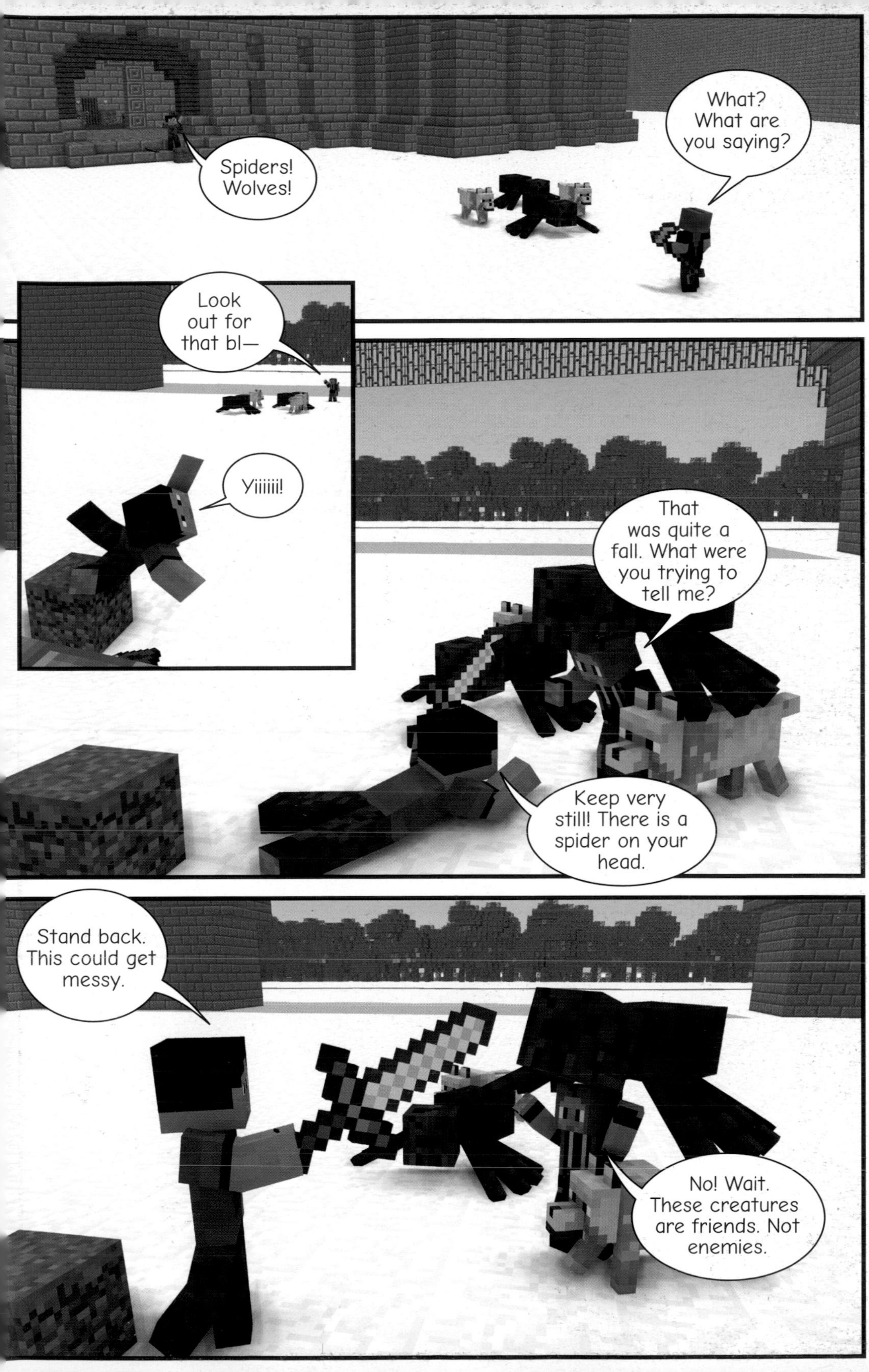
Spiders! Wolves!
What? What are you saying?
Look out for that bl—
Yiiiiii!
That was quite a fall. What were you trying to tell me?
Keep very still! There is a spider on your head.
Stand back. This could get messy.
No! Wait. These creatures are friends. Not enemies.

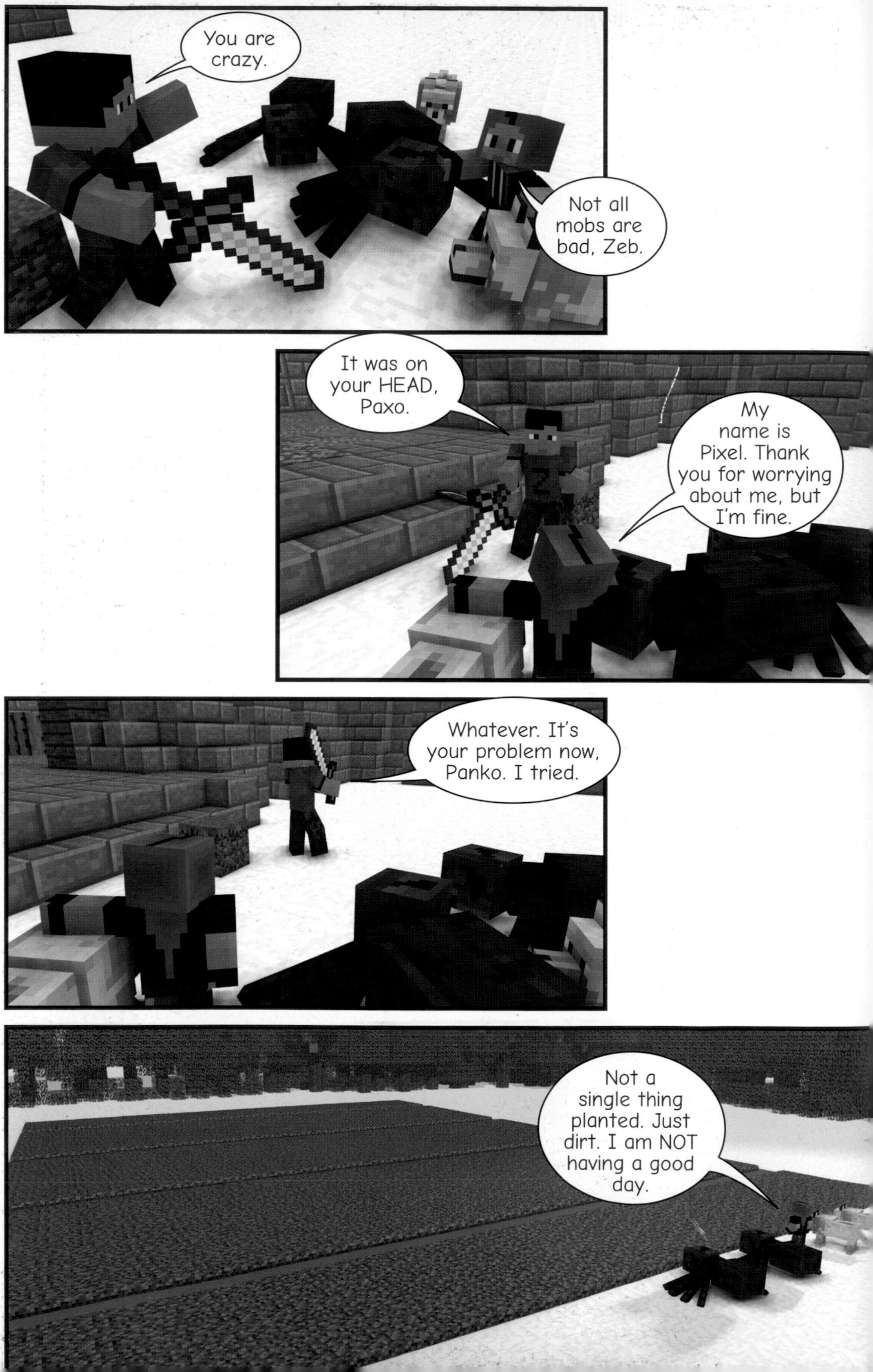
You are crazy.
Not all mobs are bad, Zeb.
It was on your HEAD, Paxo.
My name is Pixel. Thank you for worrying about me, but I'm fine.
Whatever. It's your problem now, Panko. I tried.
Not a single thing planted. Just dirt. I am NOT having a good day.

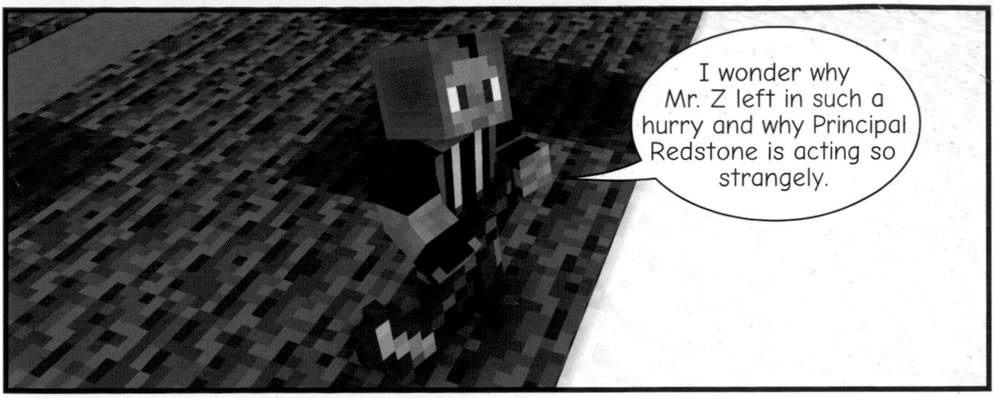
I wonder why Mr. Z left in such a hurry and why Principal Redstone is acting so strangely.

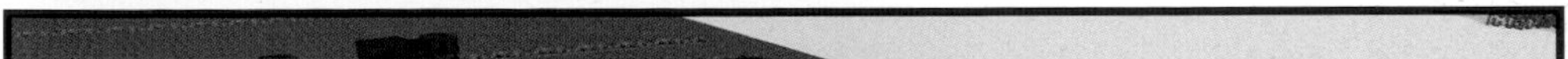
I just can't keep my mind on my chores.

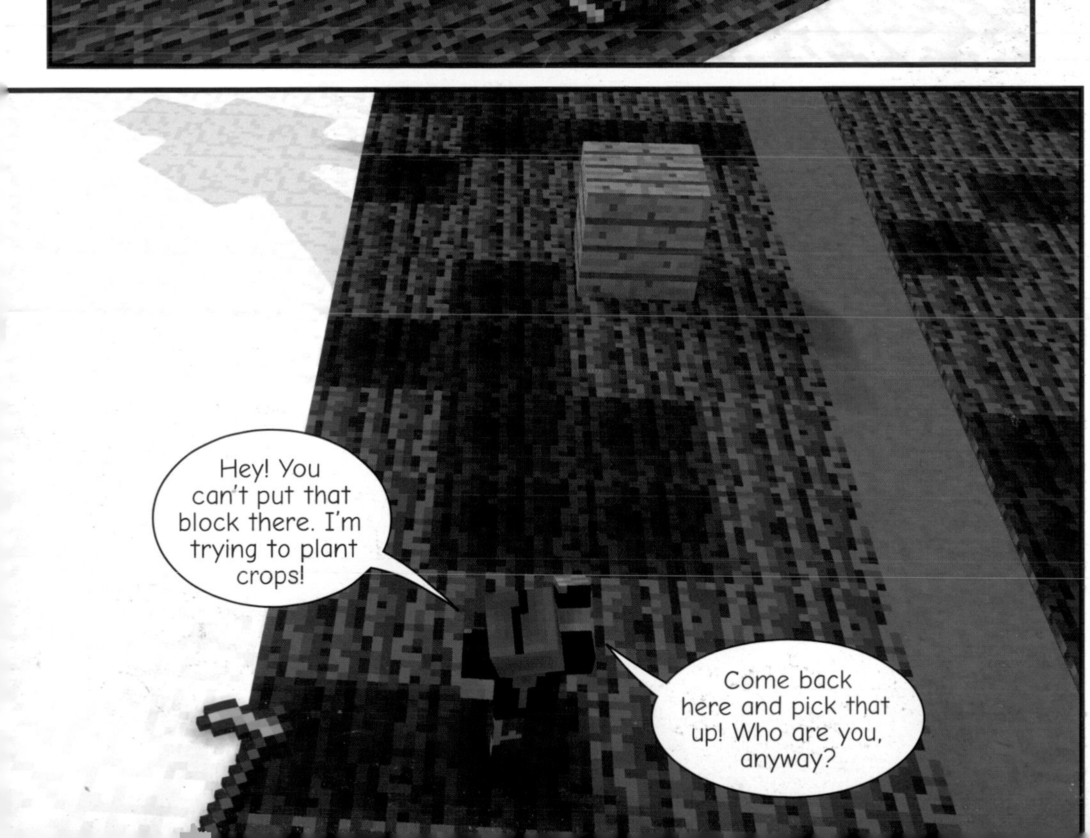
Hey! You can't put that block there. I'm trying to plant crops!
Come back here and pick that up! Who are you, anyway?

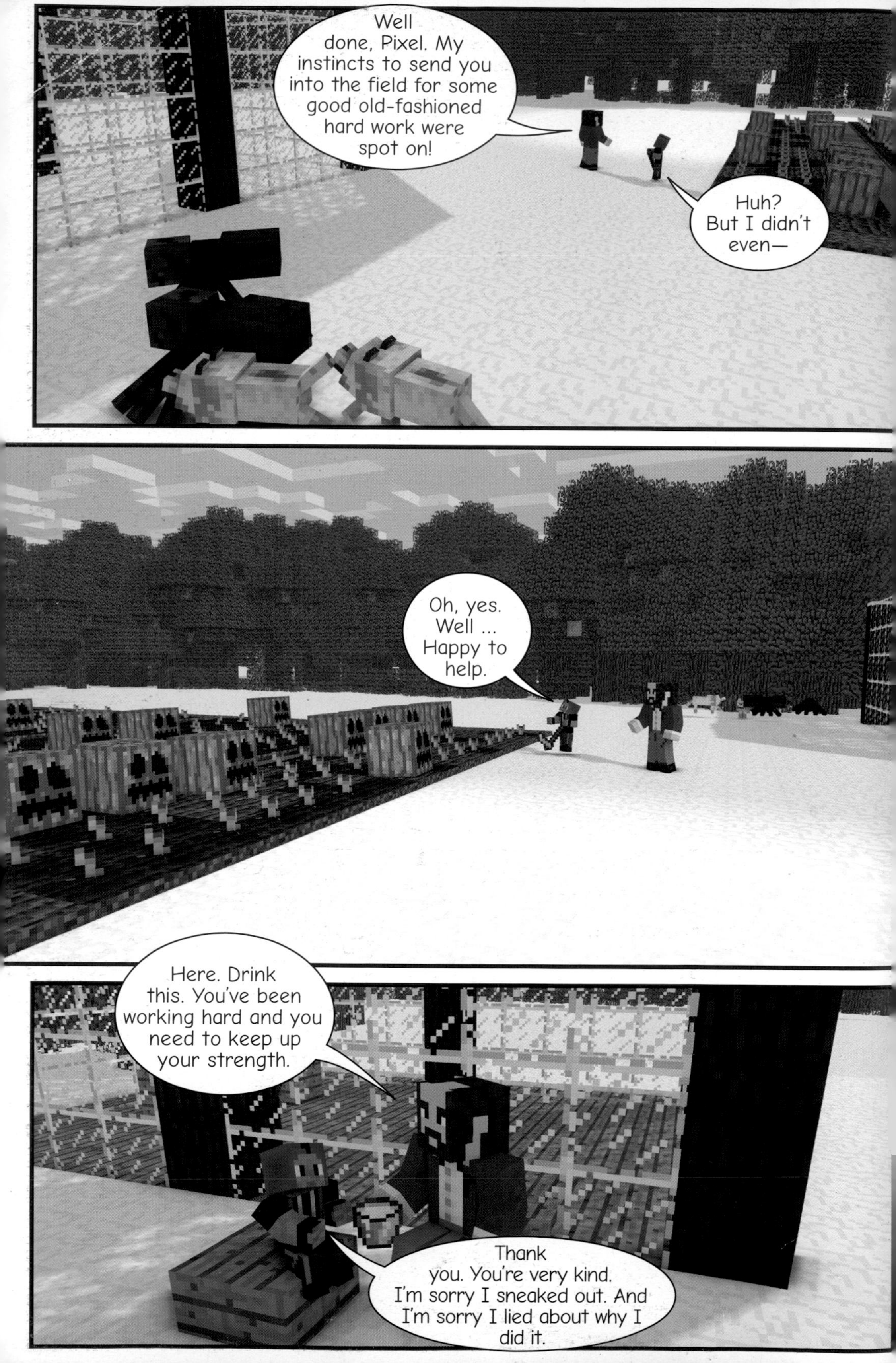
Well done, Pixel. My instincts to send you into the field for some good old-fashioned hard work were spot on!
Huh? But I didn't even—
Oh, yes. Well ... Happy to help.
Here. Drink this. You've been working hard and you need to keep up your strength.
Thank you. You're very kind. I'm sorry I sneaked out. And I'm sorry I lied about why I did it.

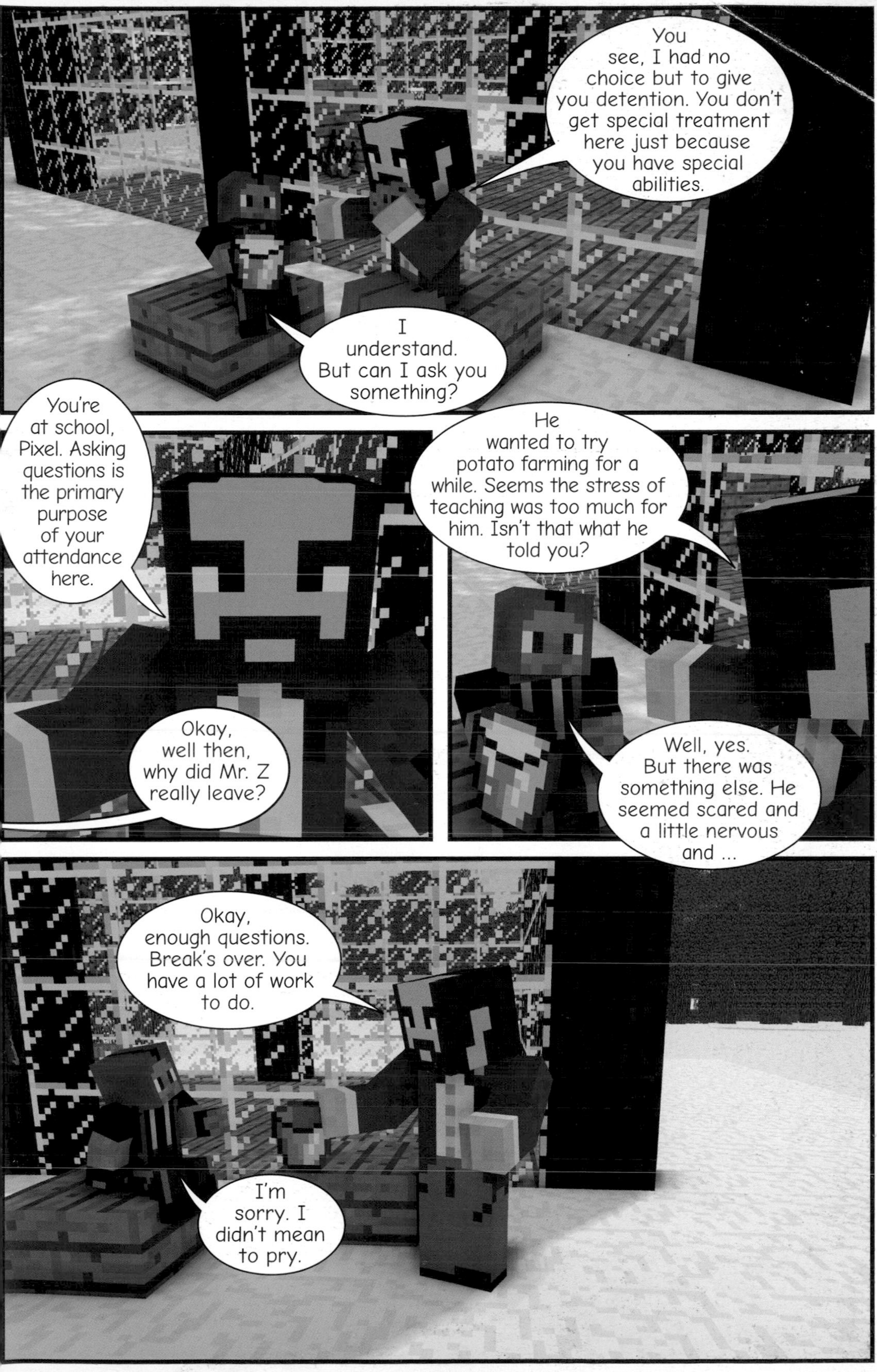
You see, I had no choice but to give you detention. You don't get special treatment here just because you have special abilities.
I understand. But can I ask you something?
You're at school, Pixel. Asking questions is the primary purpose of your attendance here.
Okay, well then, why did Mr. Z really leave?
He wanted to try potato farming for a while. Seems the stress of teaching was too much for him. Isn't that what he told you?
Well, yes. But there was something else. He seemed scared and a little nervous and ...
Okay, enough questions. Break's over. You have a lot of work to do.
I'm sorry. I didn't mean to pry.

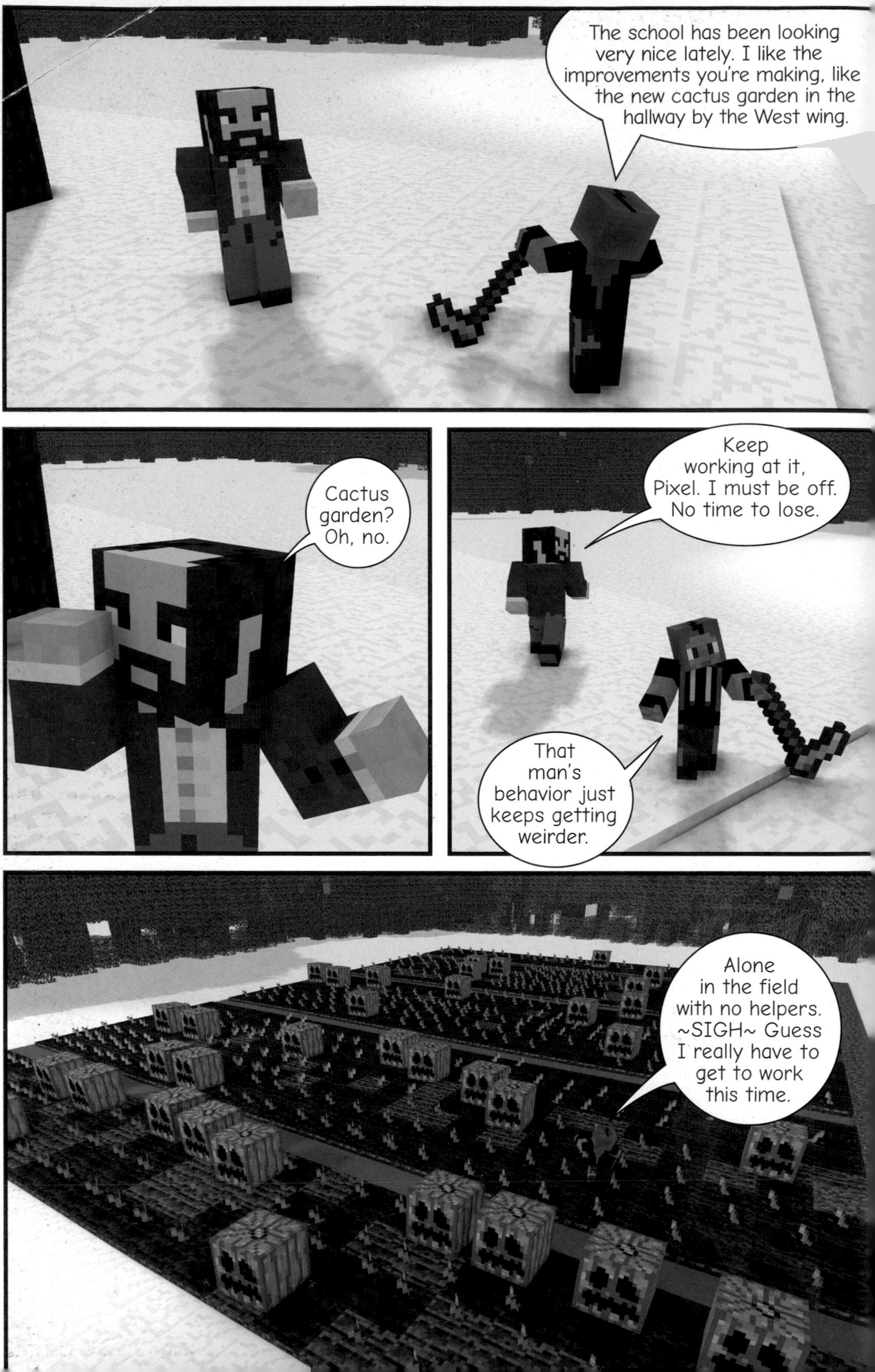
The school has been looking very nice lately. I like the improvements you're making, like the new cactus garden in the hallway by the West wing.
Cactus garden? Oh, no.
Keep working at it, Pixel. I must be off. No time to lose.
That man's behavior just keeps getting weirder.
Alone in the field with no helpers. ~SIGH~ Guess I really have to get to work this time.

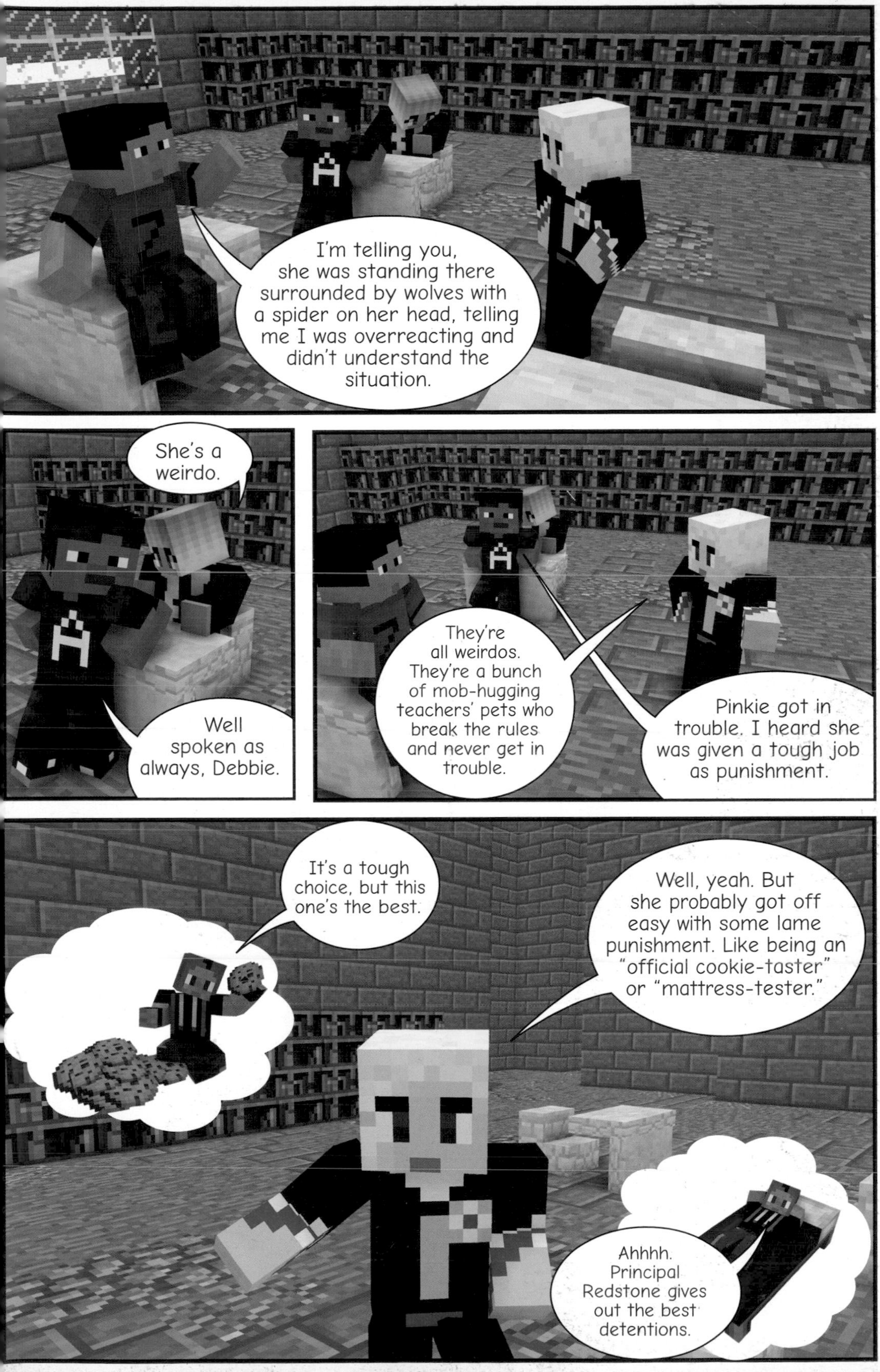
I'm telling you, she was standing there surrounded by wolves with a spider on her head, telling me I was overreacting and didn't understand the situation.
She's a weirdo.
Well spoken as always, Debbie.
They're all weirdos. They're a bunch of mob-hugging teachers' pets who break the rules and never get in trouble.
Pinkie got in trouble. I heard she was given a tough job as punishment.
Well, yeah. But she probably got off easy with some lame punishment. Like being an "official cookie-taster" or "mattress-tester."
It's a tough choice, but this one's the best.
Ahhhh. Principal Redstone gives out the best detentions.

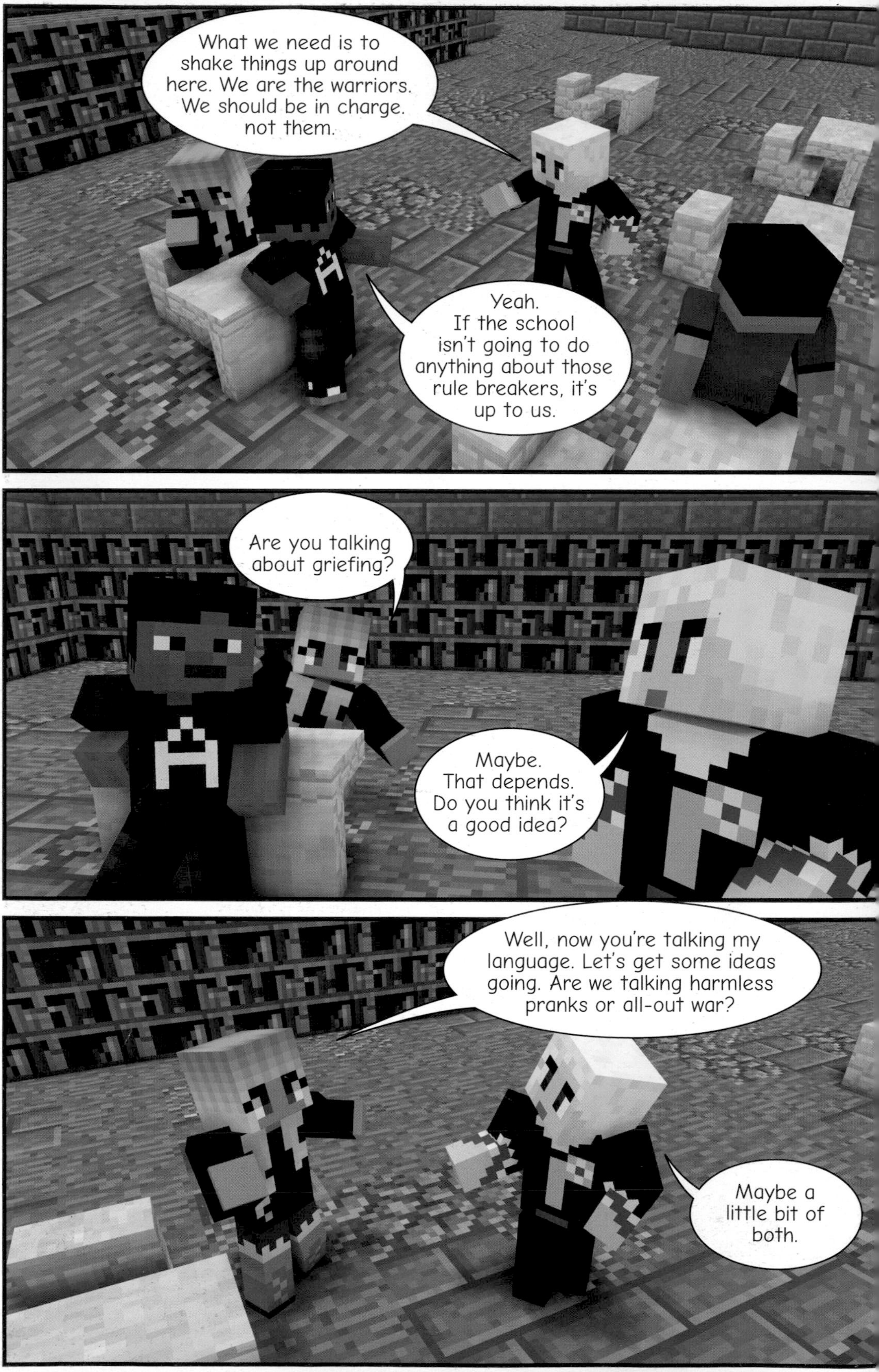
What we need is to shake things up around here. We are the warriors. We should be in charge. not them.
Yeah. If the school isn't going to do anything about those rule breakers, it's up to us.
Are you talking about griefing?
Maybe. That depends. Do you think it's a good idea?
Well, now you're talking my language. Let's get some ideas going. Are we talking harmless pranks or all-out war?
Maybe a little bit of both.

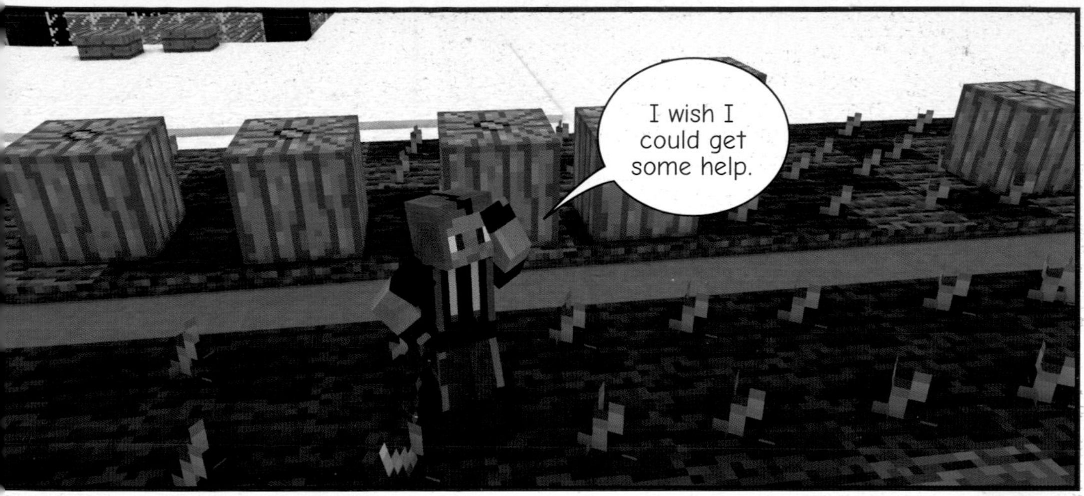
I wish I could get some help.

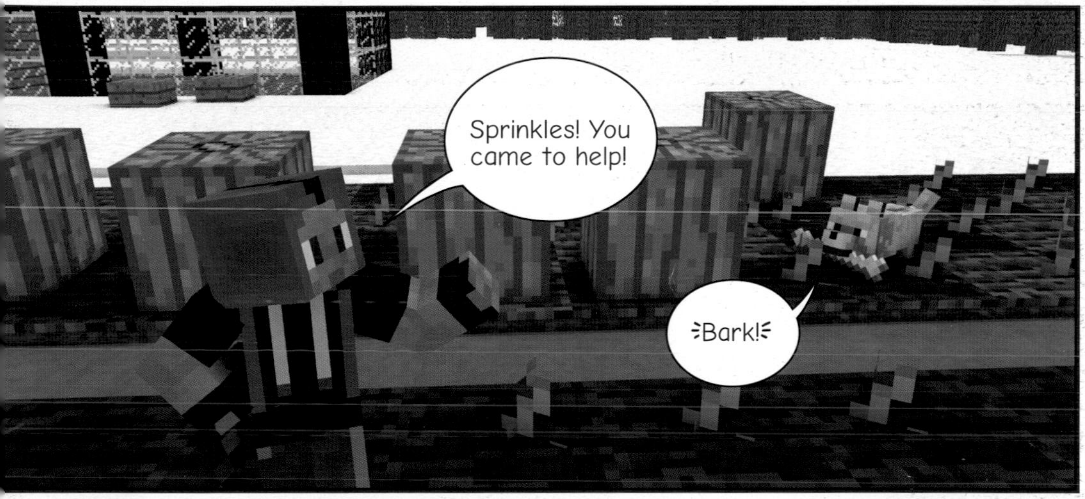
Sprinkles! You came to help!
Bark!

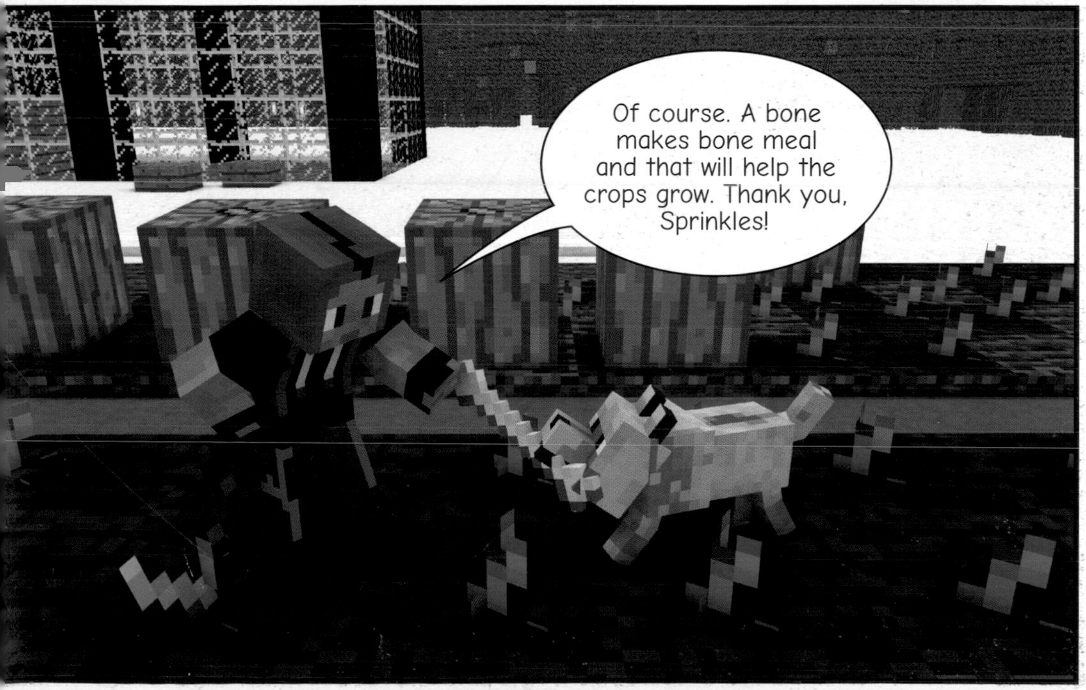
Of course. A bone makes bone meal and that will help the crops grow. Thank you, Sprinkles!

I wish we could help her.

Maybe we can.

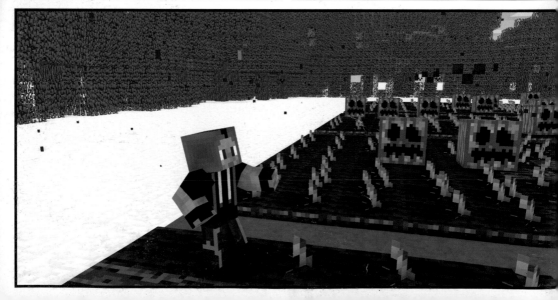

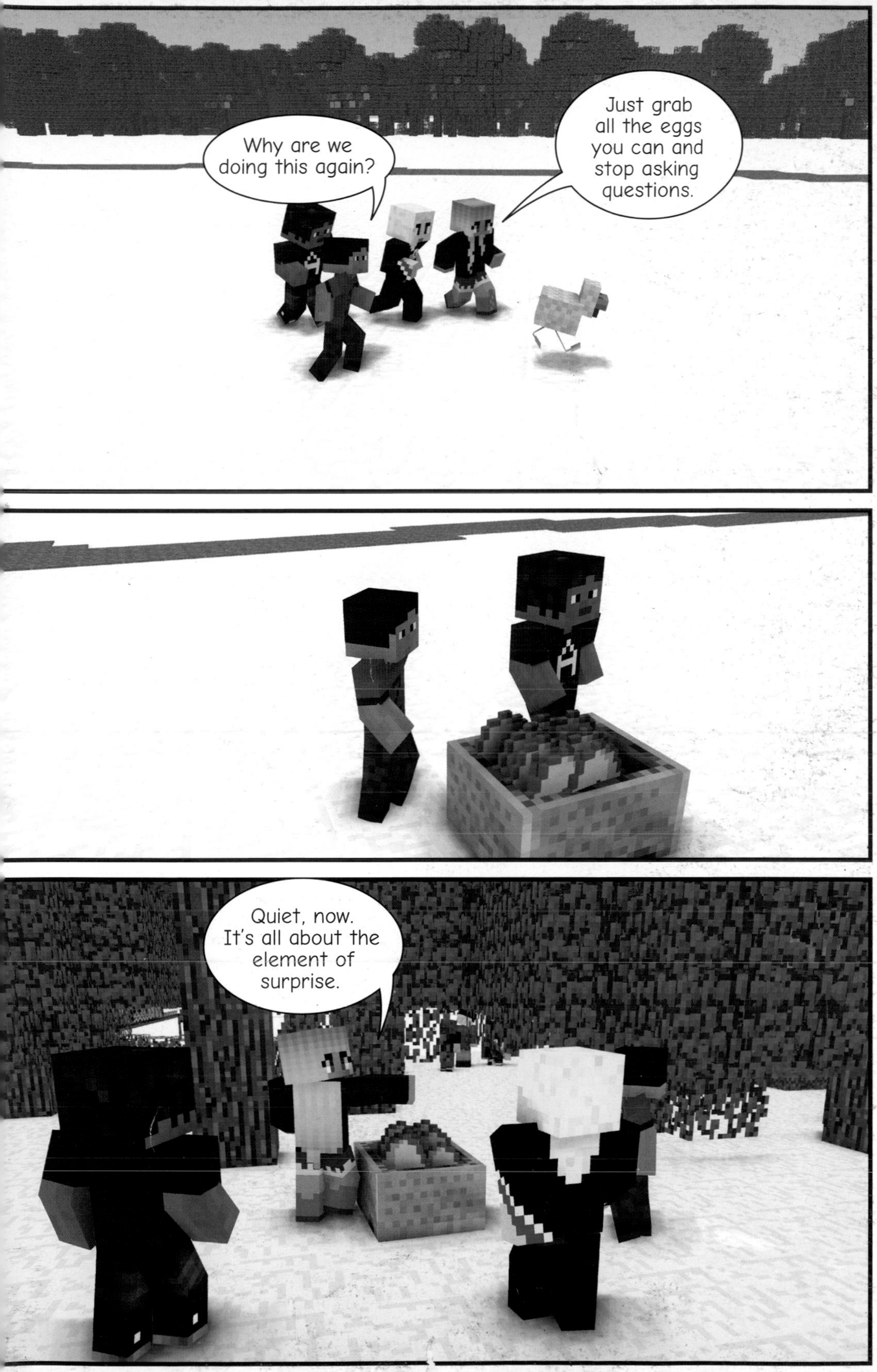
Why are we doing this again?
Just grab all the eggs you can and stop asking questions.
Quiet, now. It's all about the element of surprise.

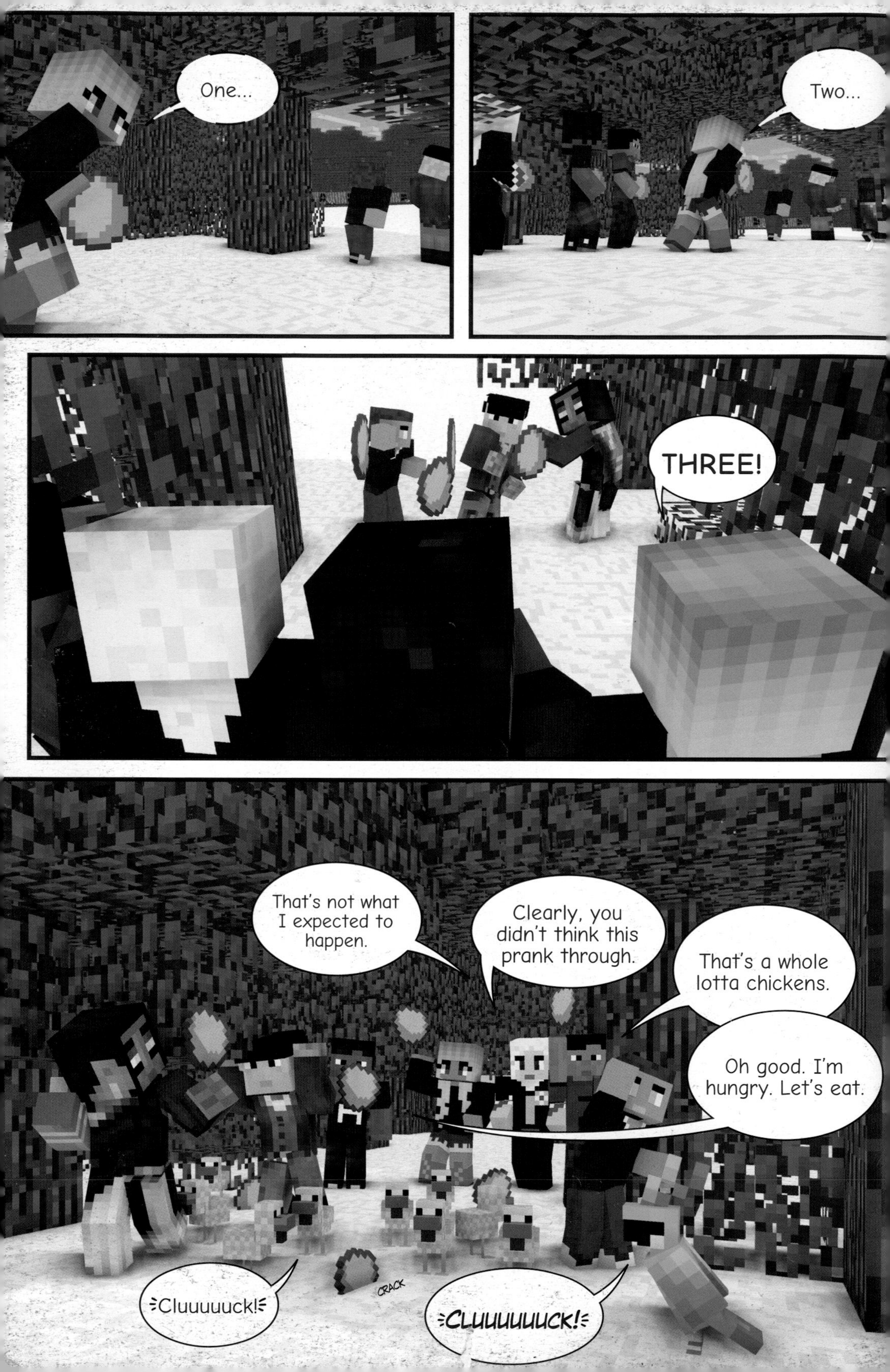
One...
Two...
THREE!
That's not what I expected to happen.
Clearly, you didn't think this prank through.
That's a whole lotta chickens.
Oh good. I'm hungry. Let's eat.
Cluuuuuck!
CRACK
CLUUUUUUCK!

CHAPTER 5

UNANSWERED QUESTIONS

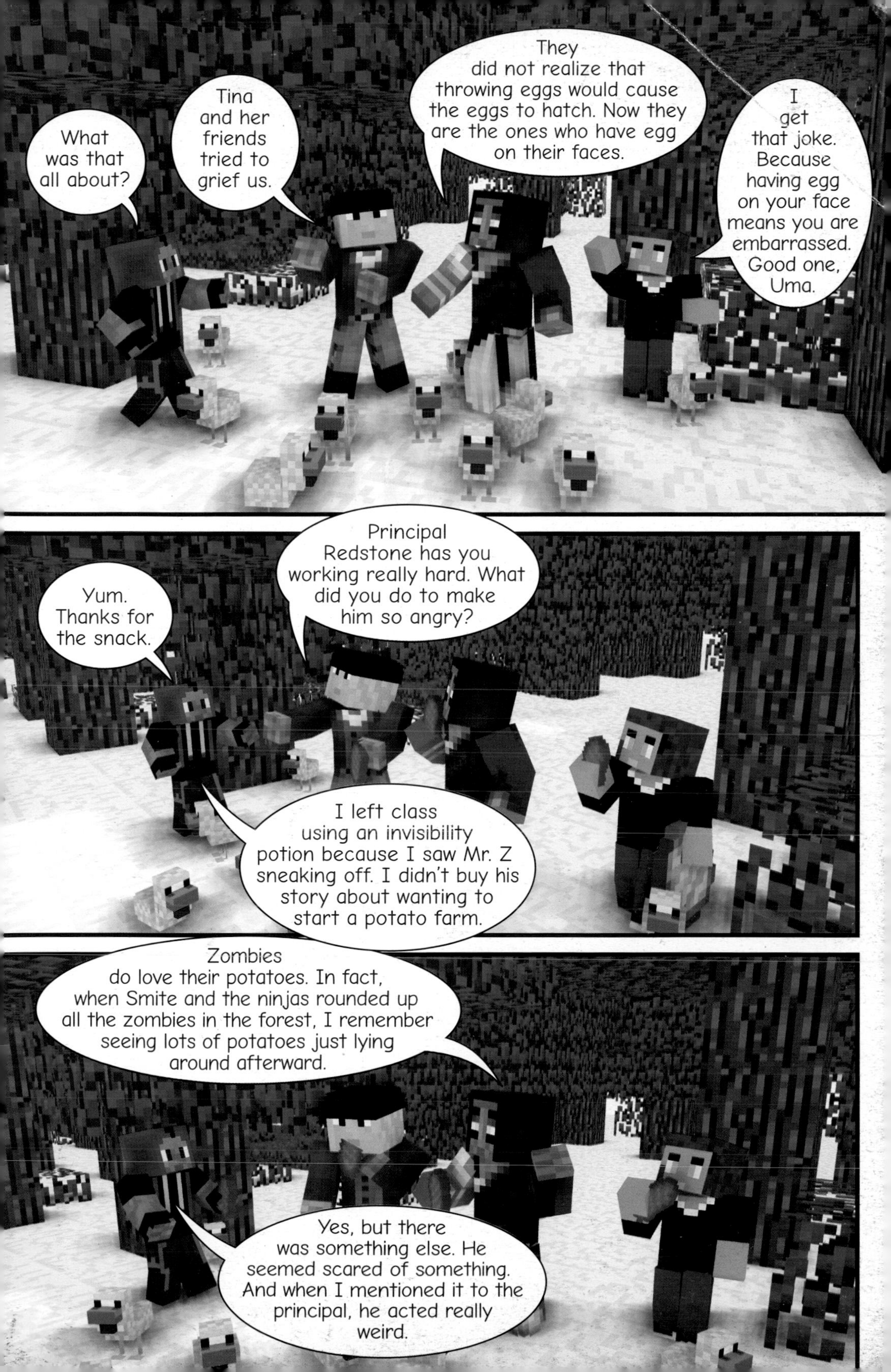
What was that all about?
Tina and her friends tried to grief us.
They did not realize that throwing eggs would cause the eggs to hatch. Now they are the ones who have egg on their faces.
I get that joke. Because having egg on your face means you are embarrassed. Good one, Uma.
Yum. Thanks for the snack.
Principal Redstone has you working really hard. What did you do to make him so angry?
I left class using an invisibility potion because I saw Mr. Z sneaking off. I didn't buy his story about wanting to start a potato farm.
Zombies do love their potatoes. In fact, when Smite and the ninjas rounded up all the zombies in the forest, I remember seeing lots of potatoes just lying around afterward.
Yes, but there was something else. He seemed scared of something. And when I mentioned it to the principal, he acted really weird.

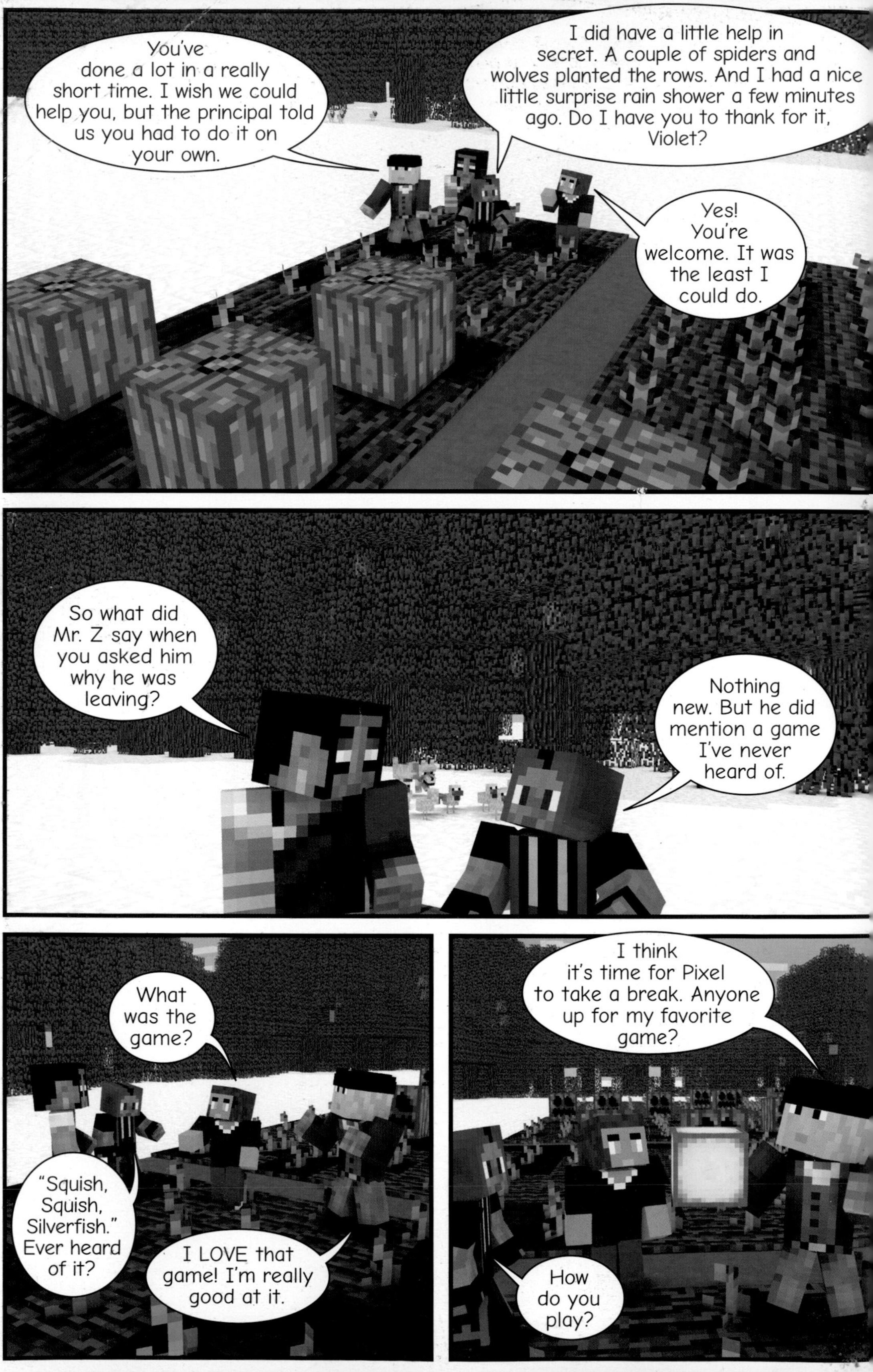
You've done a lot in a really short time. I wish we could help you, but the principal told us you had to do it on your own.
I did have a little help in secret. A couple of spiders and wolves planted the rows. And I had a nice little surprise rain shower a few minutes ago. Do I have you to thank for it, Violet?
Yes! You're welcome. It was the least I could do.
So what did Mr. Z say when you asked him why he was leaving?
Nothing new. But he did mention a game I've never heard of.
What was the game?
"Squish, Squish, Silverfish." Ever heard of it?
I LOVE that game! I'm really good at it.
I think it's time for Pixel to take a break. Anyone up for my favorite game?
How do you play?

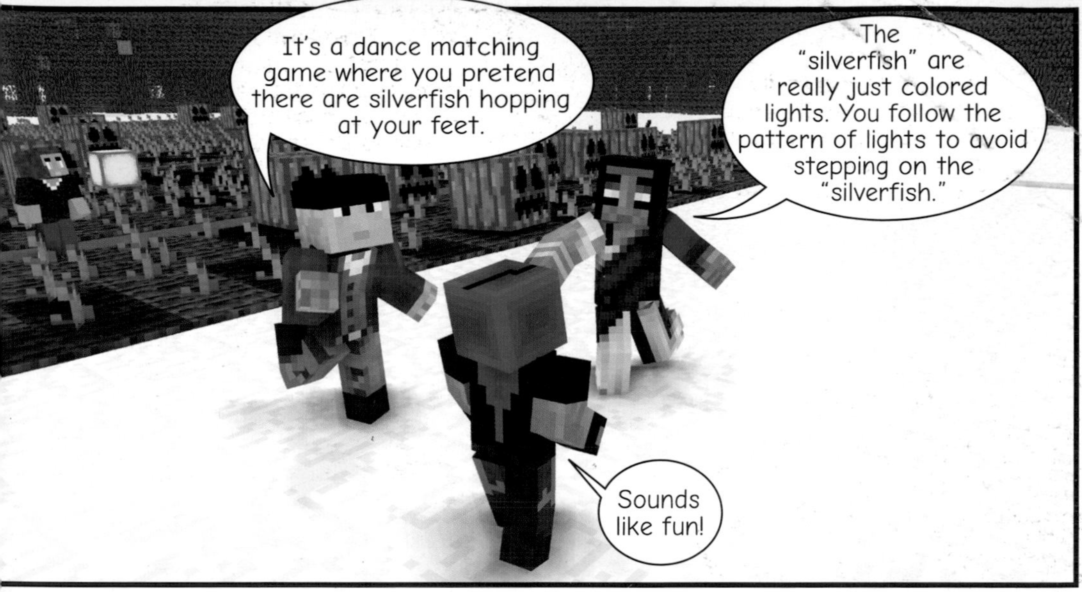
It's a dance matching game where you pretend there are silverfish hopping at your feet.
The "silverfish" are really just colored lights. You follow the pattern of lights to avoid stepping on the "silverfish."
Sounds like fun!

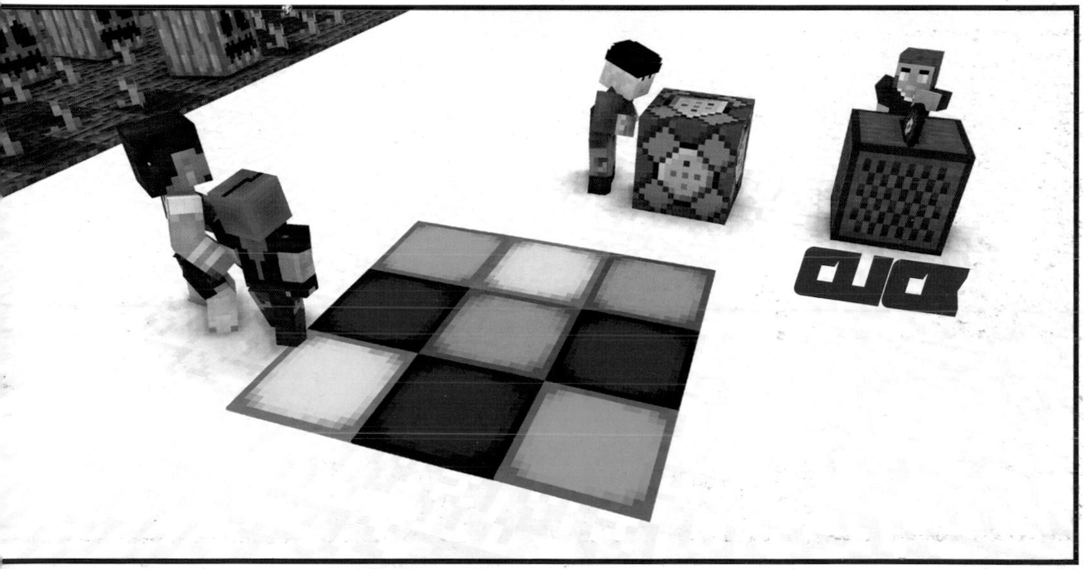
CLICK

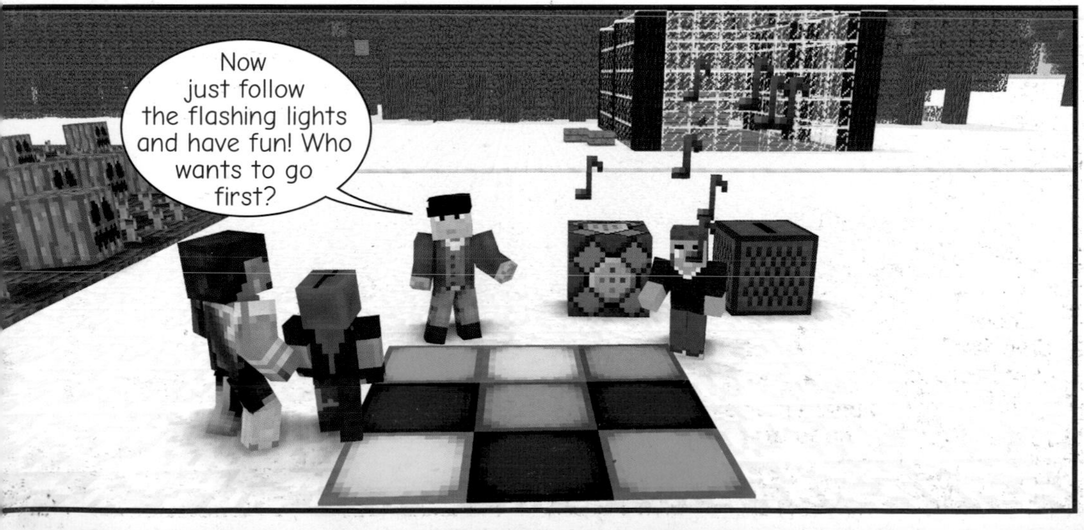
Now just follow the flashing lights and have fun! Who wants to go first?

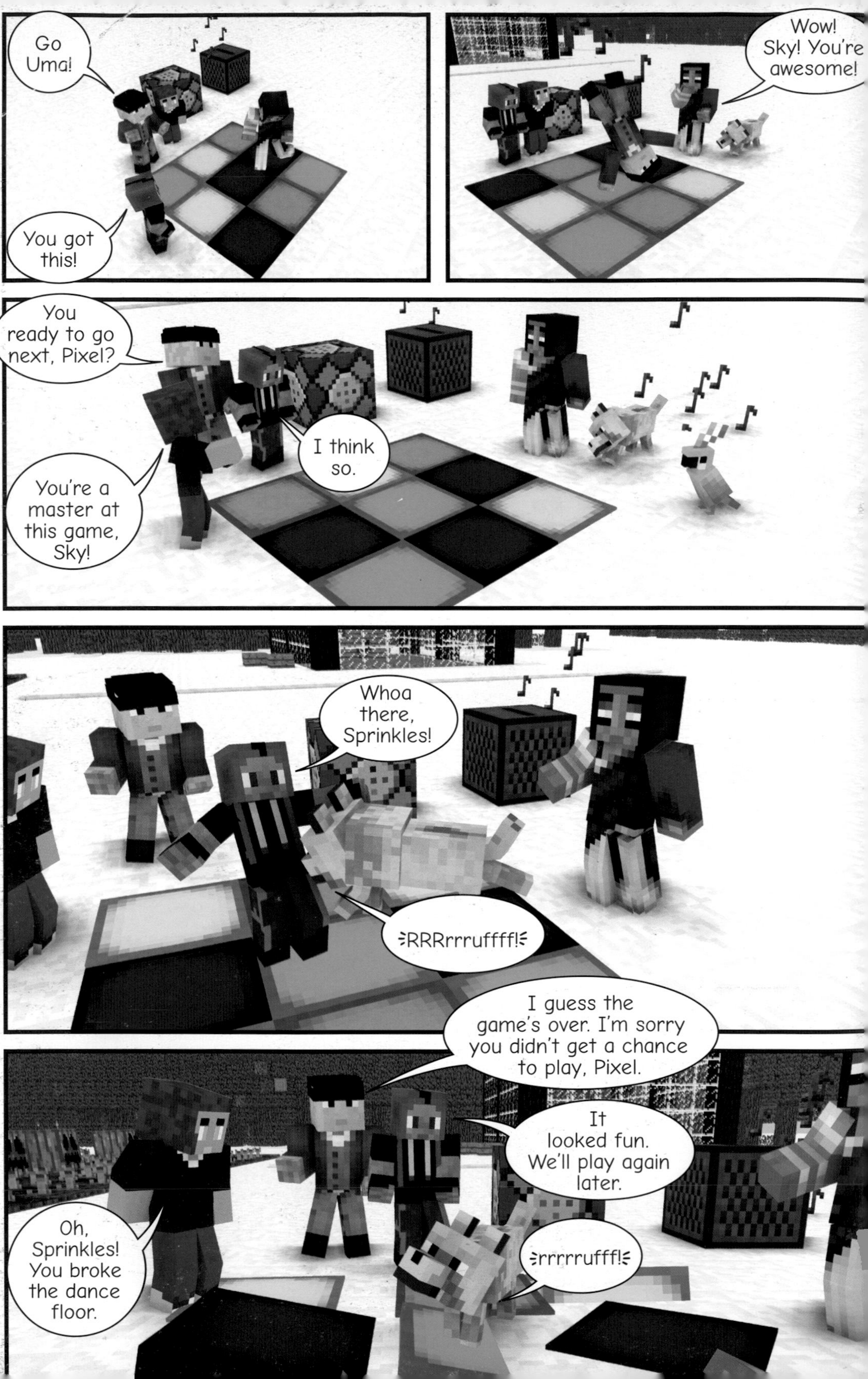

Go Uma!
You got this!
Wow! Sky! You're awesome!
You ready to go next, Pixel?
I think so.
You're a master at this game, Sky!
Whoa there, Sprinkles!
RRRrrruffff!
I guess the game's over. I'm sorry you didn't get a chance to play, Pixel.
It looked fun. We'll play again later.
Oh, Sprinkles! You broke the dance floor.
rrrrruffff!

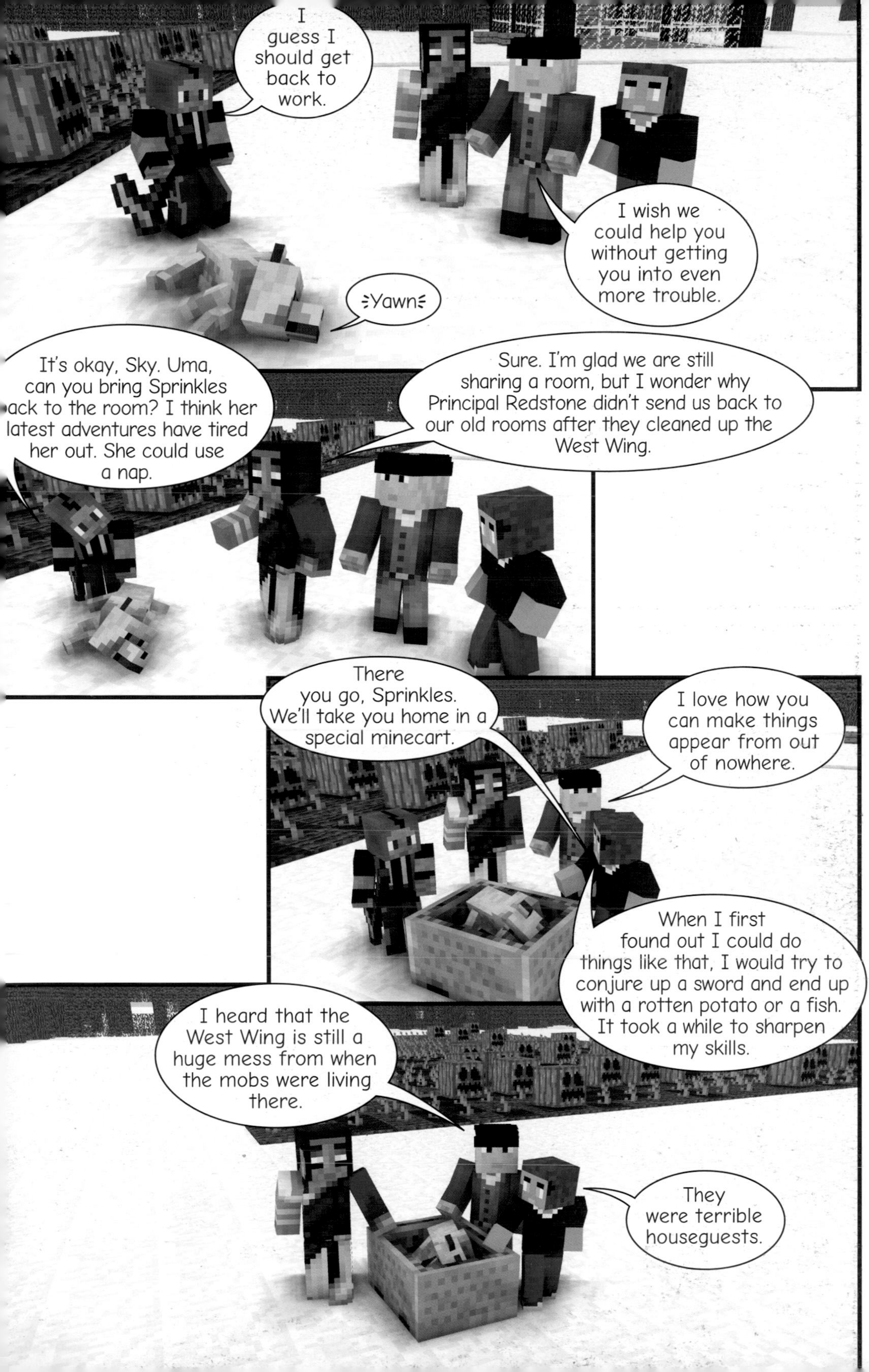

I guess I should get back to work.
I wish we could help you without getting you into even more trouble.
Yawn
It's okay, Sky. Uma, can you bring Sprinkles back to the room? I think her latest adventures have tired her out. She could use a nap.
Sure. I'm glad we are still sharing a room, but I wonder why Principal Redstone didn't send us back to our old rooms after they cleaned up the West Wing.
There you go, Sprinkles. We'll take you home in a special minecart.
I love how you can make things appear from out of nowhere.
When I first found out I could do things like that, I would try to conjure up a sword and end up with a rotten potato or a fish. It took a while to sharpen my skills.
I heard that the West Wing is still a huge mess from when the mobs were living there.
They were terrible houseguests.

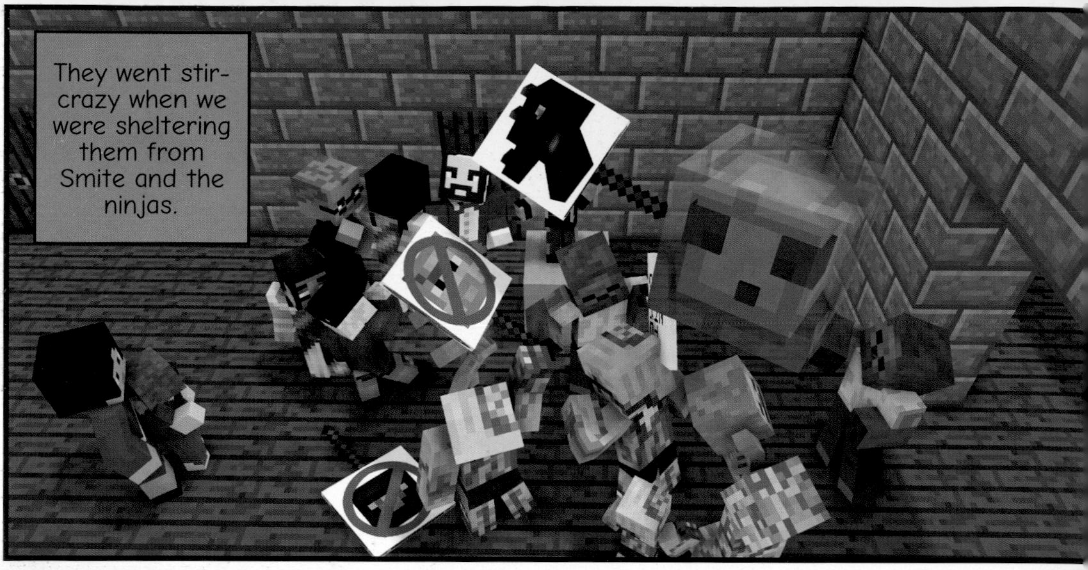
They went stir-crazy when we were sheltering them from Smite and the ninjas.

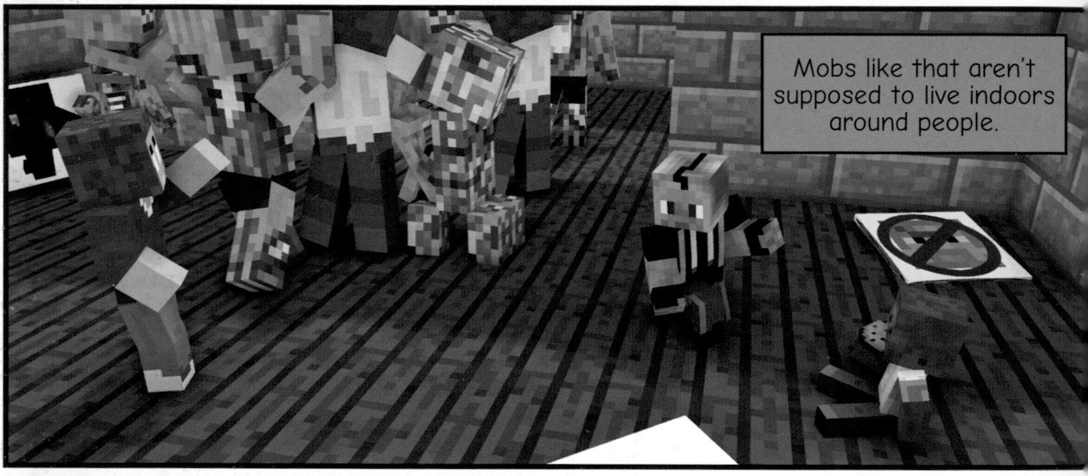
Mobs like that aren't supposed to live indoors around people.

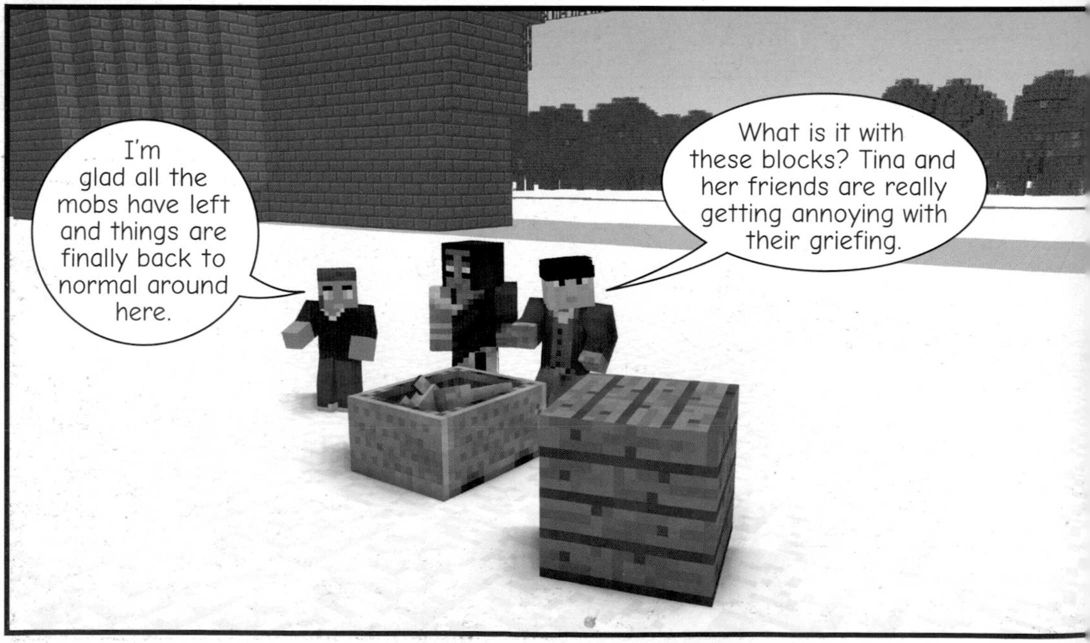
I'm glad all the mobs have left and things are finally back to normal around here.
What is it with these blocks? Tina and her friends are really getting annoying with their griefing.

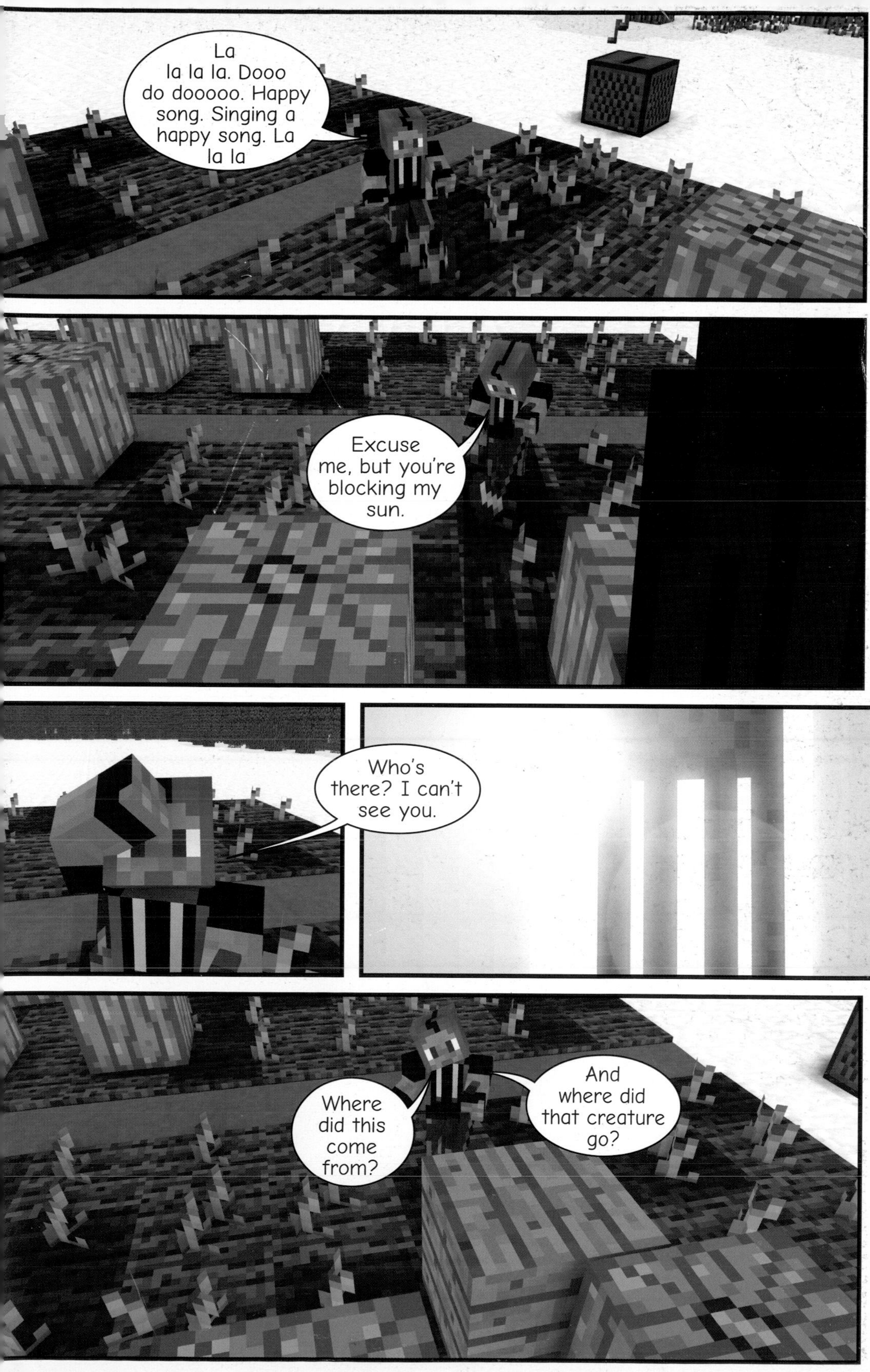
La la la la. Dooo do dooooo. Happy song. Singing a happy song. La la la
Excuse me, but you're blocking my sun.
Who's there? I can't see you.
Where did this come from?
And where did that creature go?

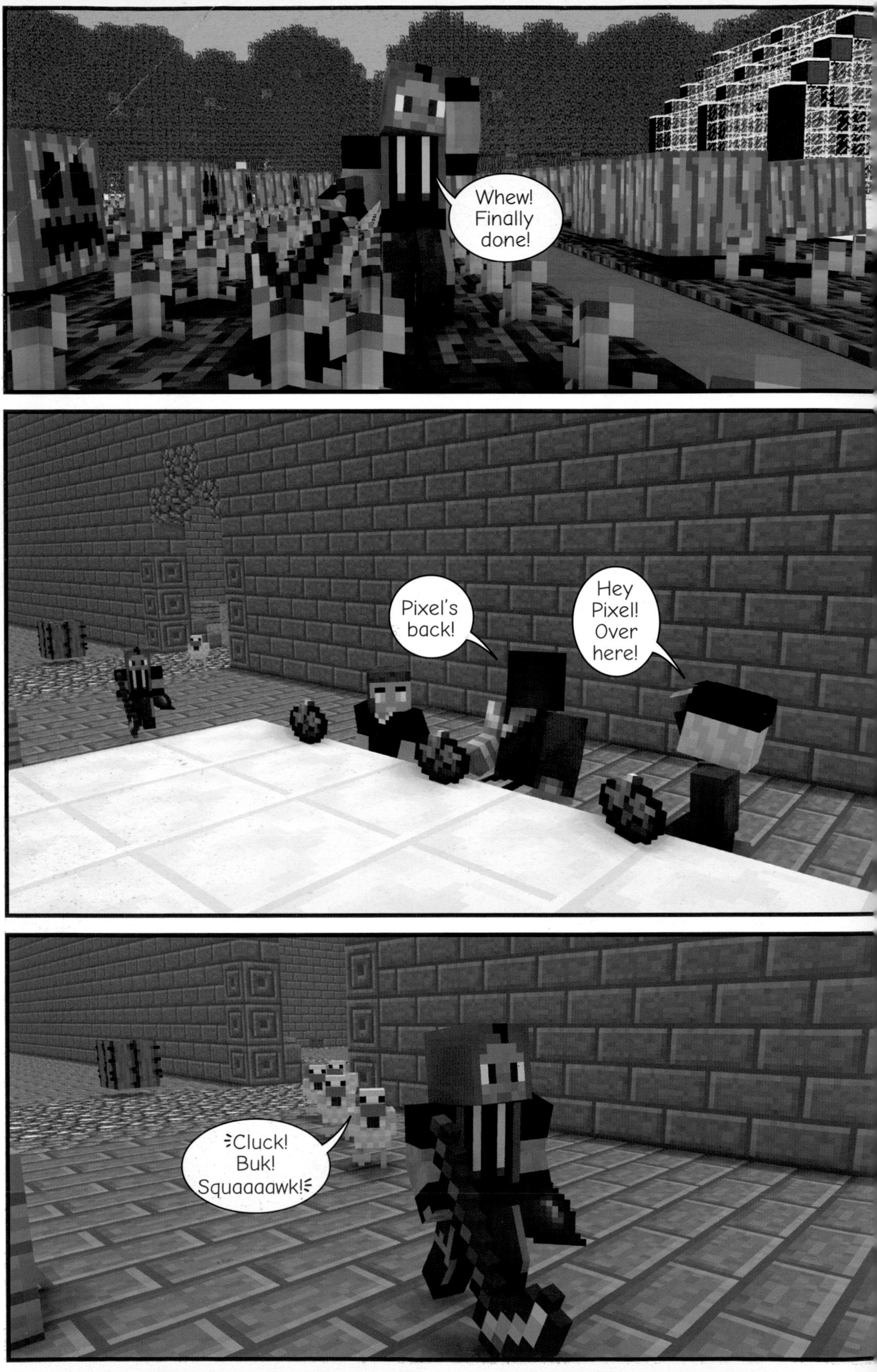
Whew! Finally done!
Pixel's back!
Hey Pixel! Over here!
Cluck! Buk! Squaaaawk!

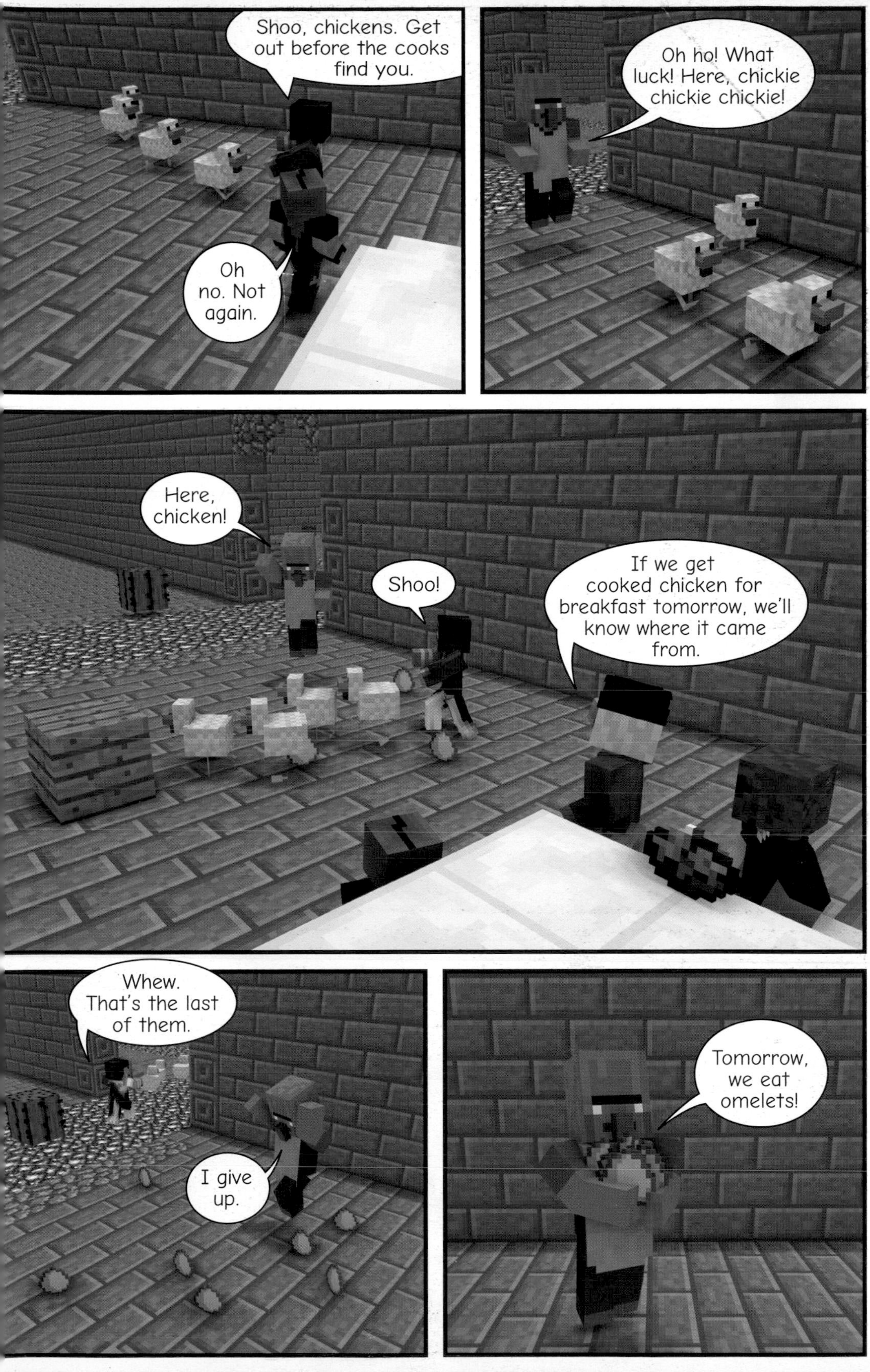
Shoo, chickens. Get out before the cooks find you.
Oh no. Not again.
Oh ho! What luck! Here, chickie chickie chickie!
Here, chicken!
Shoo!
If we get cooked chicken for breakfast tomorrow, we'll know where it came from.
Whew. That's the last of them.
I give up.
Tomorrow, we eat omelets!

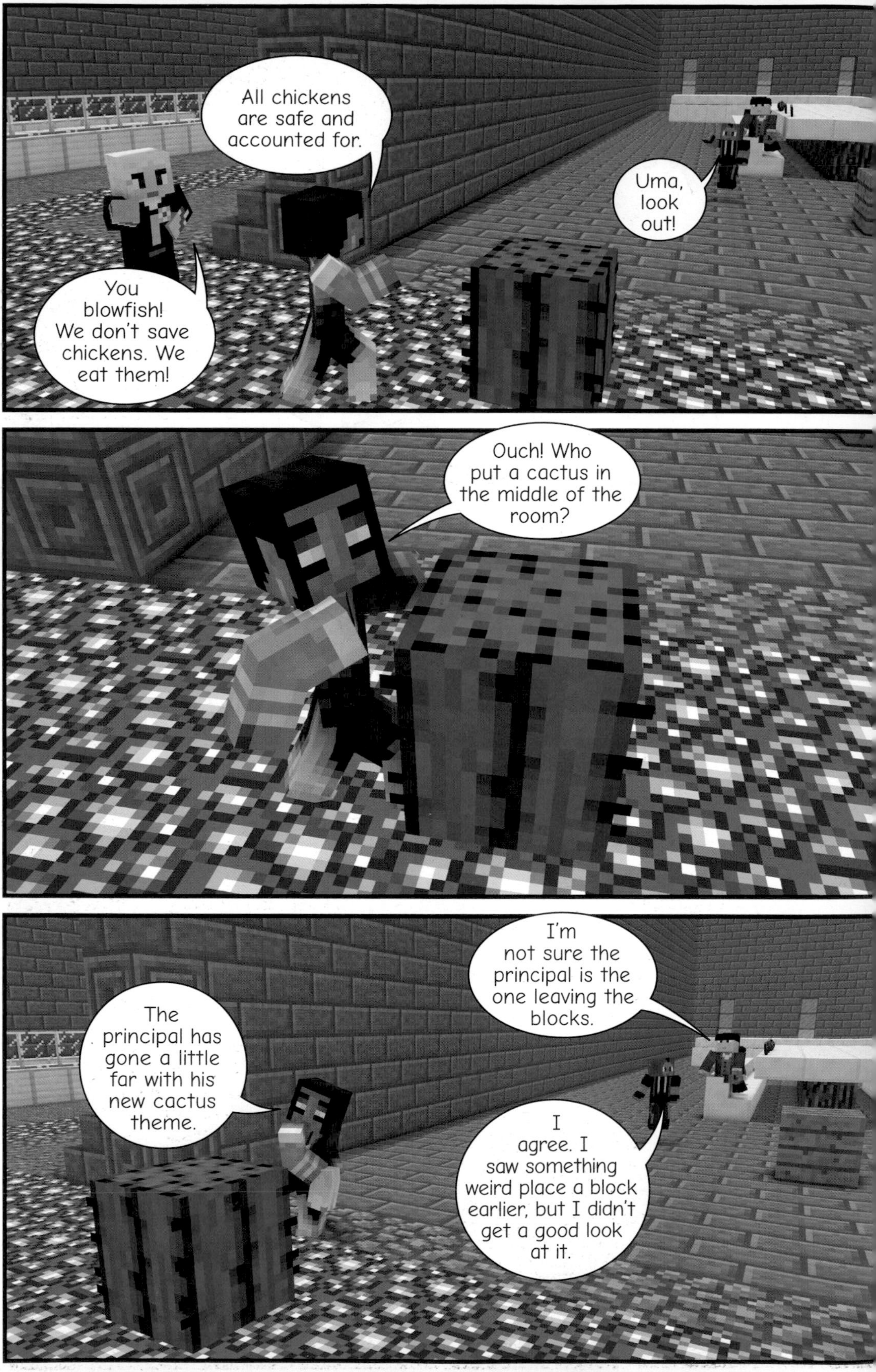
All chickens are safe and accounted for.
You blowfish! We don't save chickens. We eat them!
Uma, look out!
Ouch! Who put a cactus in the middle of the room?
The principal has gone a little far with his new cactus theme.
I'm not sure the principal is the one leaving the blocks.
I agree. I saw something weird place a block earlier, but I didn't get a good look at it.

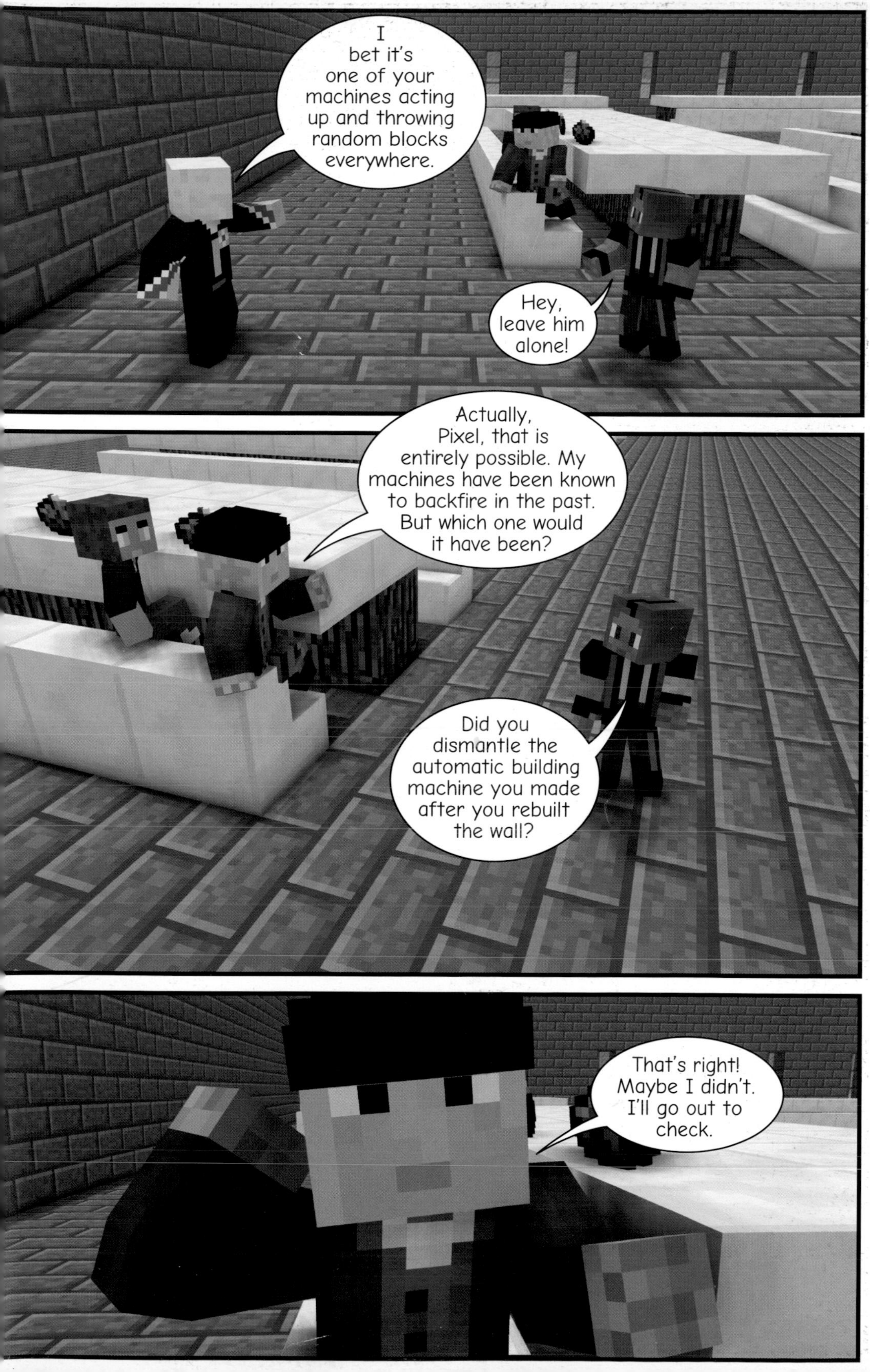
I bet it's one of your machines acting up and throwing random blocks everywhere.
Hey, leave him alone!
Actually, Pixel, that is entirely possible. My machines have been known to backfire in the past. But which one would it have been?
Did you dismantle the automatic building machine you made after you rebuilt the wall?
That's right! Maybe I didn't. I'll go out to check.

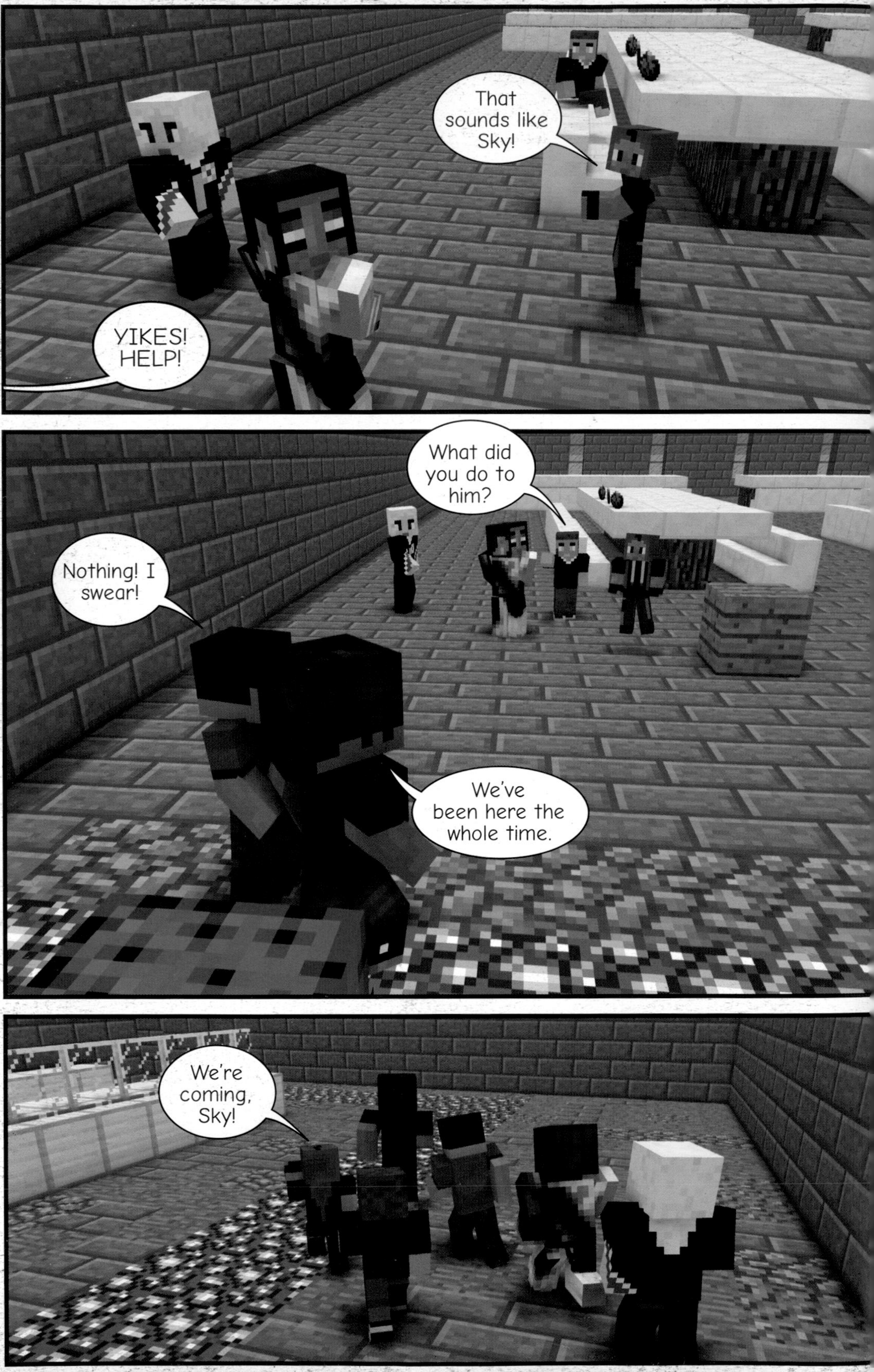
That sounds like Sky!
YIKES! HELP!
What did you do to him?
Nothing! I swear!
We've been here the whole time.
We're coming, Sky!

CHAPTER 6

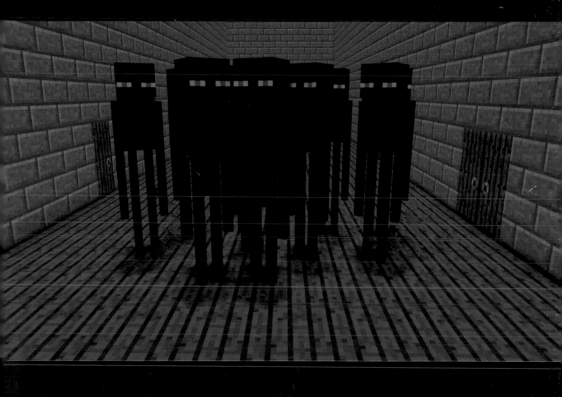

THE VISITORS

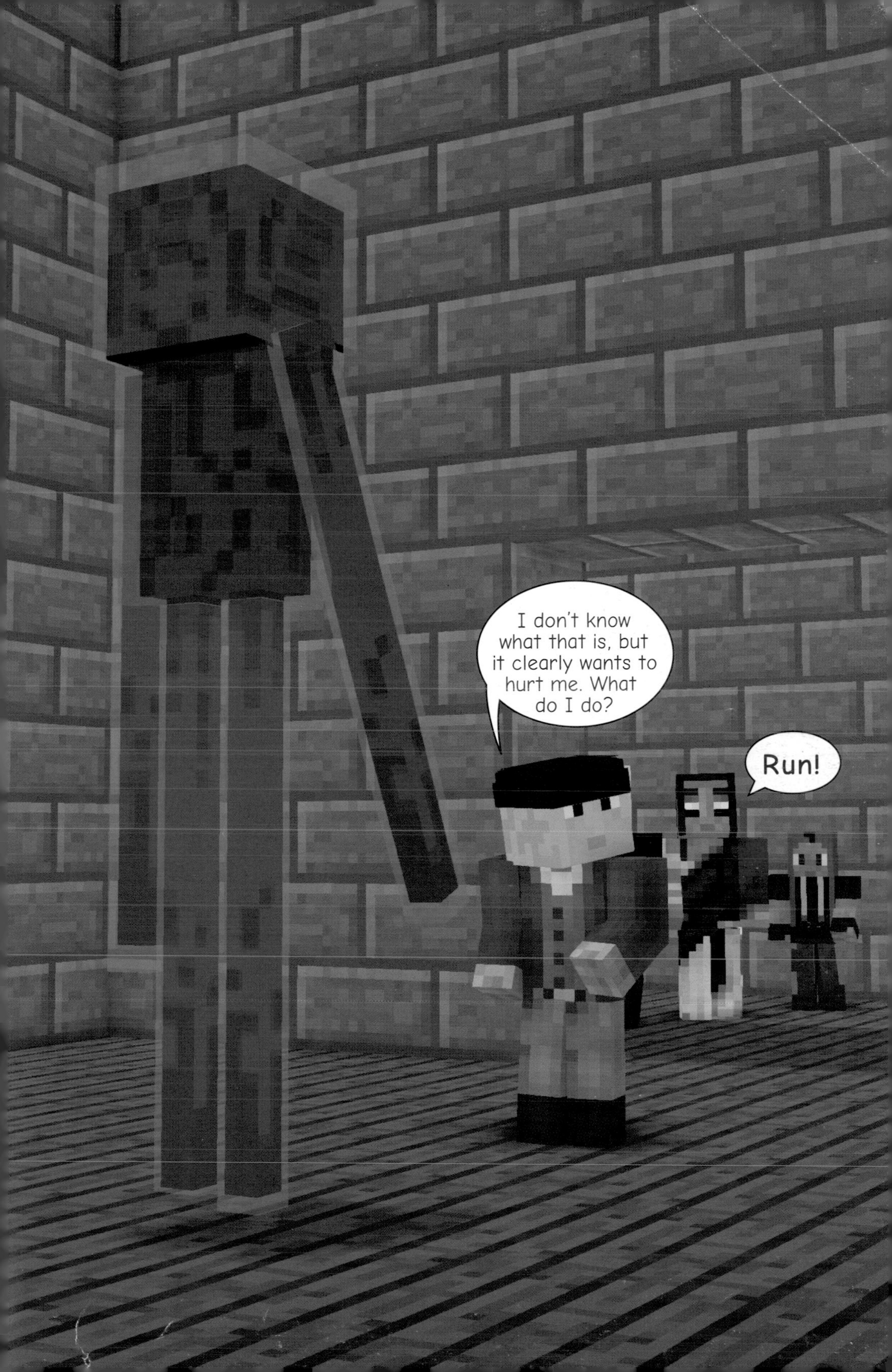
I don't know what that is, but it clearly wants to hurt me. What do I do?
Run!

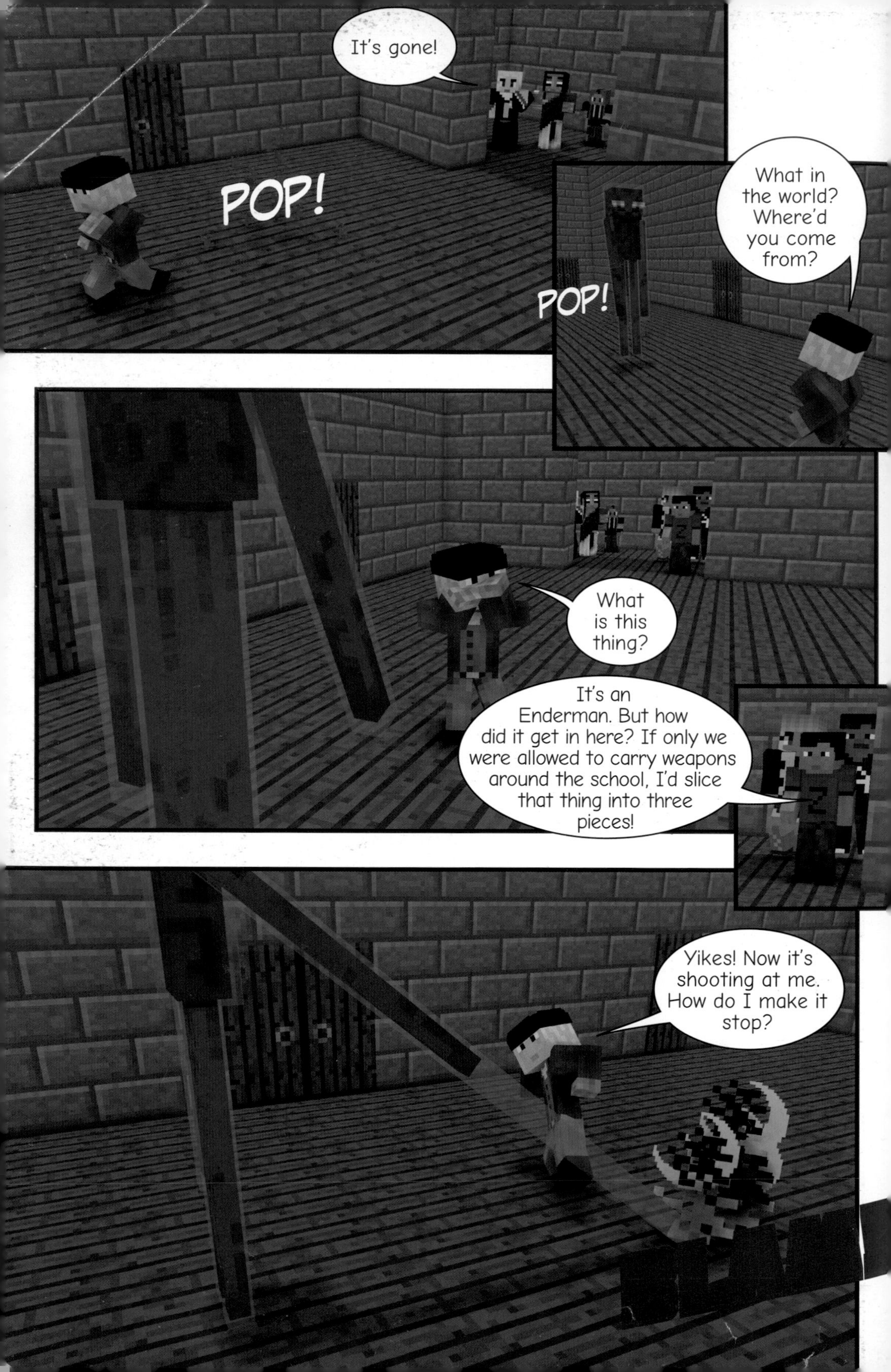
It's gone!
POP!
POP!
What in the world? Where'd you come from?
What is this thing?
It's an Enderman. But how did it get in here? If only we were allowed to carry weapons around the school, I'd slice that thing into three pieces!
Yikes! Now it's shooting at me. How do I make it stop?

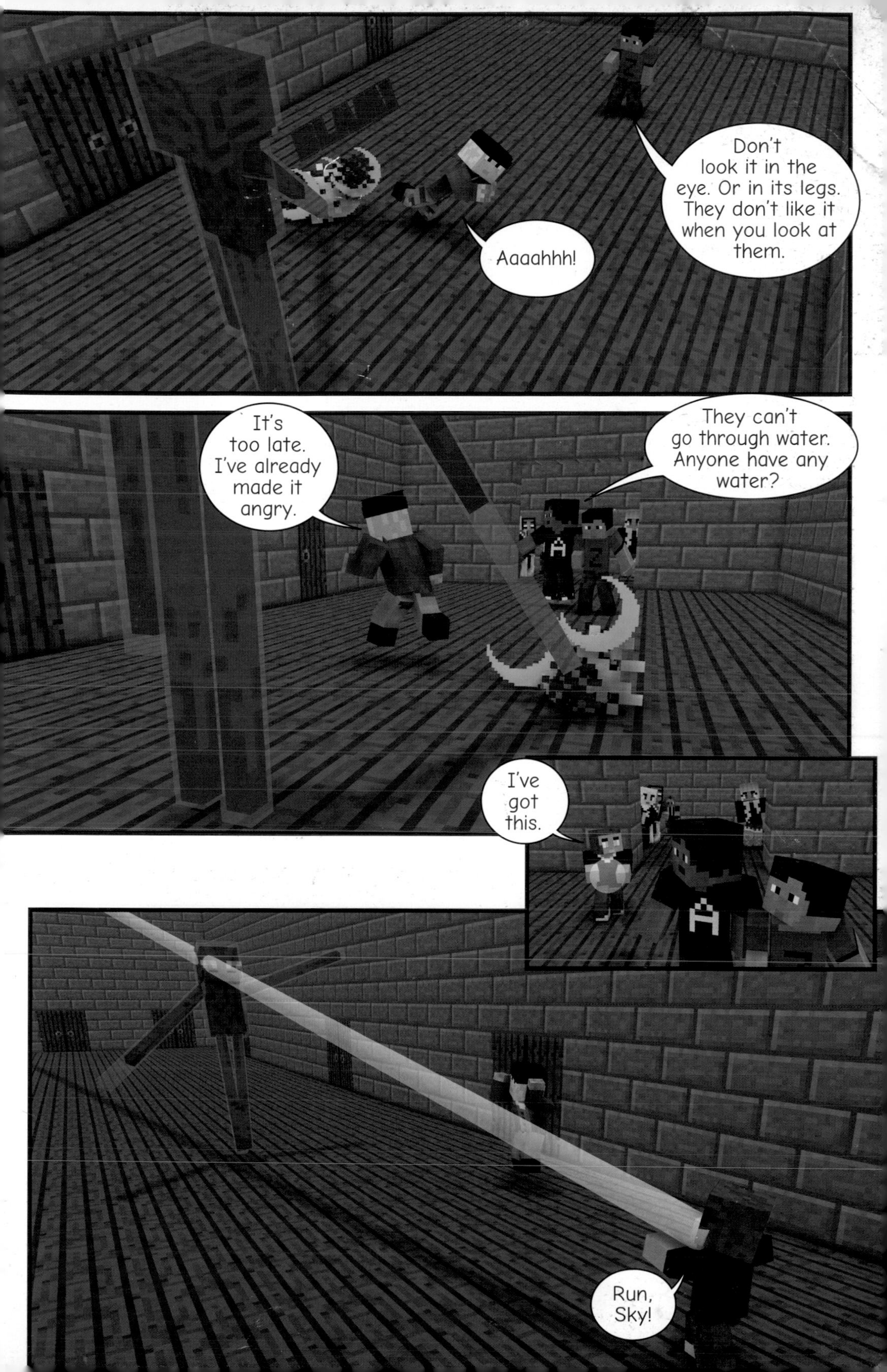
Don't look it in the eye. Or in its legs. They don't like it when you look at them.
Aaaahhh!
It's too late. I've already made it angry.
They can't go through water. Anyone have any water?
I've got this.
Run, Sky!

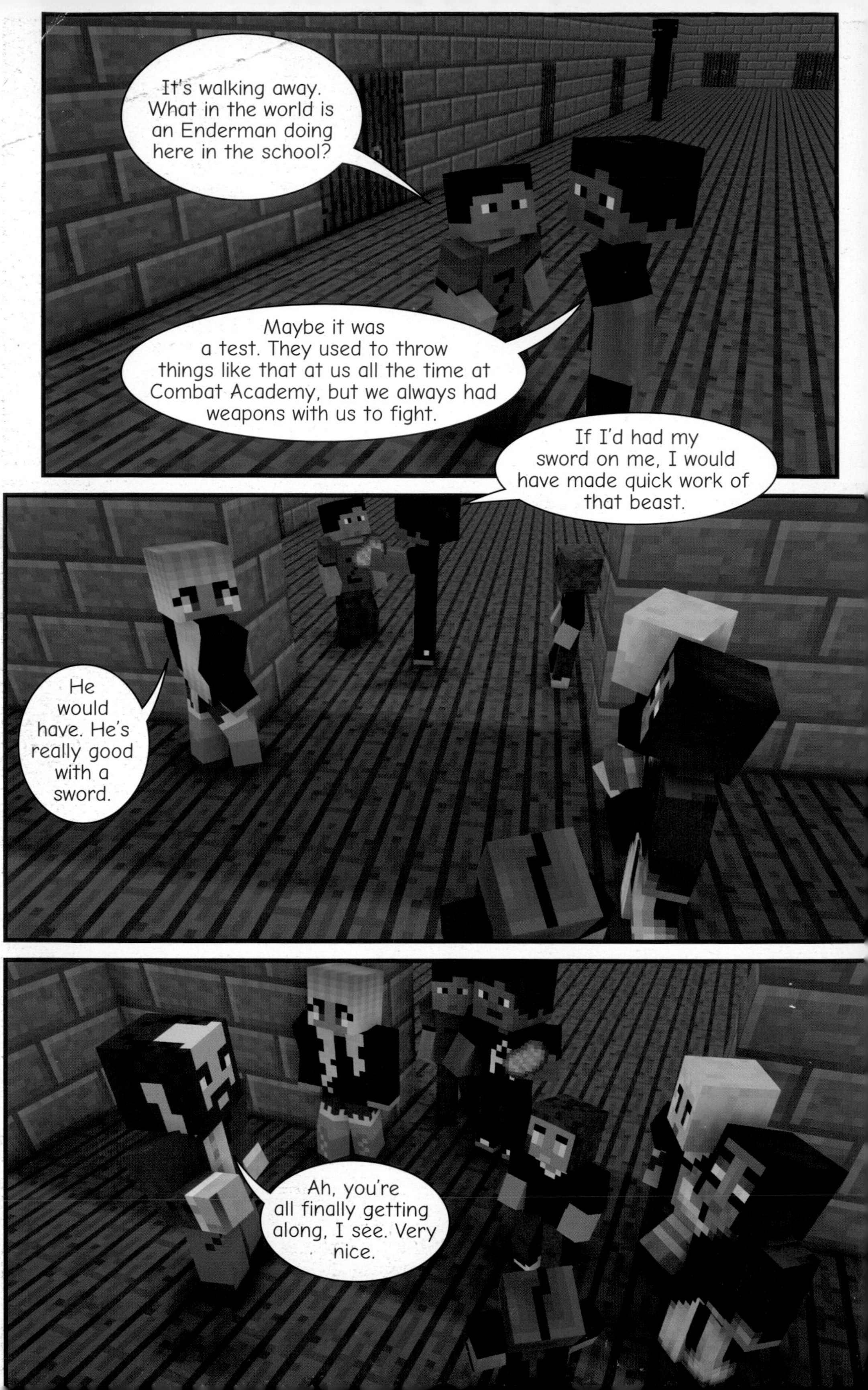
It's walking away. What in the world is an Enderman doing here in the school?
Maybe it was a test. They used to throw things like that at us all the time at Combat Academy, but we always had weapons with us to fight.
If I'd had my sword on me, I would have made quick work of that beast.
He would have. He's really good with a sword.
Ah, you're all finally getting along, I see. Very nice.

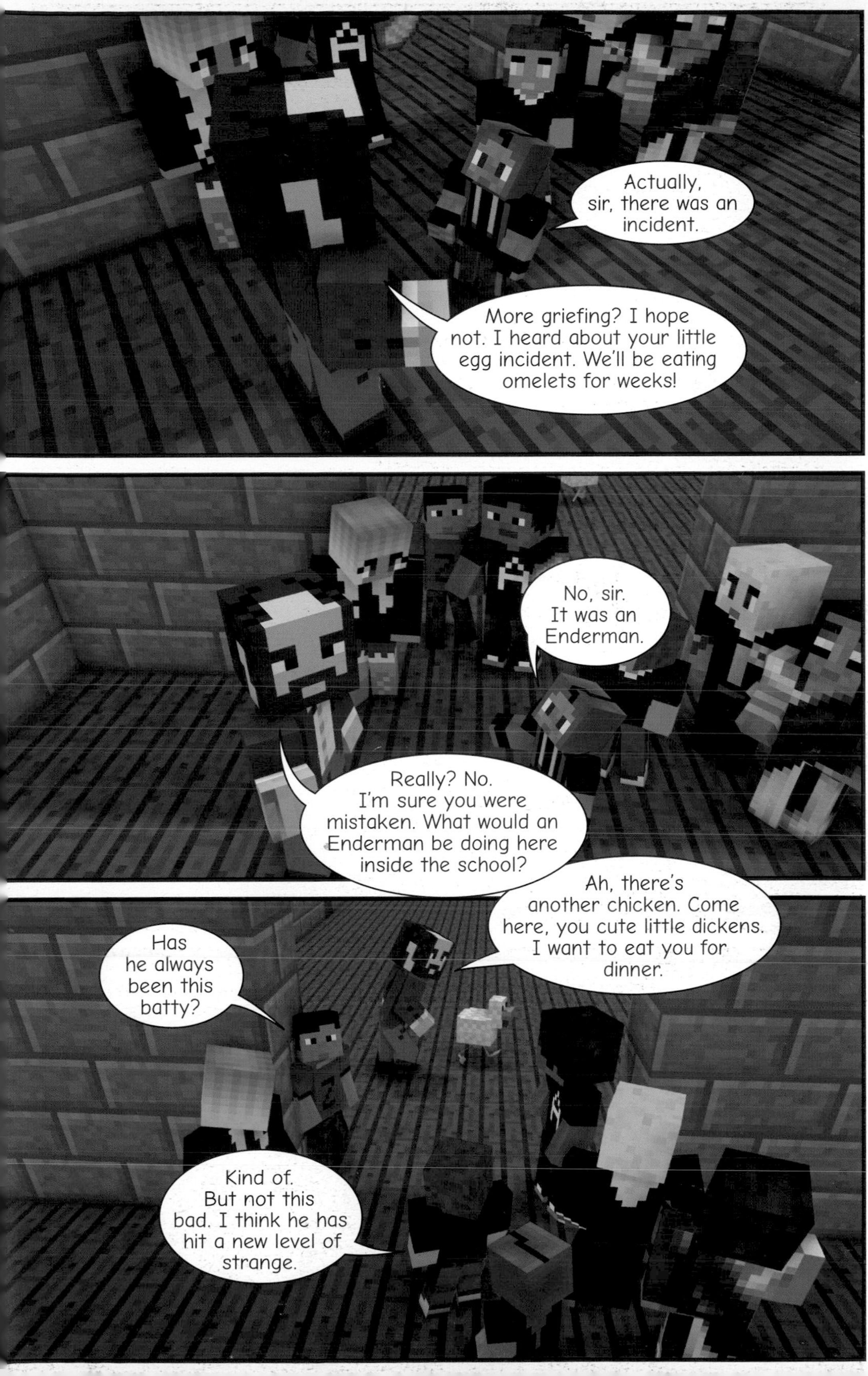
Actually, sir, there was an incident.
More griefing? I hope not. I heard about your little egg incident. We'll be eating omelets for weeks!
No, sir. It was an Enderman.
Really? No. I'm sure you were mistaken. What would an Enderman be doing here inside the school?
Ah, there's another chicken. Come here, you cute little dickens. I want to eat you for dinner.
Has he always been this batty?
Kind of. But not this bad. I think he has hit a new level of strange.

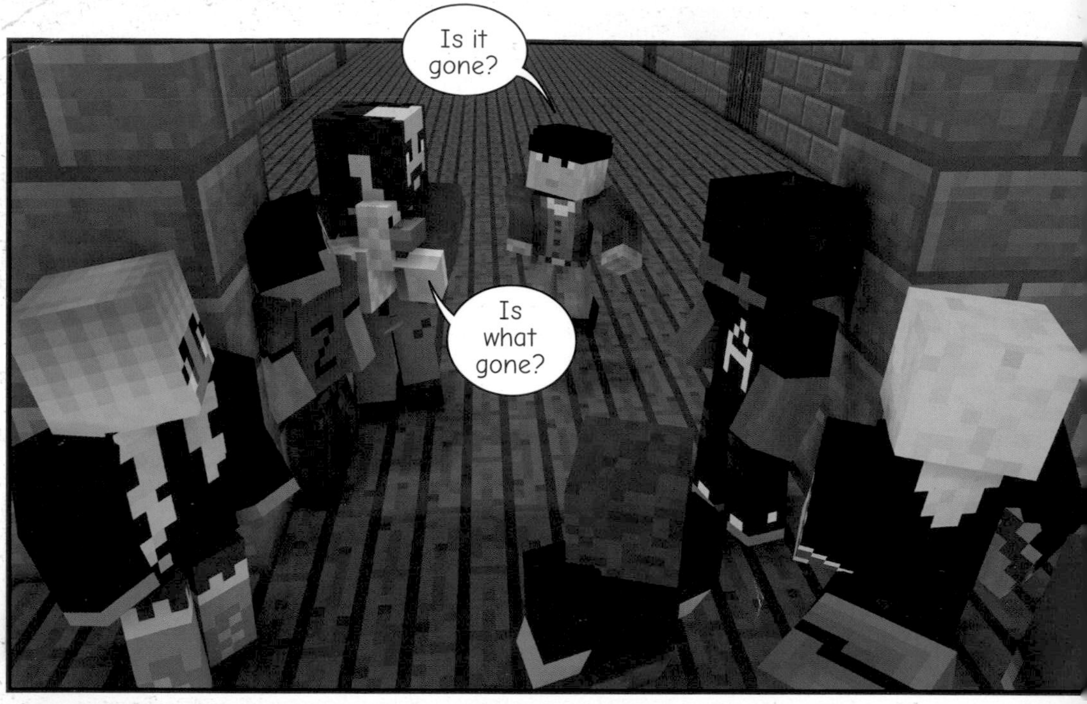
Is it gone?
Is what gone?

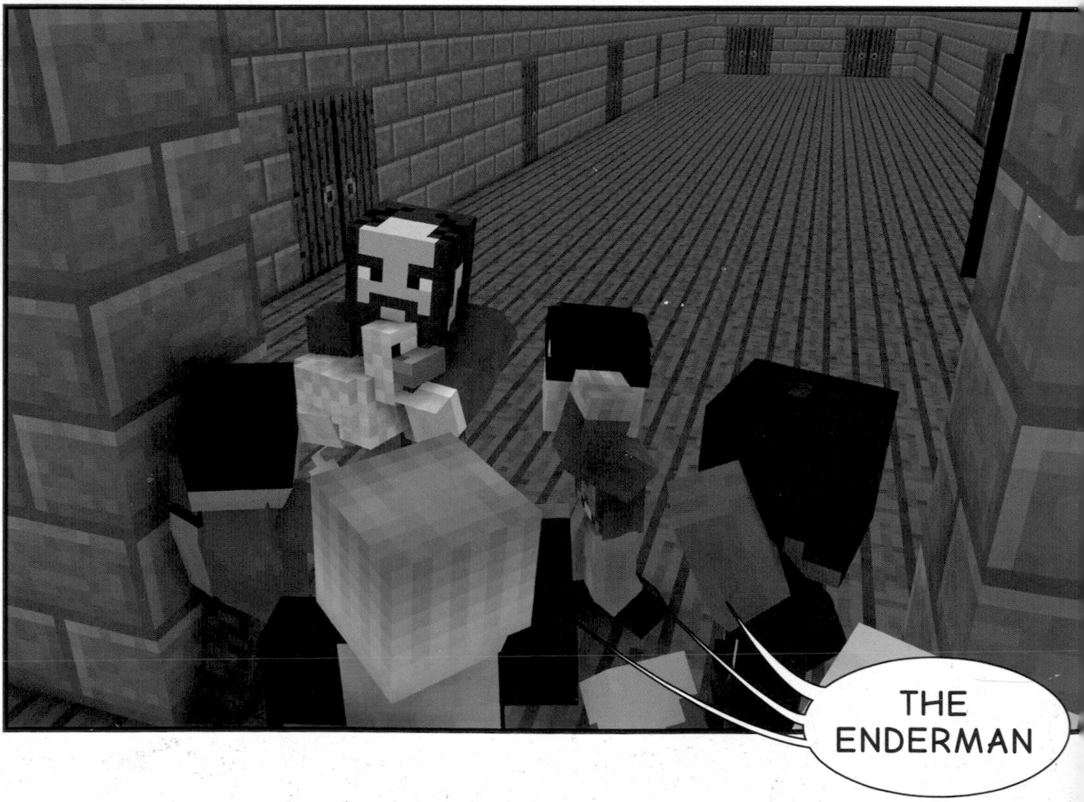
THE ENDERMAN

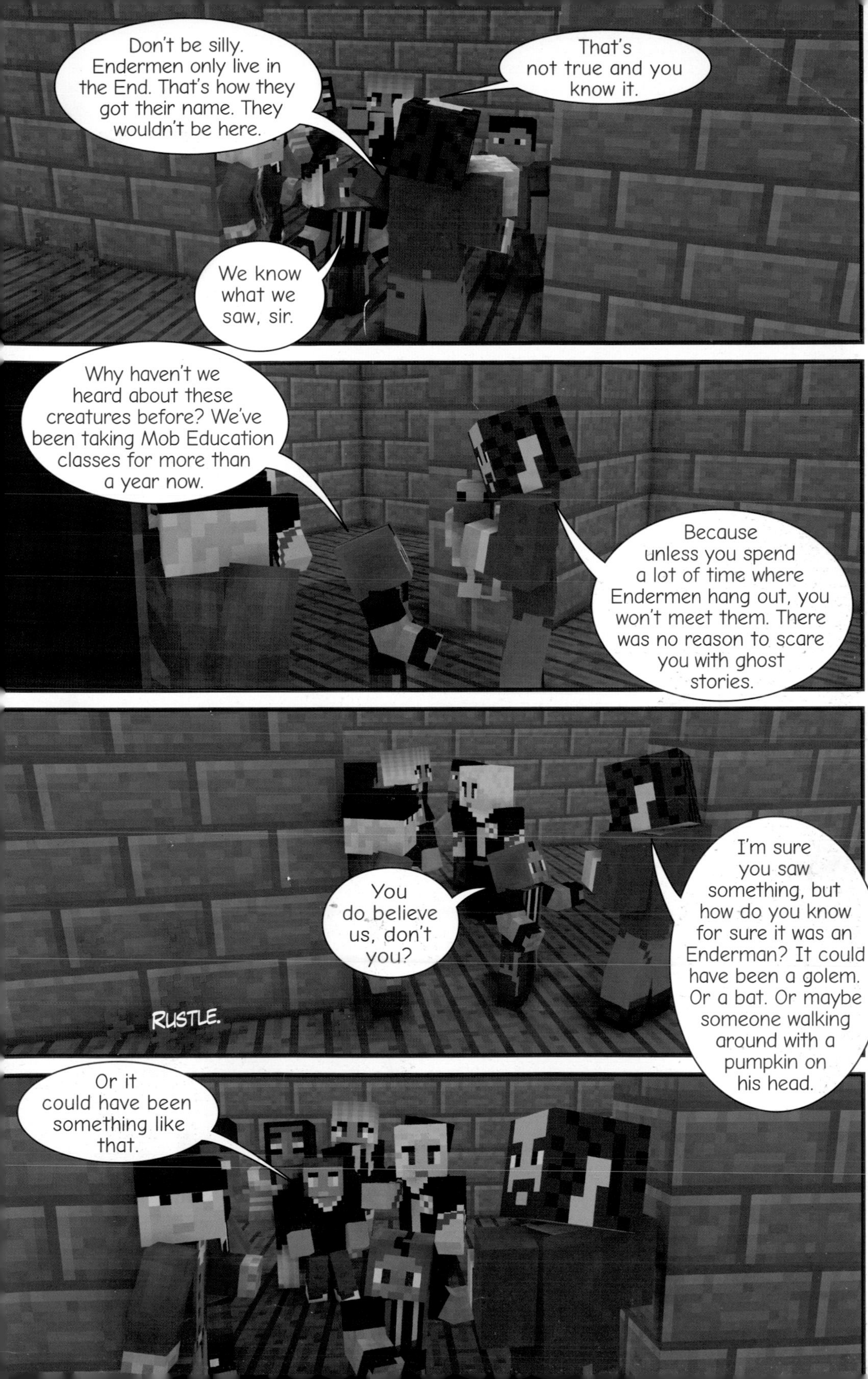
Don't be silly. Endermen only live in the End. That's how they got their name. They wouldn't be here.
That's not true and you know it.
We know what we saw, sir.
Why haven't we heard about these creatures before? We've been taking Mob Education classes for more than a year now.
Because unless you spend a lot of time where Endermen hang out, you won't meet them. There was no reason to scare you with ghost stories.
You do believe us, don't you?
I'm sure you saw something, but how do you know for sure it was an Enderman? It could have been a golem. Or a bat. Or maybe someone walking around with a pumpkin on his head.
RUSTLE.
Or it could have been something like that.

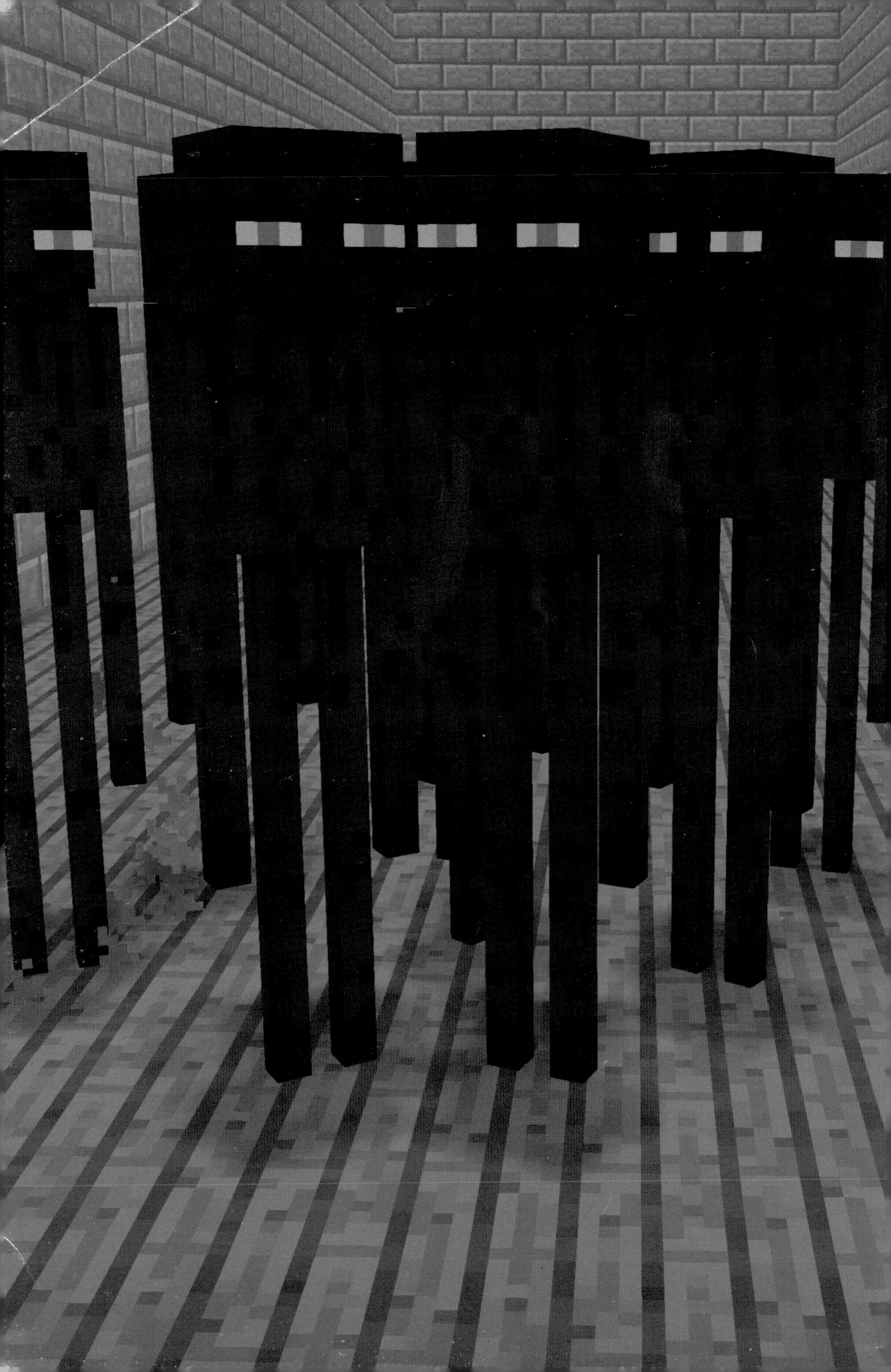

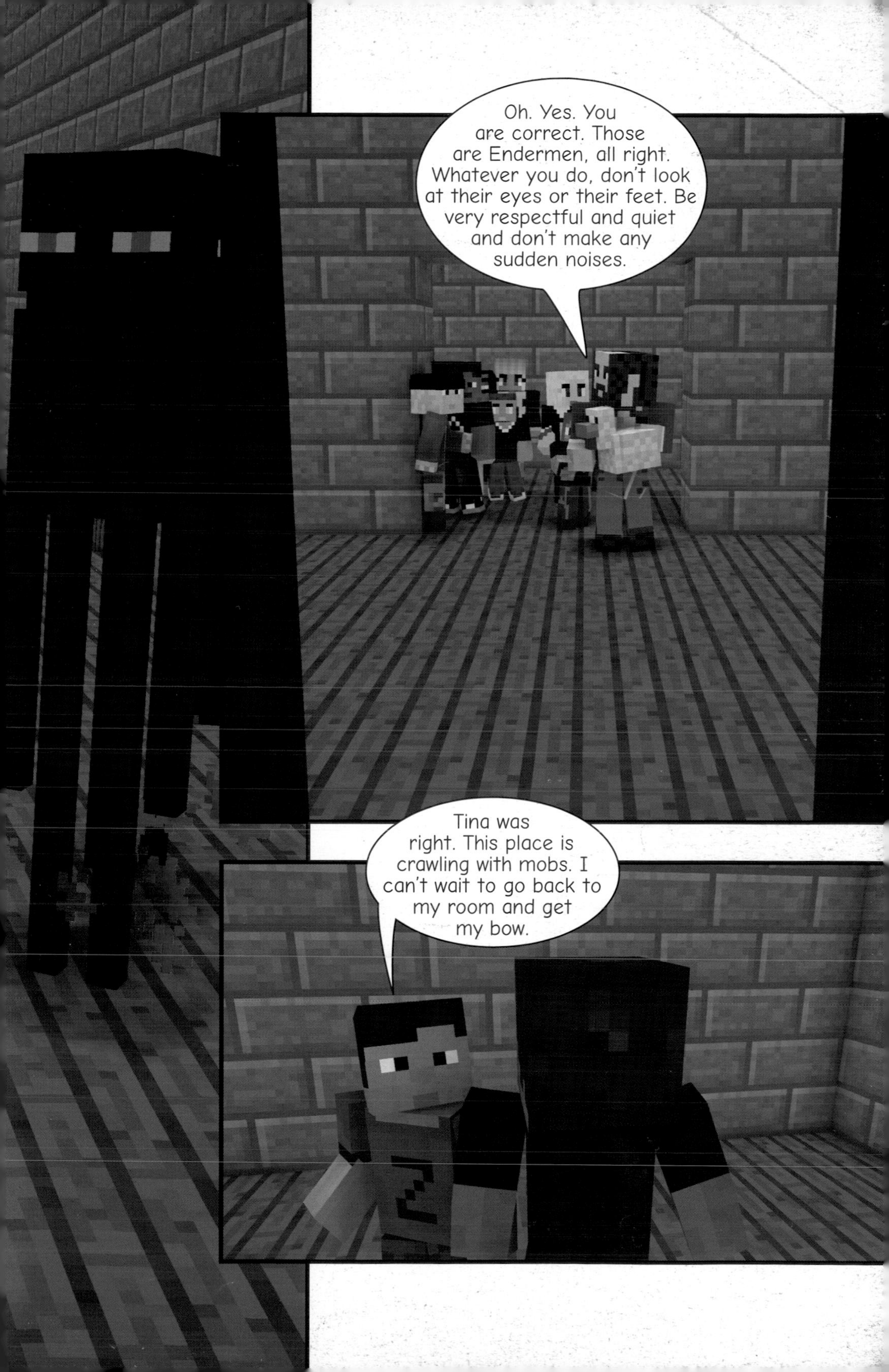
Oh. Yes. You are correct. Those are Endermen, all right. Whatever you do, don't look at their eyes or their feet. Be very respectful and quiet and don't make any sudden noises.
Tina was right. This place is crawling with mobs. I can't wait to go back to my room and get my bow.

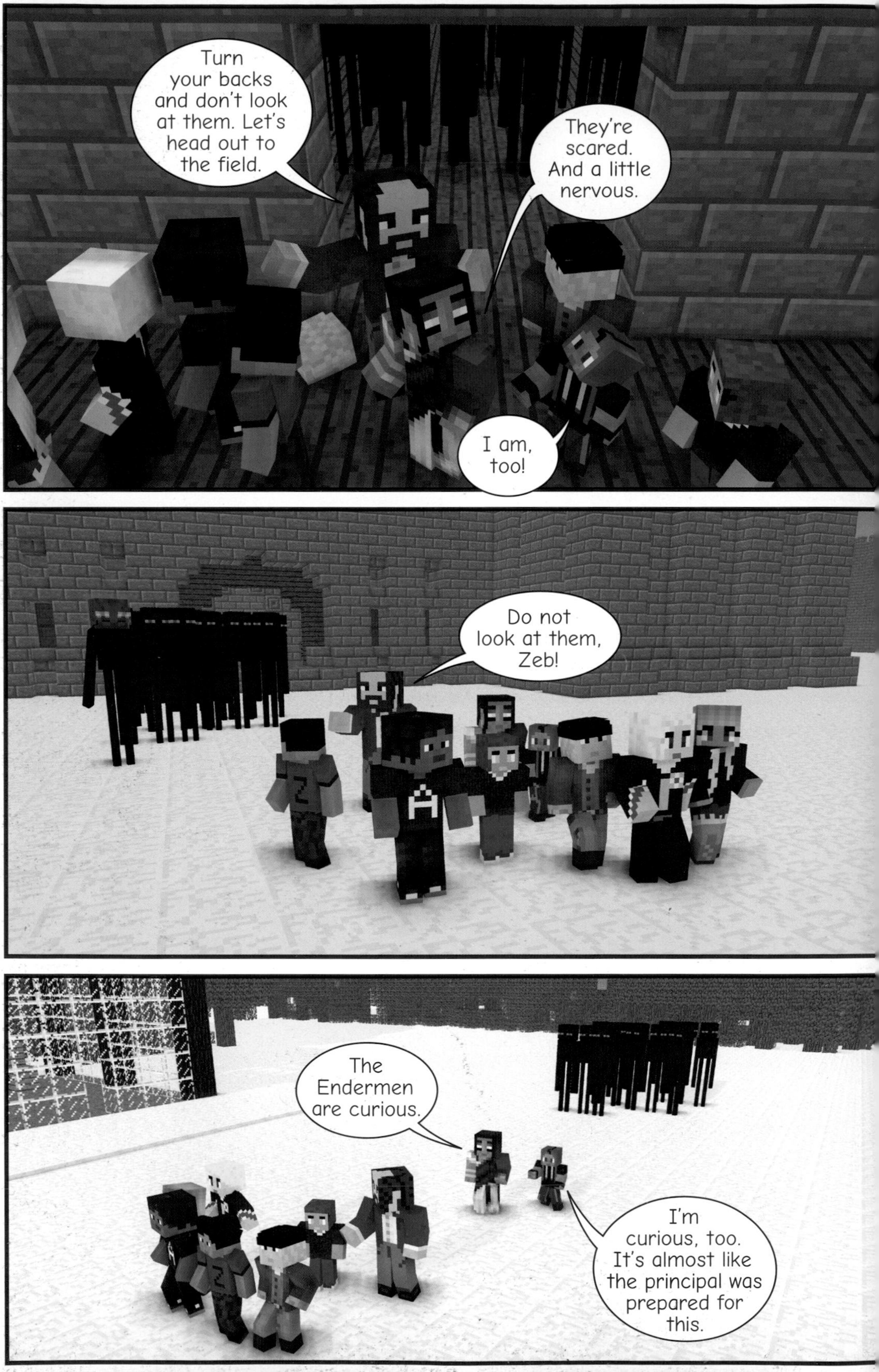
Turn your backs and don't look at them. Let's head out to the field.
They're scared. And a little nervous.
I am, too!
Do not look at them, Zeb!
The Endermen are curious.
I'm curious, too. It's almost like the principal was prepared for this.

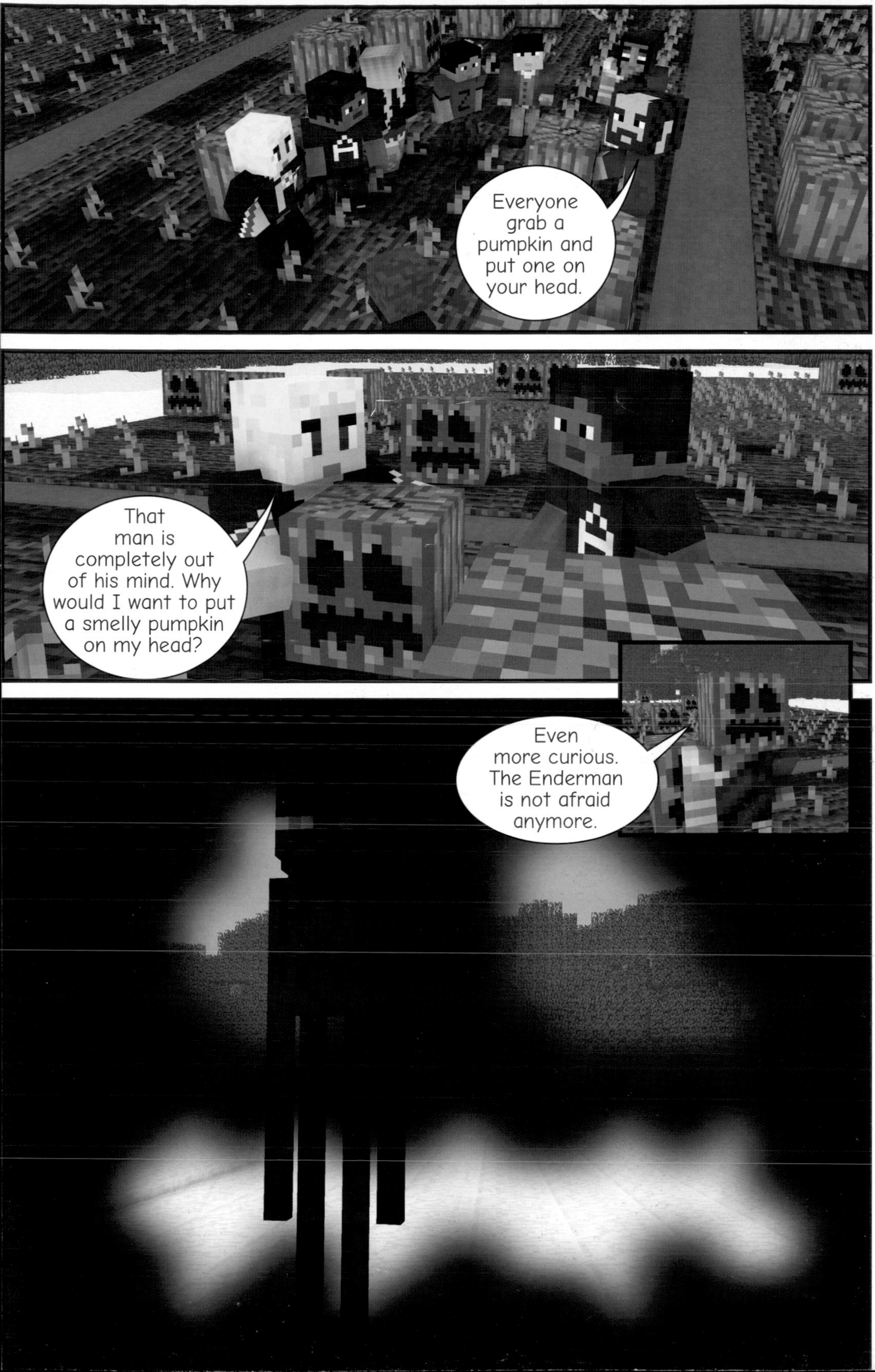
Everyone grab a pumpkin and put one on your head.
That man is completely out of his mind. Why would I want to put a smelly pumpkin on my head?
Even more curious. The Enderman is not afraid anymore.

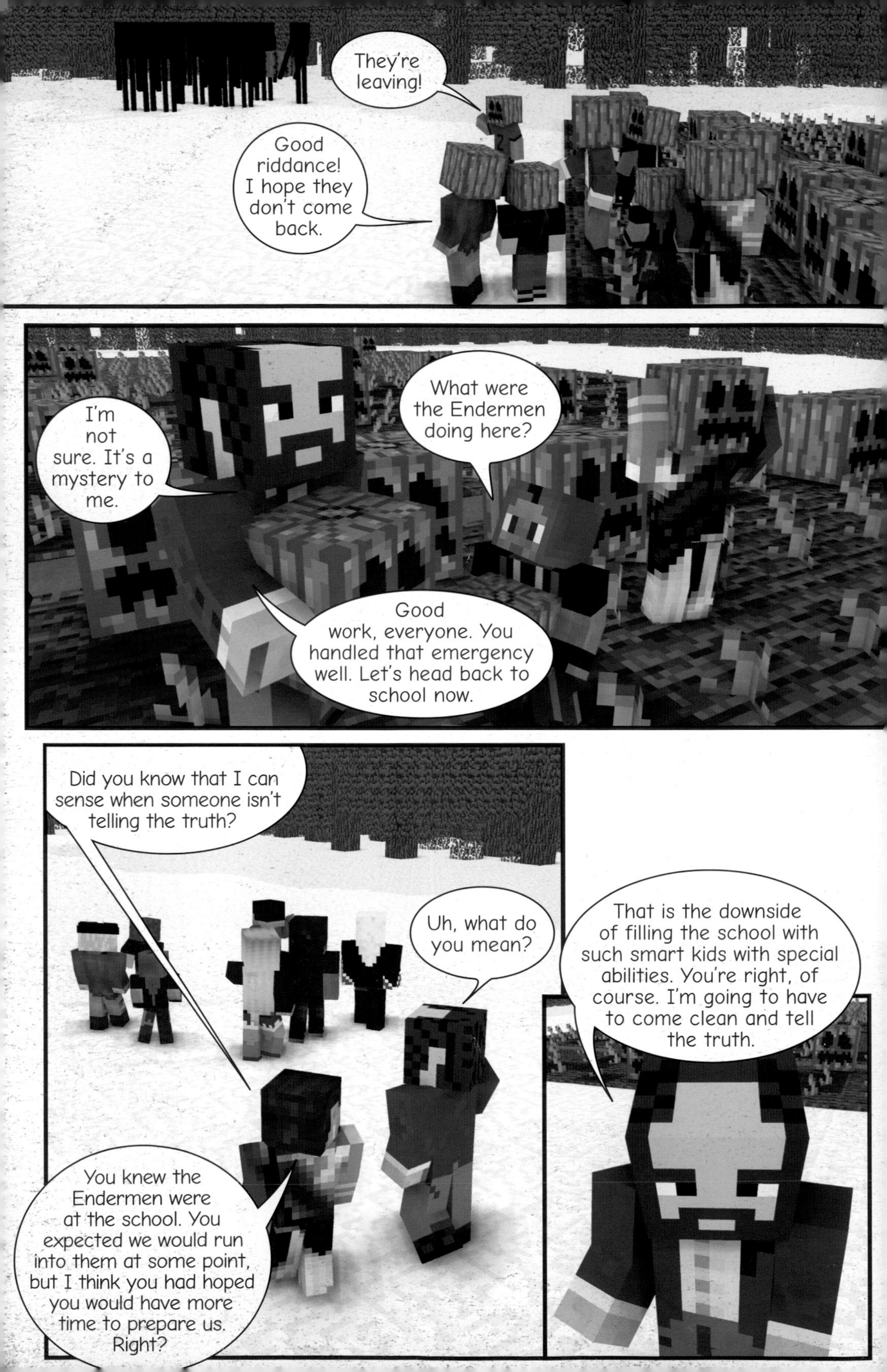

They're leaving!
Good riddance! I hope they don't come back.
I'm not sure. It's a mystery to me.
What were the Endermen doing here?
Good work, everyone. You handled that emergency well. Let's head back to school now.
Did you know that I can sense when someone isn't telling the truth?
Uh, what do you mean?
You knew the Endermen were at the school. You expected we would run into them at some point, but I think you had hoped you would have more time to prepare us. Right?
That is the downside of filling the school with such smart kids with special abilities. You're right, of course. I'm going to have to come clean and tell the truth.

CHAPTER 7

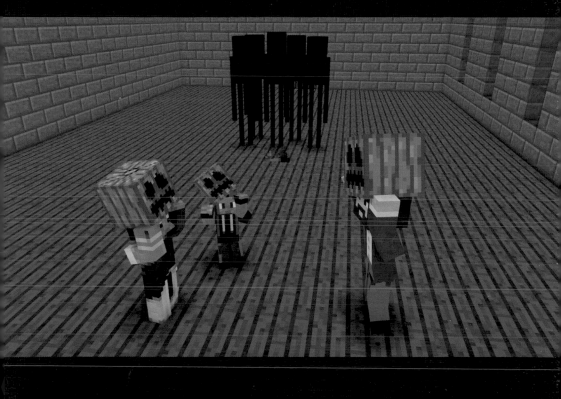

FRIENDS
OF FOES?

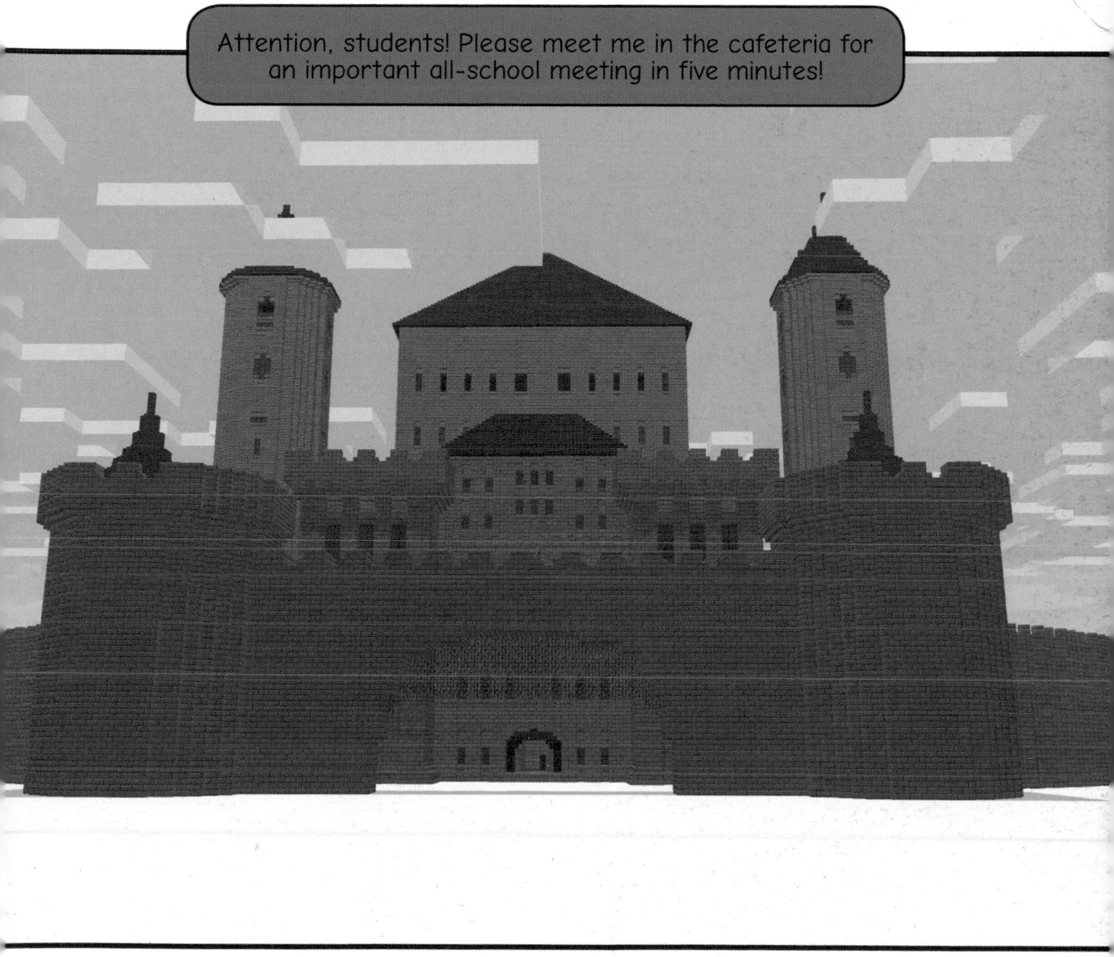
Attention, students! Please meet me in the cafeteria for an important all-school meeting in five minutes!

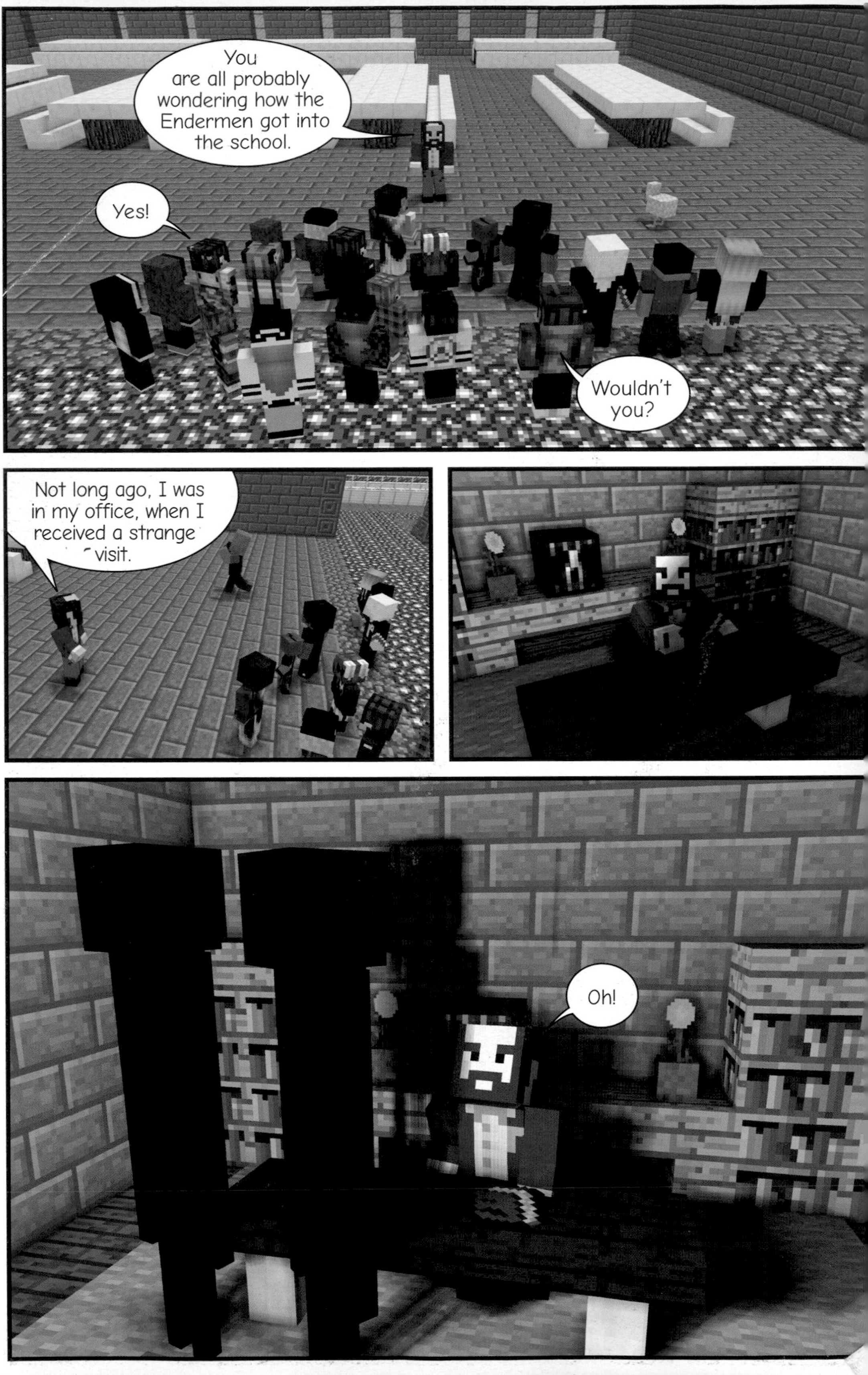
You are all probably wondering how the Endermen got into the school.
Yes!
Wouldn't you?
Not long ago, I was in my office, when I received a strange visit.
Oh!

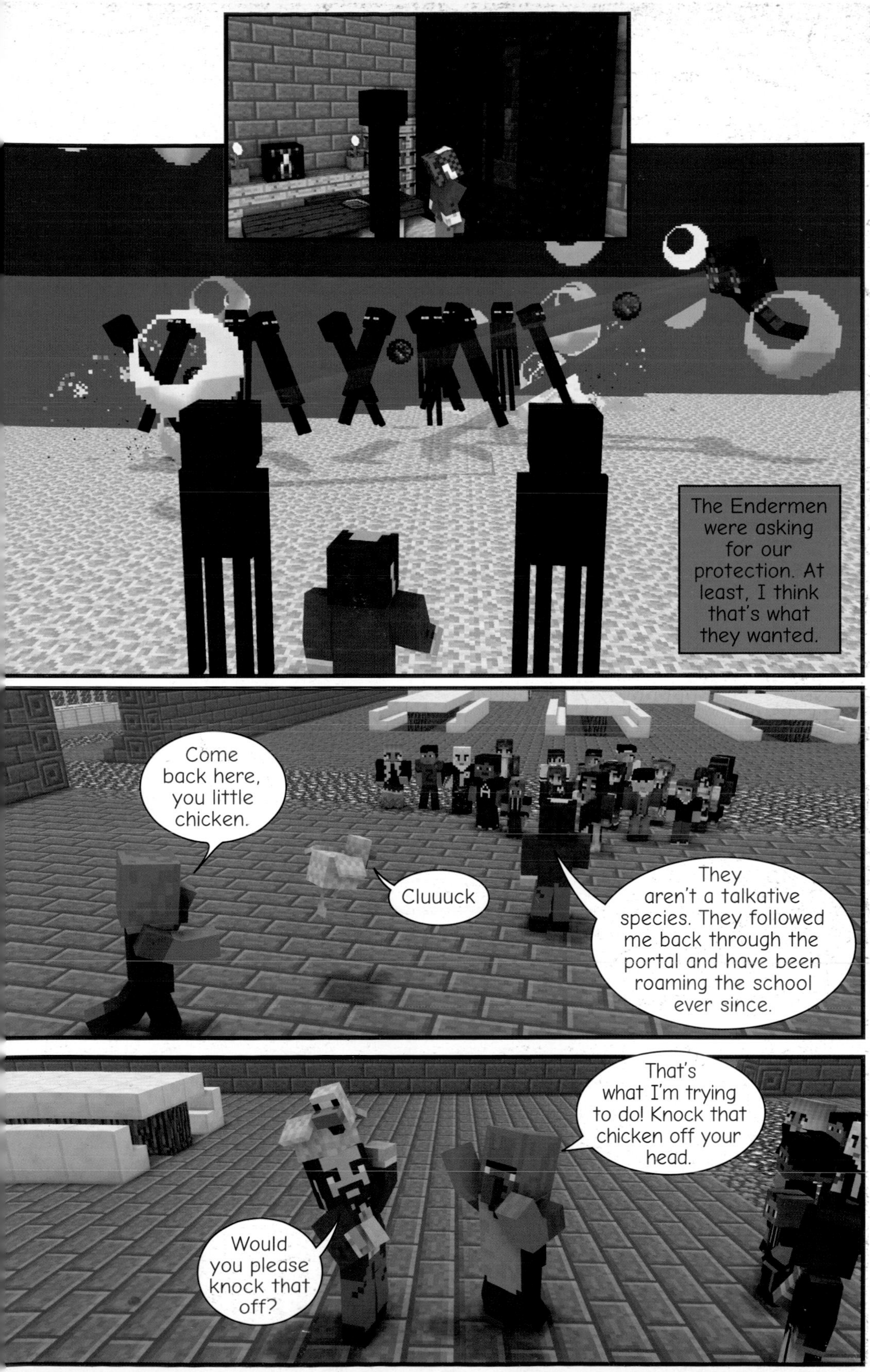
The Endermen were asking for our protection. At least, I think that's what they wanted.
Come back here, you little chicken.
Cluuuck
They aren't a talkative species. They followed me back through the portal and have been roaming the school ever since.
That's what I'm trying to do! Knock that chicken off your head.
Would you please knock that off?

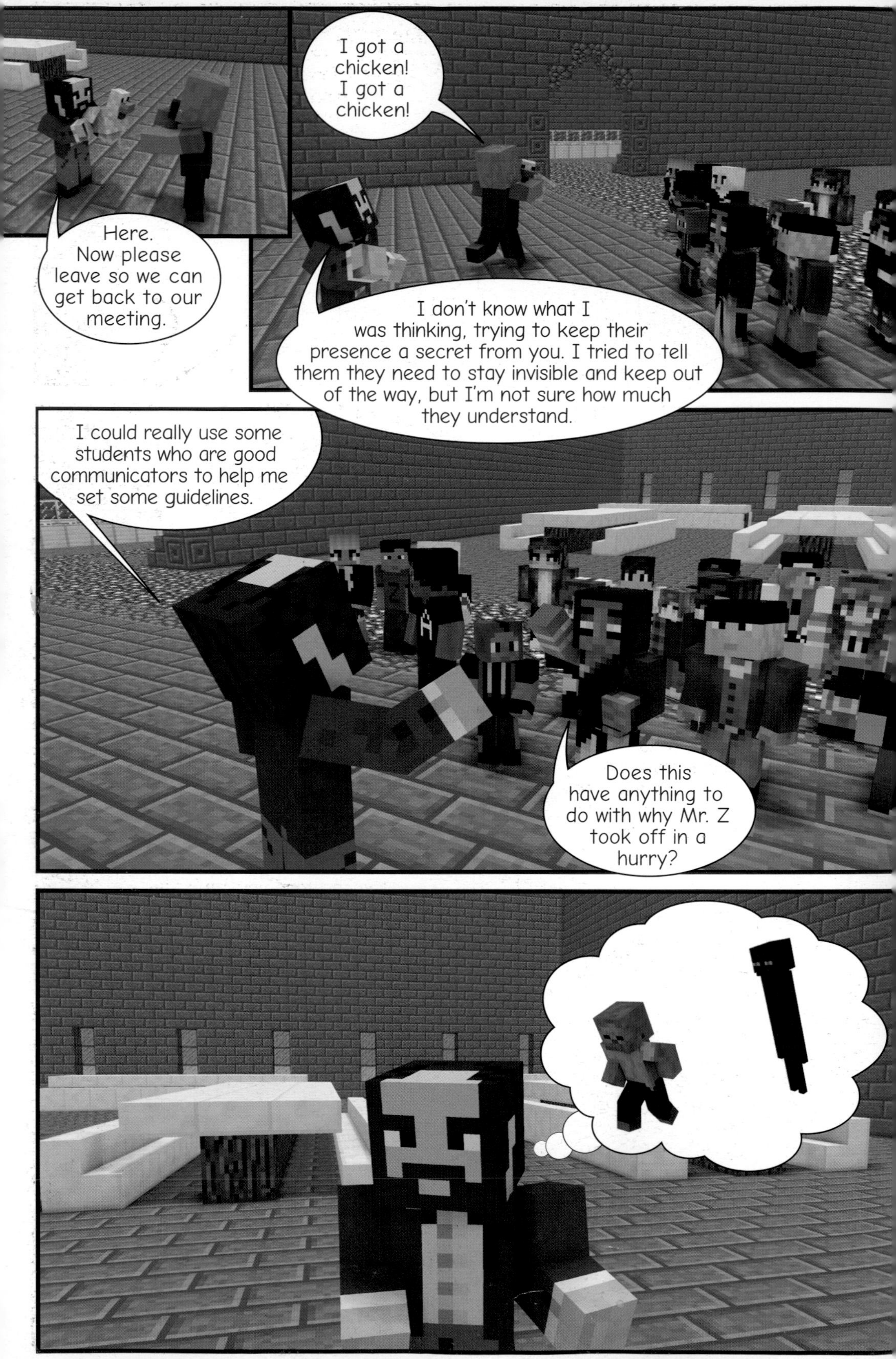
I got a chicken! I got a chicken!
Here. Now please leave so we can get back to our meeting.
I don't know what I was thinking, trying to keep their presence a secret from you. I tried to tell them they need to stay invisible and keep out of the way, but I'm not sure how much they understand.
I could really use some students who are good communicators to help me set some guidelines.
Does this have anything to do with why Mr. Z took off in a hurry?

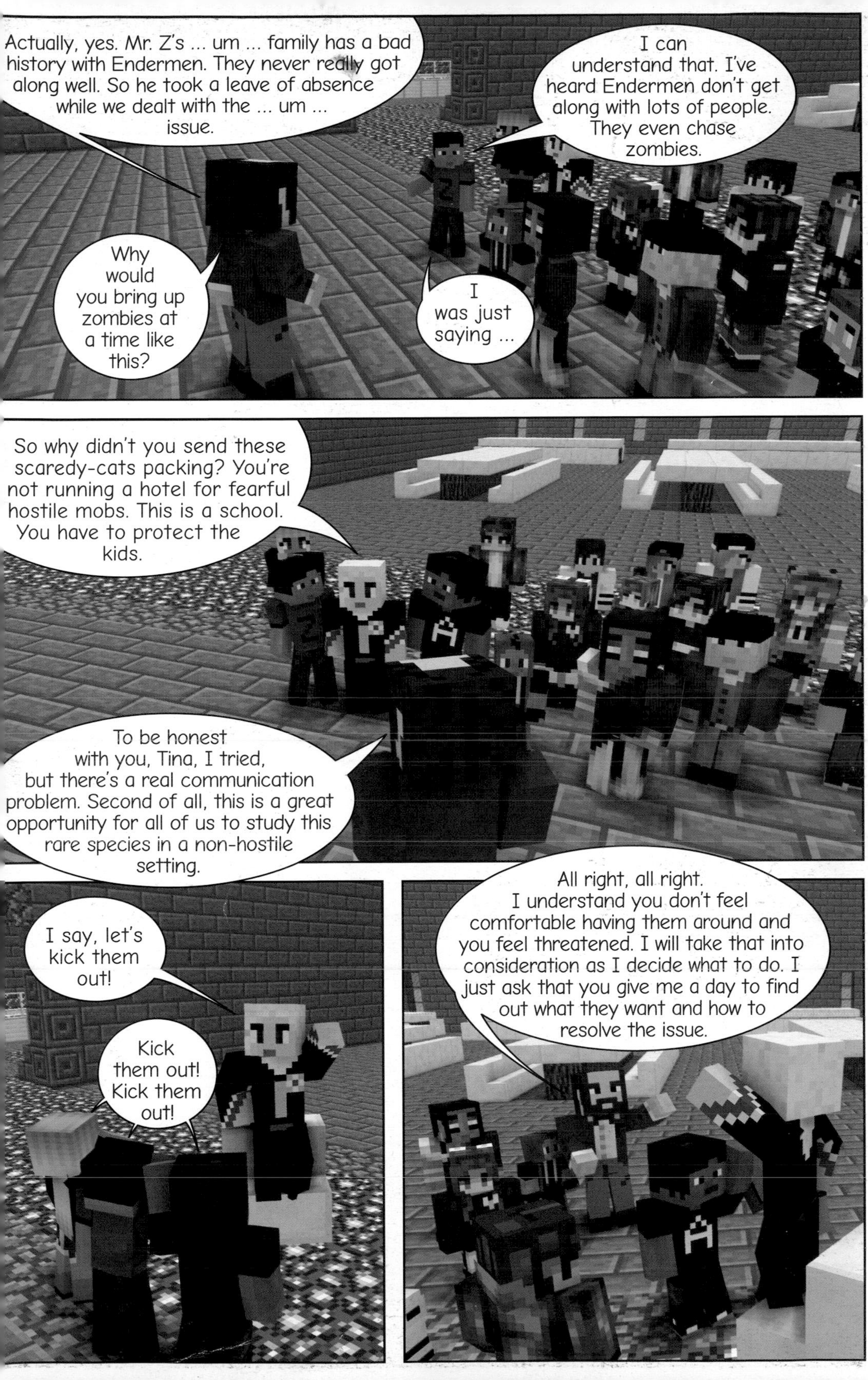
Actually, yes. Mr. Z's ... um ... family has a bad history with Endermen. They never really got along well. So he took a leave of absence while we dealt with the ... um ... issue.
I can understand that. I've heard Endermen don't get along with lots of people. They even chase zombies.
Why would you bring up zombies at a time like this?
I was just saying ...
So why didn't you send these scaredy-cats packing? You're not running a hotel for fearful hostile mobs. This is a school. You have to protect the kids.
To be honest with you, Tina, I tried, but there's a real communication problem. Second of all, this is a great opportunity for all of us to study this rare species in a non-hostile setting.
I say, let's kick them out!
Kick them out! Kick them out!
All right, all right. I understand you don't feel comfortable having them around and you feel threatened. I will take that into consideration as I decide what to do. I just ask that you give me a day to find out what they want and how to resolve the issue.

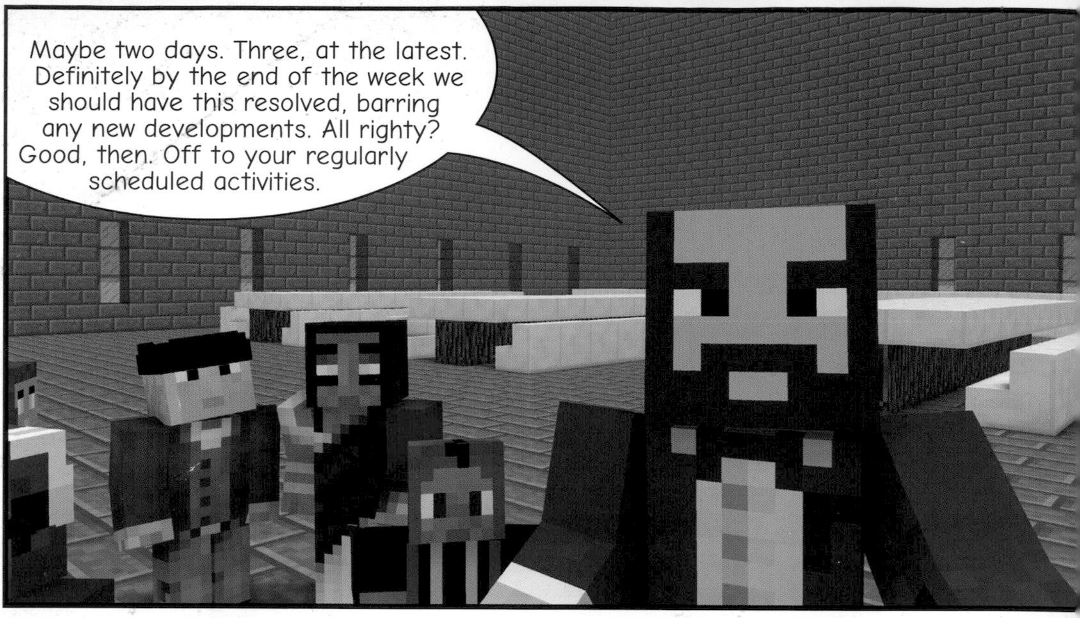
Maybe two days. Three, at the latest. Definitely by the end of the week we should have this resolved, barring any new developments. All righty? Good, then. Off to your regularly scheduled activities.

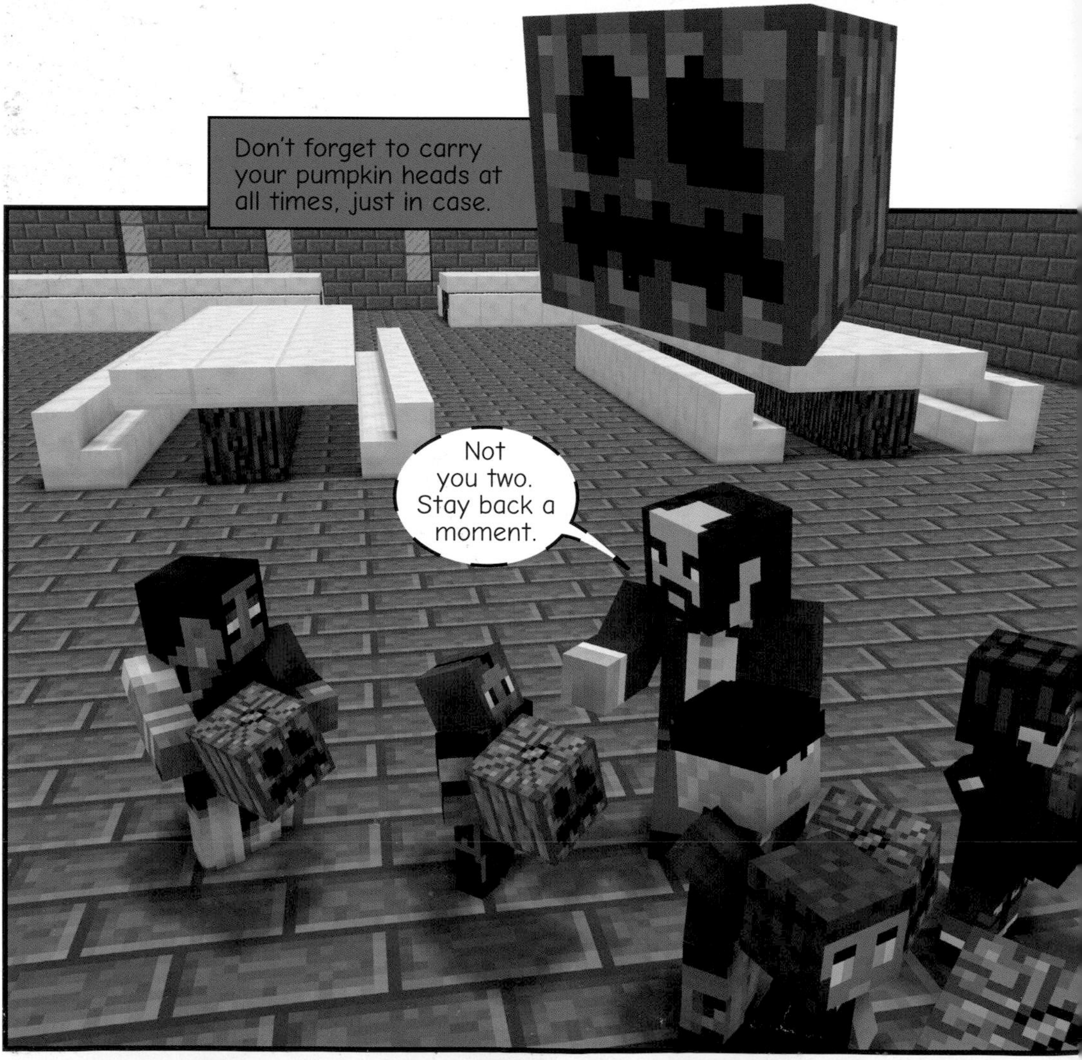
Don't forget to carry your pumpkin heads at all times, just in case.
Not you two. Stay back a moment.

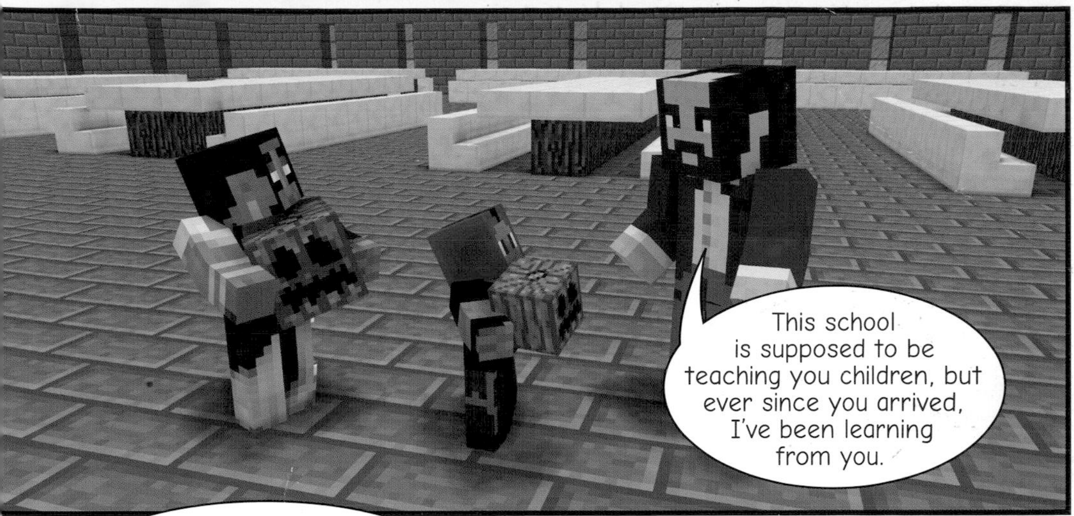
This school is supposed to be teaching you children, but ever since you arrived, I've been learning from you.

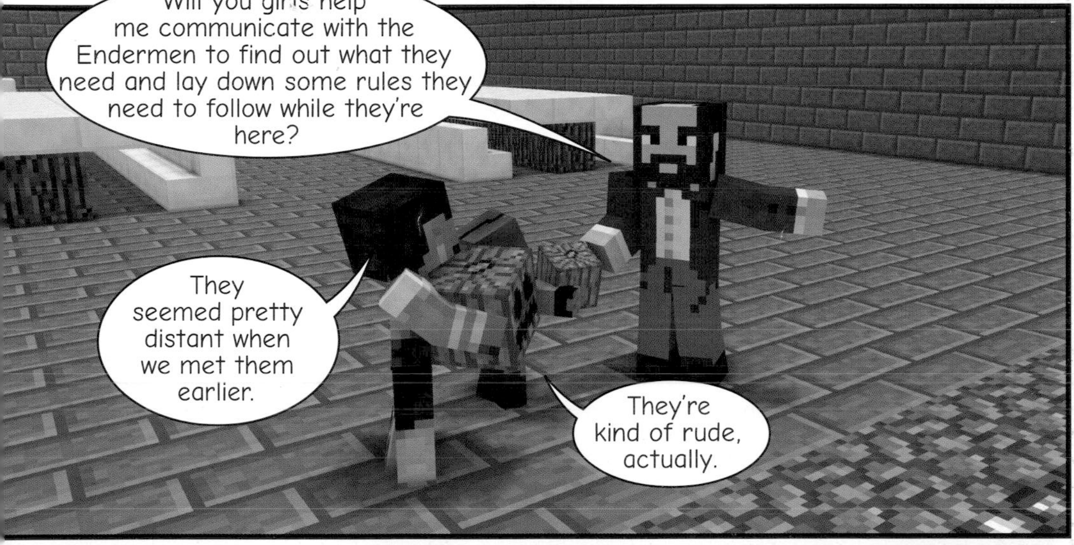
Will you girls help me communicate with the Endermen to find out what they need and lay down some rules they need to follow while they're here?
They seemed pretty distant when we met them earlier.
They're kind of rude, actually.

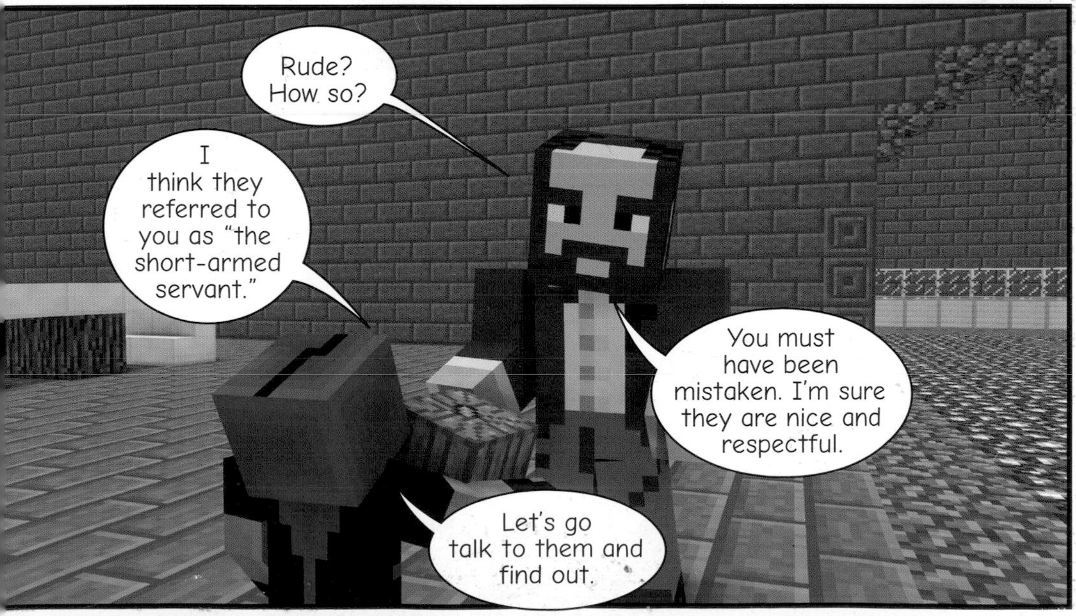
Rude? How so?
I think they referred to you as "the short-armed servant."
You must have been mistaken. I'm sure they are nice and respectful.
Let's go talk to them and find out.

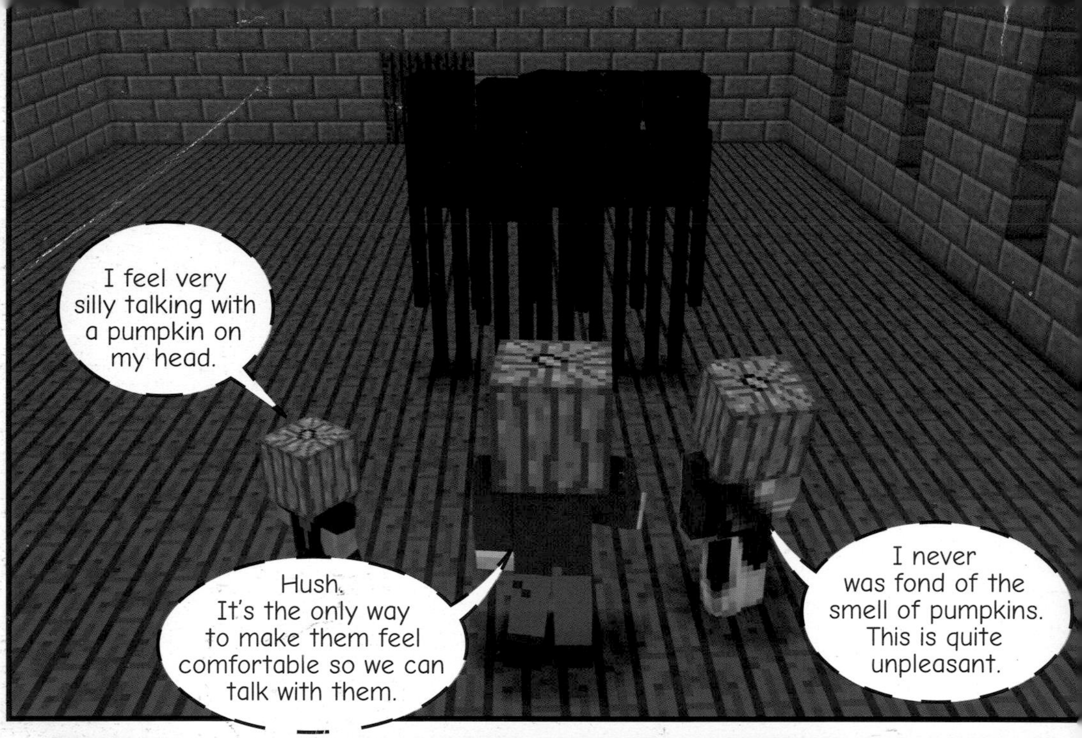
I feel very silly talking with a pumpkin on my head.
Hush. It's the only way to make them feel comfortable so we can talk with them.
I never was fond of the smell of pumpkins. This is quite unpleasant.

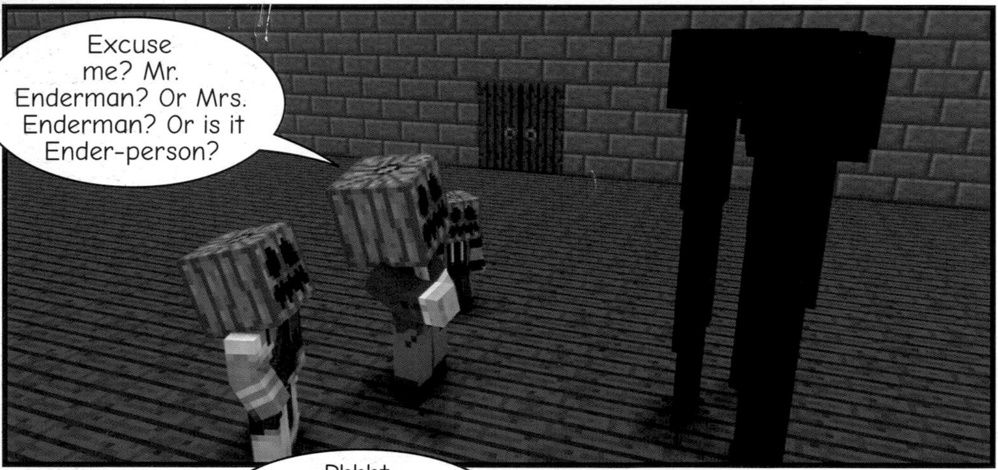
Excuse me? Mr. Enderman? Or Mrs. Enderman? Or is it Ender-person?

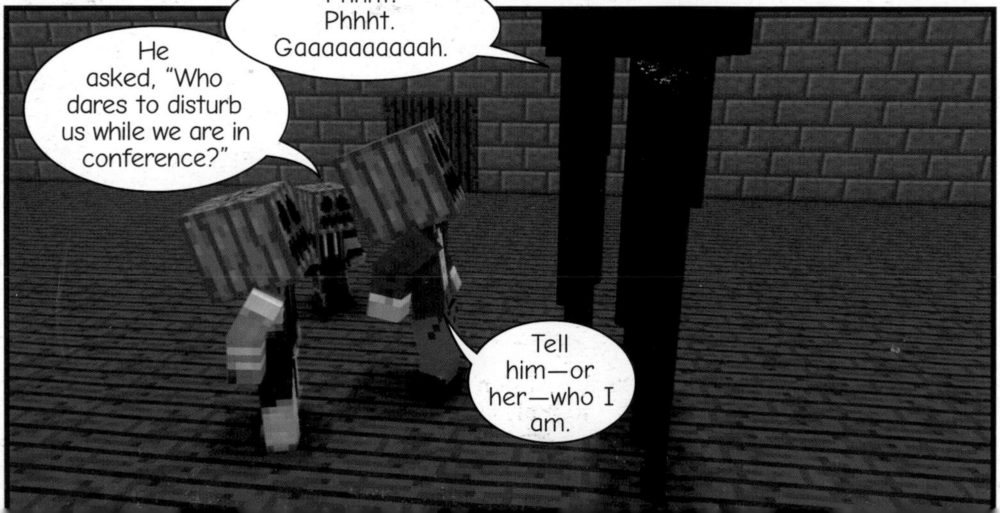
Phhht. Phhht. Gaaaaaaaaaah.
He asked, "Who dares to disturb us while we are in conference?"
Tell him—or her—who I am.

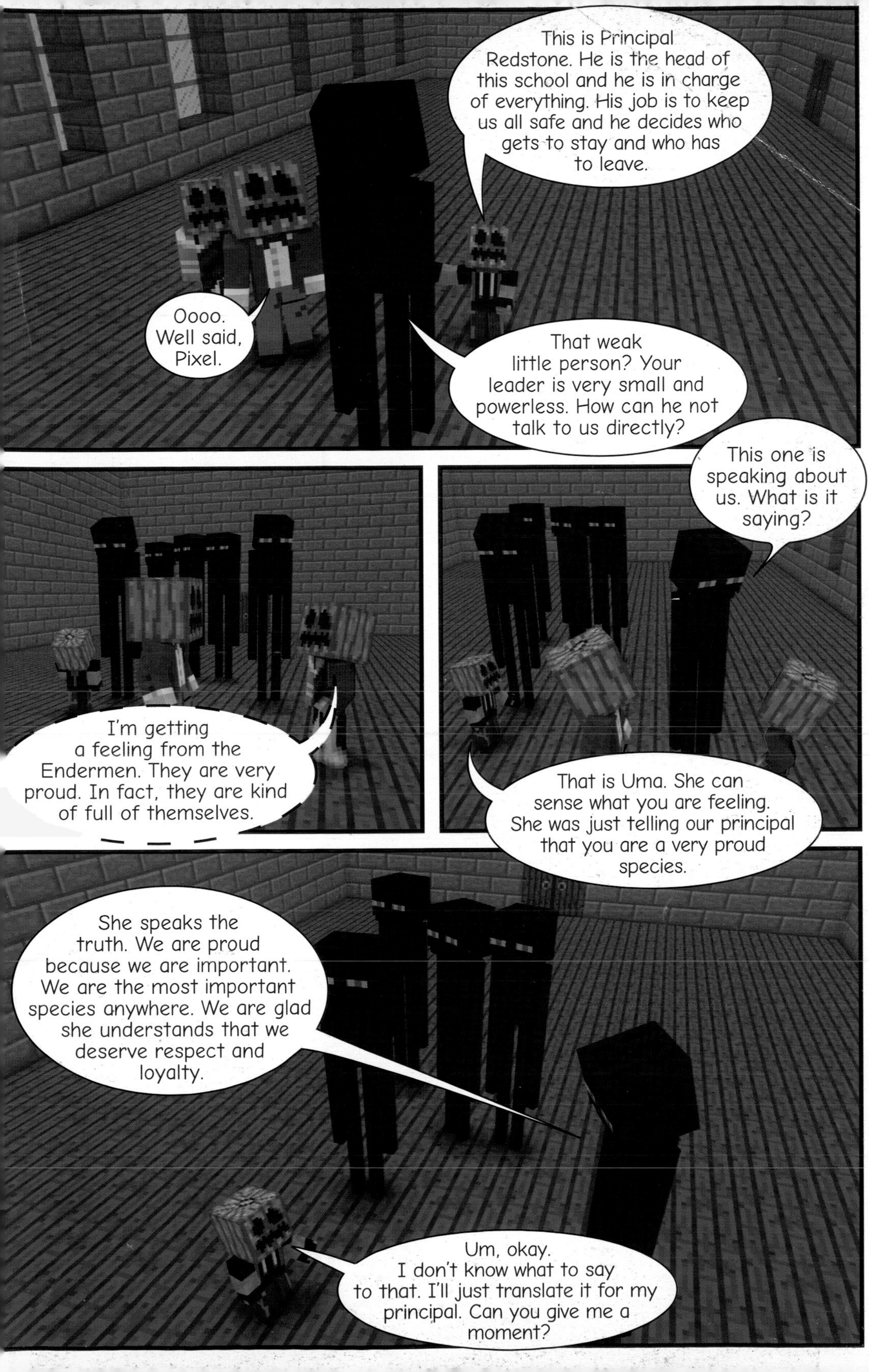
This is Principal Redstone. He is the head of this school and he is in charge of everything. His job is to keep us all safe and he decides who gets to stay and who has to leave.
Oooo. Well said, Pixel.
That weak little person? Your leader is very small and powerless. How can he not talk to us directly?
I'm getting a feeling from the Endermen. They are very proud. In fact, they are kind of full of themselves.
This one is speaking about us. What is it saying?
That is Uma. She can sense what you are feeling. She was just telling our principal that you are a very proud species.
She speaks the truth. We are proud because we are important. We are the most important species anywhere. We are glad she understands that we deserve respect and loyalty.
Um, okay. I don't know what to say to that. I'll just translate it for my principal. Can you give me a moment?

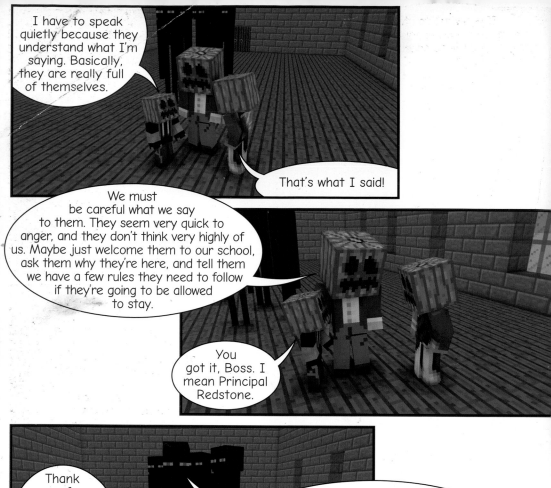

I have to speak quietly because they understand what I'm saying. Basically, they are really full of themselves.

That's what I said!

We must be careful what we say to them. They seem very quick to anger, and they don't think very highly of us. Maybe just welcome them to our school, ask them why they're here, and tell them we have a few rules they need to follow if they're going to be allowed to stay.

You got it, Boss. I mean Principal Redstone.

Thank you for waiting. We would like to know what brought you here to our school.

We had managed to escape the Wither for many moons. When he found us, we needed a place where he would never think to look. Your little community here is filled with weak young ones and talks of peace. It is the last place the Wither will look for us.

That's not very nice of you!

Careful, Pixel. He doesn't like it when you get angry.

We do not need to be nice. We need to be safe. This place will do. For now.

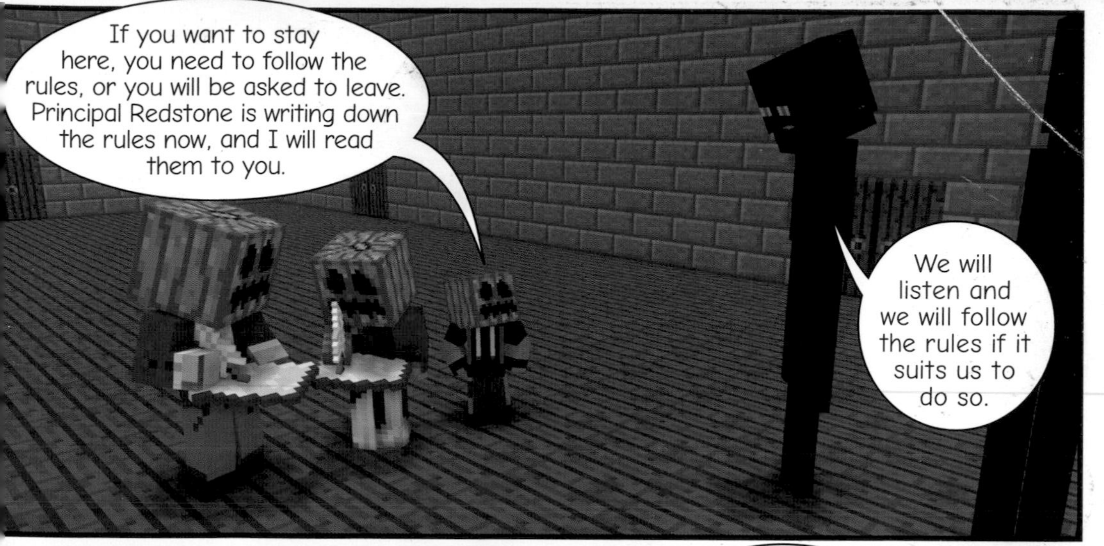
If you want to stay here, you need to follow the rules, or you will be asked to leave. Principal Redstone is writing down the rules now, and I will read them to you.
We will listen and we will follow the rules if it suits us to do so.

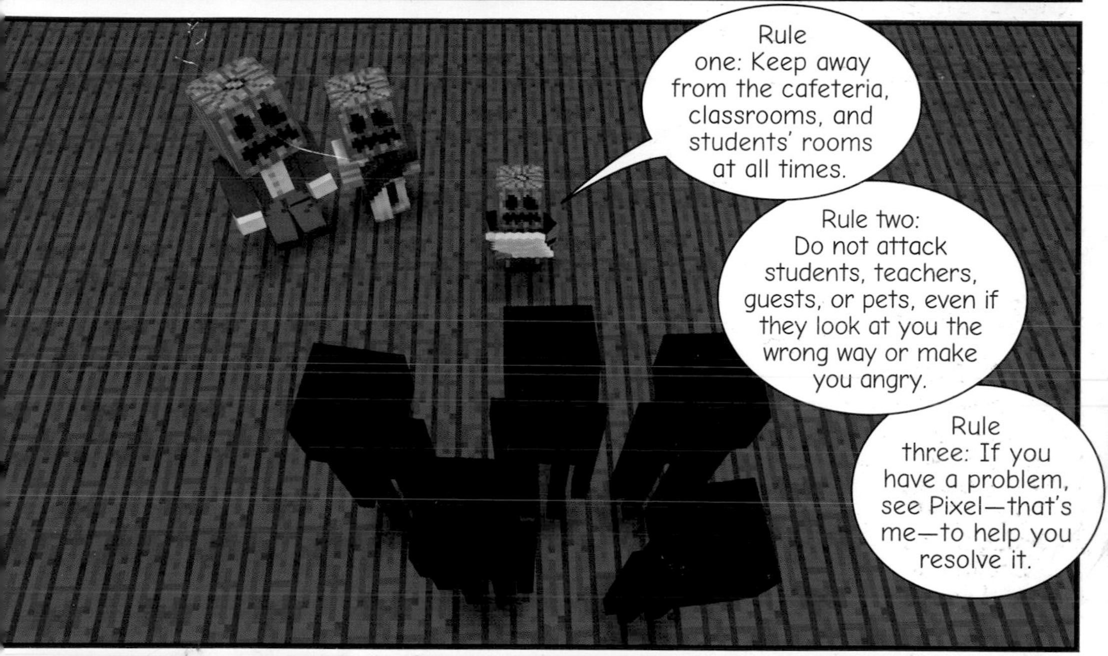
Rule one: Keep away from the cafeteria, classrooms, and students' rooms at all times.
Rule two: Do not attack students, teachers, guests, or pets, even if they look at you the wrong way or make you angry.
Rule three: If you have a problem, see Pixel—that's me—to help you resolve it.

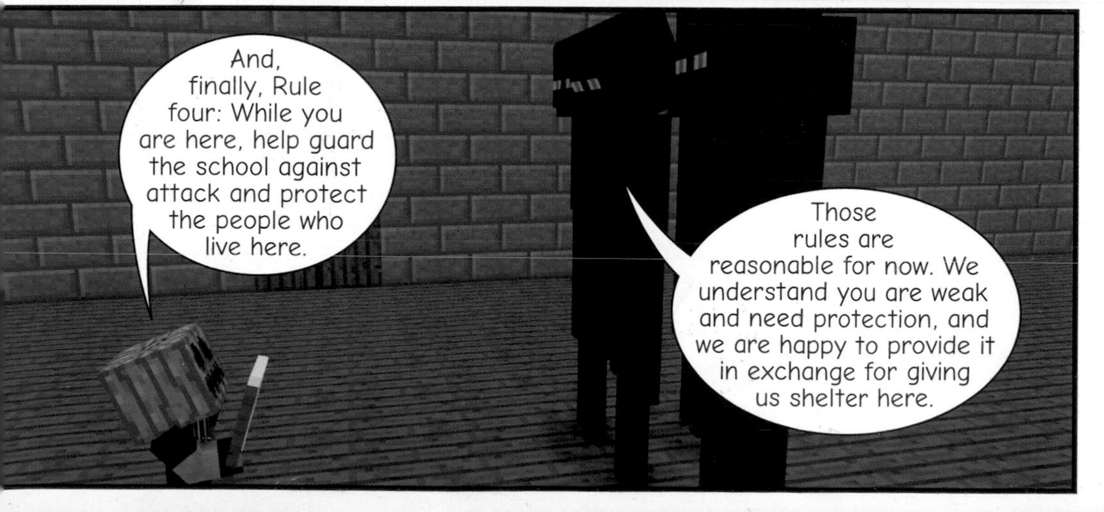
And, finally, Rule four: While you are here, help guard the school against attack and protect the people who live here.
Those rules are reasonable for now. We understand you are weak and need protection, and we are happy to provide it in exchange for giving us shelter here.

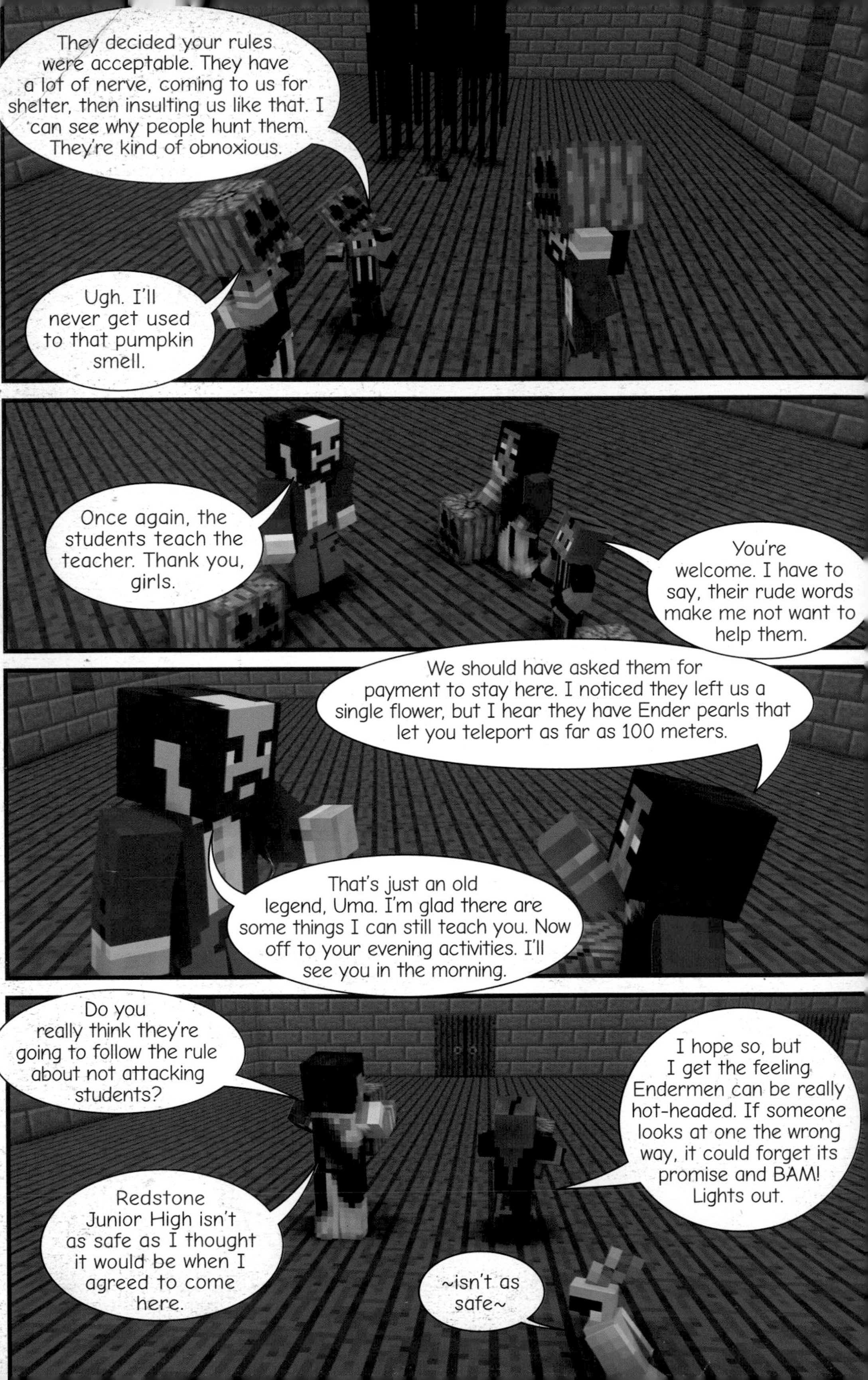
They decided your rules were acceptable. They have a lot of nerve, coming to us for shelter, then insulting us like that. I can see why people hunt them. They're kind of obnoxious.
Ugh. I'll never get used to that pumpkin smell.
Once again, the students teach the teacher. Thank you, girls.
You're welcome. I have to say, their rude words make me not want to help them.
We should have asked them for payment to stay here. I noticed they left us a single flower, but I hear they have Ender pearls that let you teleport as far as 100 meters.
That's just an old legend, Uma. I'm glad there are some things I can still teach you. Now off to your evening activities. I'll see you in the morning.
Do you really think they're going to follow the rule about not attacking students?
I hope so, but I get the feeling Endermen can be really hot-headed. If someone looks at one the wrong way, it could forget its promise and BAM! Lights out.
Redstone Junior High isn't as safe as I thought it would be when I agreed to come here.
~isn't as safe~

CHAPTER 8

CHAOS IN
THE SCHOOL

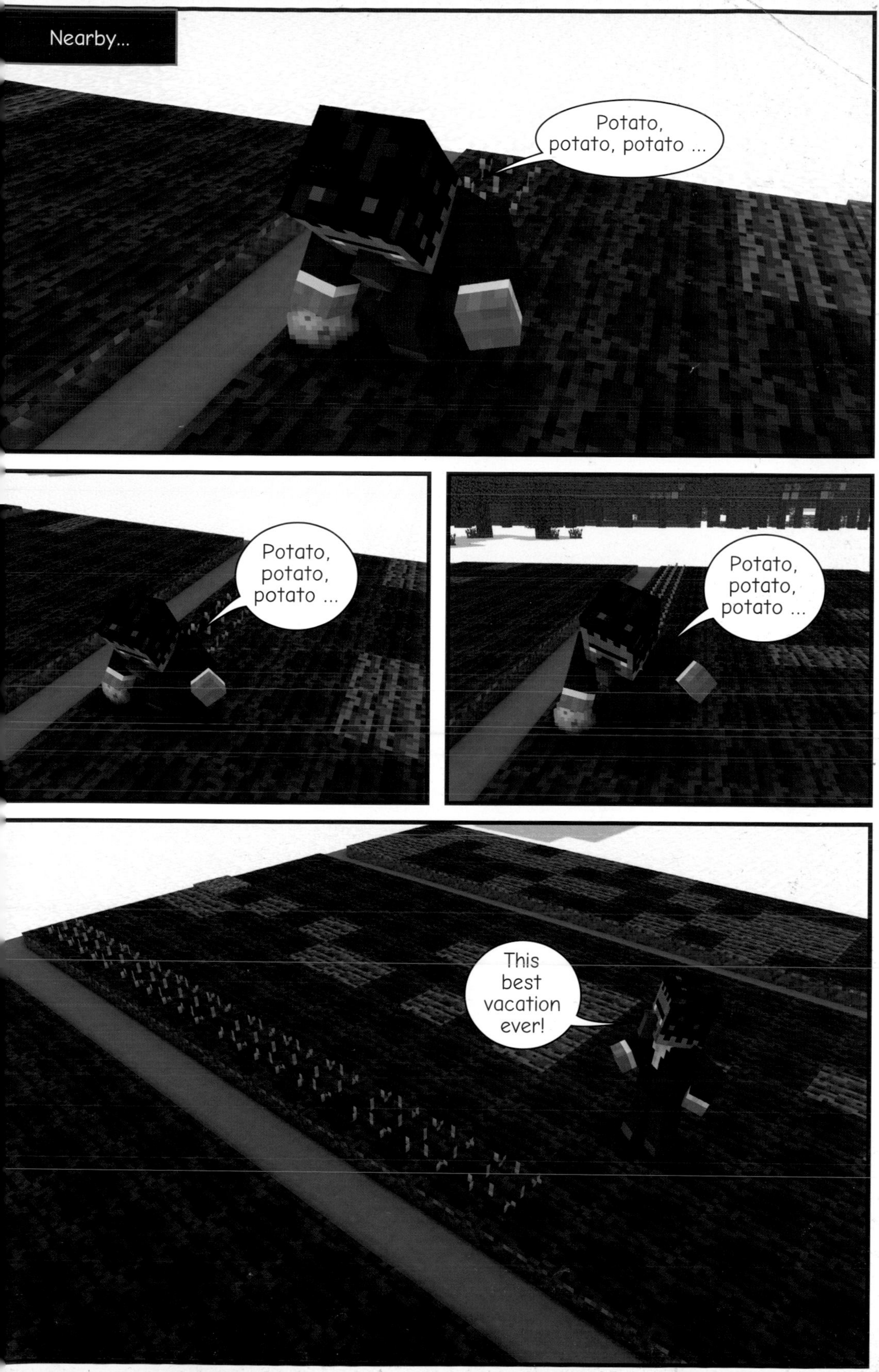
Nearby...
Potato, potato, potato ...
Potato, potato, potato ...
Potato, potato, potato ...
This best vacation ever!

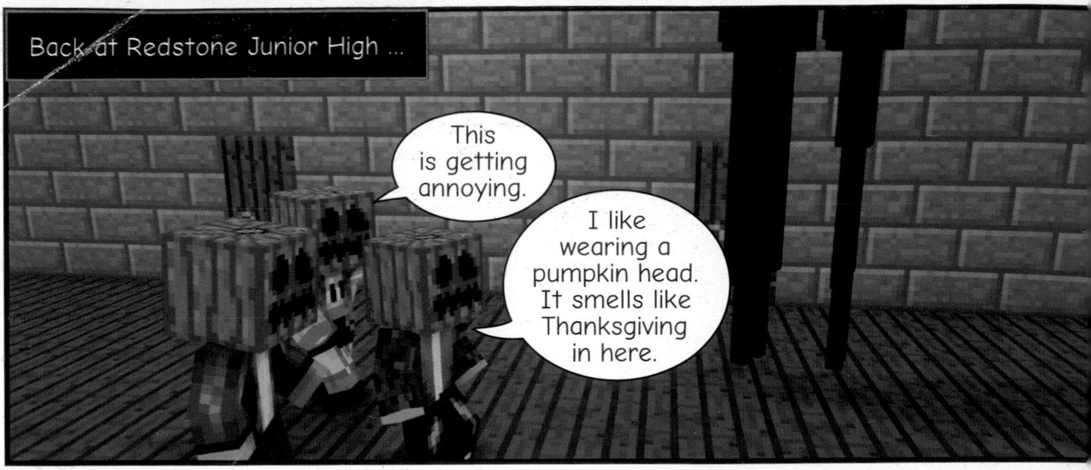
Back at Redstone Junior High ...
This is getting annoying.
I like wearing a pumpkin head. It smells like Thanksgiving in here.

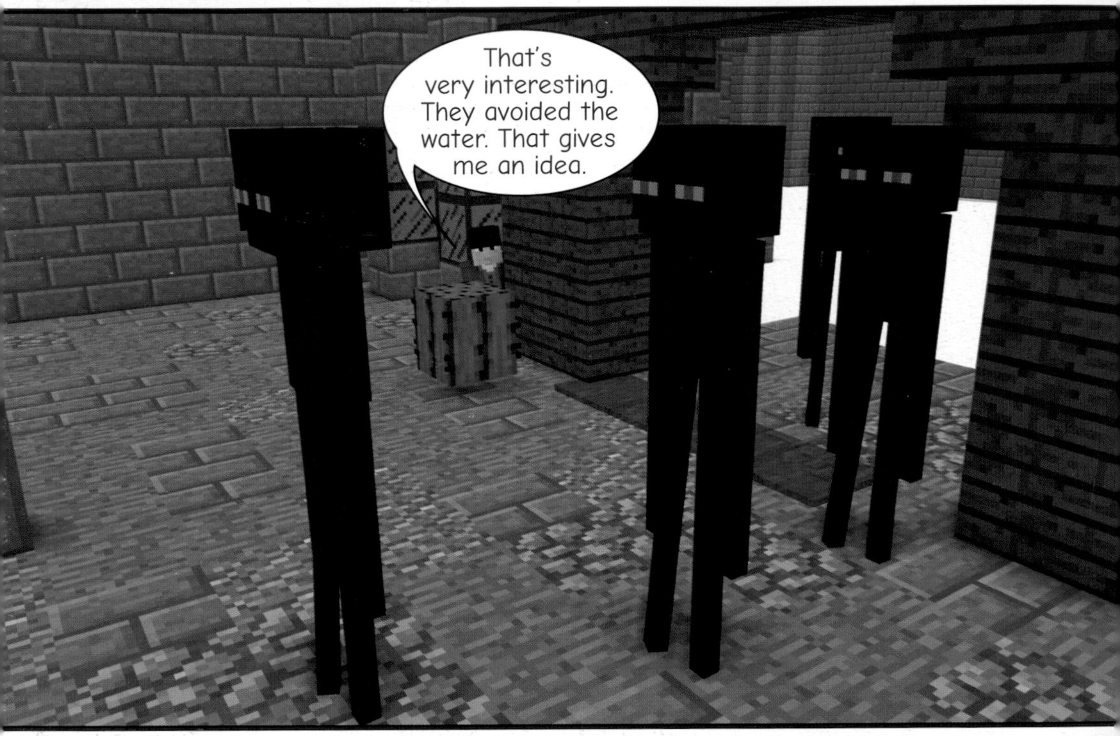
That's very interesting. They avoided the water. That gives me an idea.

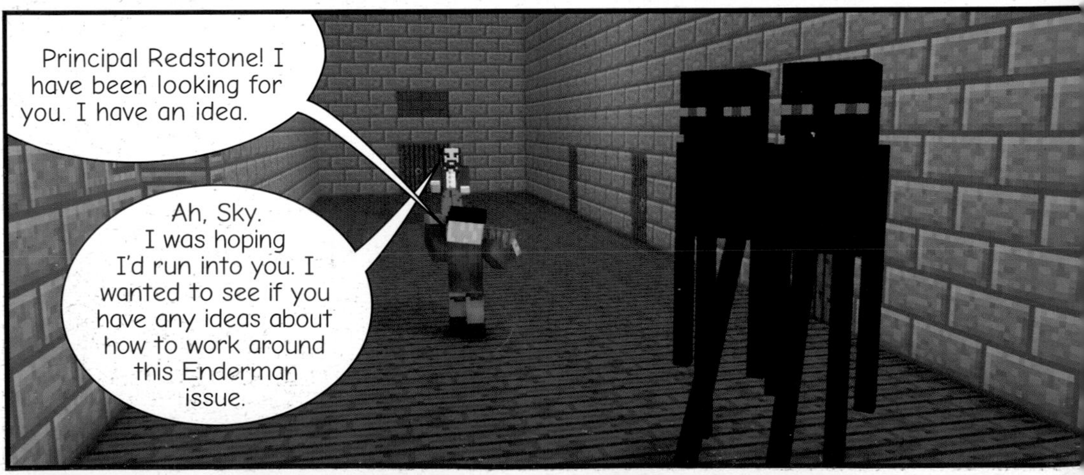
Principal Redstone! I have been looking for you. I have an idea.
Ah, Sky. I was hoping I'd run into you. I wanted to see if you have any ideas about how to work around this Enderman issue.

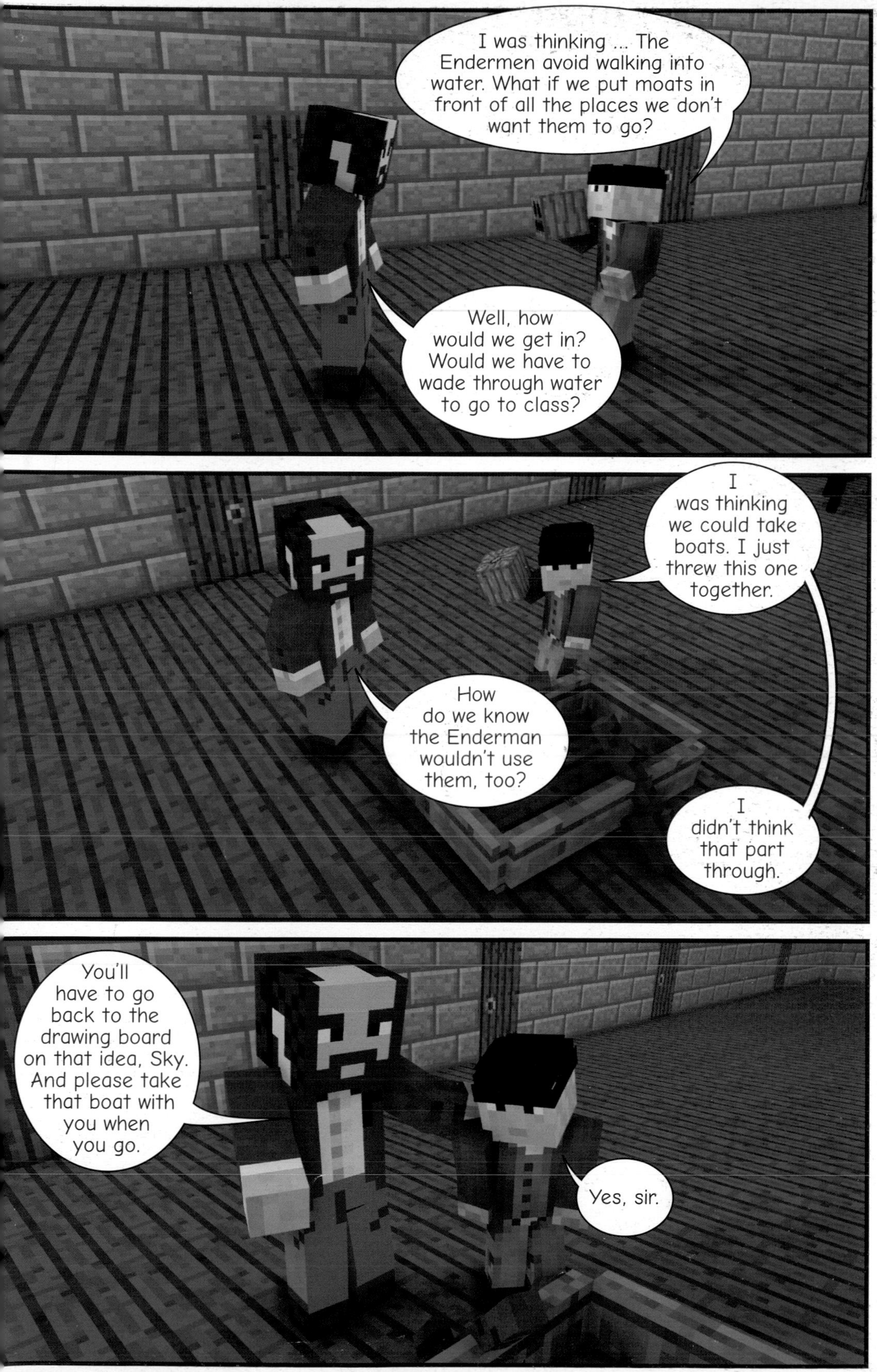
I was thinking ... The Endermen avoid walking into water. What if we put moats in front of all the places we don't want them to go?
Well, how would we get in? Would we have to wade through water to go to class?
I was thinking we could take boats. I just threw this one together.
How do we know the Enderman wouldn't use them, too?
I didn't think that part through.
You'll have to go back to the drawing board on that idea, Sky. And please take that boat with you when you go.
Yes, sir.

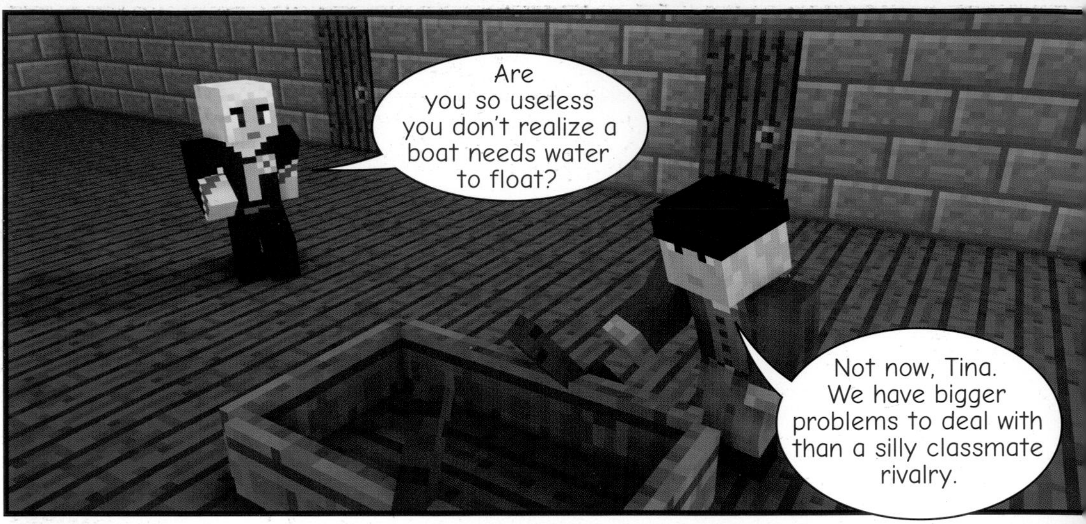
Are you so useless you don't realize a boat needs water to float?
Not now, Tina. We have bigger problems to deal with than a silly classmate rivalry.

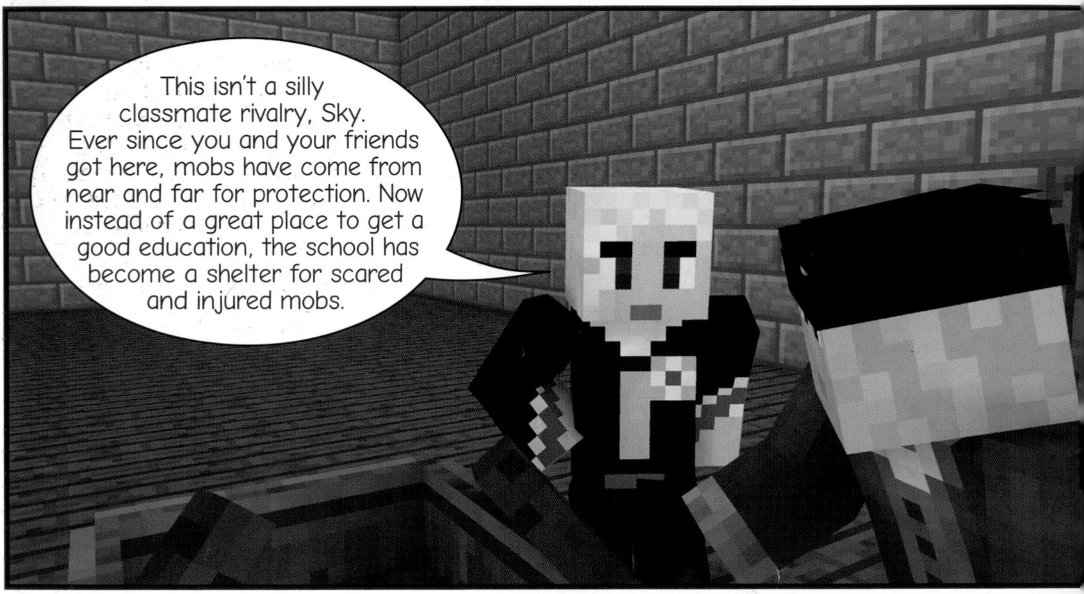
This isn't a silly classmate rivalry, Sky. Ever since you and your friends got here, mobs have come from near and far for protection. Now instead of a great place to get a good education, the school has become a shelter for scared and injured mobs.

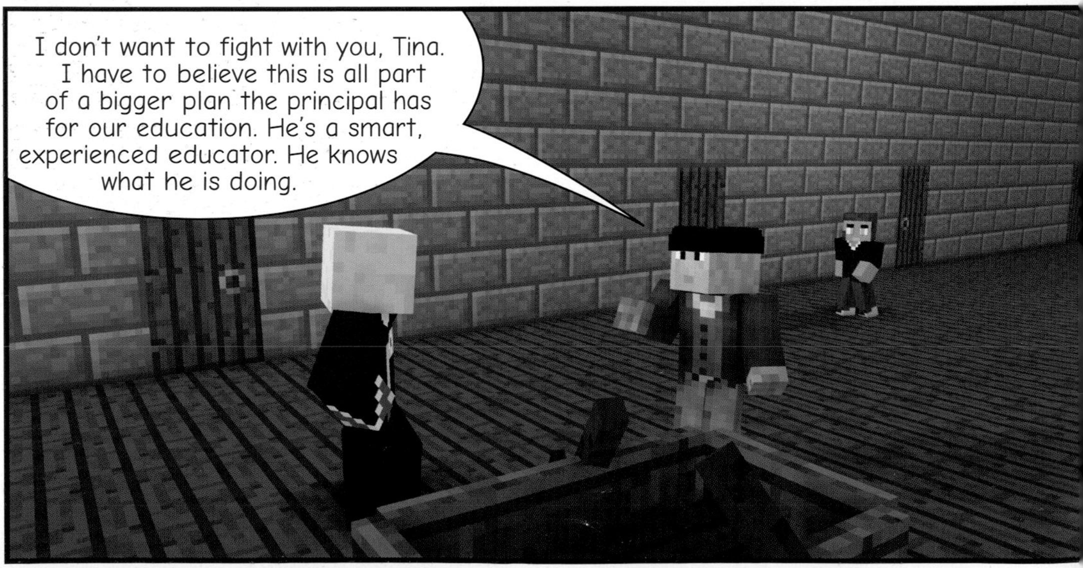
I don't want to fight with you, Tina. I have to believe this is all part of a bigger plan the principal has for our education. He's a smart, experienced educator. He knows what he is doing.

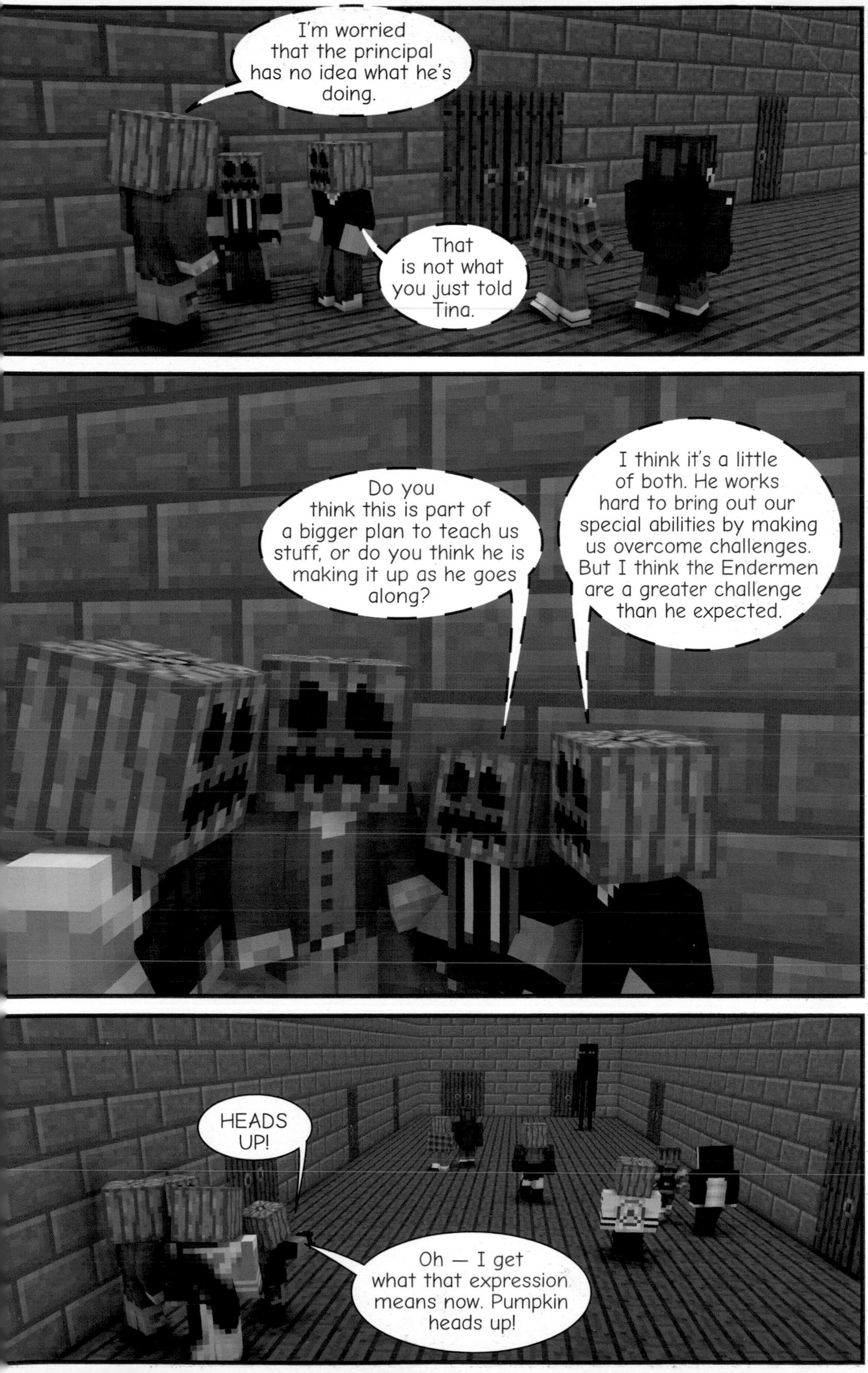
I'm worried that the principal has no idea what he's doing.
That is not what you just told Tina.
Do you think this is part of a bigger plan to teach us stuff, or do you think he is making it up as he goes along?
I think it's a little of both. He works hard to bring out our special abilities by making us overcome challenges. But I think the Endermen are a greater challenge than he expected.
HEADS UP!
Oh — I get what that expression means now. Pumpkin heads up!

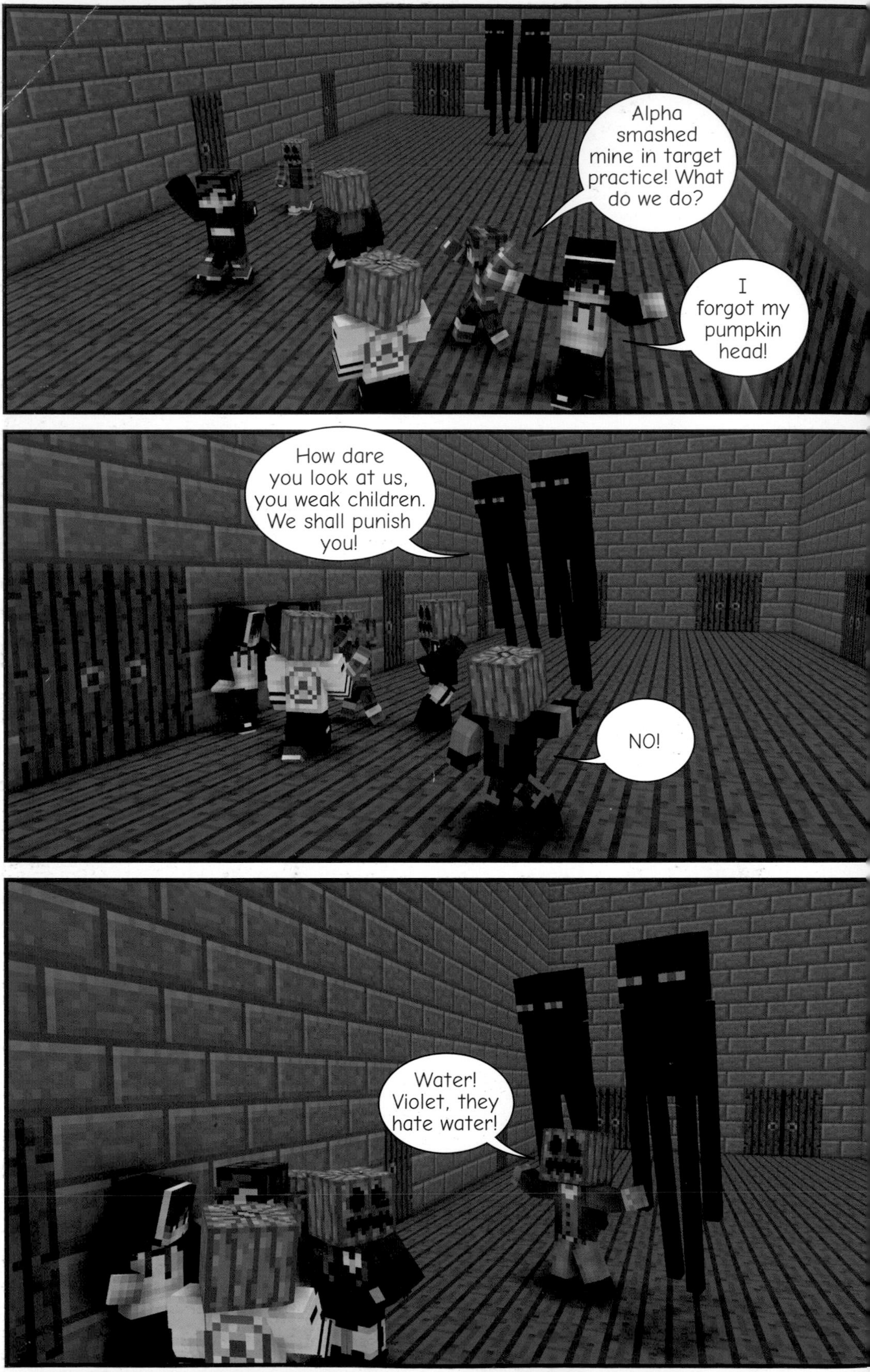
Alpha smashed mine in target practice! What do we do?
I forgot my pumpkin head!
How dare you look at us, you weak children. We shall punish you!
NO!
Water! Violet, they hate water!

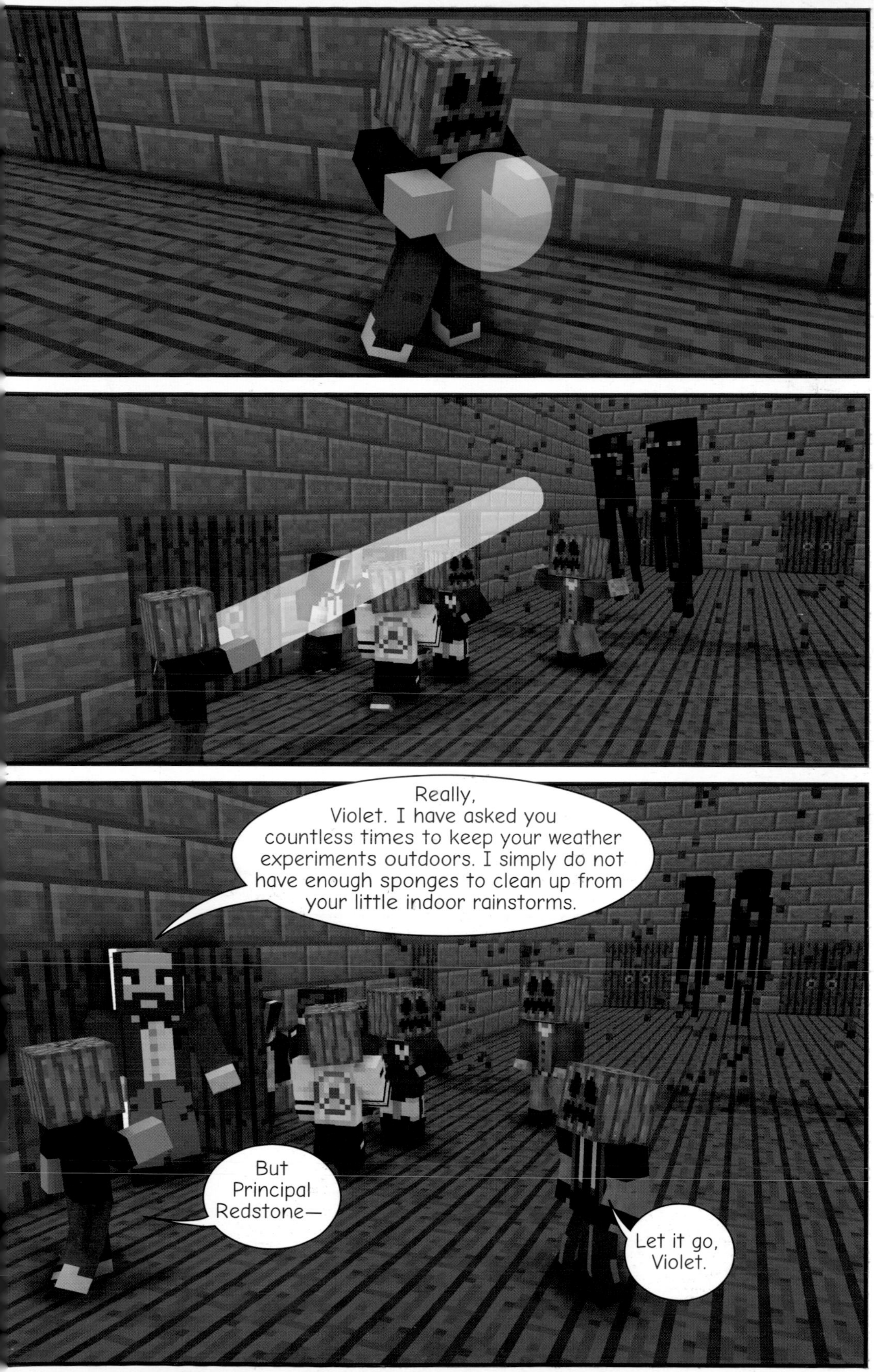

Really, Violet. I have asked you countless times to keep your weather experiments outdoors. I simply do not have enough sponges to clean up from your little indoor rainstorms.
But Principal Redstone—
Let it go, Violet.

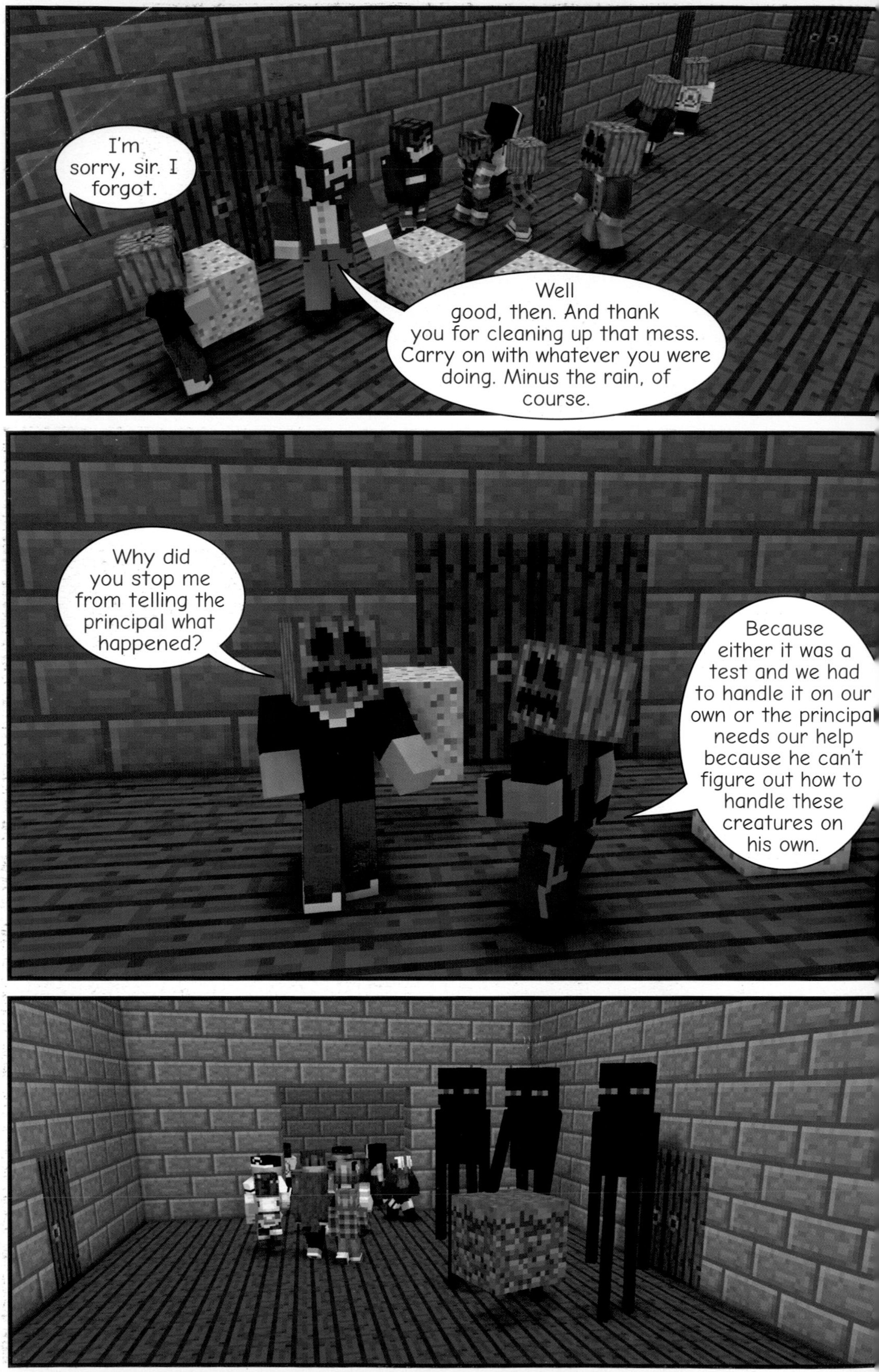
I'm sorry, sir. I forgot.
Well good, then. And thank you for cleaning up that mess. Carry on with whatever you were doing. Minus the rain, of course.
Why did you stop me from telling the principal what happened?
Because either it was a test and we had to handle it on our own or the principa needs our help because he can't figure out how to handle these creatures on his own.

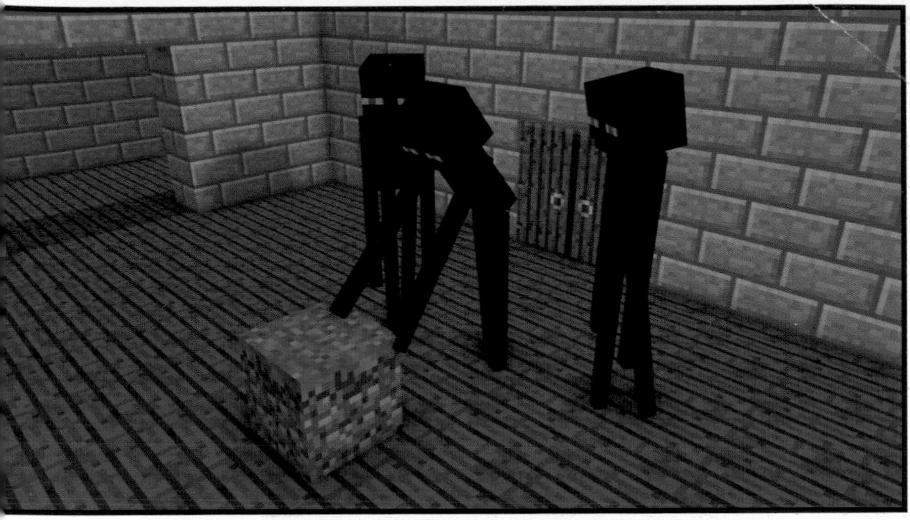

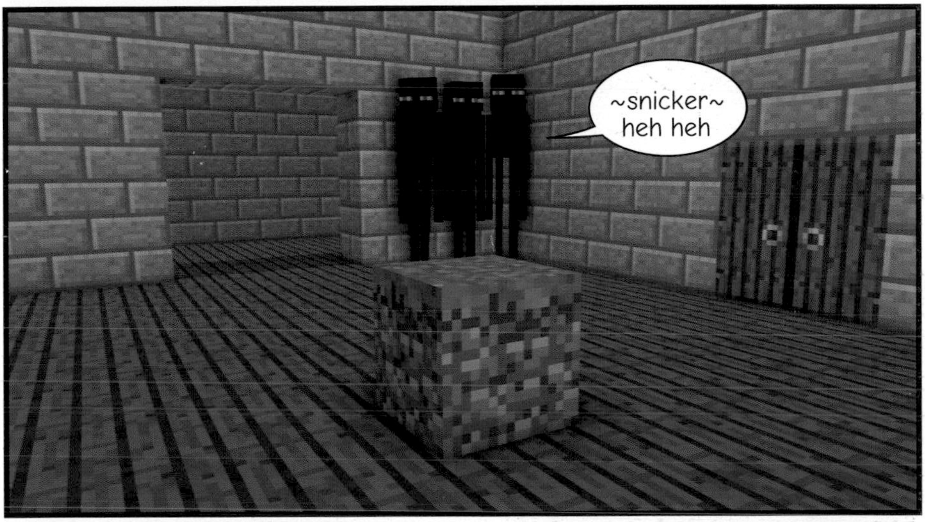
~snicker~
heh heh

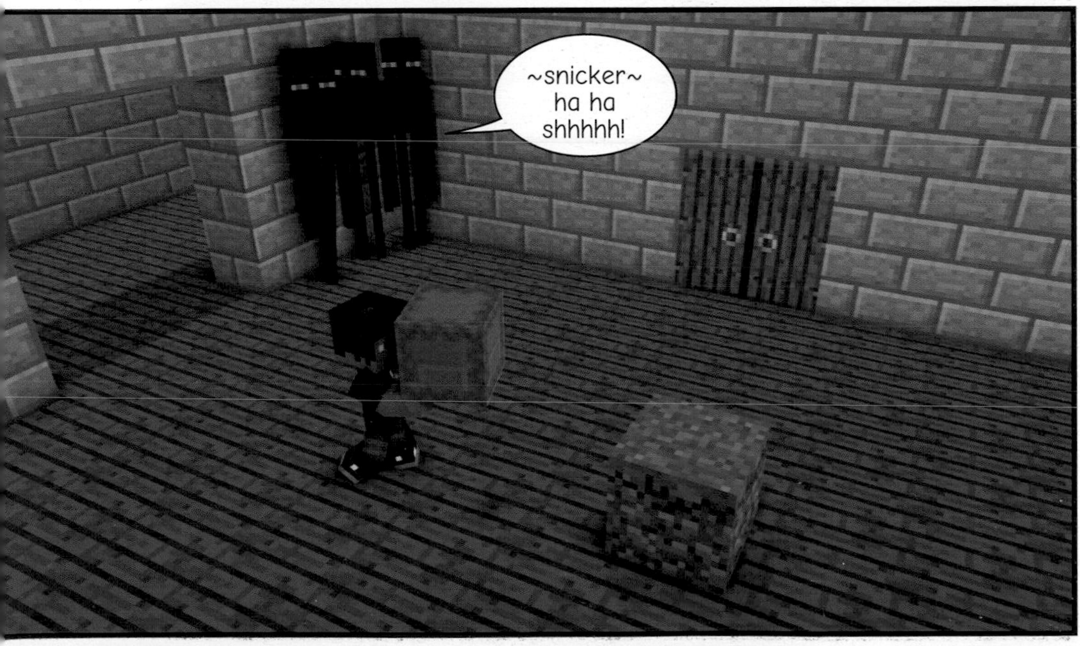
~snicker~
ha ha
shhhhh!

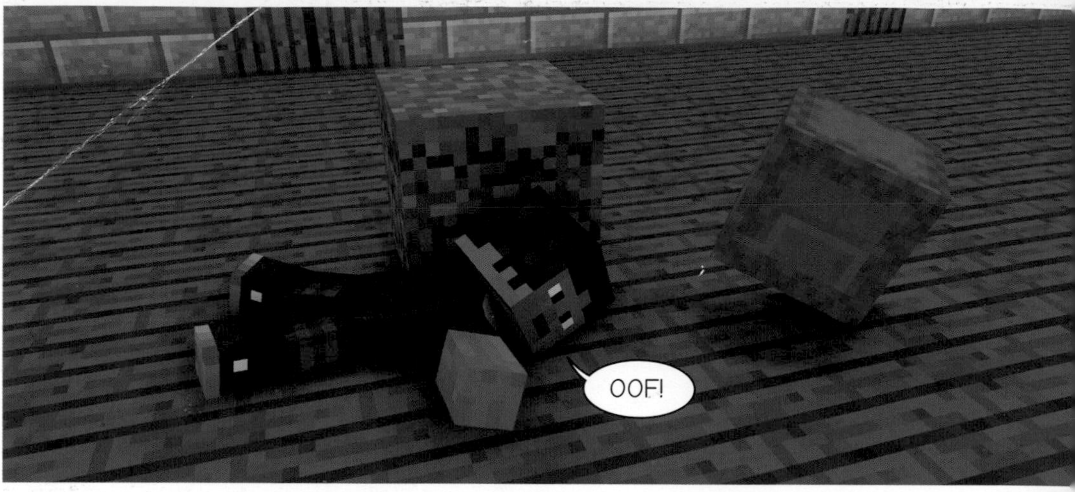
OOF!

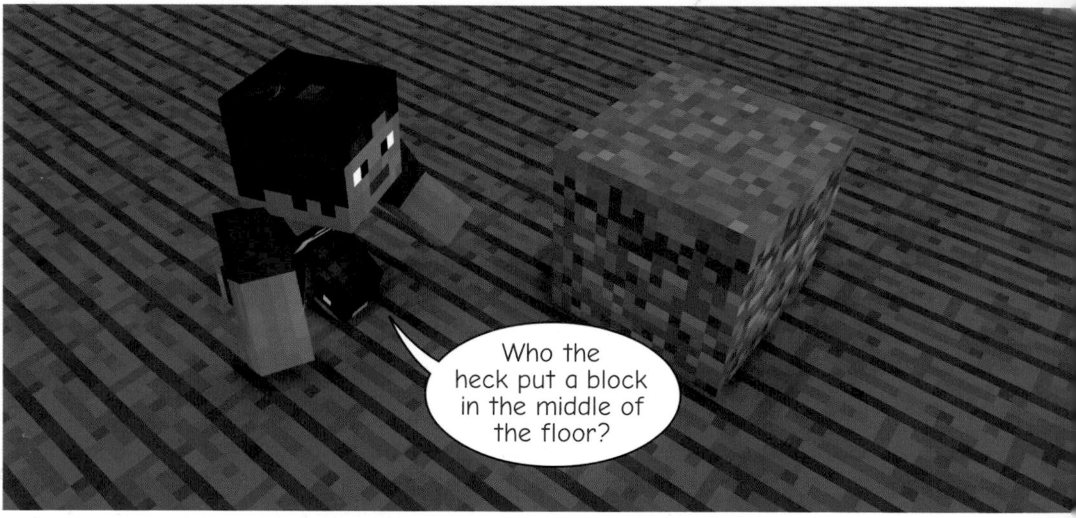
Who the heck put a block in the middle of the floor?

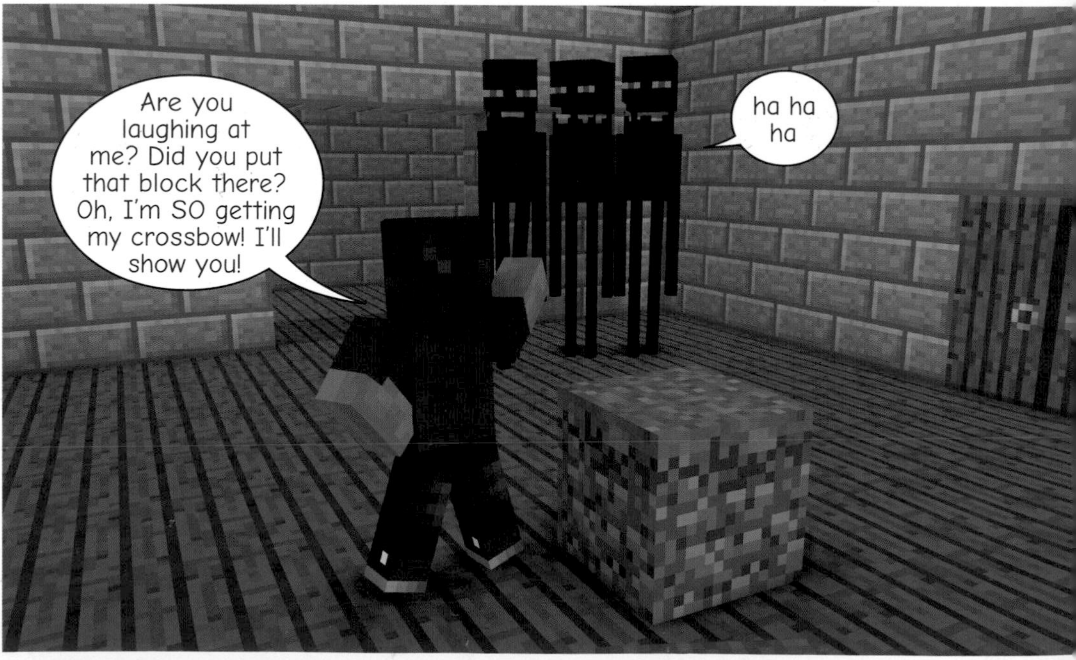
Are you laughing at me? Did you put that block there? Oh, I'm SO getting my crossbow! I'll show you!
ha ha ha

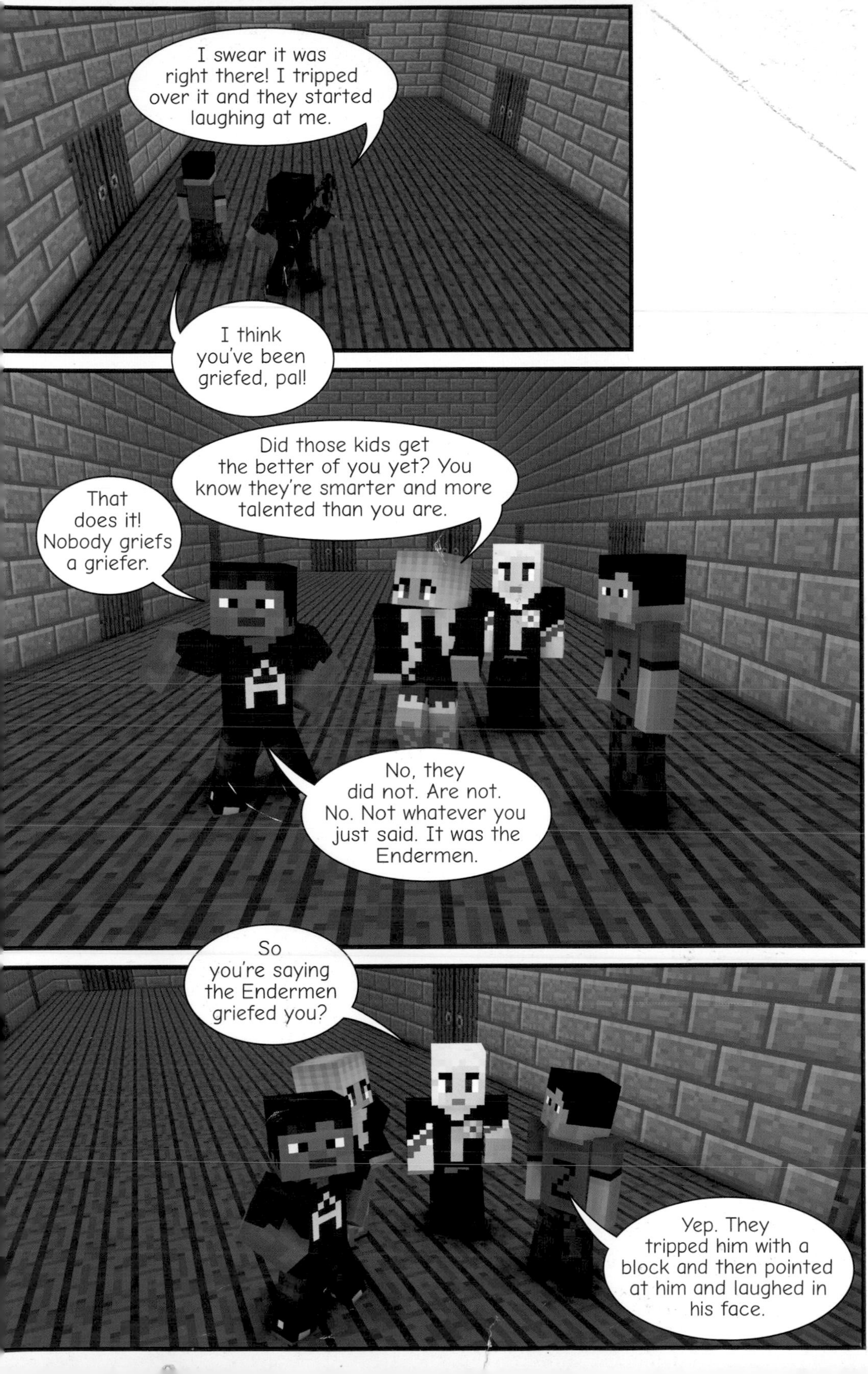
I swear it was right there! I tripped over it and they started laughing at me.
I think you've been griefed, pal!
Did those kids get the better of you yet? You know they're smarter and more talented than you are.
That does it! Nobody griefs a griefer.
No, they did not. Are not. No. Not whatever you just said. It was the Endermen.
So you're saying the Endermen griefed you?
Yep. They tripped him with a block and then pointed at him and laughed in his face.

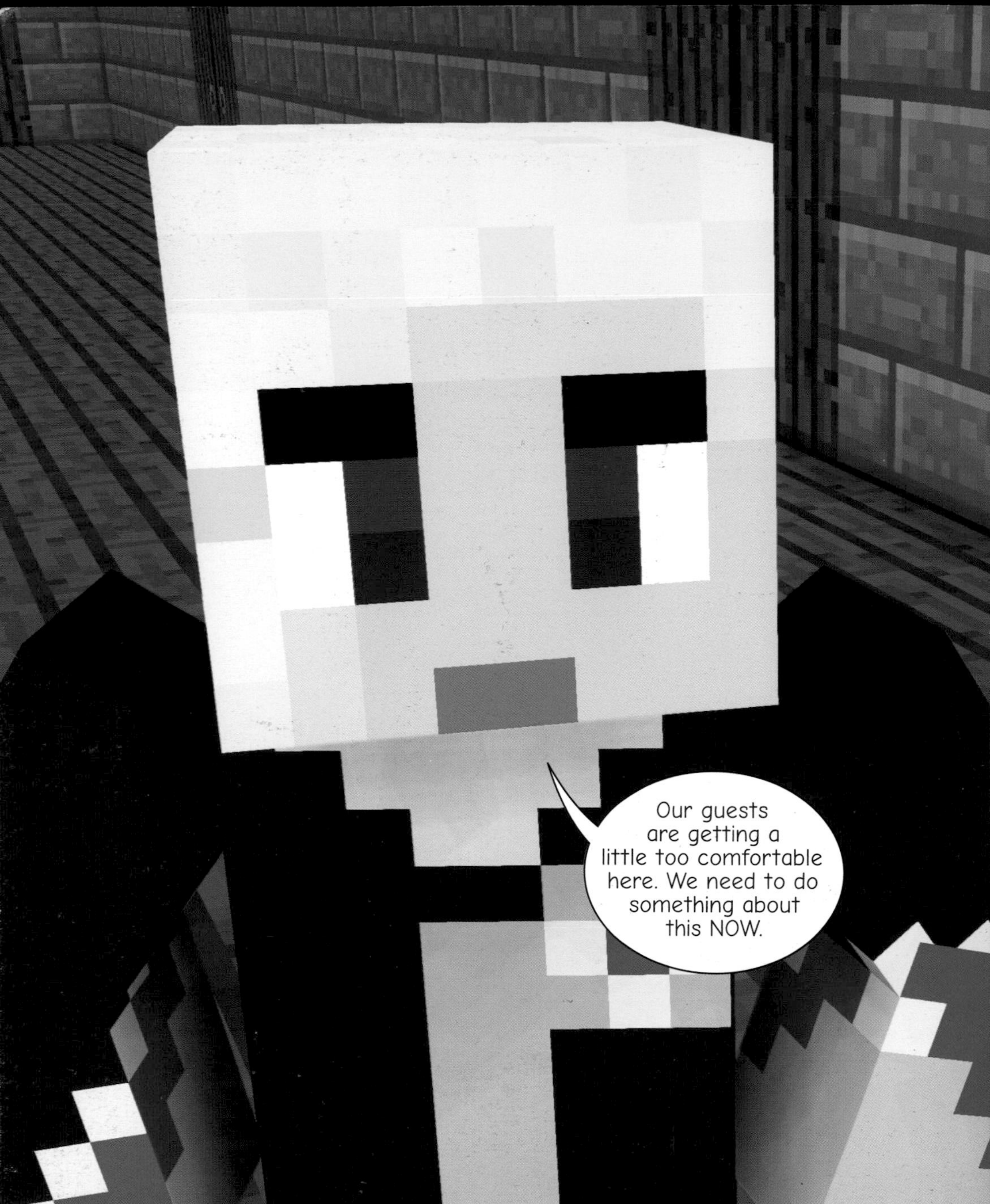
Our guests are getting a little too comfortable here. We need to do something about this NOW.

CHAPTER 9

KNOW YOUR ENEMY

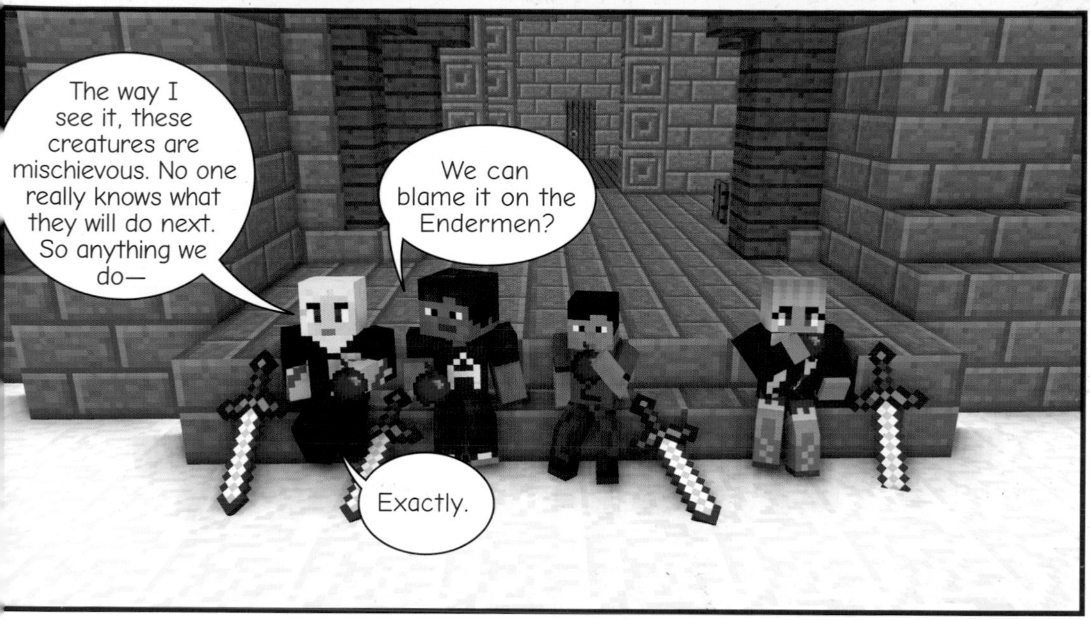
The way I see it, these creatures are mischievous. No one really knows what they will do next. So anything we do—
We can blame it on the Endermen?
Exactly.

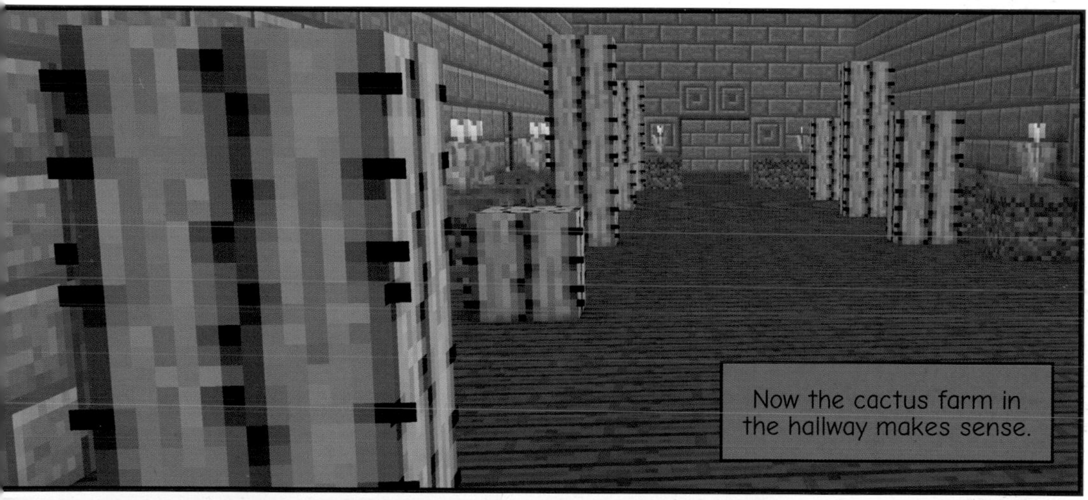
Now the cactus farm in the hallway makes sense.

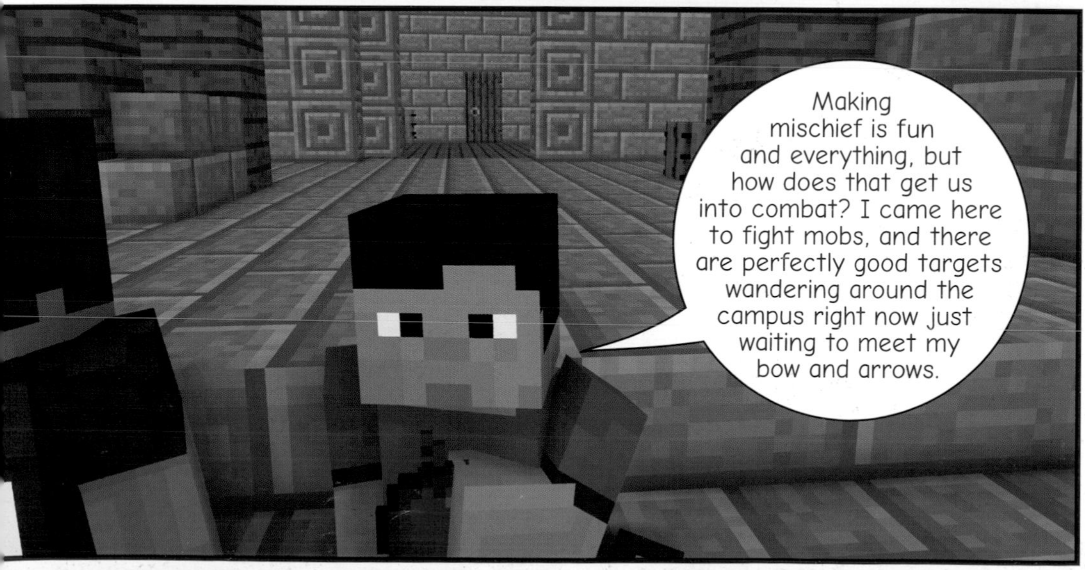
Making mischief is fun and everything, but how does that get us into combat? I came here to fight mobs, and there are perfectly good targets wandering around the campus right now just waiting to meet my bow and arrows.

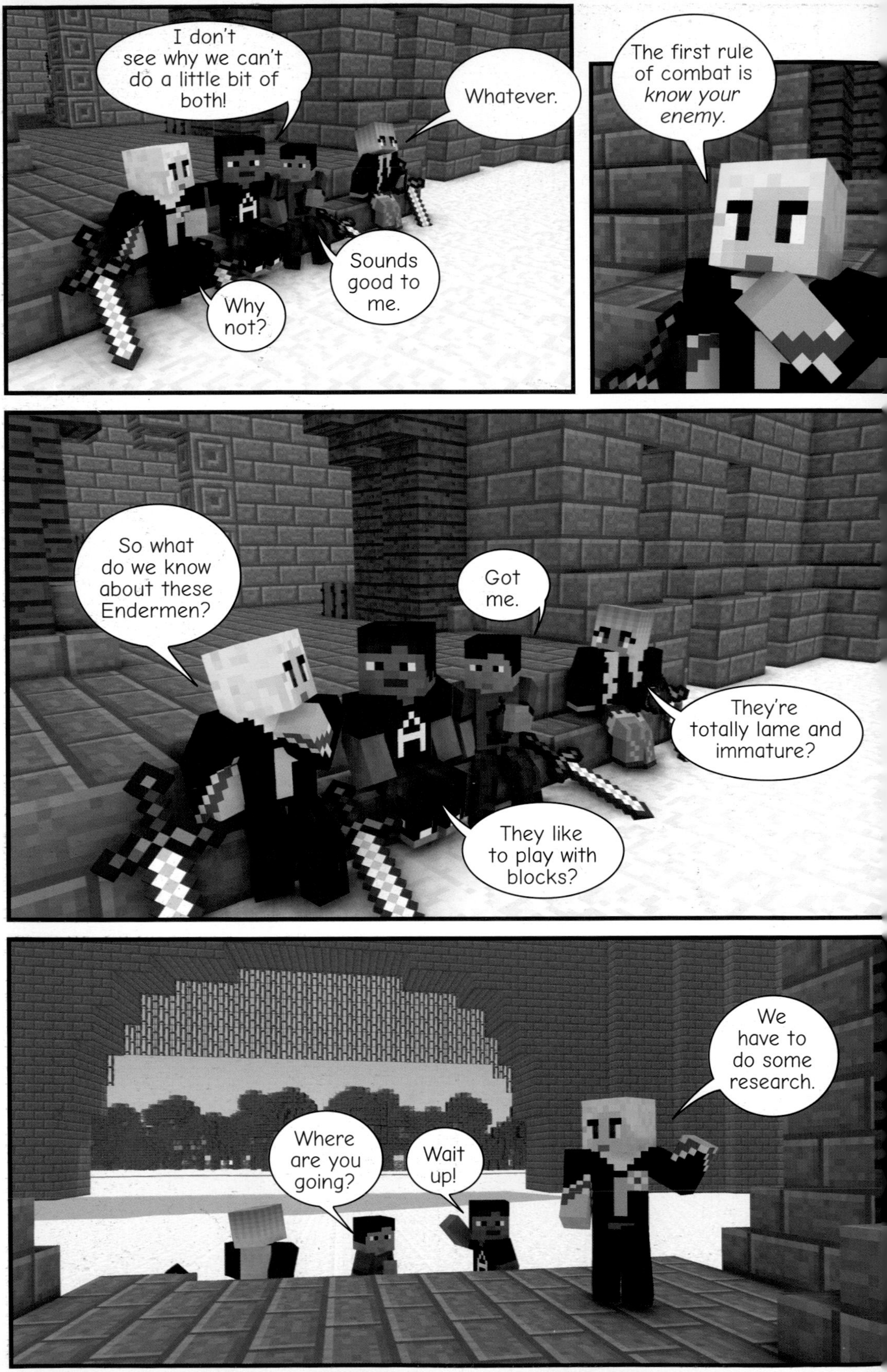
I don't see why we can't do a little bit of both!
Whatever.
Sounds good to me.
Why not?
The first rule of combat is *know your enemy.*
So what do we know about these Endermen?
Got me.
They're totally lame and immature?
They like to play with blocks?
We have to do some research.
Where are you going?
Wait up!

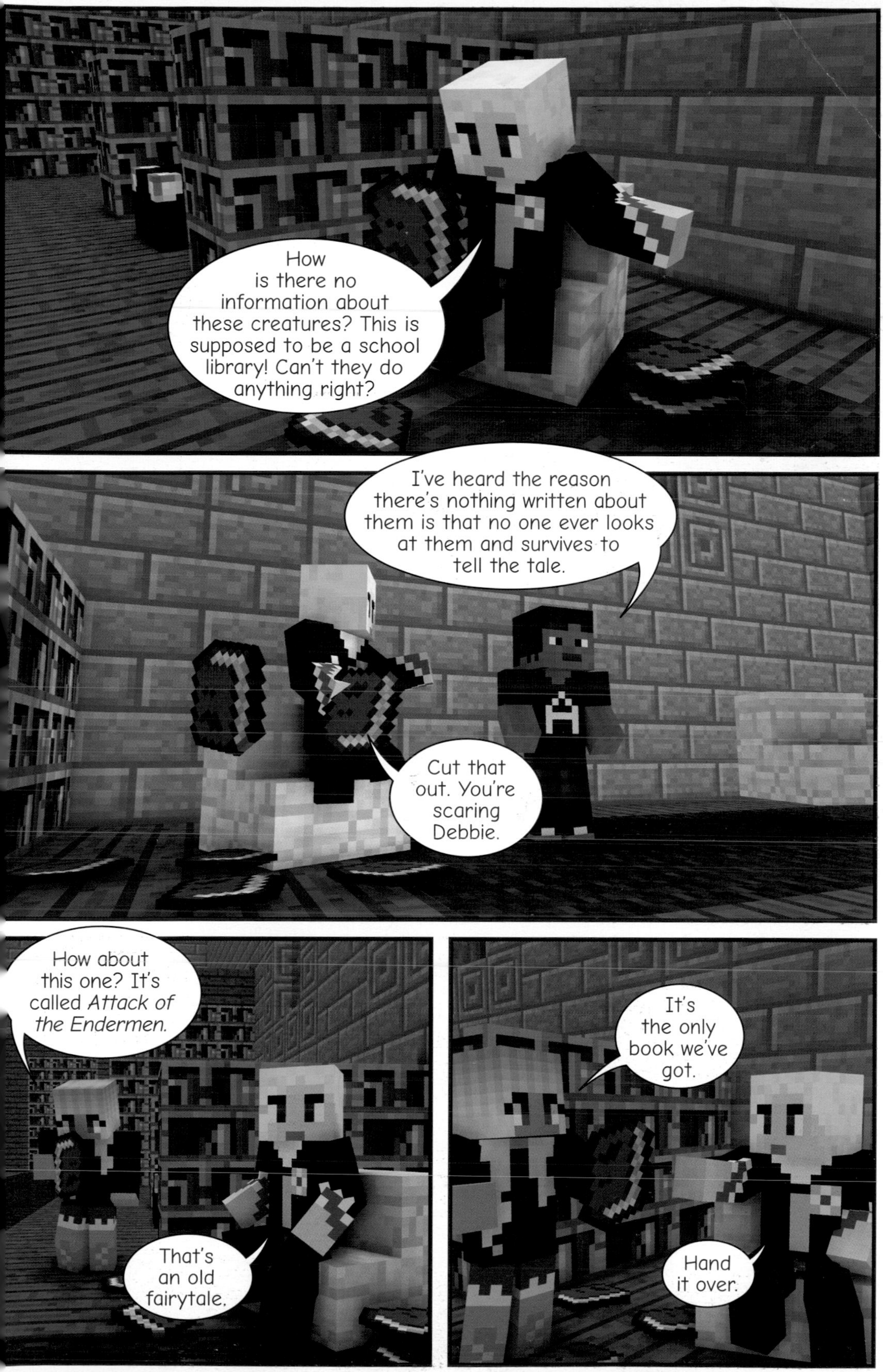
How is there no information about these creatures? This is supposed to be a school library! Can't they do anything right?
I've heard the reason there's nothing written about them is that no one ever looks at them and survives to tell the tale.
Cut that out. You're scaring Debbie.
How about this one? It's called *Attack of the Endermen.*
That's an old fairytale.
It's the only book we've got.
Hand it over.

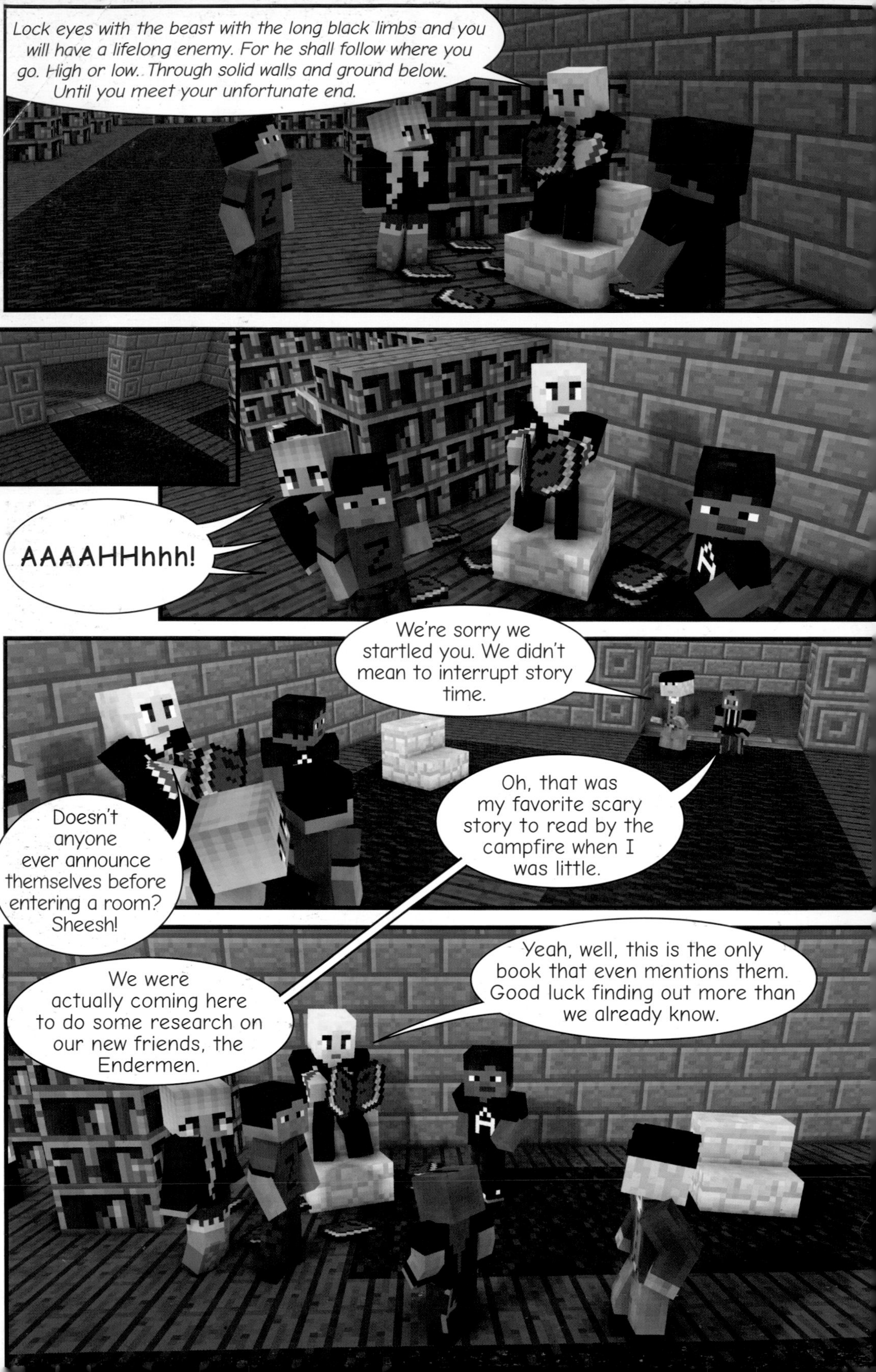
Lock eyes with the beast with the long black limbs and you will have a lifelong enemy. For he shall follow where you go. High or low. Through solid walls and ground below. Until you meet your unfortunate end.
AAAAHHhhh!
We're sorry we startled you. We didn't mean to interrupt story time.
Doesn't anyone ever announce themselves before entering a room? Sheesh!
Oh, that was my favorite scary story to read by the campfire when I was little.
We were actually coming here to do some research on our new friends, the Endermen.
Yeah, well, this is the only book that even mentions them. Good luck finding out more than we already know.

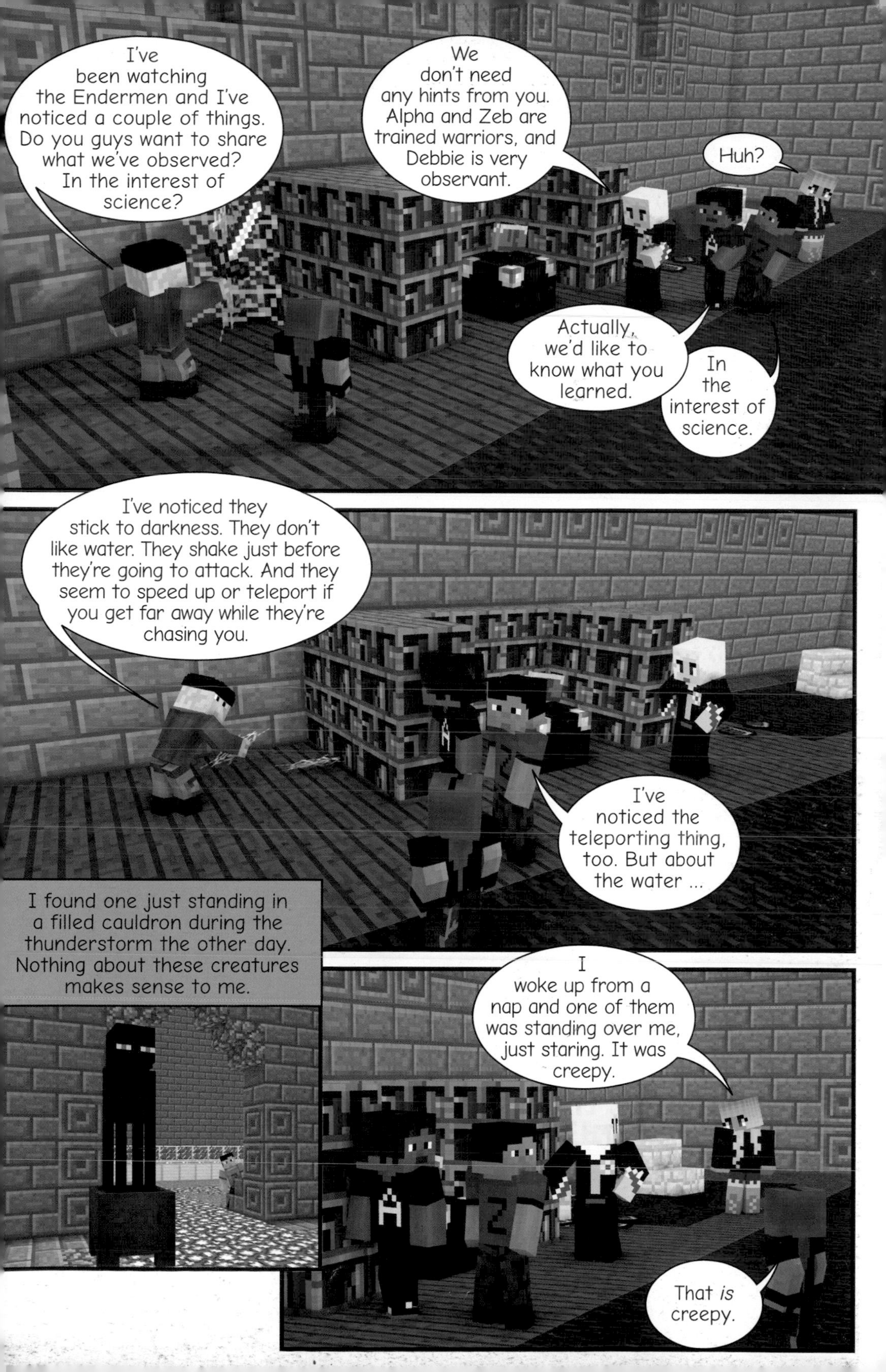
I've been watching the Endermen and I've noticed a couple of things. Do you guys want to share what we've observed? In the interest of science?
We don't need any hints from you. Alpha and Zeb are trained warriors, and Debbie is very observant.
Huh?
Actually, we'd like to know what you learned.
In the interest of science.
I've noticed they stick to darkness. They don't like water. They shake just before they're going to attack. And they seem to speed up or teleport if you get far away while they're chasing you.
I've noticed the teleporting thing, too. But about the water ...
I found one just standing in a filled cauldron during the thunderstorm the other day. Nothing about these creatures makes sense to me.
I woke up from a nap and one of them was standing over me, just staring. It was creepy.
That *is* creepy.

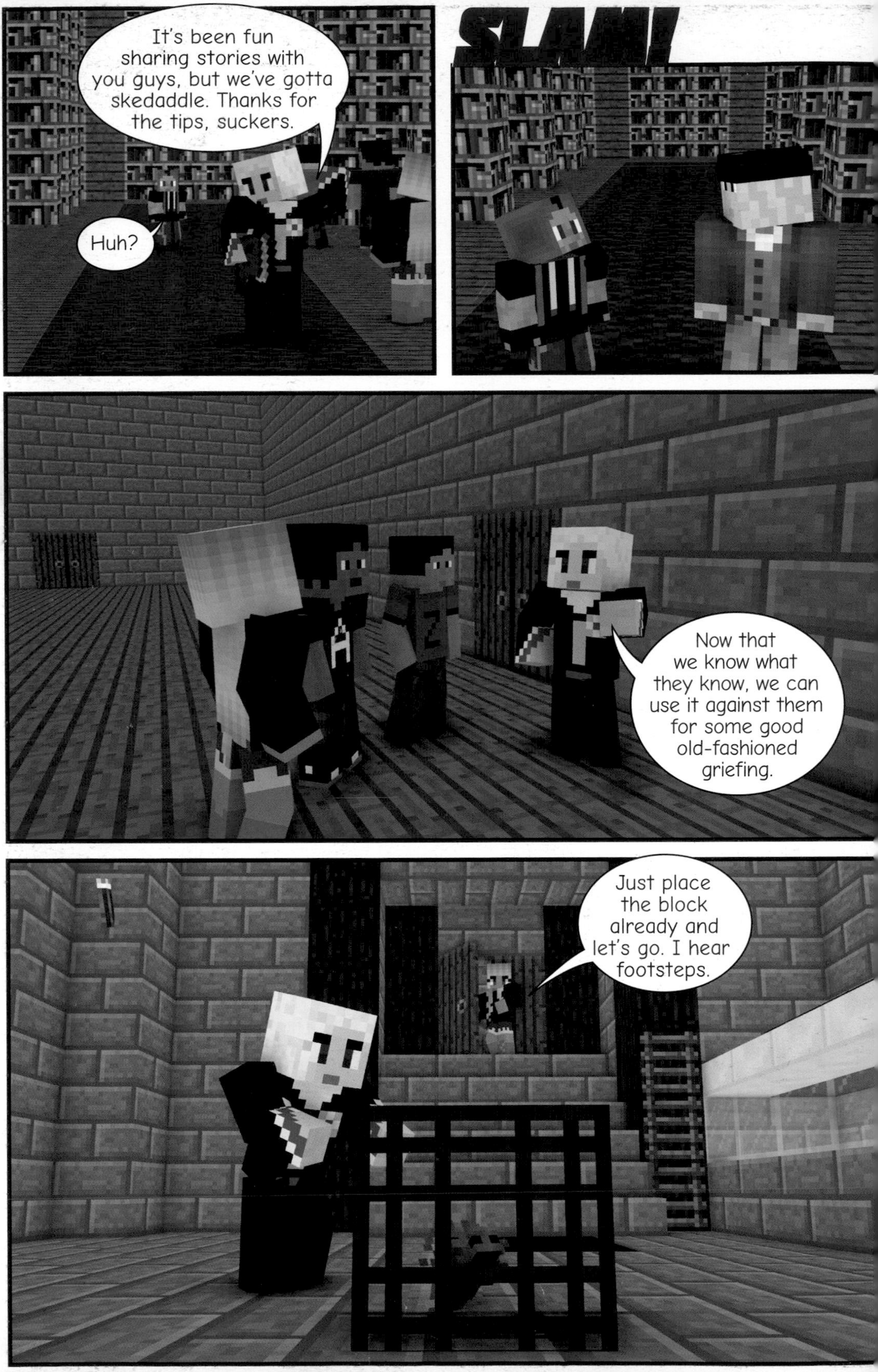
It's been fun sharing stories with you guys, but we've gotta skedaddle. Thanks for the tips, suckers.
Huh?
SLAM!
Now that we know what they know, we can use it against them for some good old-fashioned griefing.
Just place the block already and let's go. I hear footsteps.

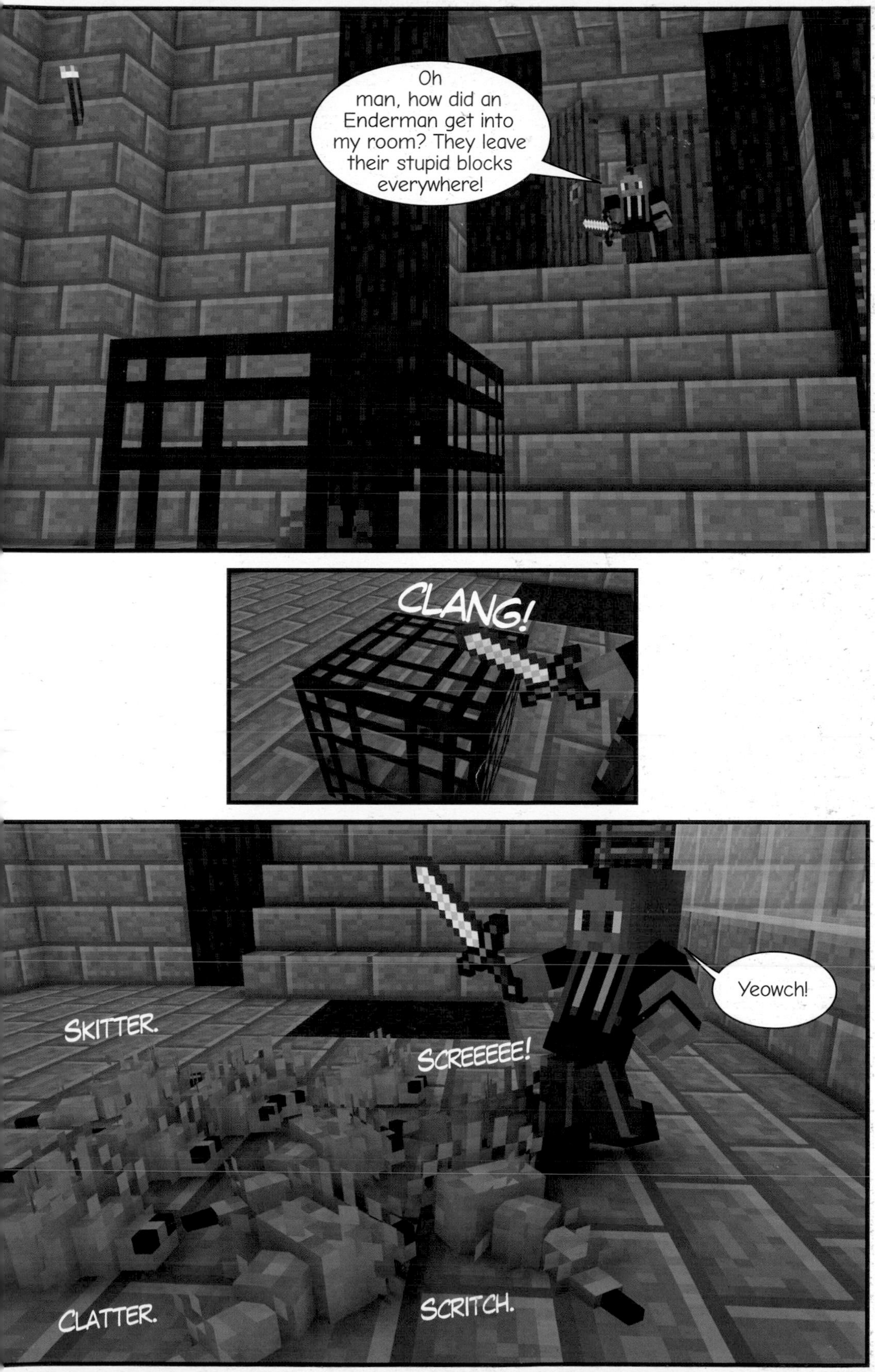
Oh man, how did an Enderman get into my room? They leave their stupid blocks everywhere!
CLANG!
Yeowch!
SKITTER.
SCREEEEEE!
CLATTER.
SCRITCH.

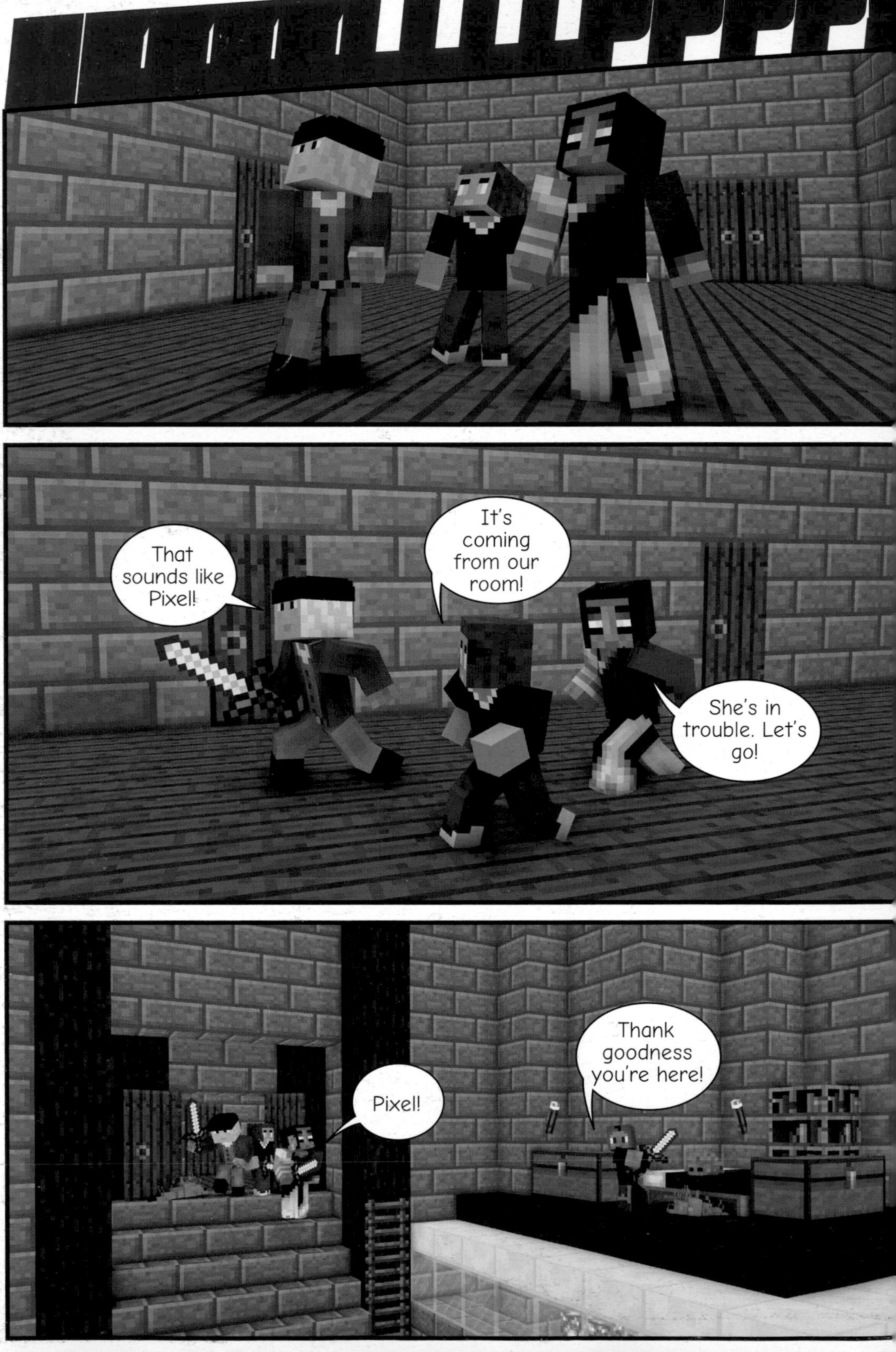
That sounds like Pixel!
It's coming from our room!
She's in trouble. Let's go!
Pixel!
Thank goodness you're here!

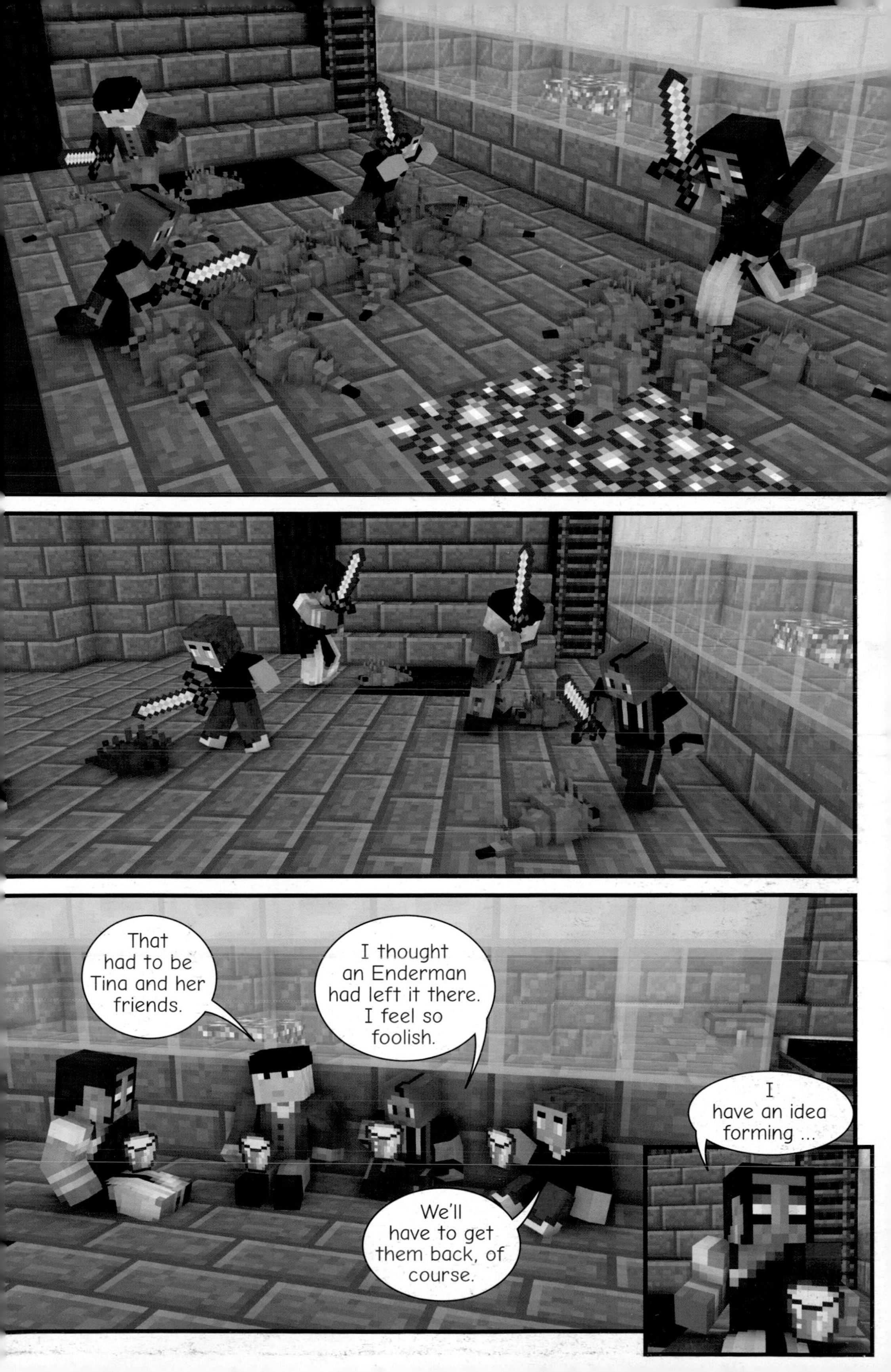
That had to be Tina and her friends.
I thought an Enderman had left it there. I feel so foolish.
We'll have to get them back, of course.
I have an idea forming ...

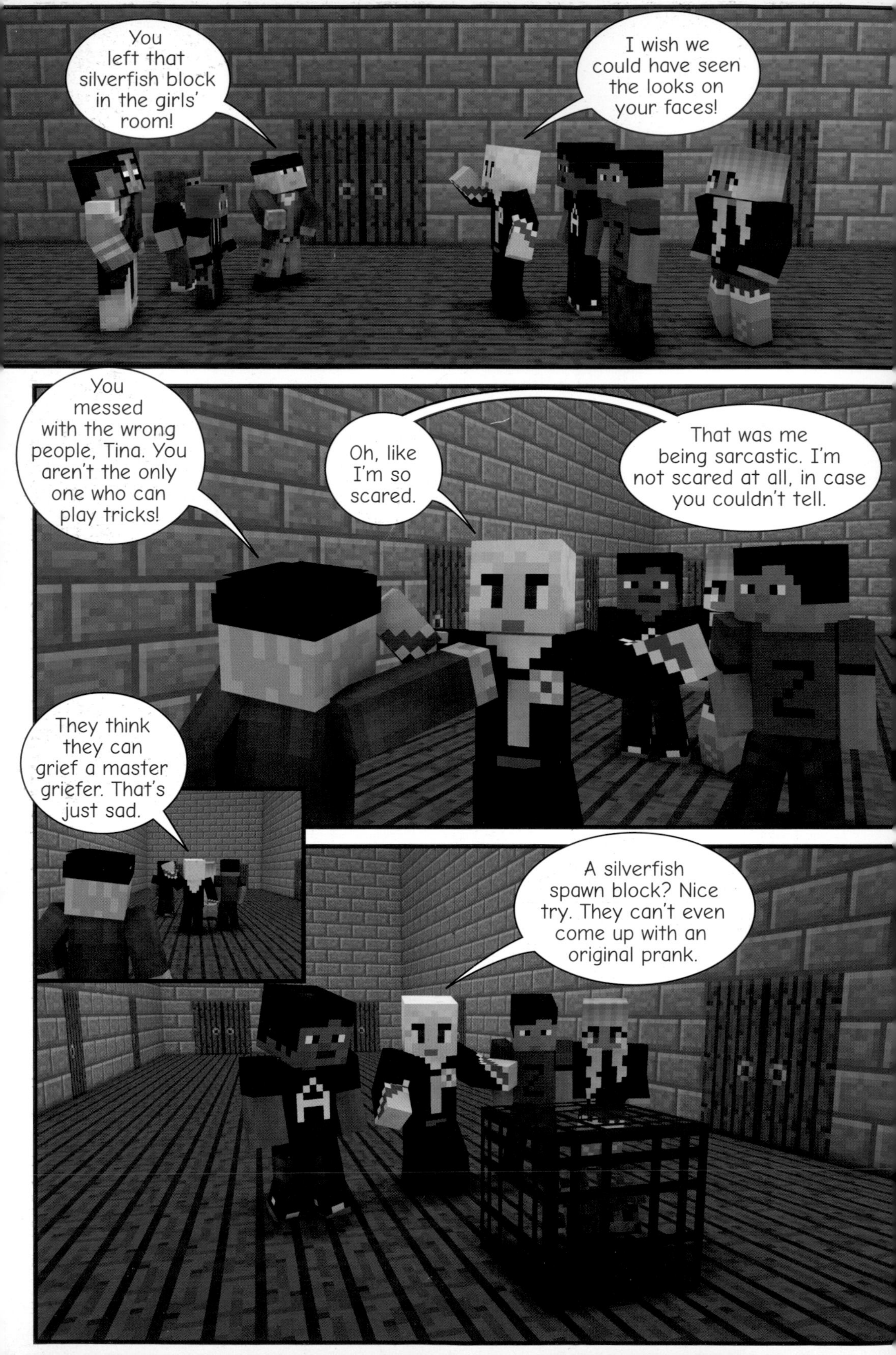
You left that silverfish block in the girls' room!
I wish we could have seen the looks on your faces!
You messed with the wrong people, Tina. You aren't the only one who can play tricks!
Oh, like I'm so scared.
That was me being sarcastic. I'm not scared at all, in case you couldn't tell.
They think they can grief a master griefer. That's just sad.
A silverfish spawn block? Nice try. They can't even come up with an original prank.

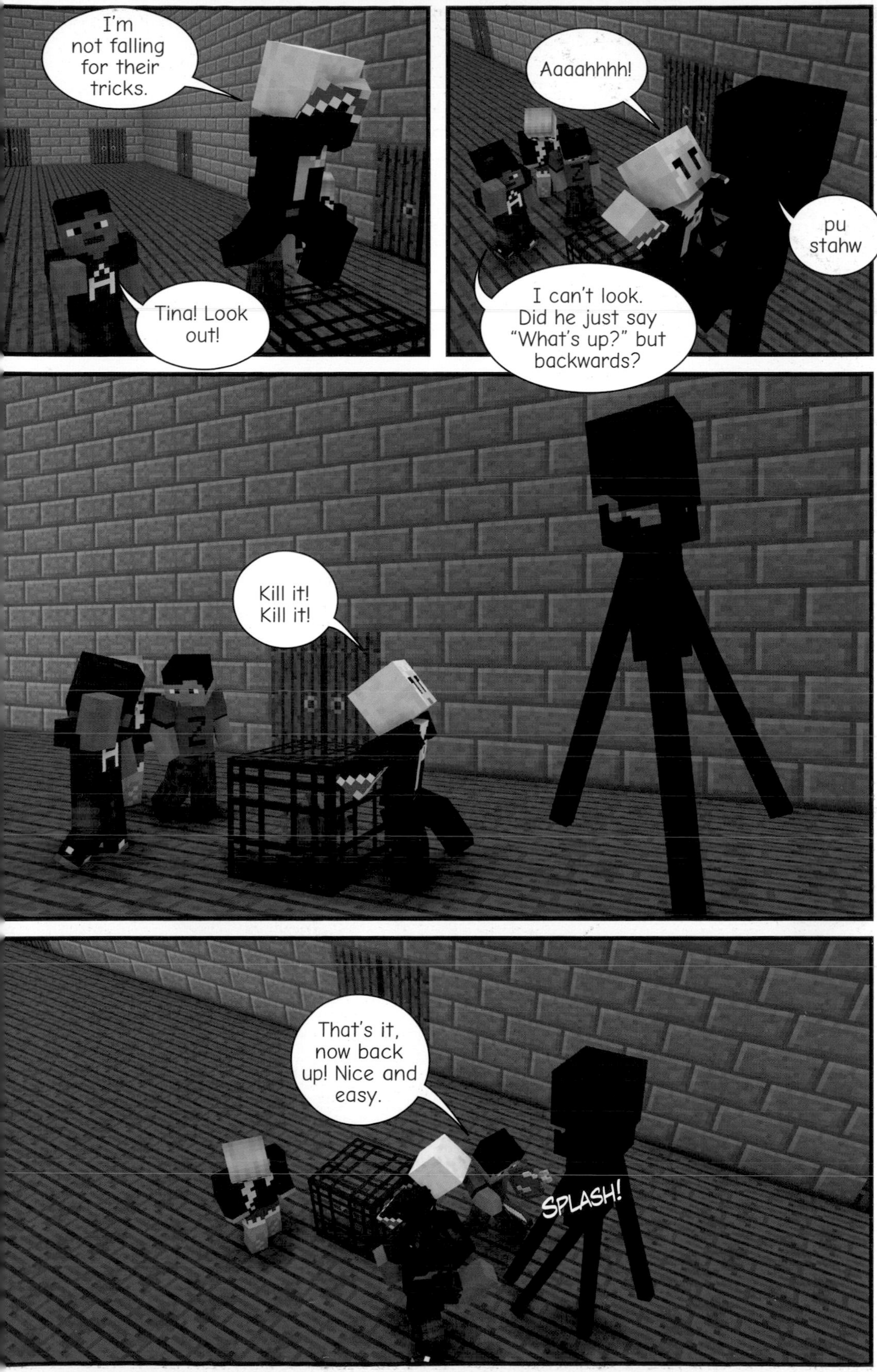
I'm not falling for their tricks.
Tina! Look out!
Aaaahhhh!
pu stahw
I can't look. Did he just say "What's up?" but backwards?
Kill it! Kill it!
That's it, now back up! Nice and easy.
SPLASH!

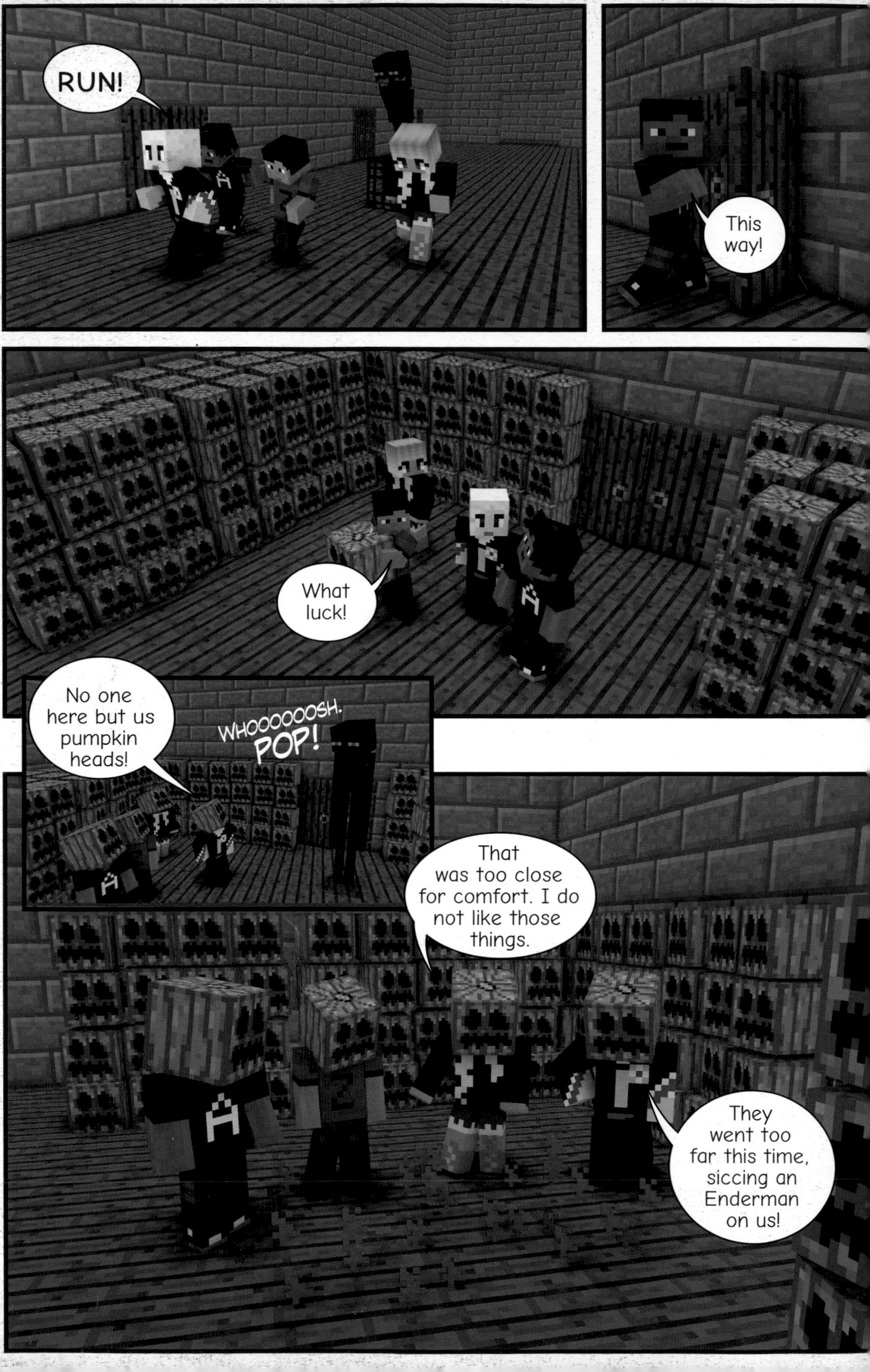
RUN!
This way!
What luck!
No one here but us pumpkin heads!
WHOOOOOOSH. POP!
That was too close for comfort. I do not like those things.
They went too far this time, siccing an Enderman on us!

CHAPTER 10

GOOD GRIEF

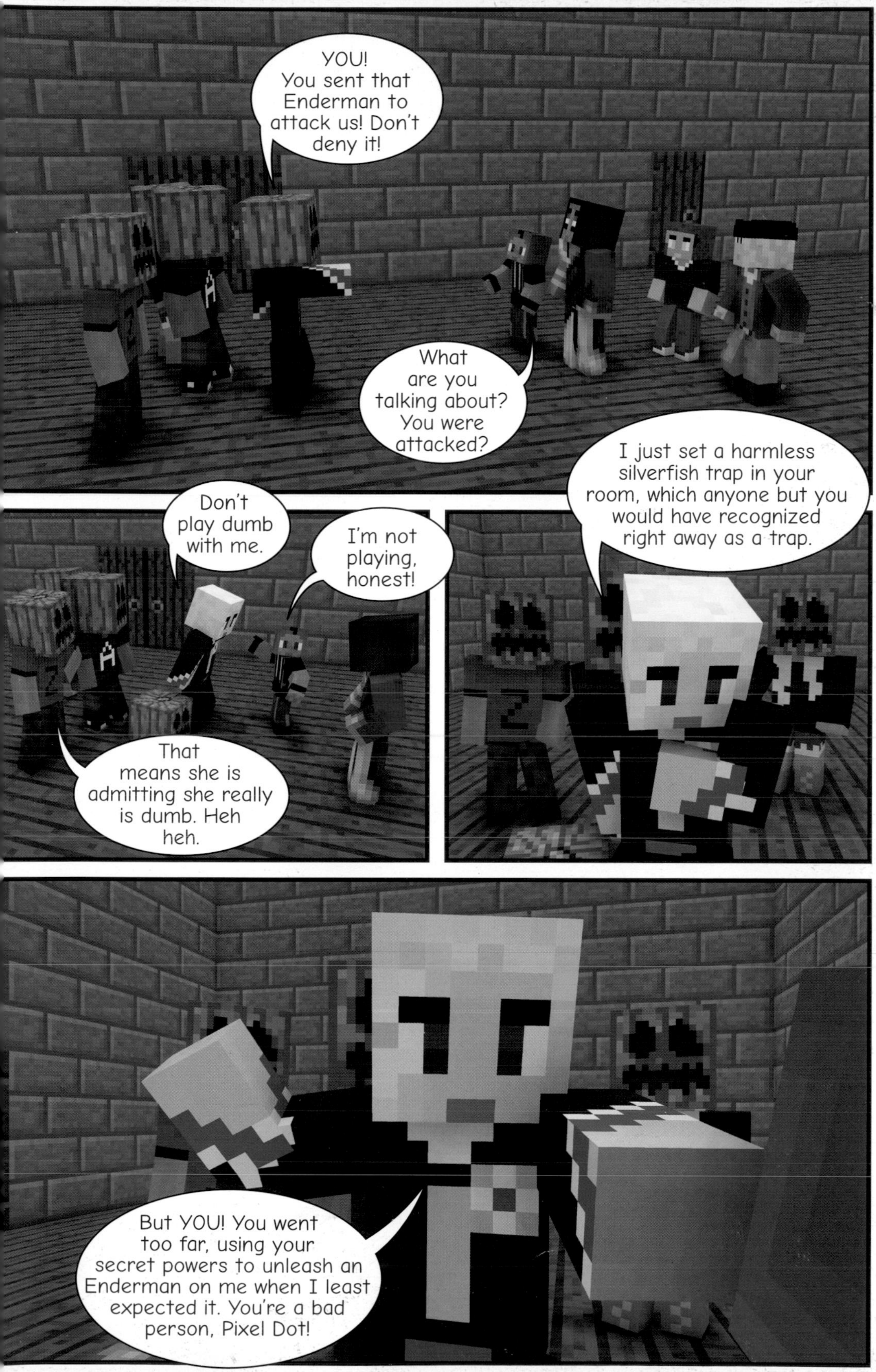
YOU! You sent that Enderman to attack us! Don't deny it!
What are you talking about? You were attacked?
I just set a harmless silverfish trap in your room, which anyone but you would have recognized right away as a trap.
Don't play dumb with me.
I'm not playing, honest!
That means she is admitting she really is dumb. Heh heh.
But YOU! You went too far, using your secret powers to unleash an Enderman on me when I least expected it. You're a bad person, Pixel Dot!

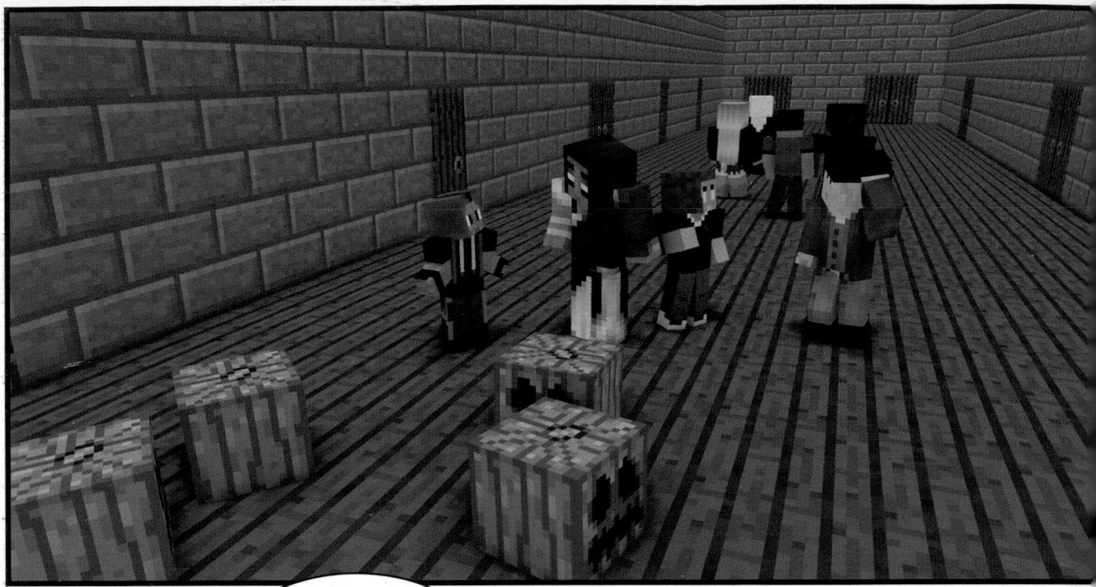

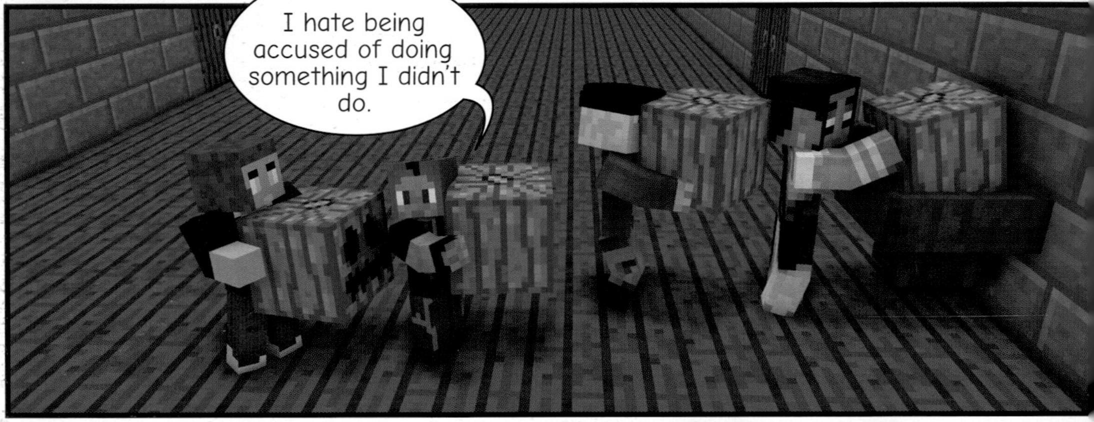
I hate being accused of doing something I didn't do.

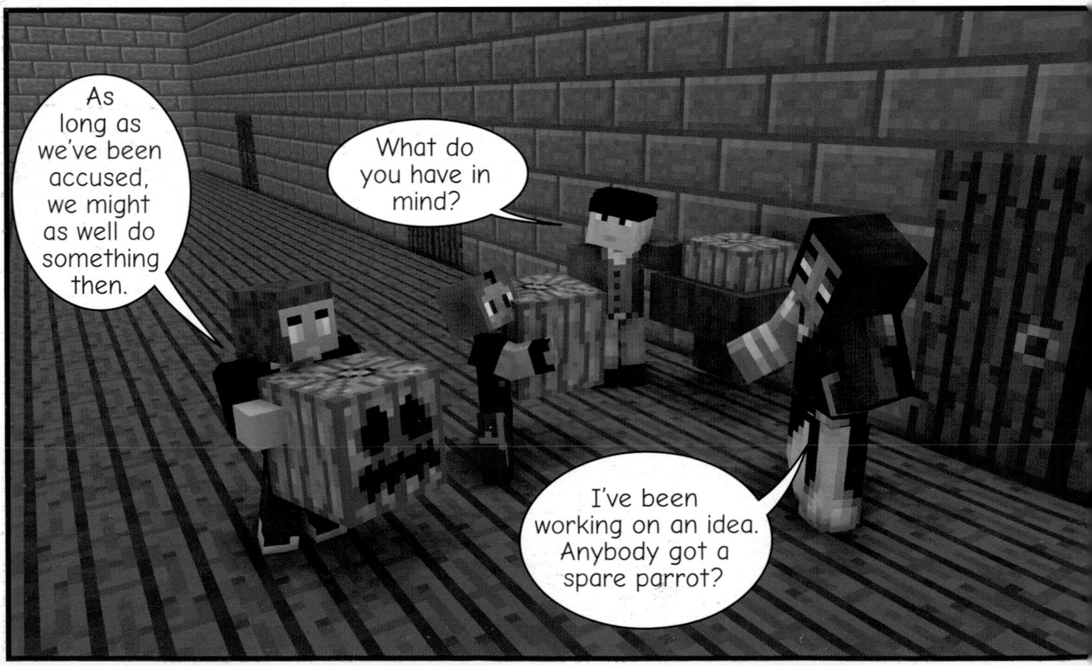
As long as we've been accused, we might as well do something then.
What do you have in mind?
I've been working on an idea. Anybody got a spare parrot?

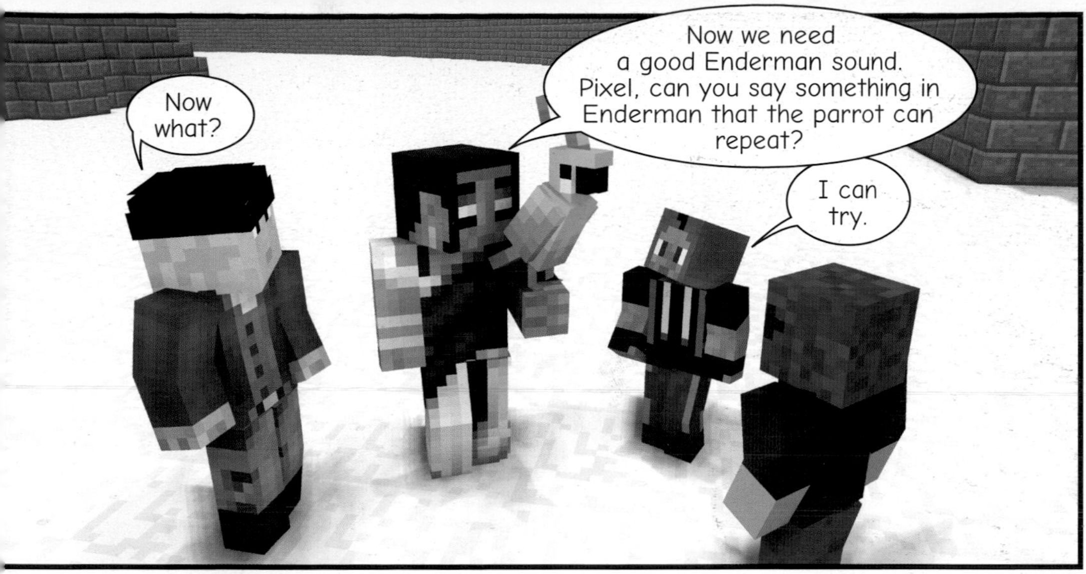
Now what?
Now we need a good Enderman sound. Pixel, can you say something in Enderman that the parrot can repeat?
I can try.

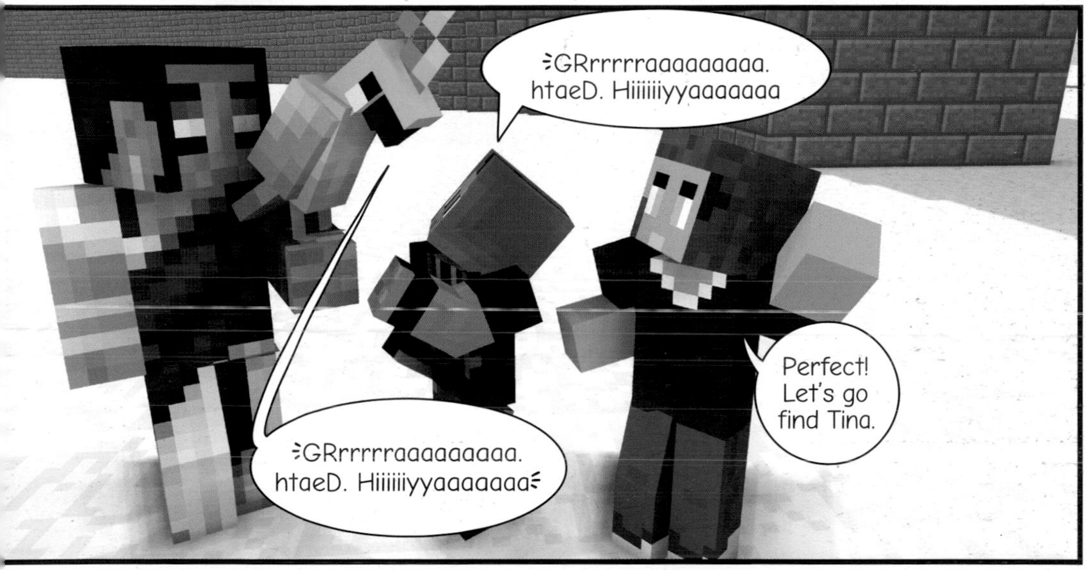
GRrrrrraaaaaaaaa. htaeD. Hiiiiiiyyaaaaaaa
GRrrrrraaaaaaaaa. htaeD. Hiiiiiiyyaaaaaaa
Perfect! Let's go find Tina.

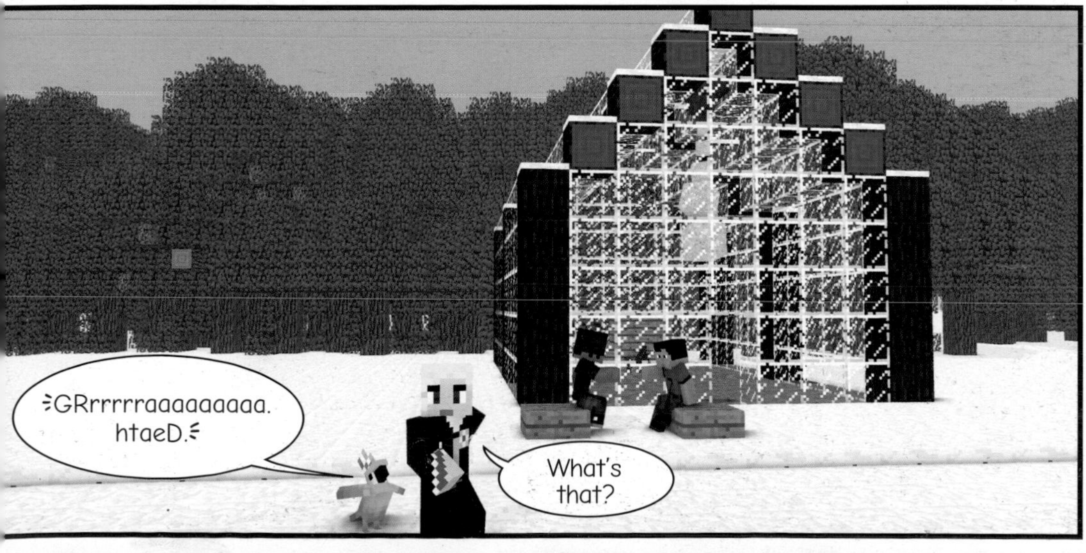
GRrrrrraaaaaaaaa. htaeD.
What's that?

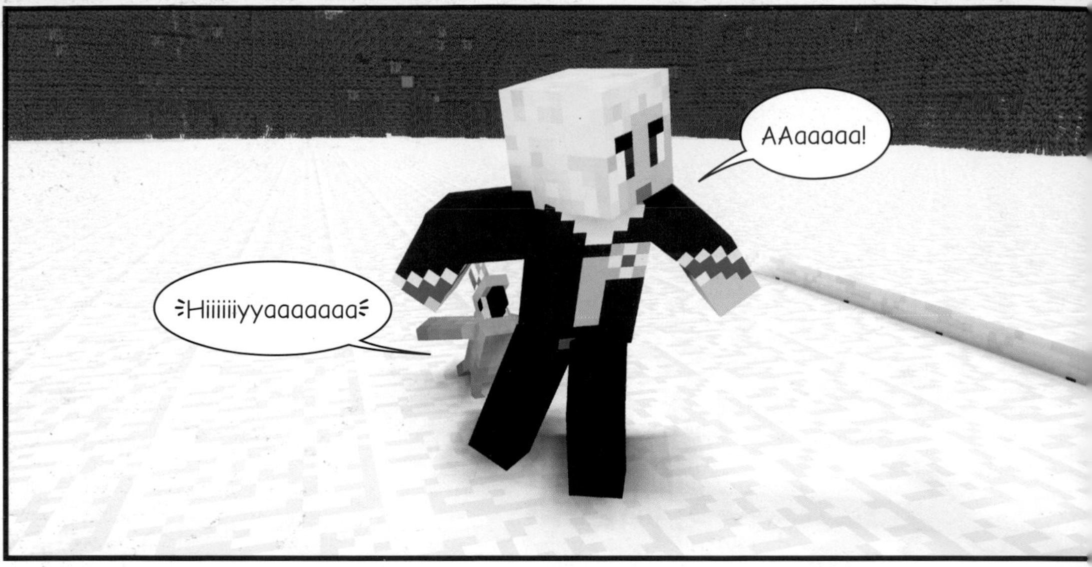
AAaaaaa!
Hiiiiiiyyaaaaaaa

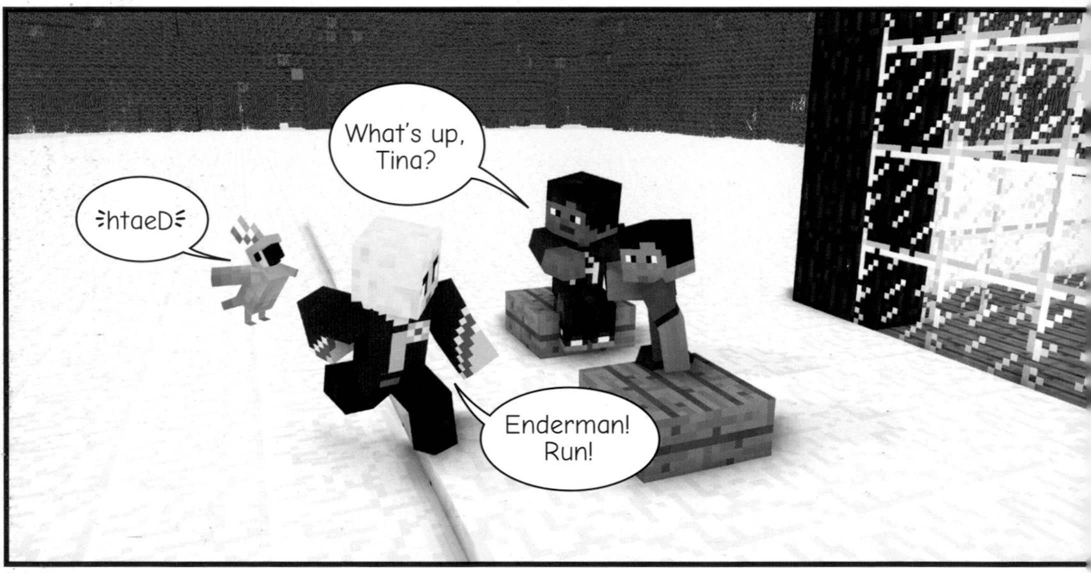
What's up, Tina?
htaeD
Enderman! Run!

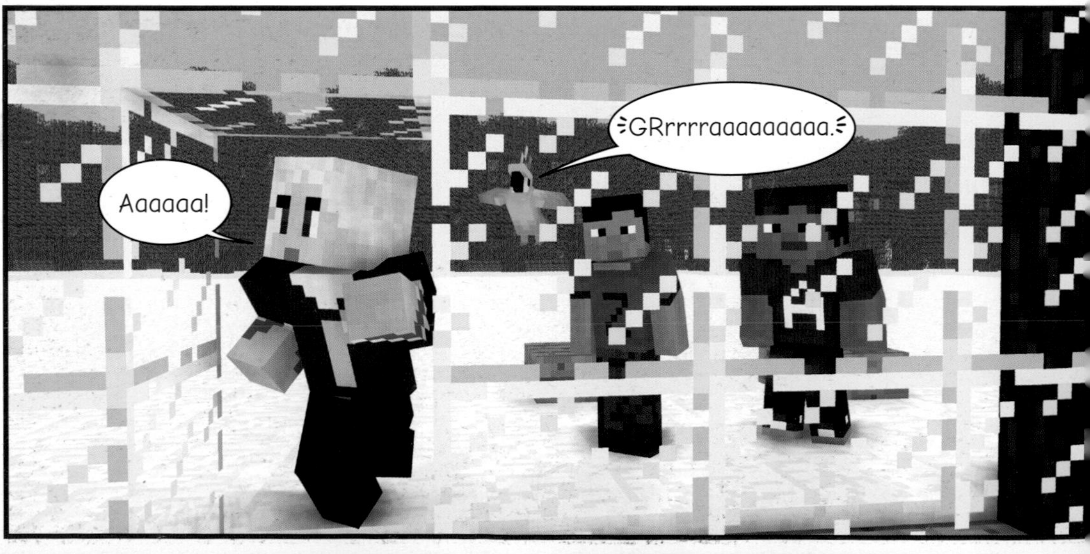
GRrrrraaaaaaaaa.
Aaaaaa!

CLICK!

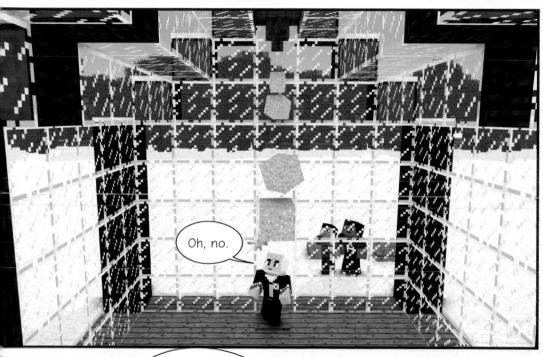

Oh, no.

Grrrrraaaaa. I'm an Enderman. Hahaha.

Ha hahaha ha!

Grrrr! That does it!

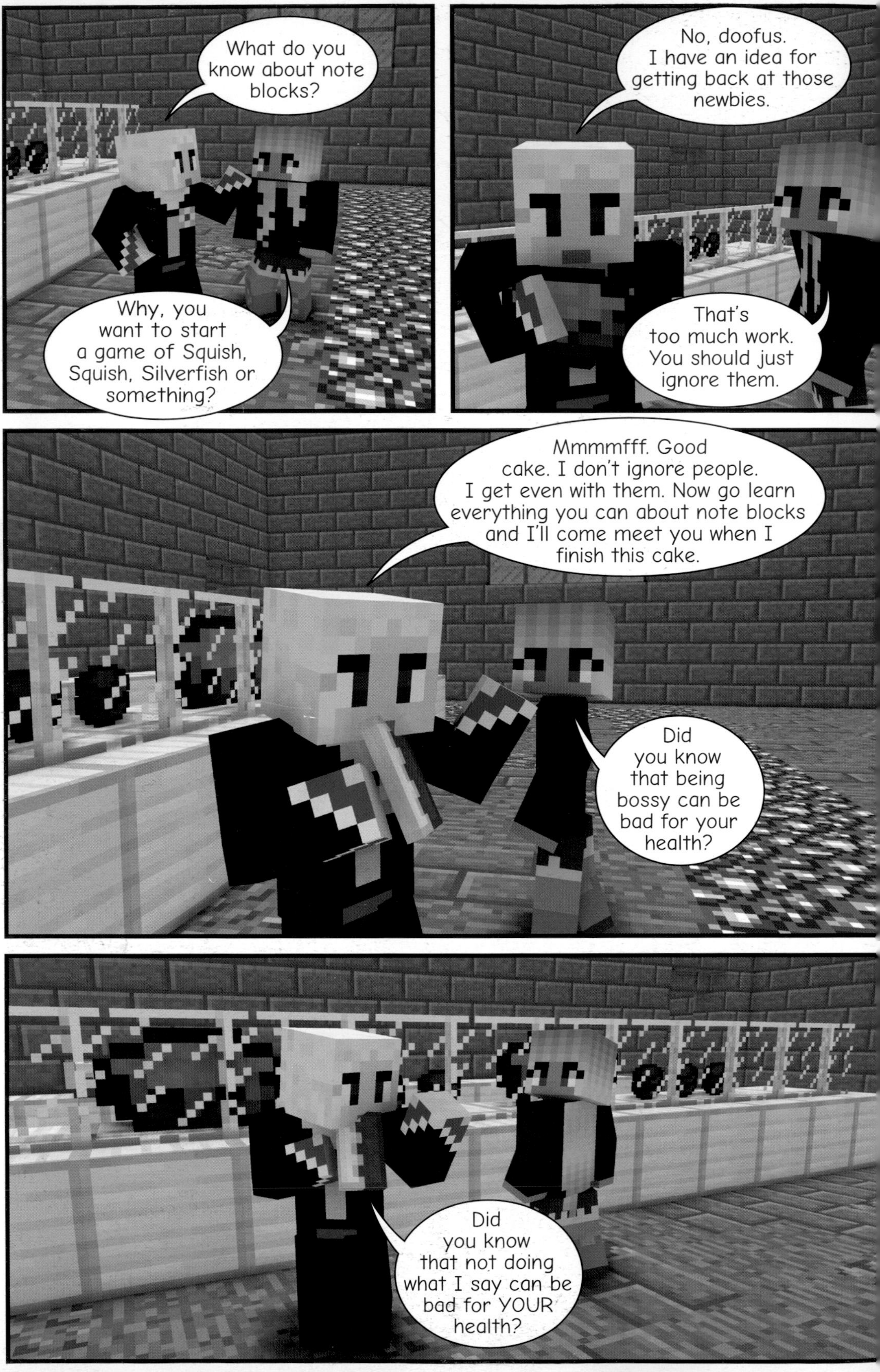
What do you know about note blocks?
Why, you want to start a game of Squish, Squish, Silverfish or something?
No, doofus. I have an idea for getting back at those newbies.
That's too much work. You should just ignore them.
Mmmmfff. Good cake. I don't ignore people. I get even with them. Now go learn everything you can about note blocks and I'll come meet you when I finish this cake.
Did you know that being bossy can be bad for your health?
Did you know that not doing what I say can be bad for YOUR health?

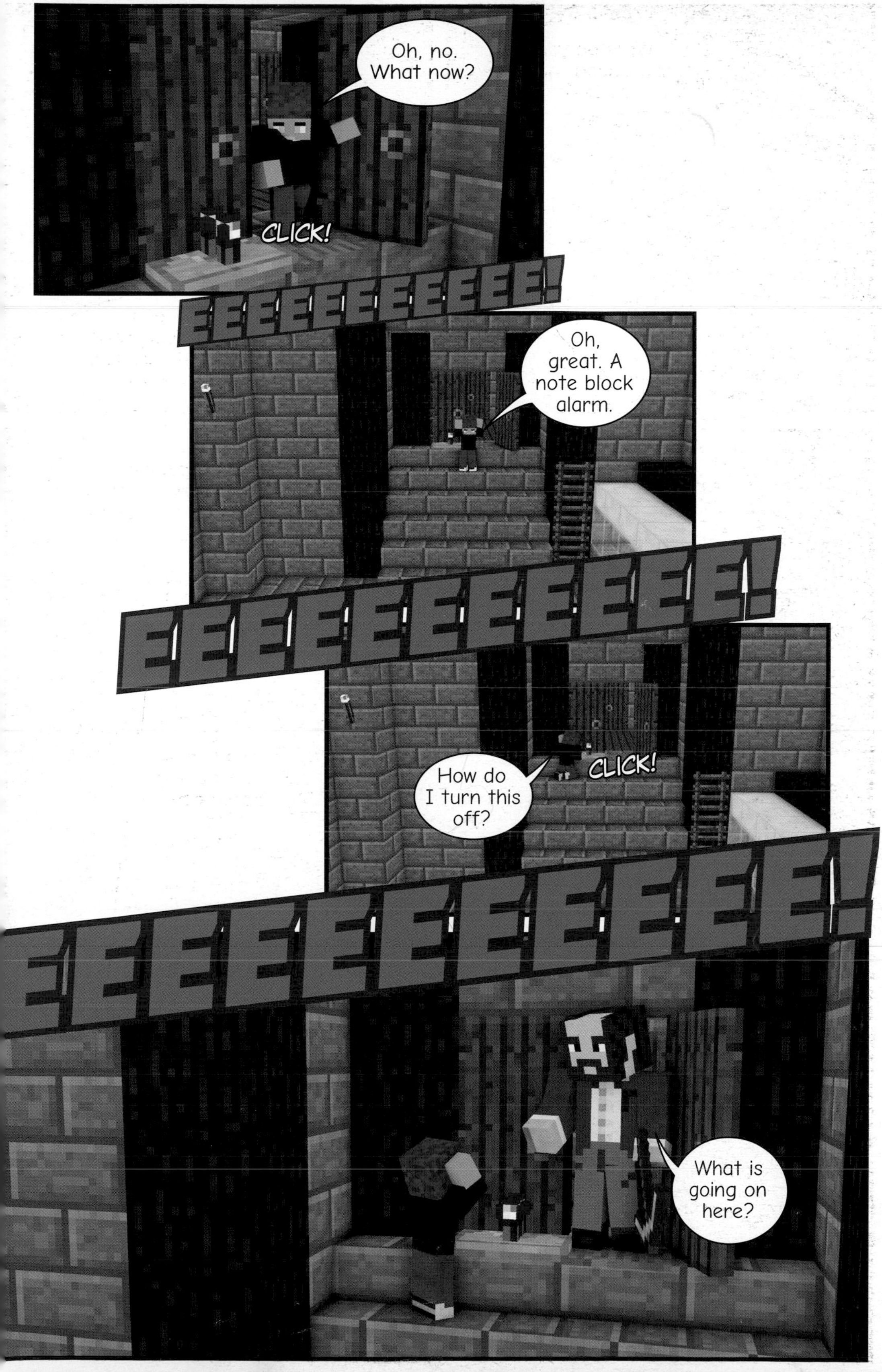
Oh, no.
What now?
CLICK!
EEEEEEEEEEE!
Oh,
great. A
note block
alarm.
EEEEEEEEEEEE!
How do
I turn this
off?
CLICK!
EEEEEEEEEEEEEE!
What is
going on
here?

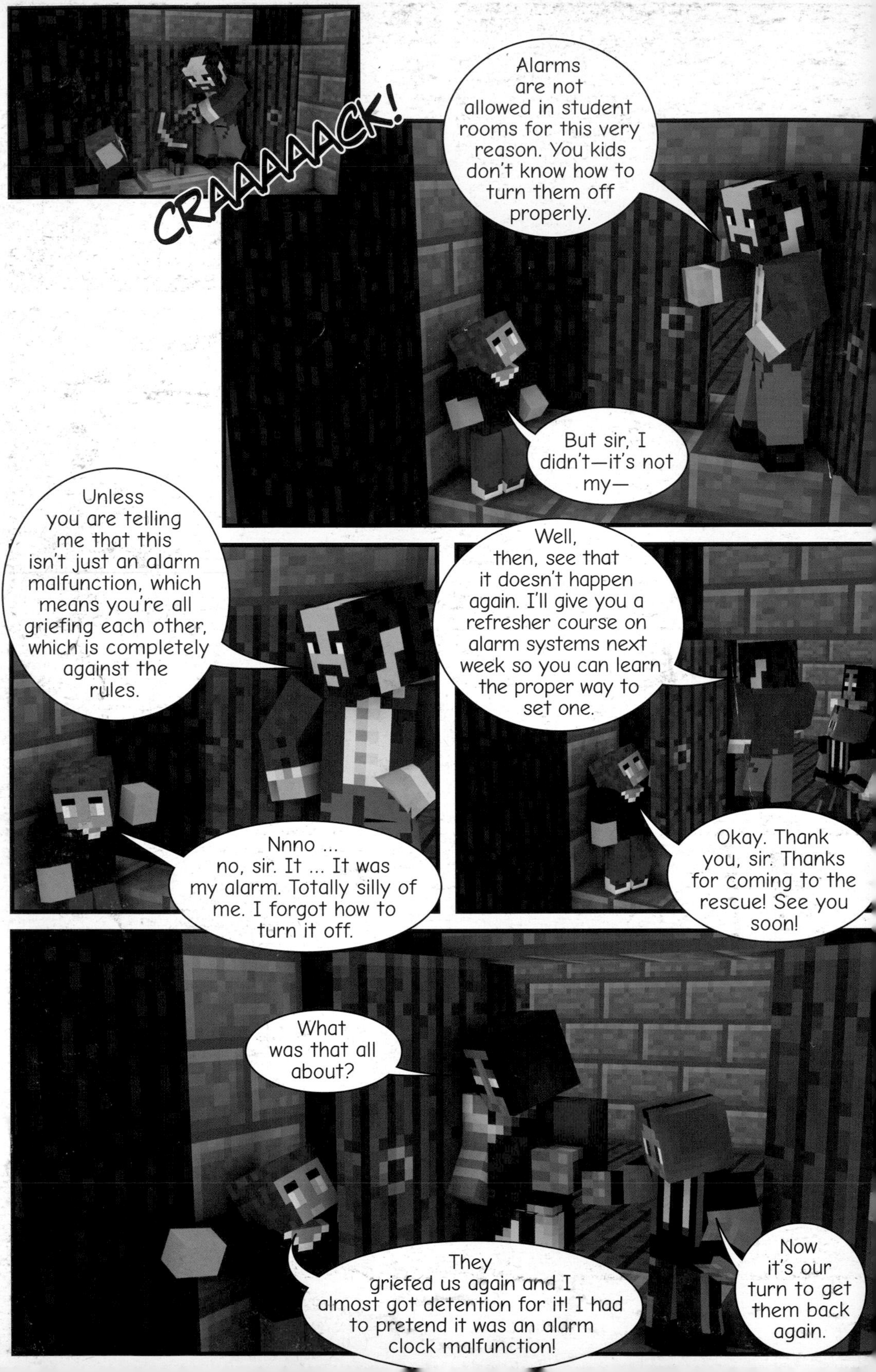
CRAAAAACK!
Alarms are not allowed in student rooms for this very reason. You kids don't know how to turn them off properly.
But sir, I didn't—it's not my—
Unless you are telling me that this isn't just an alarm malfunction, which means you're all griefing each other, which is completely against the rules.
Nnno ... no, sir. It ... It was my alarm. Totally silly of me. I forgot how to turn it off.
Well, then, see that it doesn't happen again. I'll give you a refresher course on alarm systems next week so you can learn the proper way to set one.
Okay. Thank you, sir. Thanks for coming to the rescue! See you soon!
What was that all about?
They griefed us again and I almost got detention for it! I had to pretend it was an alarm clock malfunction!
Now it's our turn to get them back again.

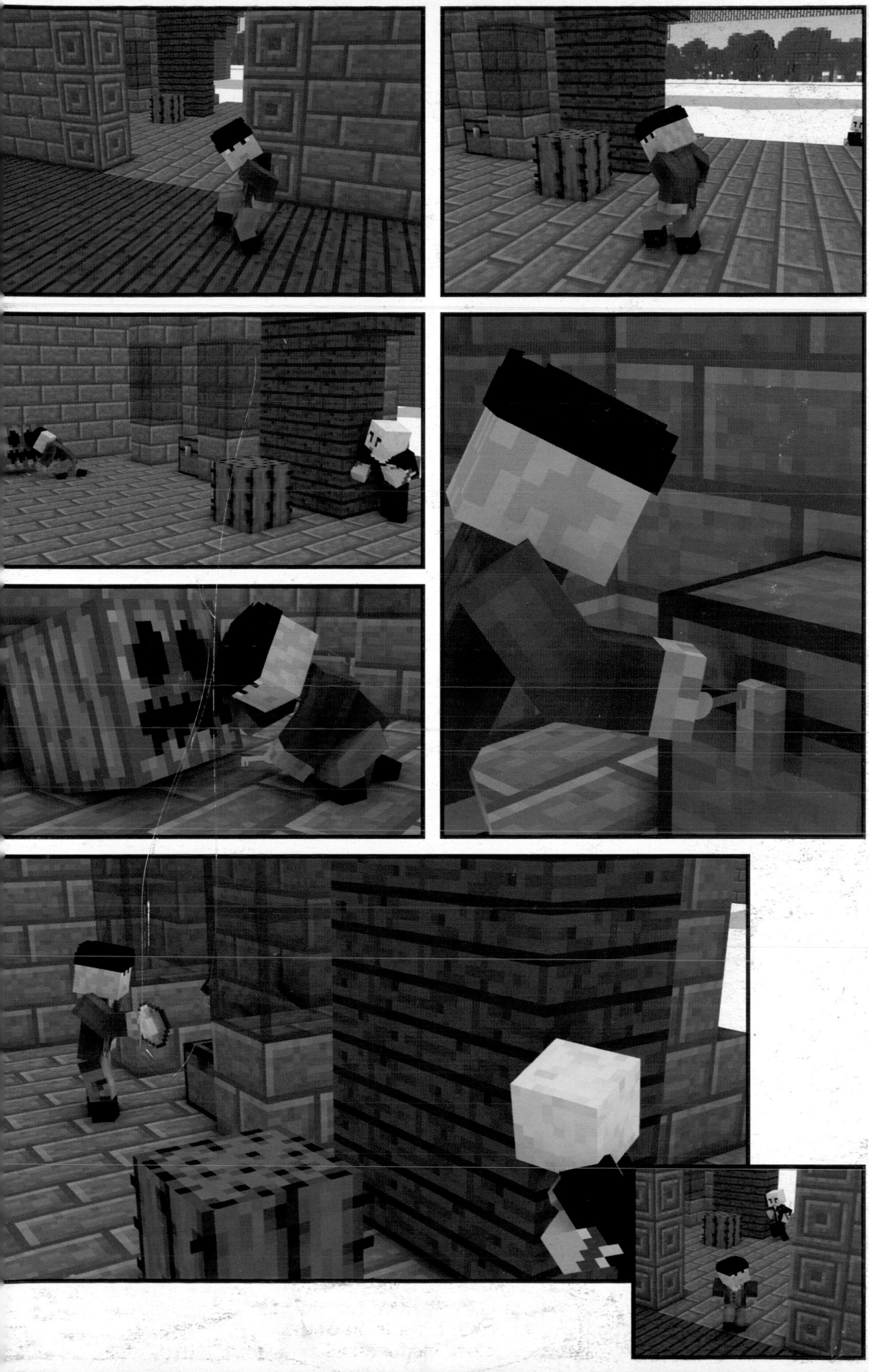

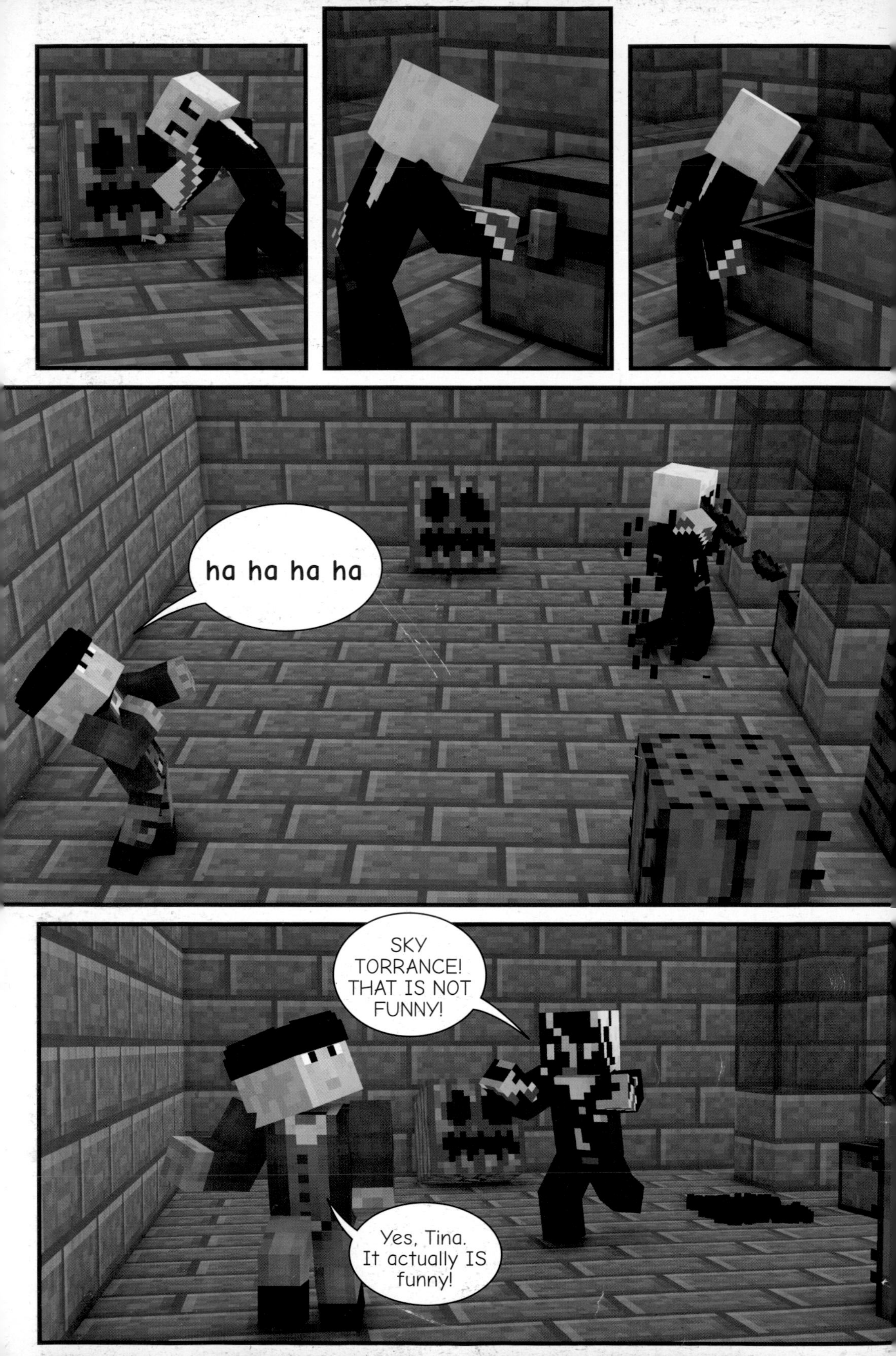
ha ha ha ha
SKY TORRANCE! THAT IS NOT FUNNY!
Yes, Tina. It actually IS funny!

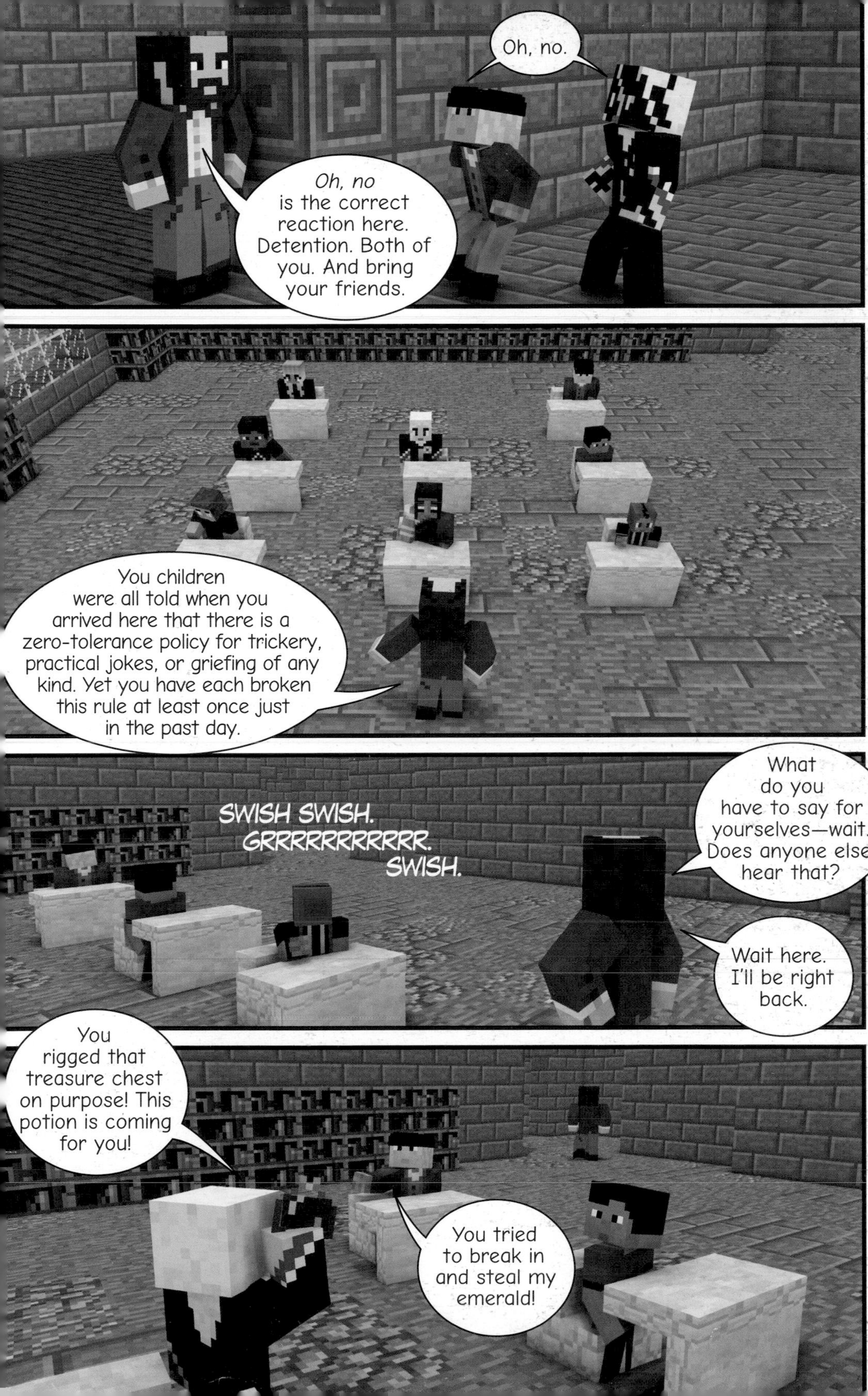

Oh, no.
Oh, no is the correct reaction here. Detention. Both of you. And bring your friends.
You children were all told when you arrived here that there is a zero-tolerance policy for trickery, practical jokes, or griefing of any kind. Yet you have each broken this rule at least once just in the past day.
SWISH SWISH. GRRRRRRRRRR. SWISH.
What do you have to say for yourselves—wait. Does anyone else hear that?
Wait here. I'll be right back.
You rigged that treasure chest on purpose! This potion is coming for you!
You tried to break in and steal my emerald!

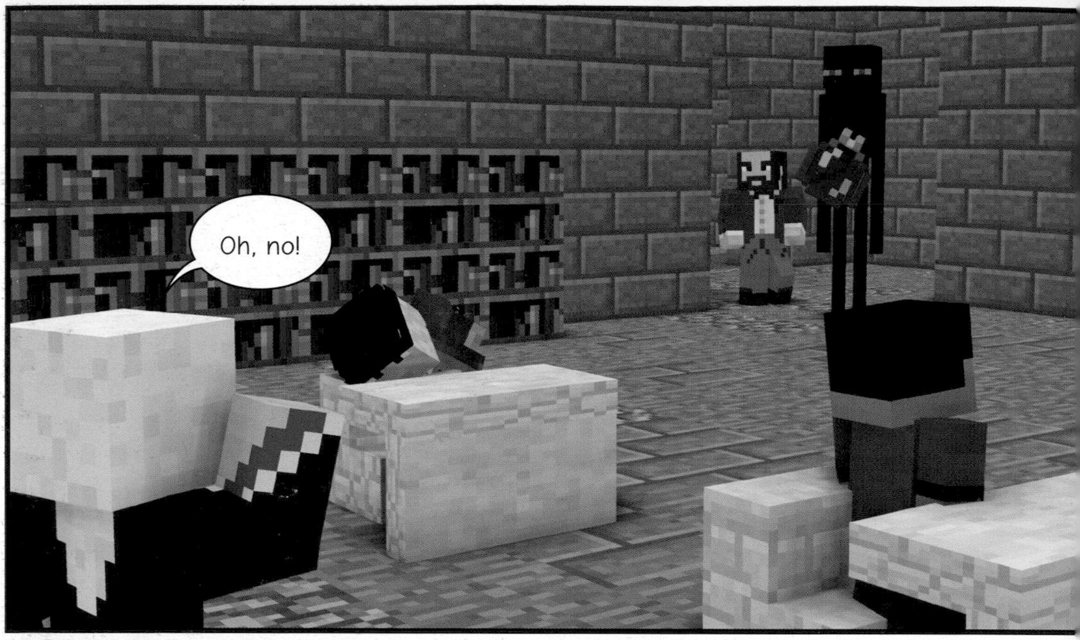
Oh, no!

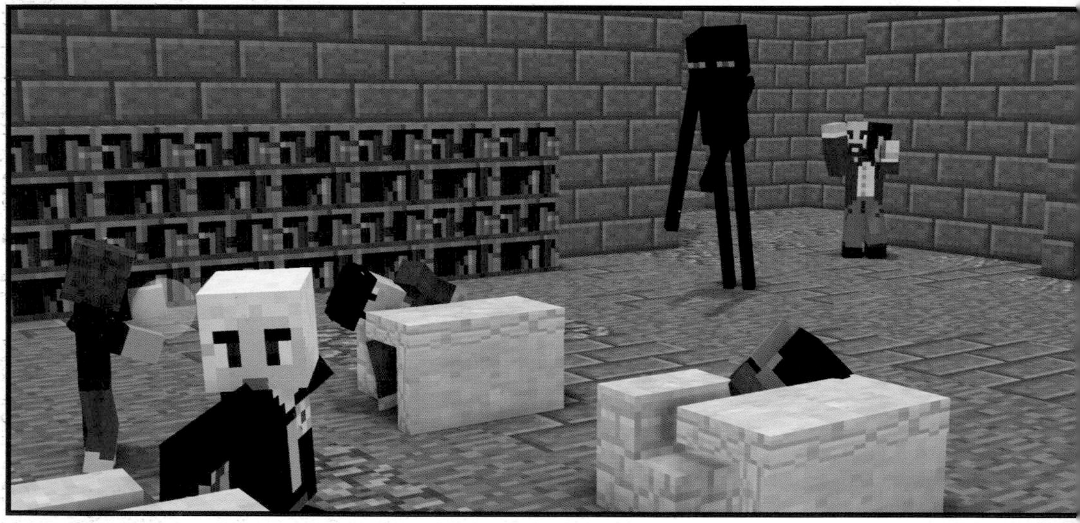

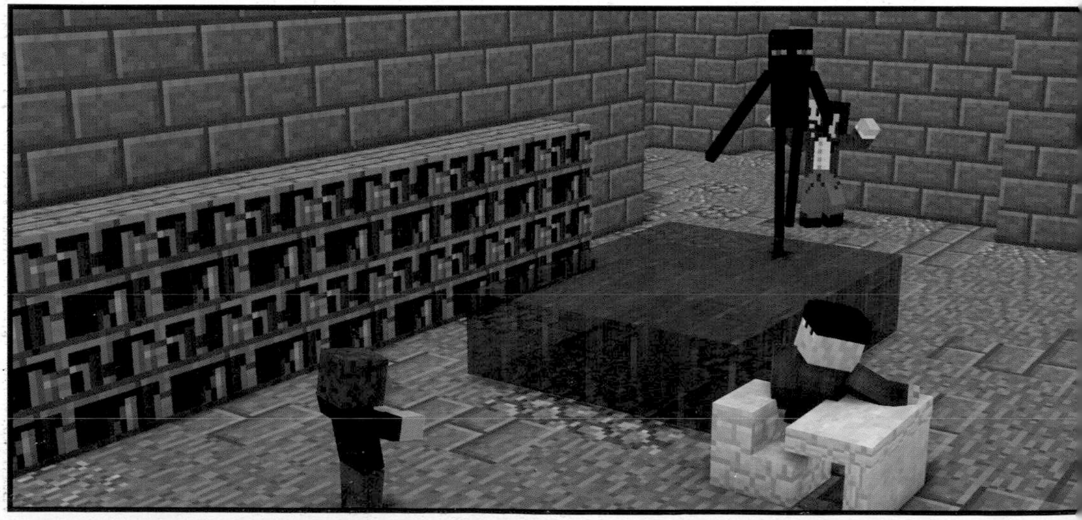

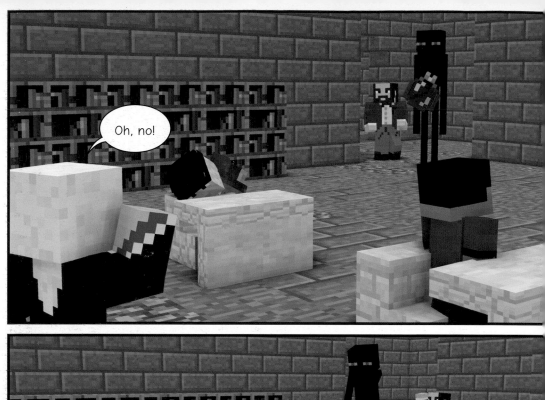

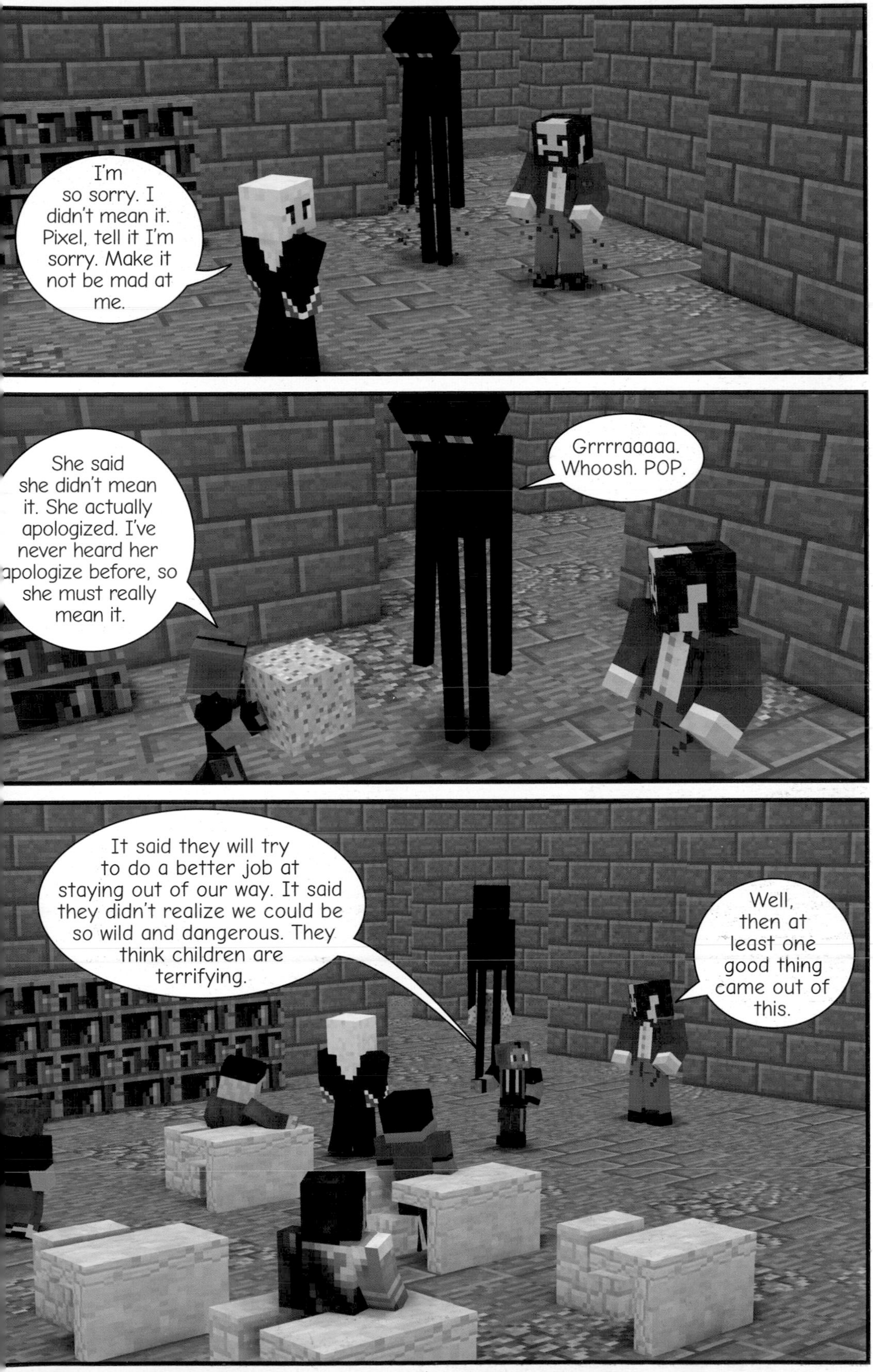
I'm so sorry. I didn't mean it. Pixel, tell it I'm sorry. Make it not be mad at me.
She said she didn't mean it. She actually apologized. I've never heard her apologize before, so she must really mean it.
Grrrraaaaa. Whoosh. POP.
It said they will try to do a better job at staying out of our way. It said they didn't realize we could be so wild and dangerous. They think children are terrifying.
Well, then at least one good thing came out of this.

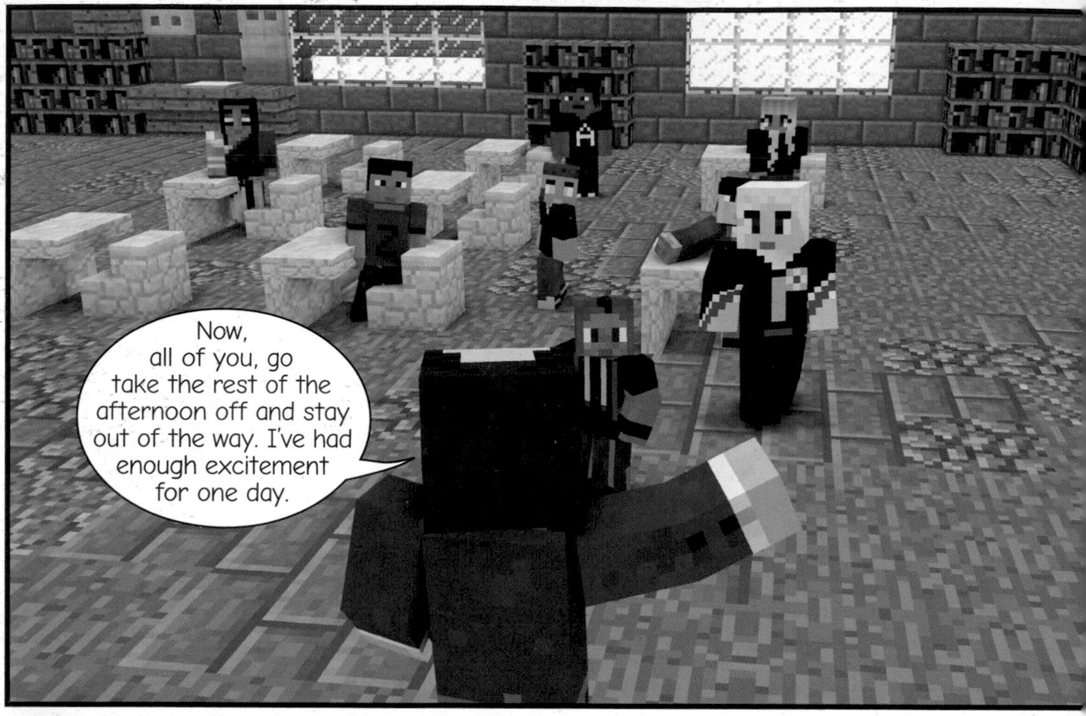
Now, all of you, go take the rest of the afternoon off and stay out of the way. I've had enough excitement for one day.

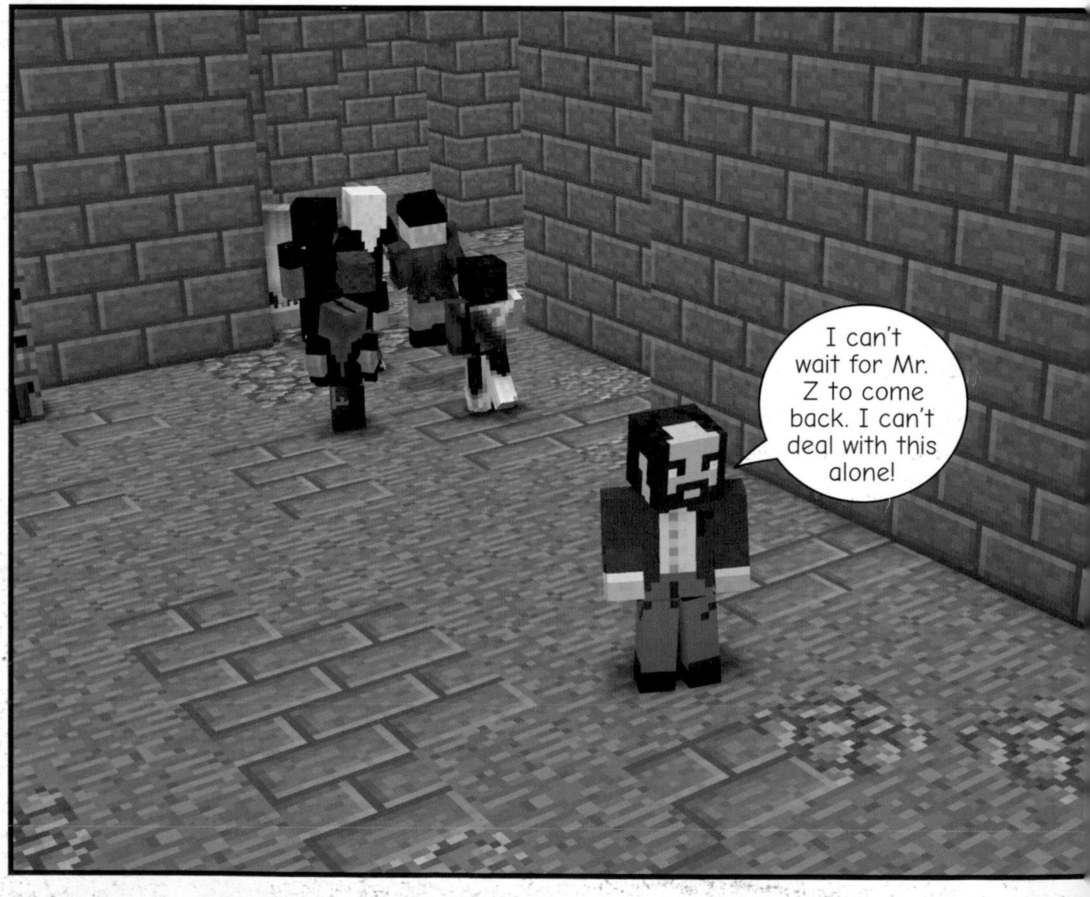
I can't wait for Mr. Z to come back. I can't deal with this alone!

CHAPTER II

LIVING THE
DREAM

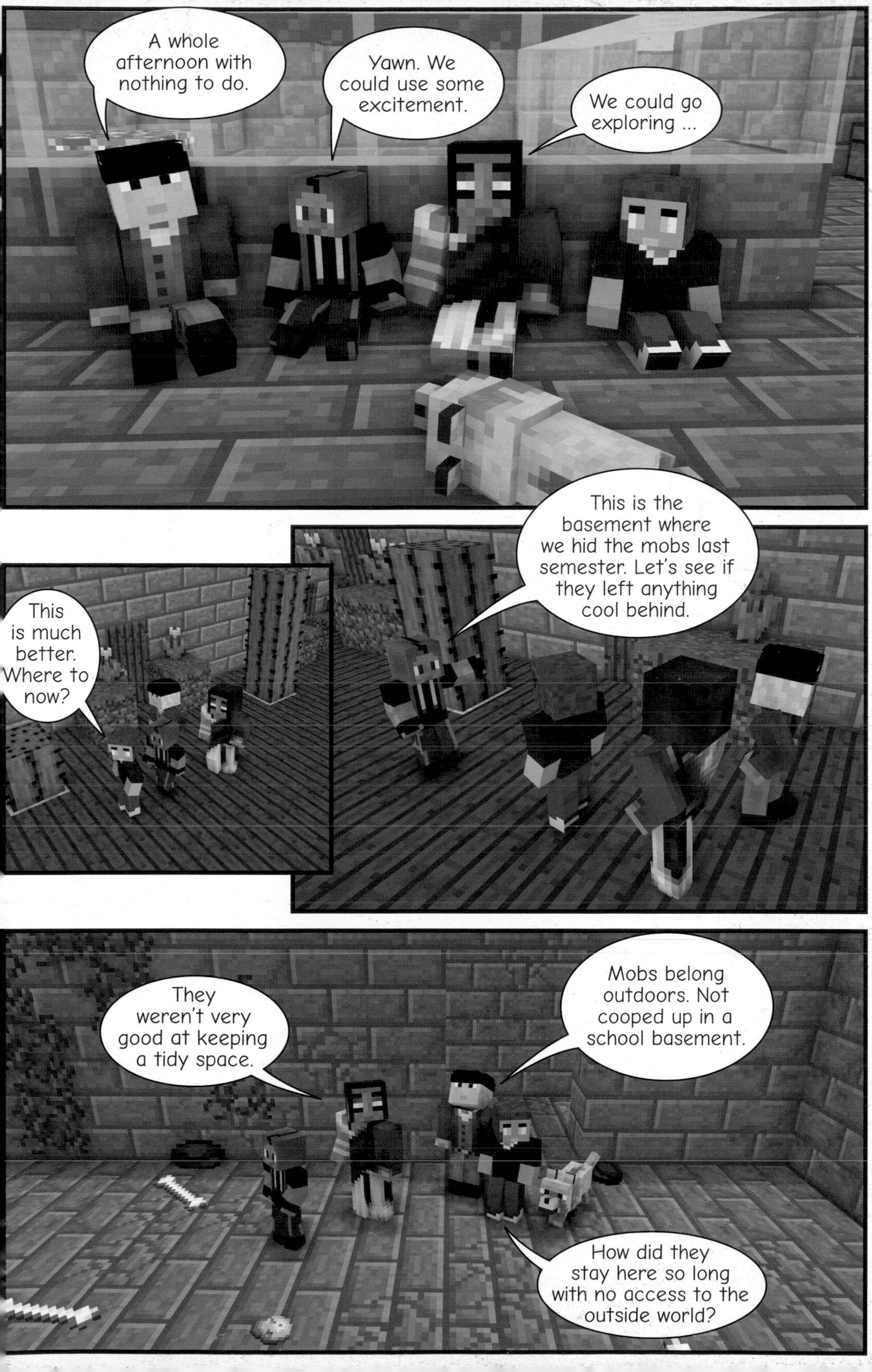

A whole afternoon with nothing to do.
Yawn. We could use some excitement.
We could go exploring ...
This is much better. Where to now?
This is the basement where we hid the mobs last semester. Let's see if they left anything cool behind.
They weren't very good at keeping a tidy space.
Mobs belong outdoors. Not cooped up in a school basement.
How did they stay here so long with no access to the outside world?

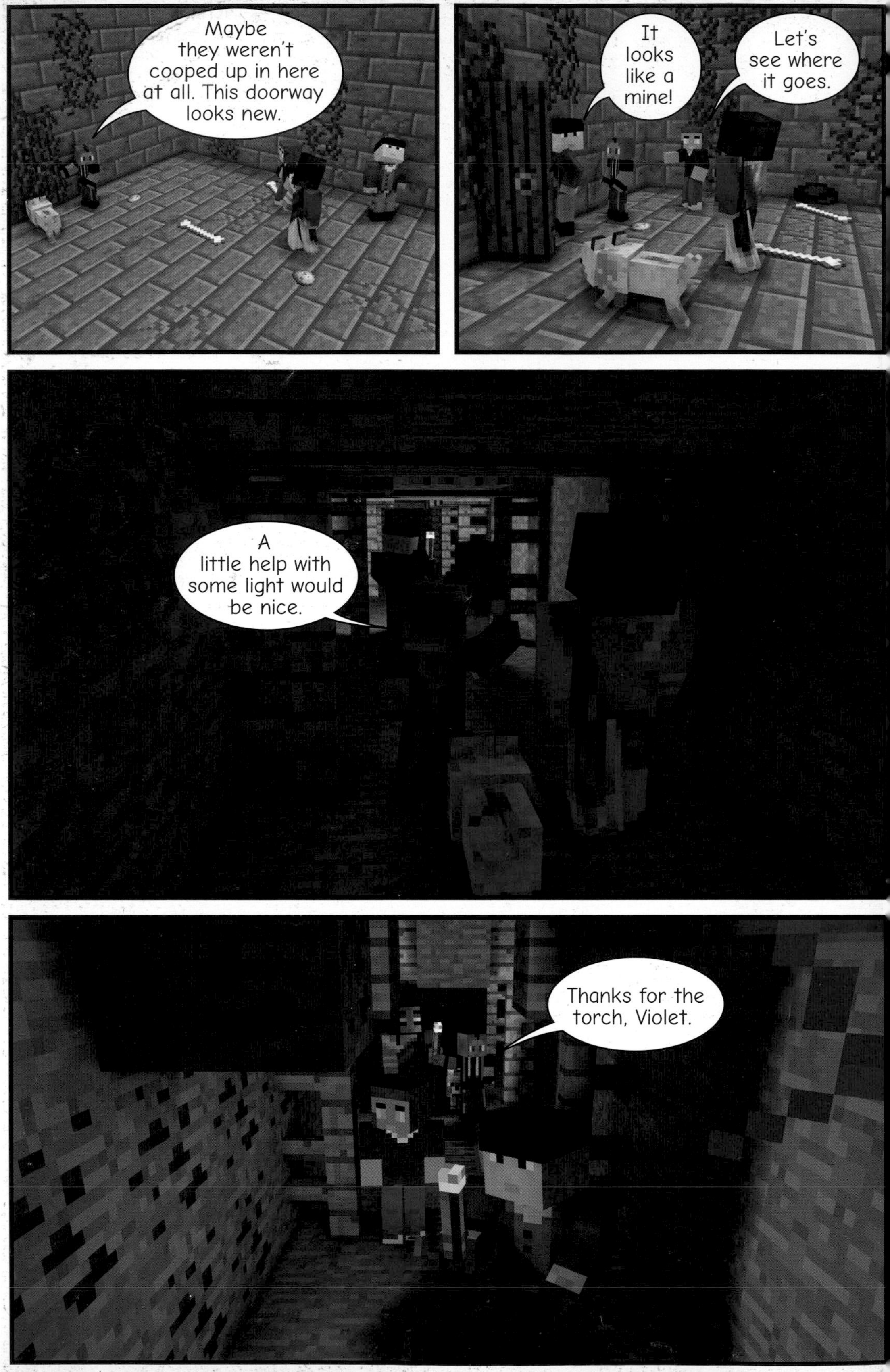
Maybe they weren't cooped up in here at all. This doorway looks new.
It looks like a mine!
Let's see where it goes.
A little help with some light would be nice.
Thanks for the torch, Violet.

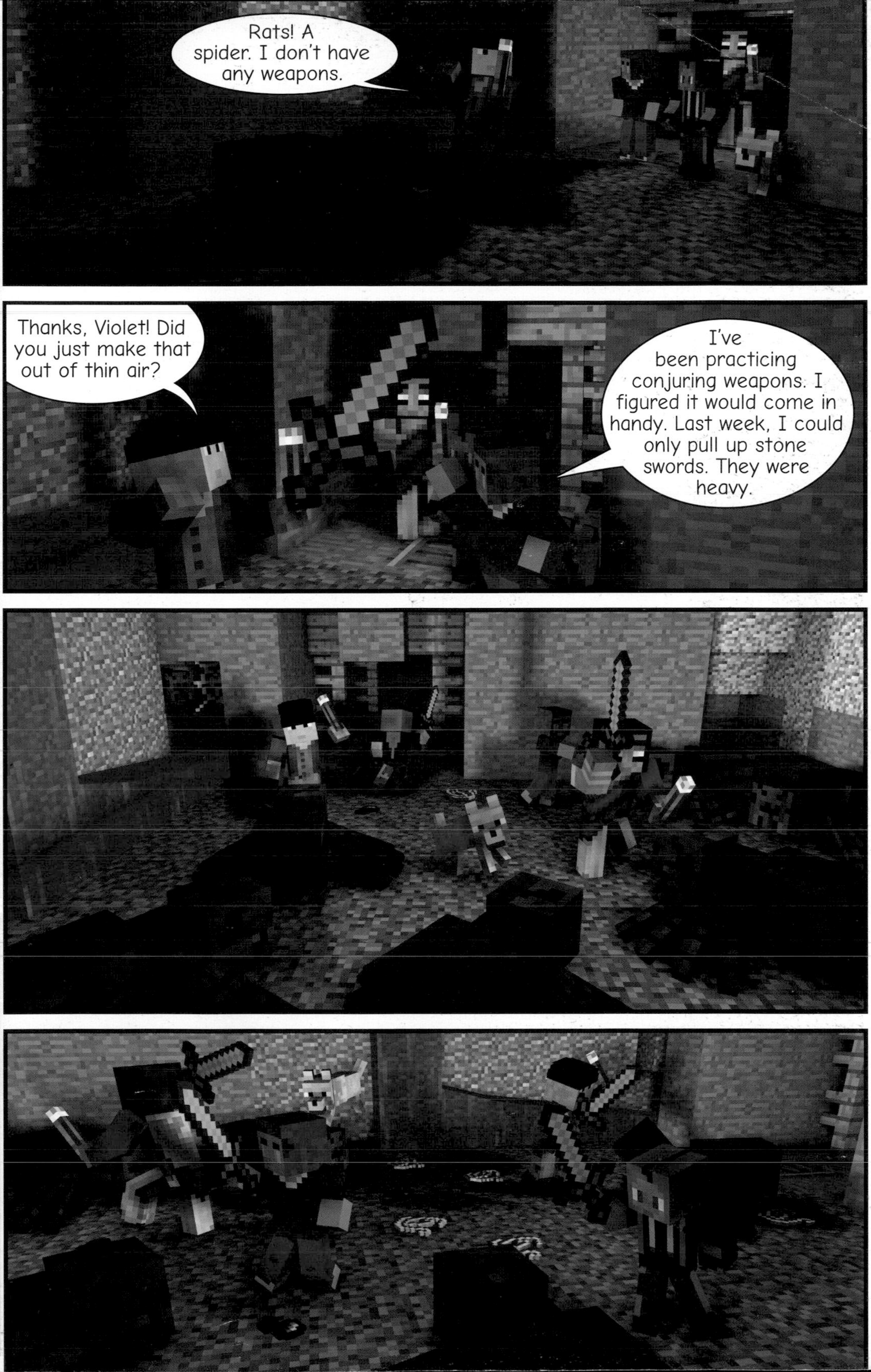
Rats! A spider. I don't have any weapons.
Thanks, Violet! Did you just make that out of thin air?
I've been practicing conjuring weapons. I figured it would come in handy. Last week, I could only pull up stone swords. They were heavy.

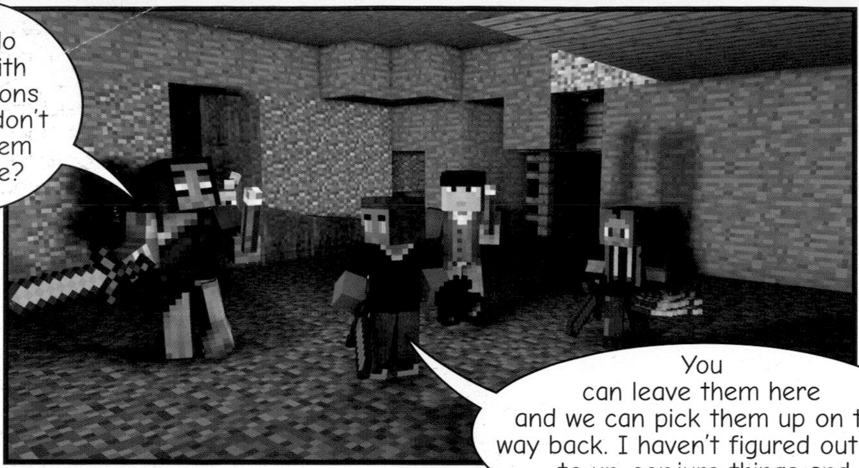
What do we do with our weapons when we don't need them anymore?
You can leave them here and we can pick them up on the way back. I haven't figured out how to un-conjure things and disappear them.

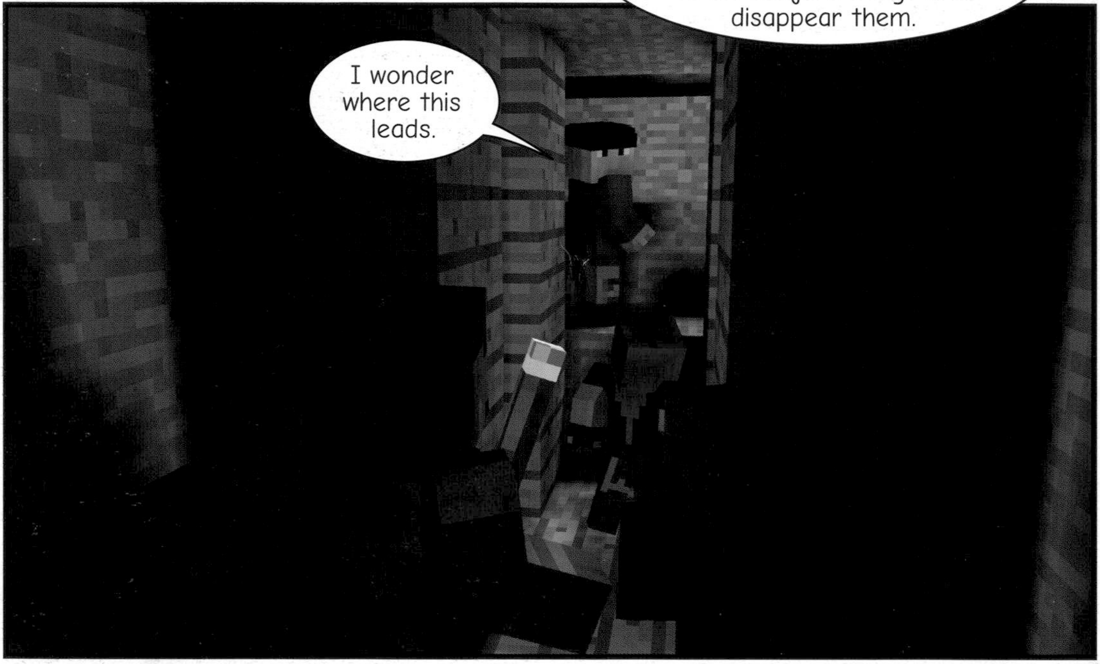
I wonder where this leads.

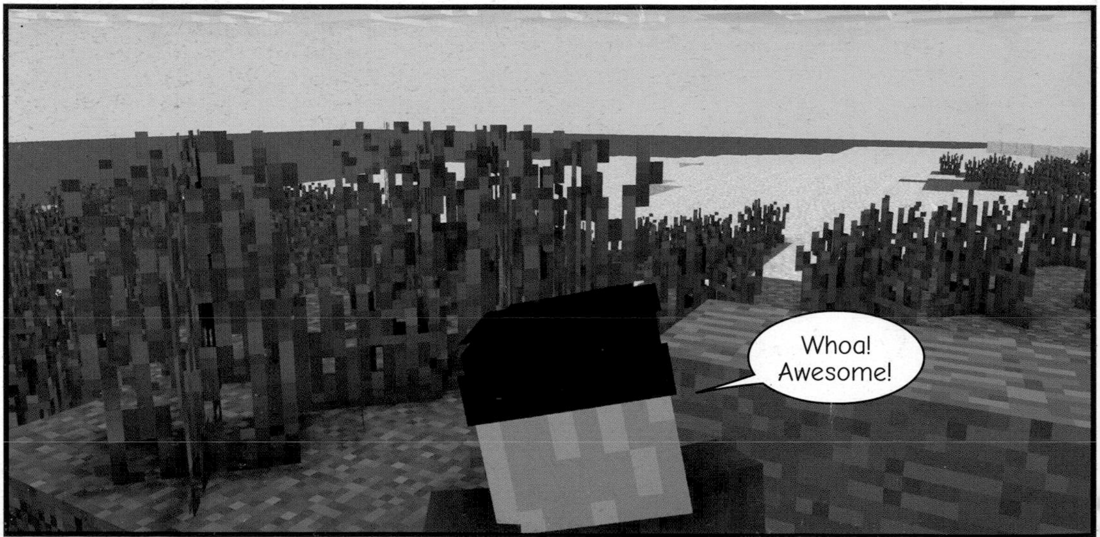
Whoa! Awesome!

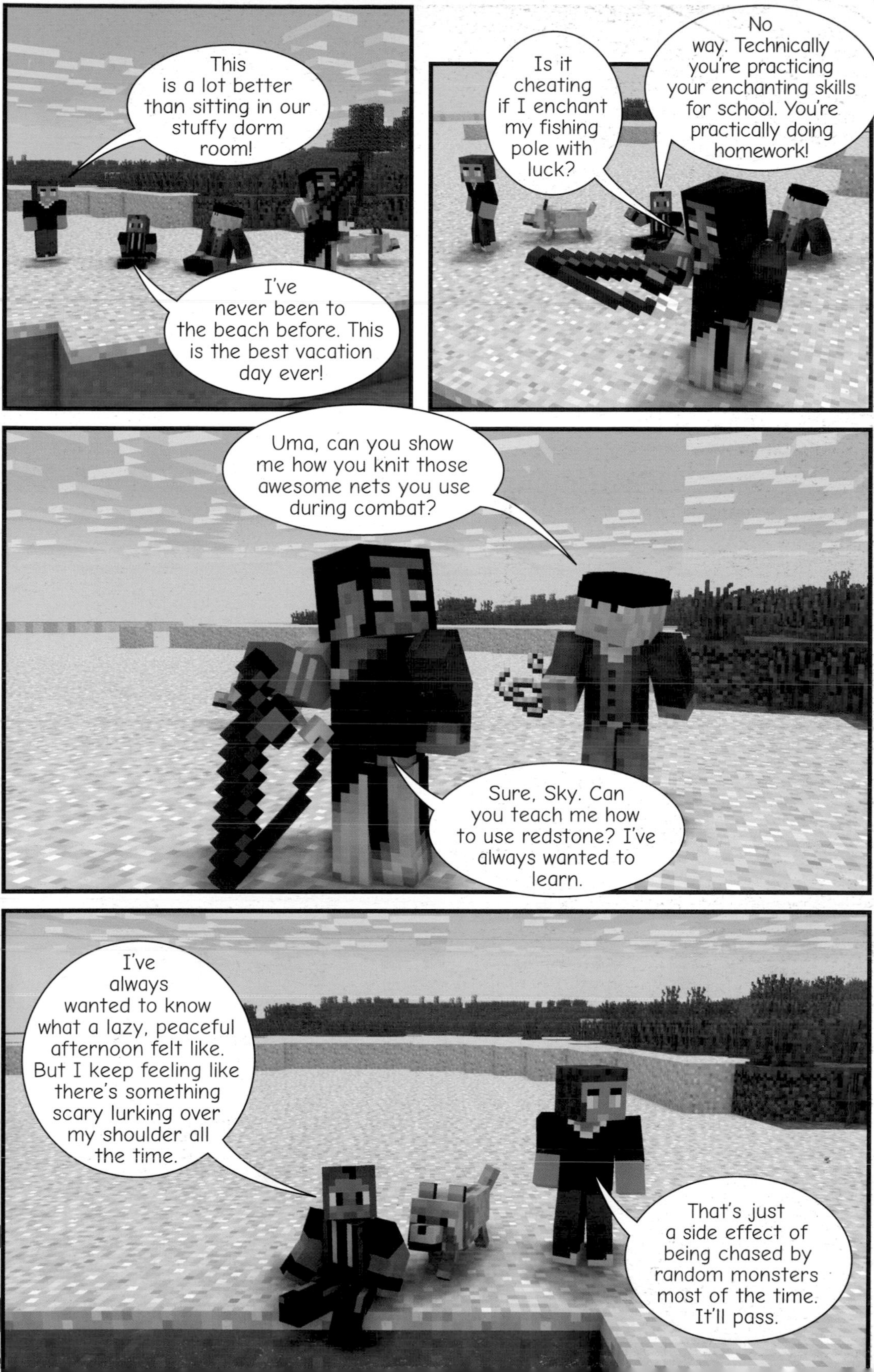
This is a lot better than sitting in our stuffy dorm room!
I've never been to the beach before. This is the best vacation day ever!
Is it cheating if I enchant my fishing pole with luck?
No way. Technically you're practicing your enchanting skills for school. You're practically doing homework!
Uma, can you show me how you knit those awesome nets you use during combat?
Sure, Sky. Can you teach me how to use redstone? I've always wanted to learn.
I've always wanted to know what a lazy, peaceful afternoon felt like. But I keep feeling like there's something scary lurking over my shoulder all the time.
That's just a side effect of being chased by random monsters most of the time. It'll pass.

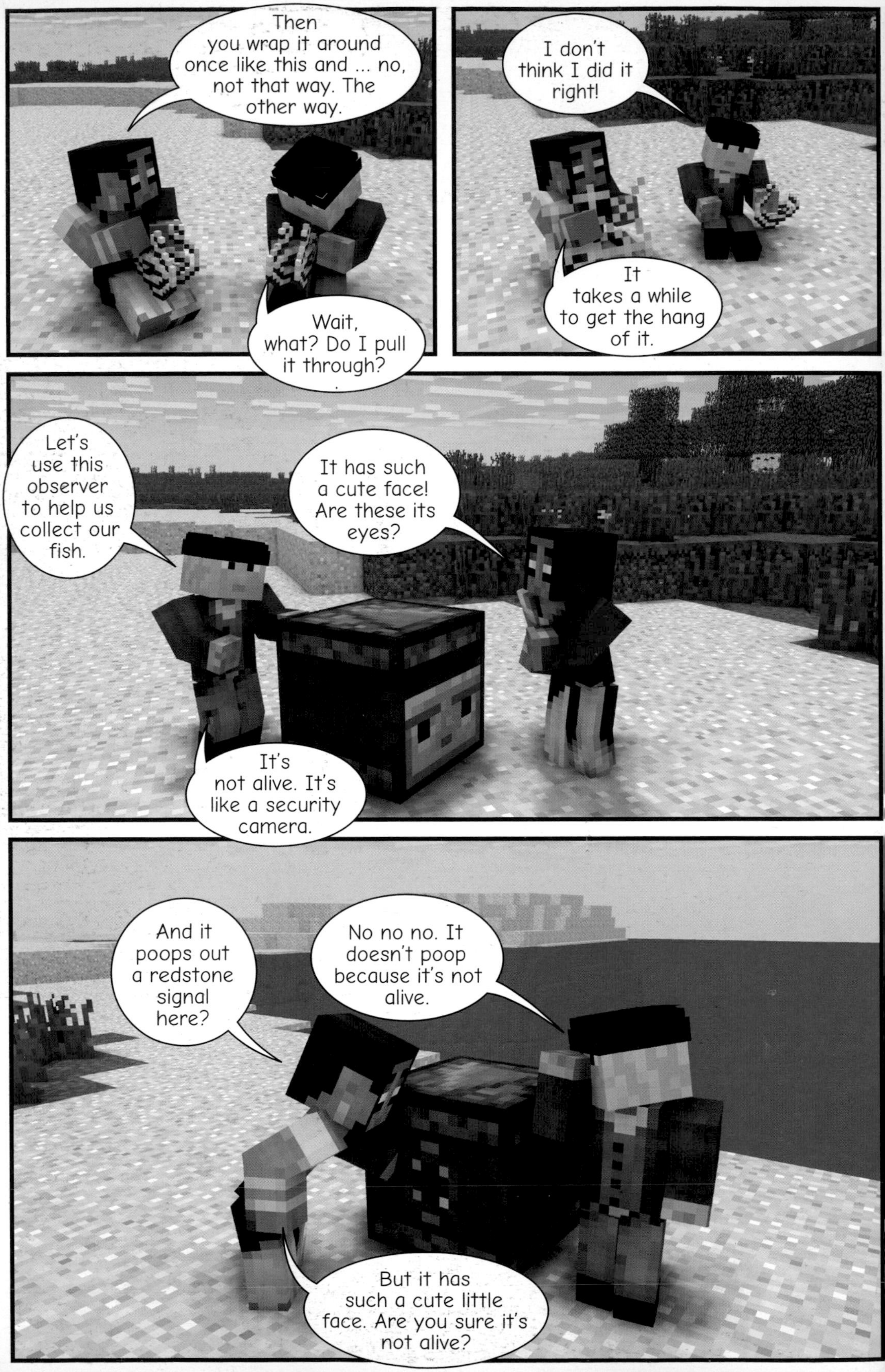
Then you wrap it around once like this and ... no, not that way. The other way.
Wait, what? Do I pull it through?
I don't think I did it right!
It takes a while to get the hang of it.
Let's use this observer to help us collect our fish.
It has such a cute face! Are these its eyes?
It's not alive. It's like a security camera.
And it poops out a redstone signal here?
No no no. It doesn't poop because it's not alive.
But it has such a cute little face. Are you sure it's not alive?

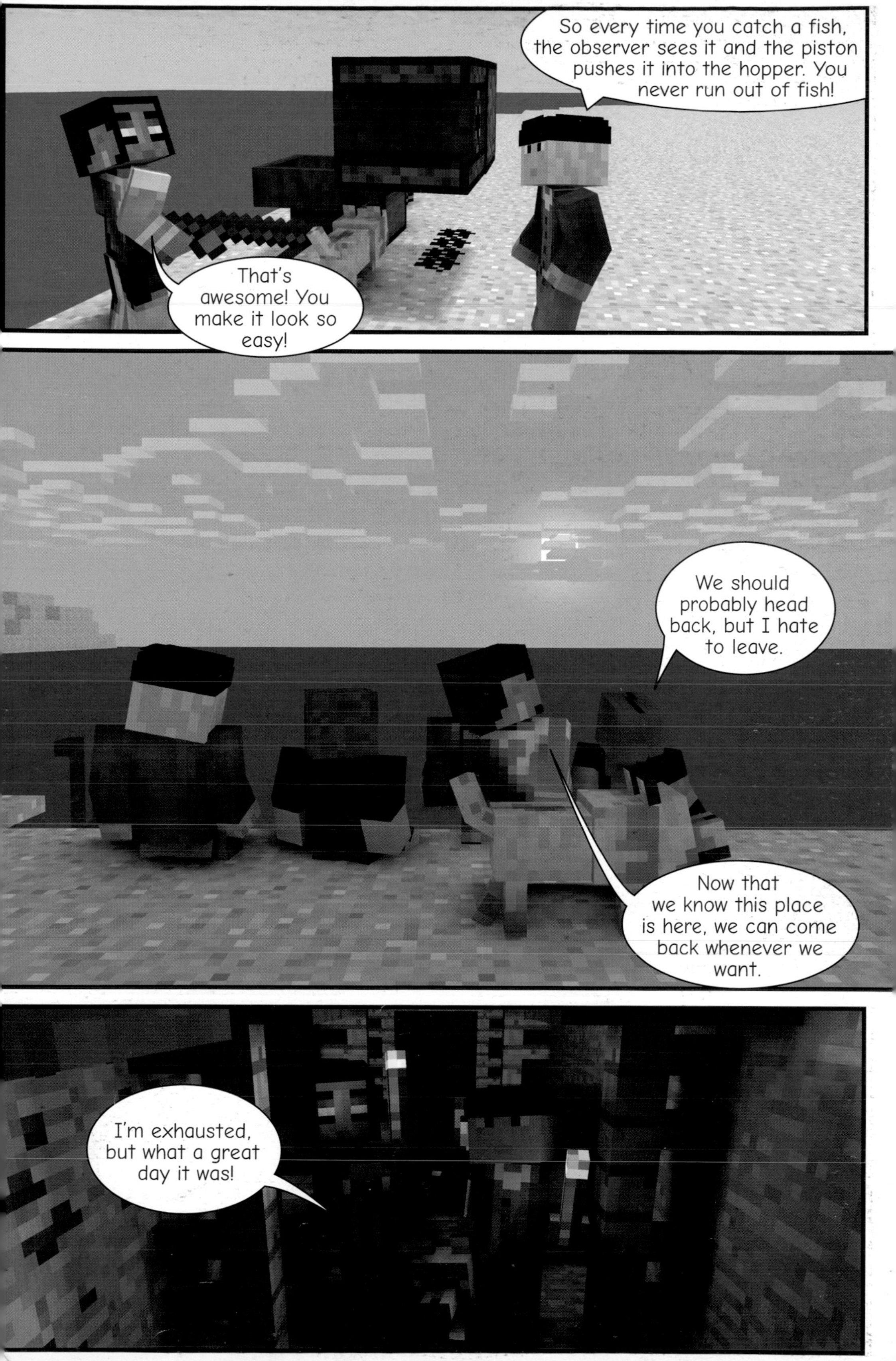
So every time you catch a fish, the observer sees it and the piston pushes it into the hopper. You never run out of fish!
That's awesome! You make it look so easy!
We should probably head back, but I hate to leave.
Now that we know this place is here, we can come back whenever we want.
I'm exhausted, but what a great day it was!

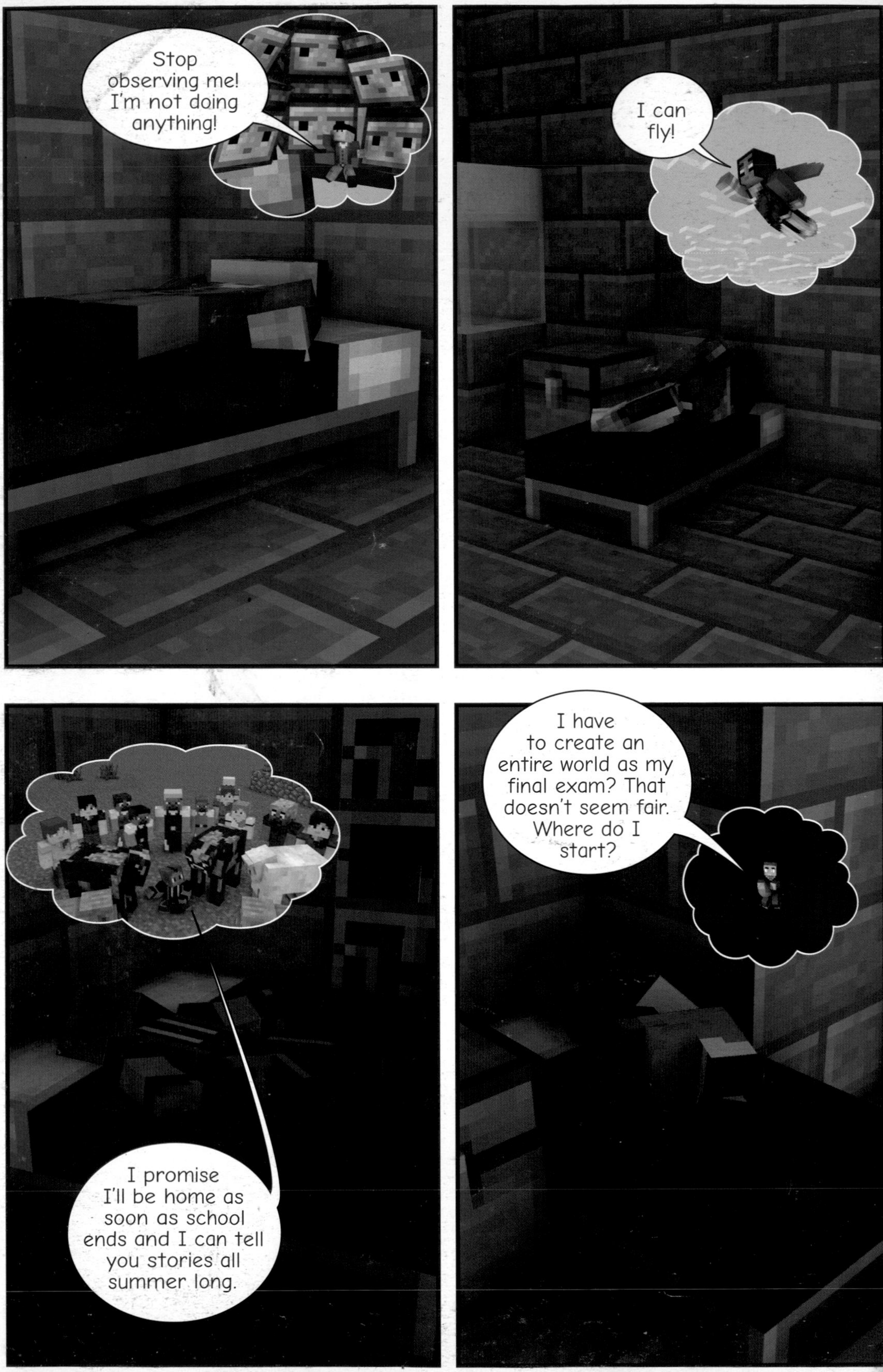
Stop observing me! I'm not doing anything!
I can fly!
I promise I'll be home as soon as school ends and I can tell you stories all summer long.
I have to create an entire world as my final exam? That doesn't seem fair. Where do I start?

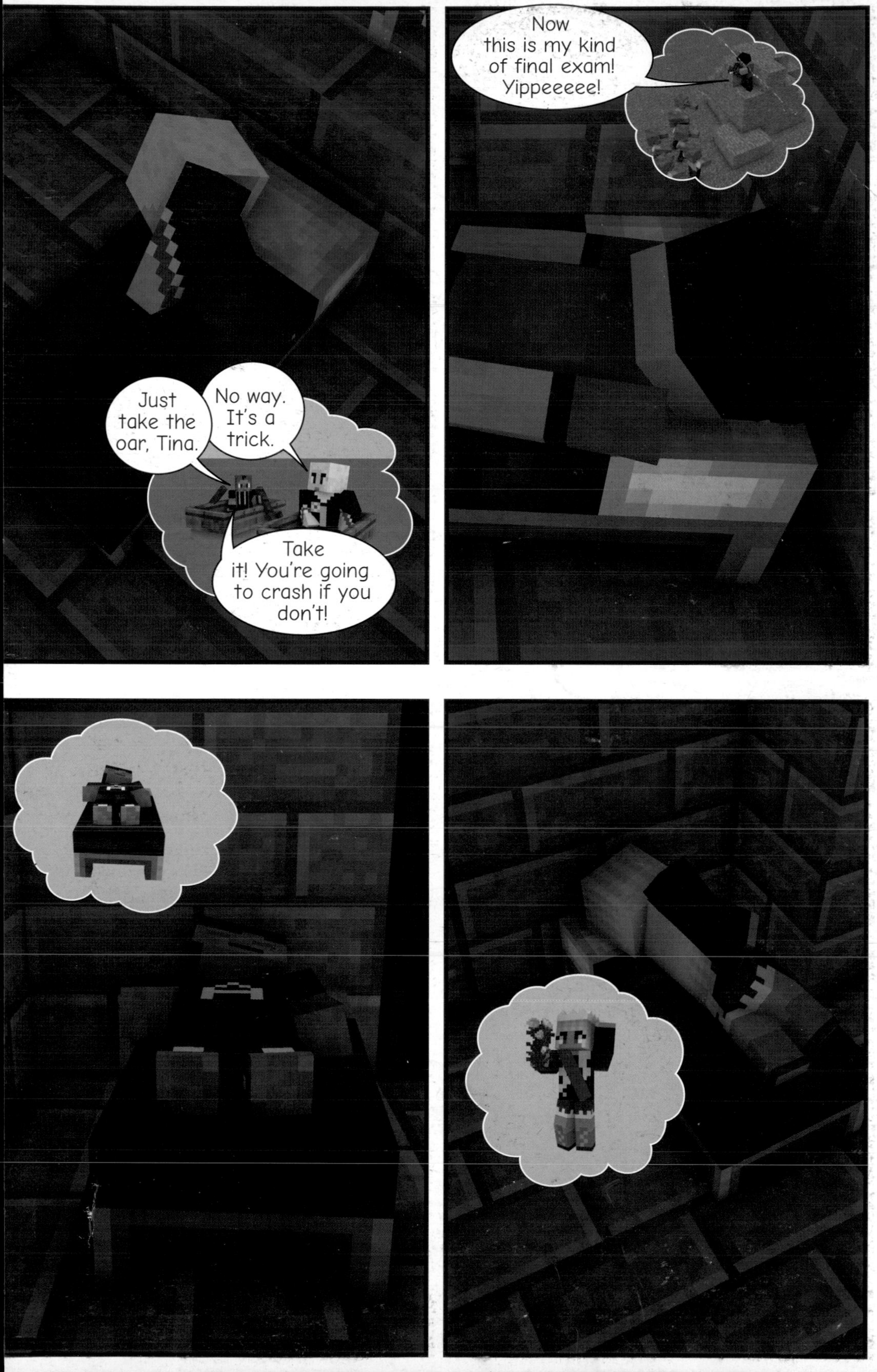
Just take the oar, Tina.
No way. It's a trick.
Take it! You're going to crash if you don't!
Now this is my kind of final exam! Yippeeeee!

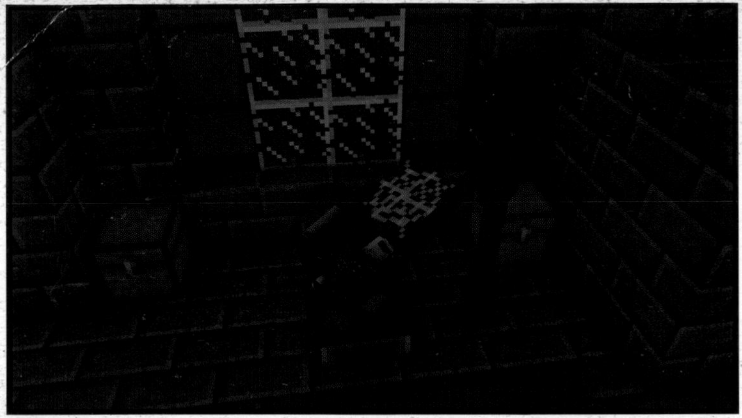

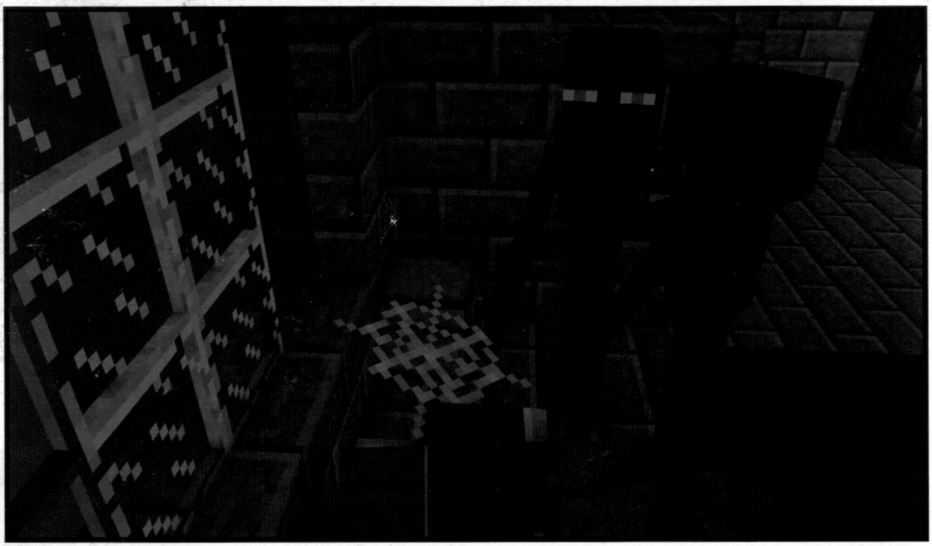

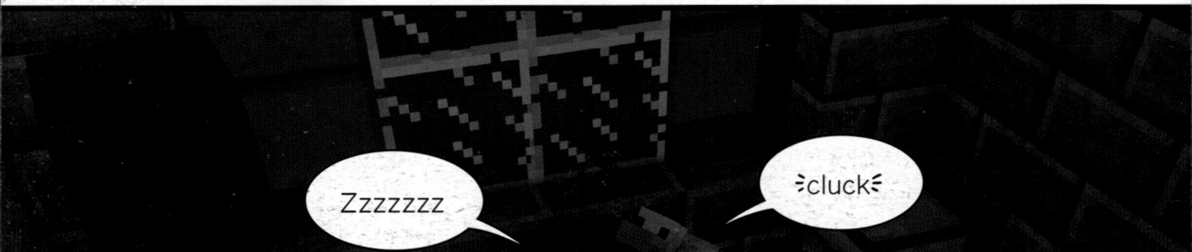
Zzzzzzz
cluck

CHAPTER 12

TEAMING UP

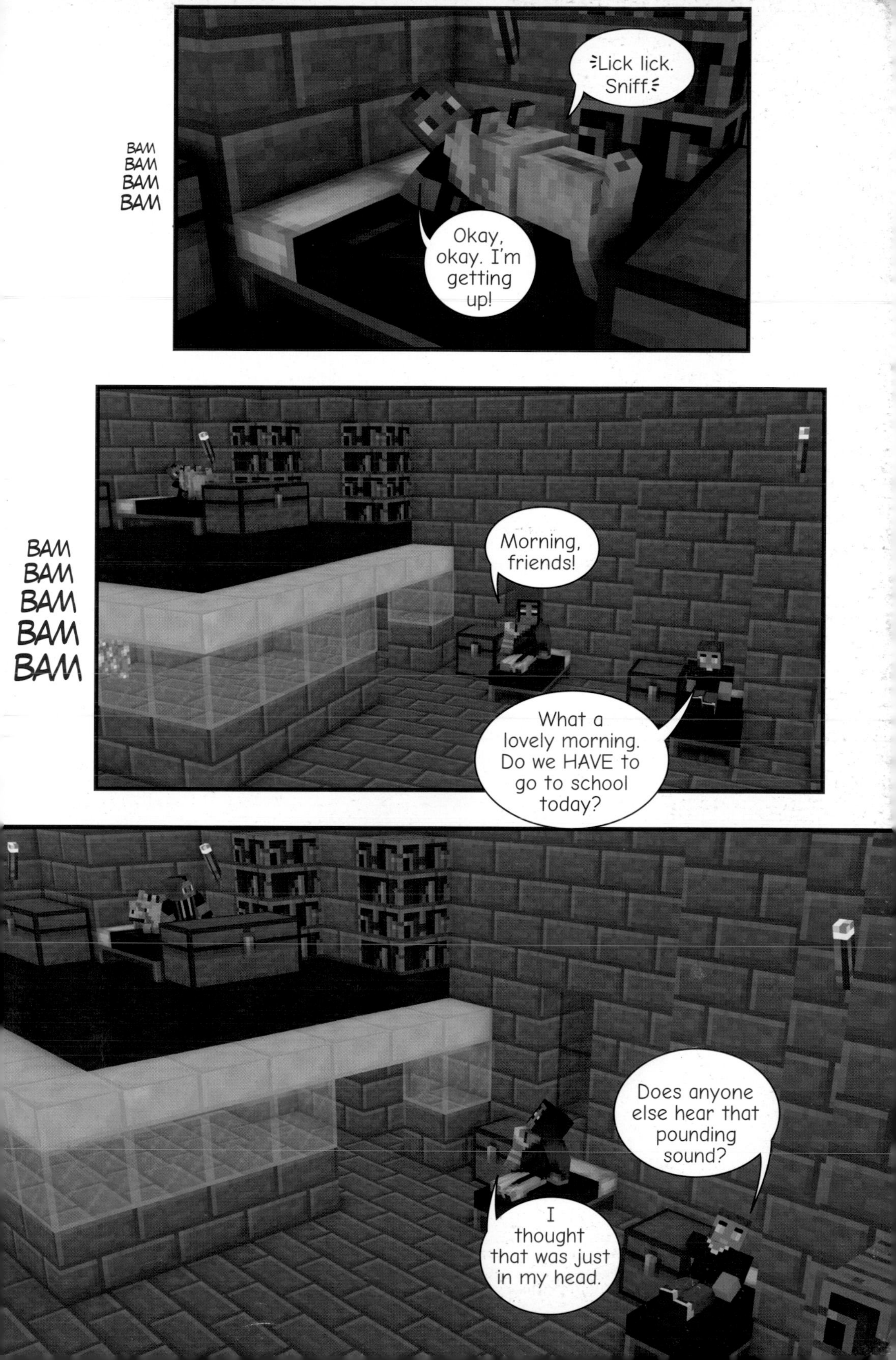
BAM BAM BAM BAM
Lick lick. Sniff.
Okay, okay. I'm getting up!
BAM BAM BAM BAM BAM
Morning, friends!
What a lovely morning. Do we HAVE to go to school today?
Does anyone else hear that pounding sound?
I thought that was just in my head.

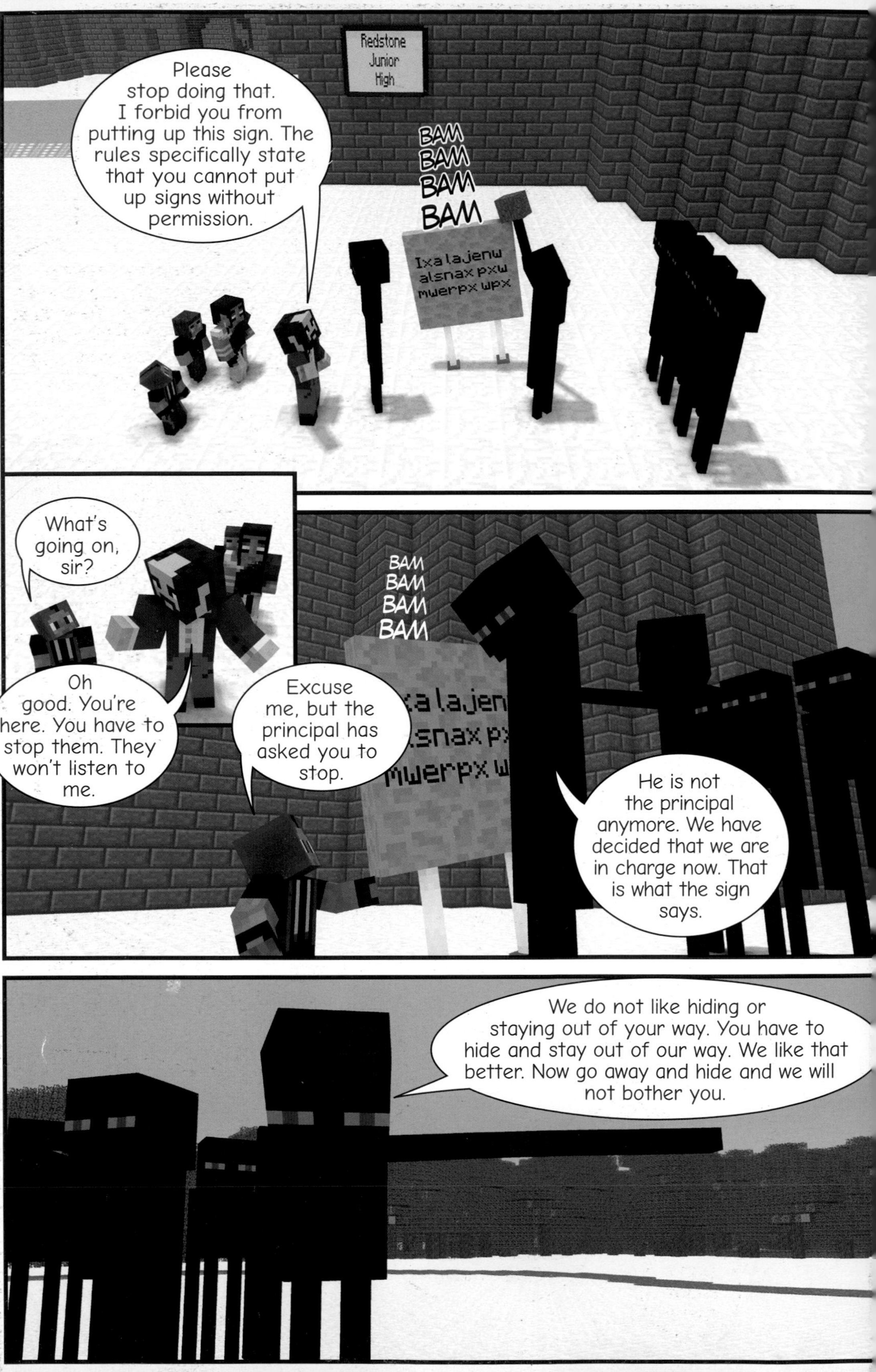
Redstone Junior High
Please stop doing that. I forbid you from putting up this sign. The rules specifically state that you cannot put up signs without permission.
BAM BAM BAM BAM
Ixa lajenw alsnax pxw mwerpx wpx
What's going on, sir?
Oh good. You're here. You have to stop them. They won't listen to me.
BAM BAM BAM BAM
Excuse me, but the principal has asked you to stop.
He is not the principal anymore. We have decided that we are in charge now. That is what the sign says.
We do not like hiding or staying out of your way. You have to hide and stay out of our way. We like that better. Now go away and hide and we will not bother you.

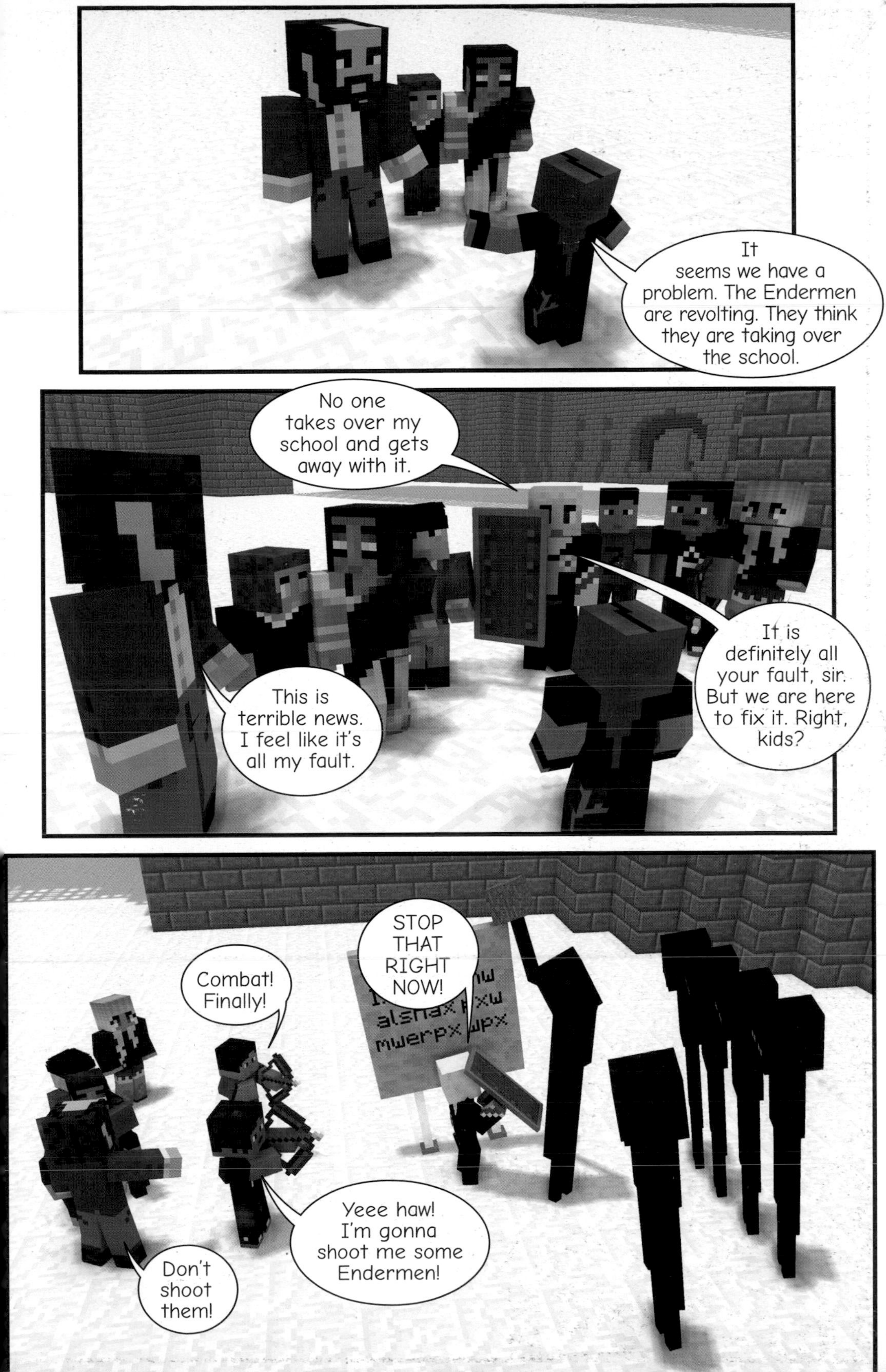
It seems we have a problem. The Endermen are revolting. They think they are taking over the school.
No one takes over my school and gets away with it.
This is terrible news. I feel like it's all my fault.
It is definitely all your fault, sir. But we are here to fix it. Right, kids?
Combat! Finally!
STOP THAT RIGHT NOW!
Yeee haw! I'm gonna shoot me some Endermen!
Don't shoot them!

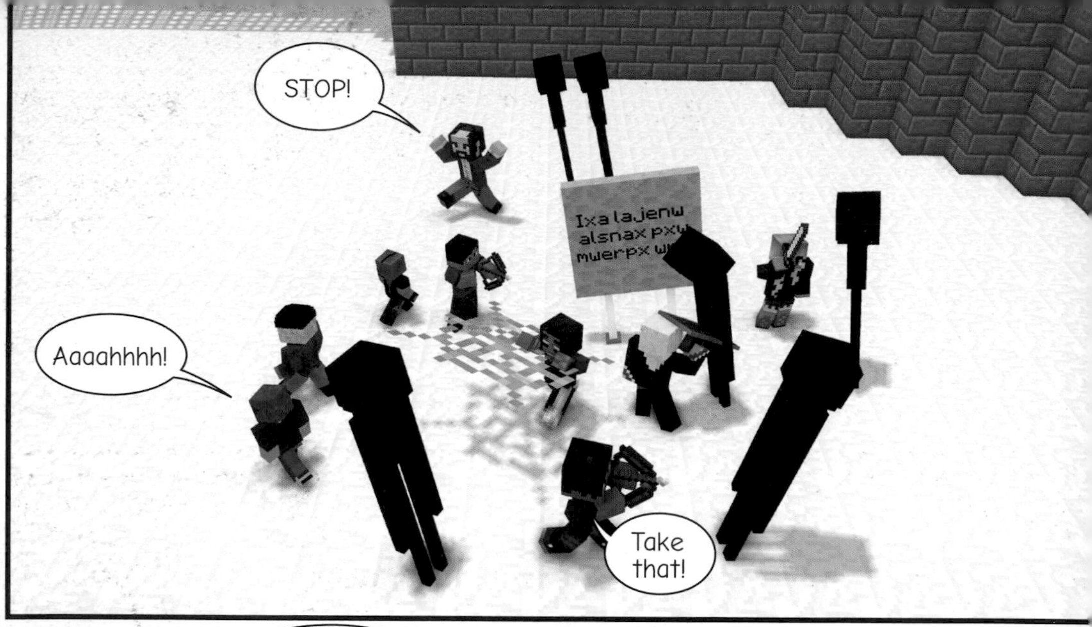
STOP!
Ixa lajenw alsnax pxw mwerpx wp
Aaaahhhh!
Take that!

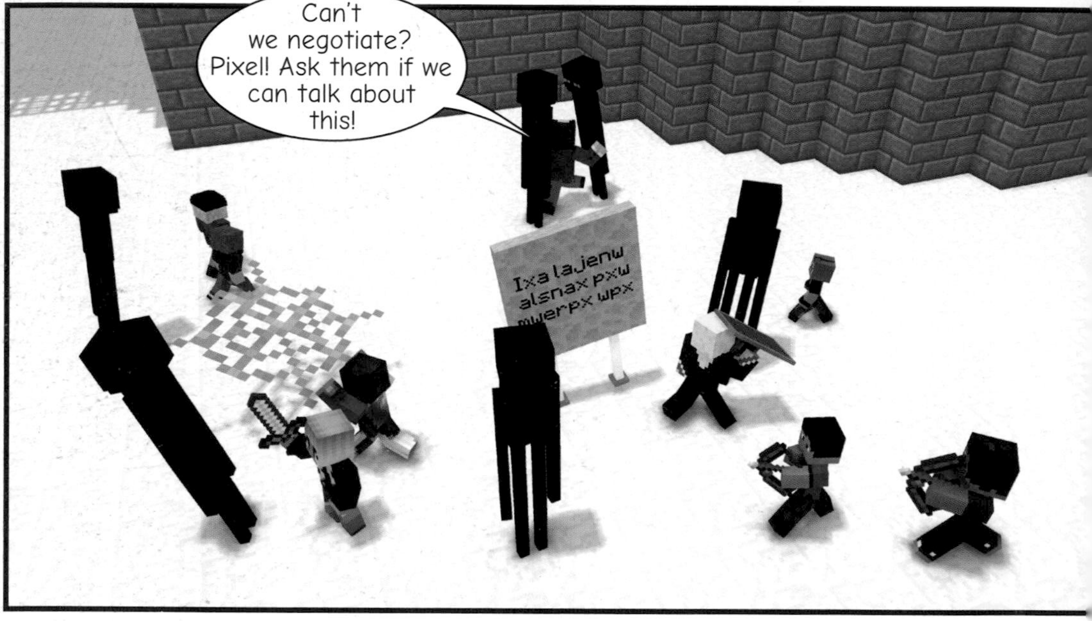
Can't we negotiate? Pixel! Ask them if we can talk about this!
Ixa lajenw alsnax pxw mwerpx wpx

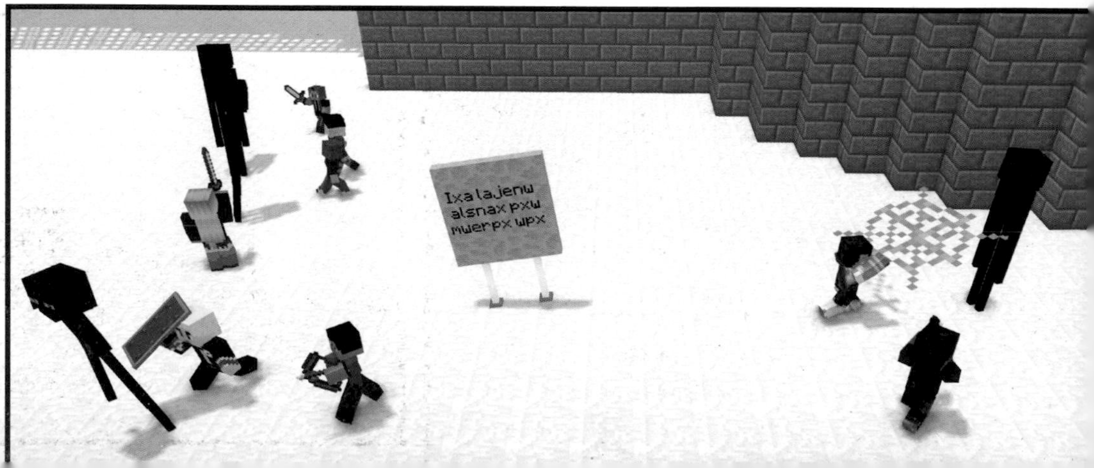
Ixa lajenw alsnax pxw mwerpx wpx

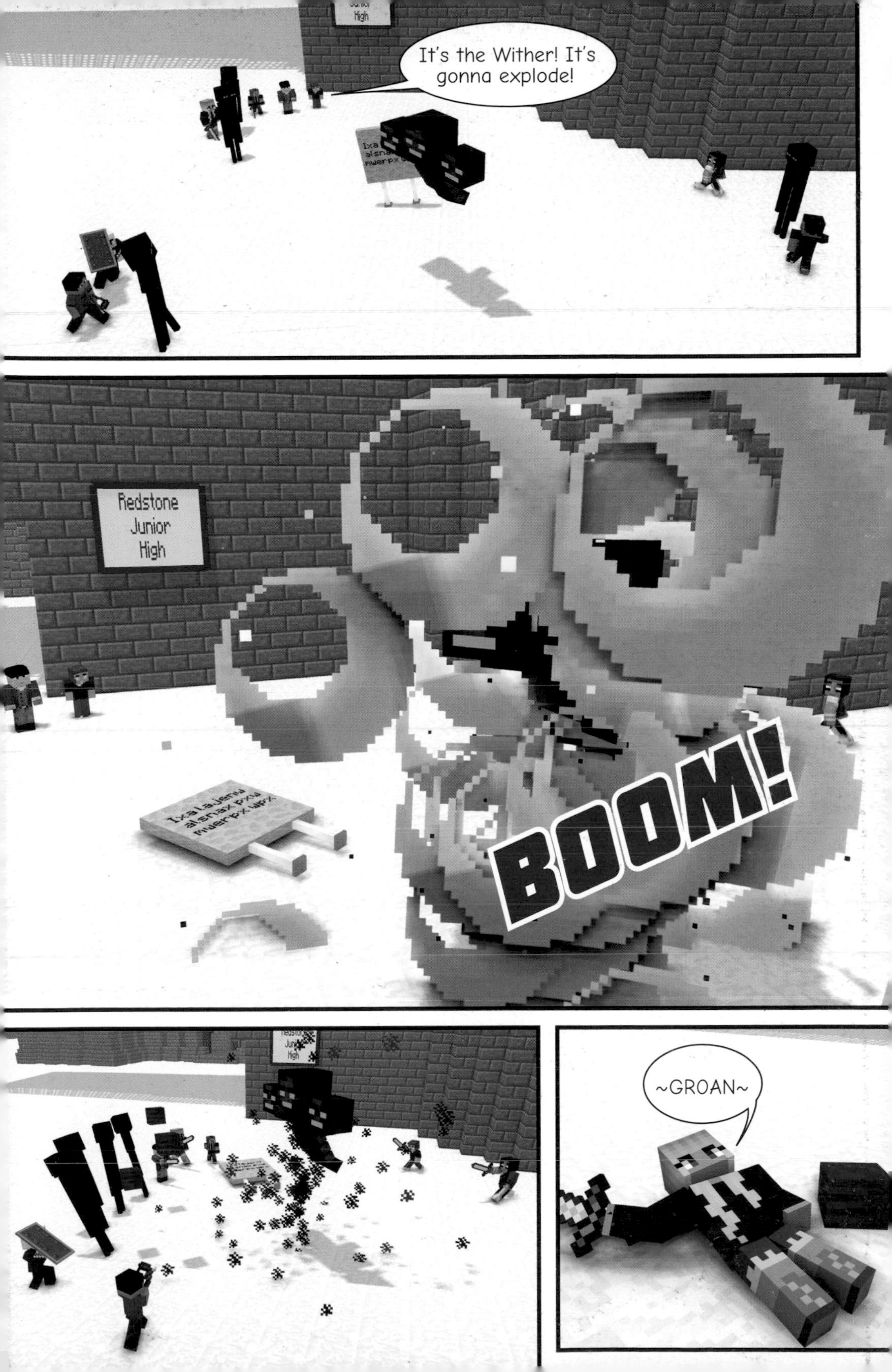
It's the Wither! It's gonna explode!
Redstone Junior High
BOOM!
~GROAN~

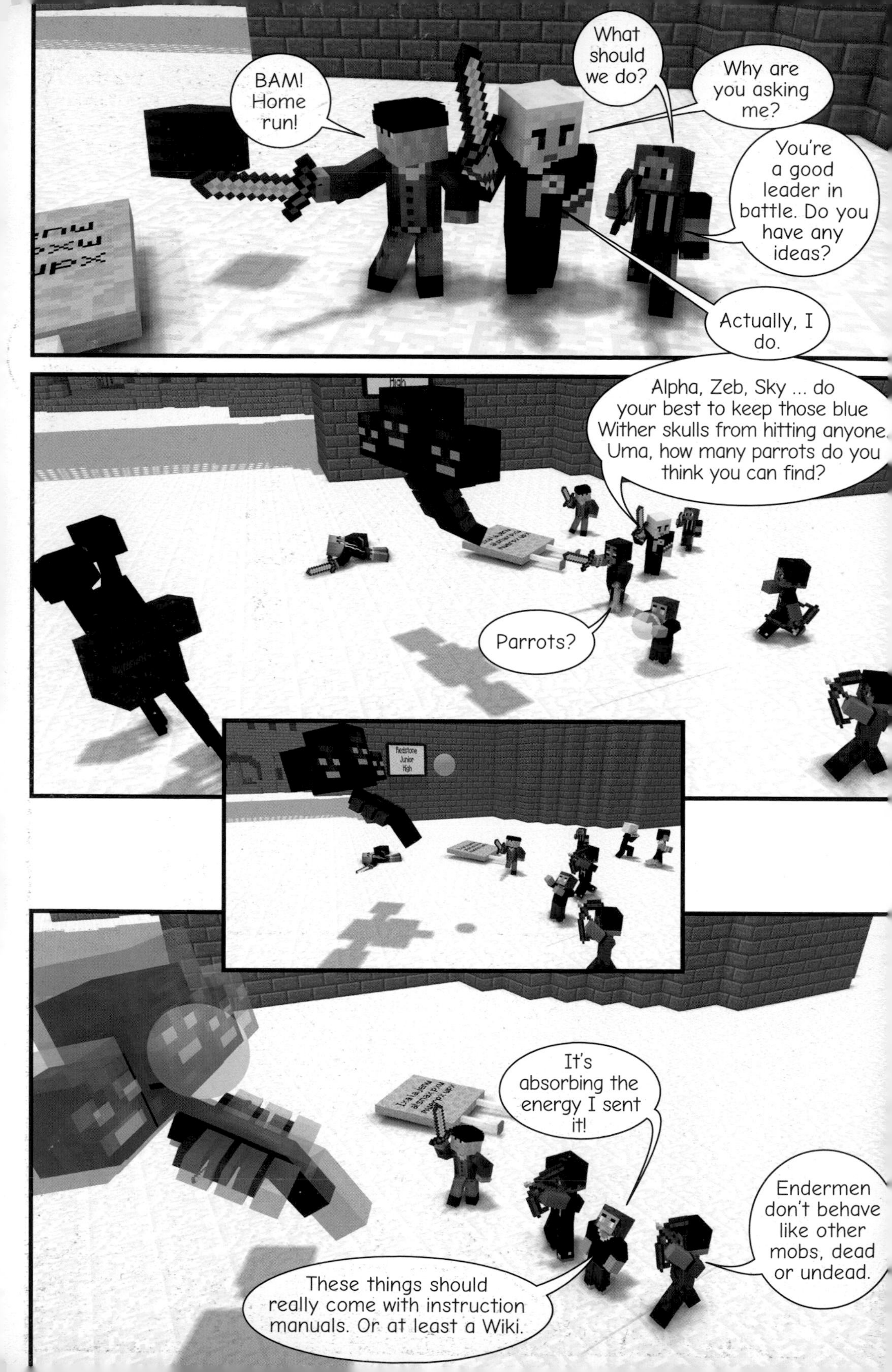

BAM! Home run!
What should we do?
Why are you asking me?
You're a good leader in battle. Do you have any ideas?
Actually, I do.
Alpha, Zeb, Sky ... do your best to keep those blue Wither skulls from hitting anyone. Uma, how many parrots do you think you can find?
Parrots?
Redstone Junior High
It's absorbing the energy I sent it!
Endermen don't behave like other mobs, dead or undead.
These things should really come with instruction manuals. Or at least a Wiki.

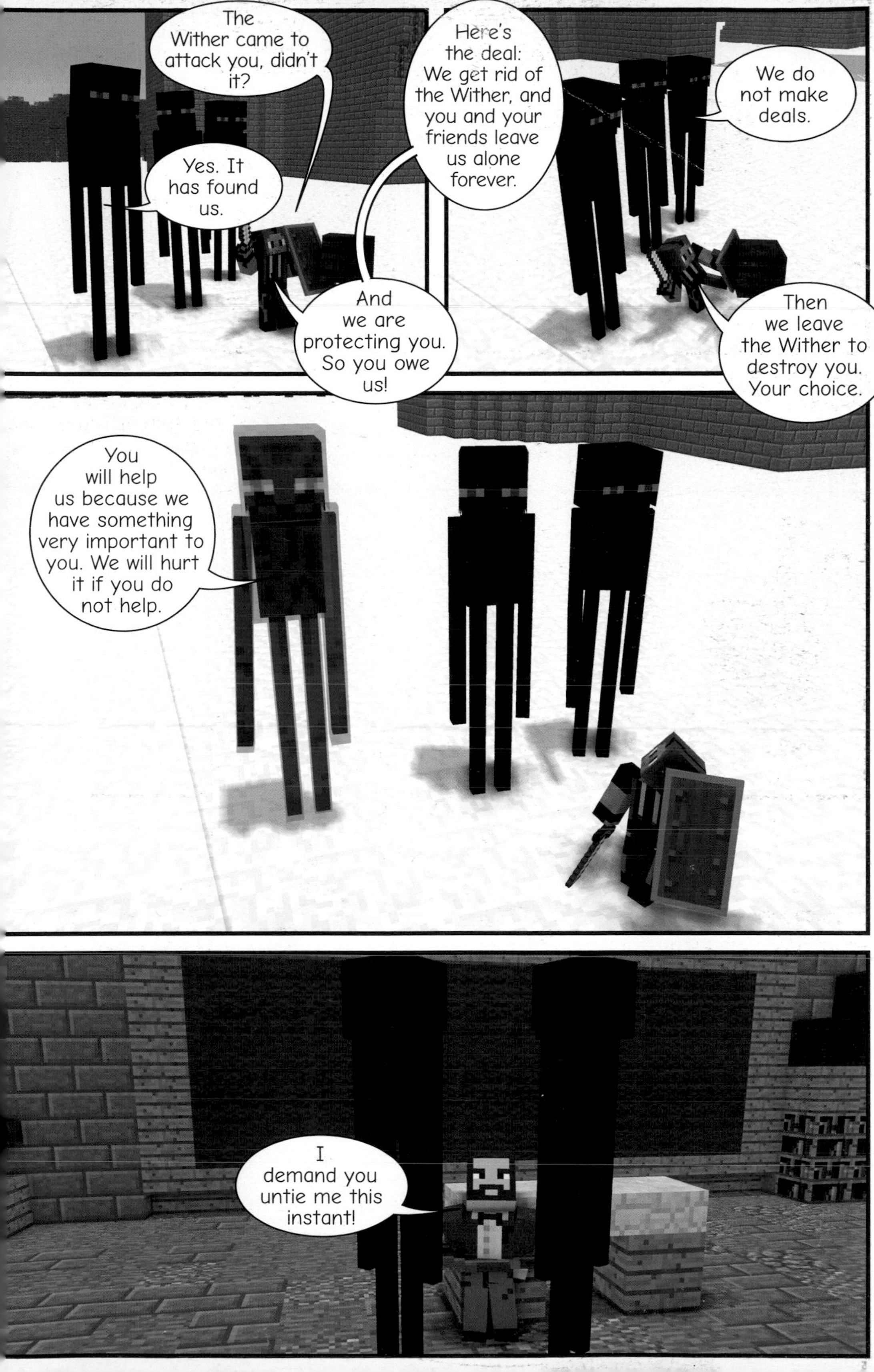
The Wither came to attack you, didn't it?
Yes. It has found us.
And we are protecting you. So you owe us!
Here's the deal: We get rid of the Wither, and you and your friends leave us alone forever.
We do not make deals.
Then we leave the Wither to destroy you. Your choice.
You will help us because we have something very important to you. We will hurt it if you do not help.
I demand you untie me this instant!

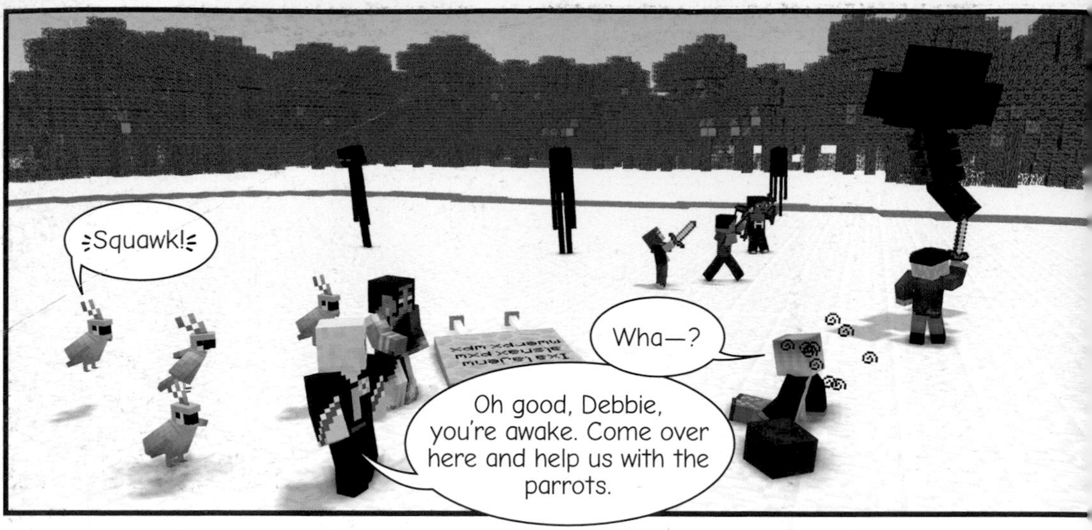
Squawk!
Wha—?
Oh good, Debbie, you're awake. Come over here and help us with the parrots.

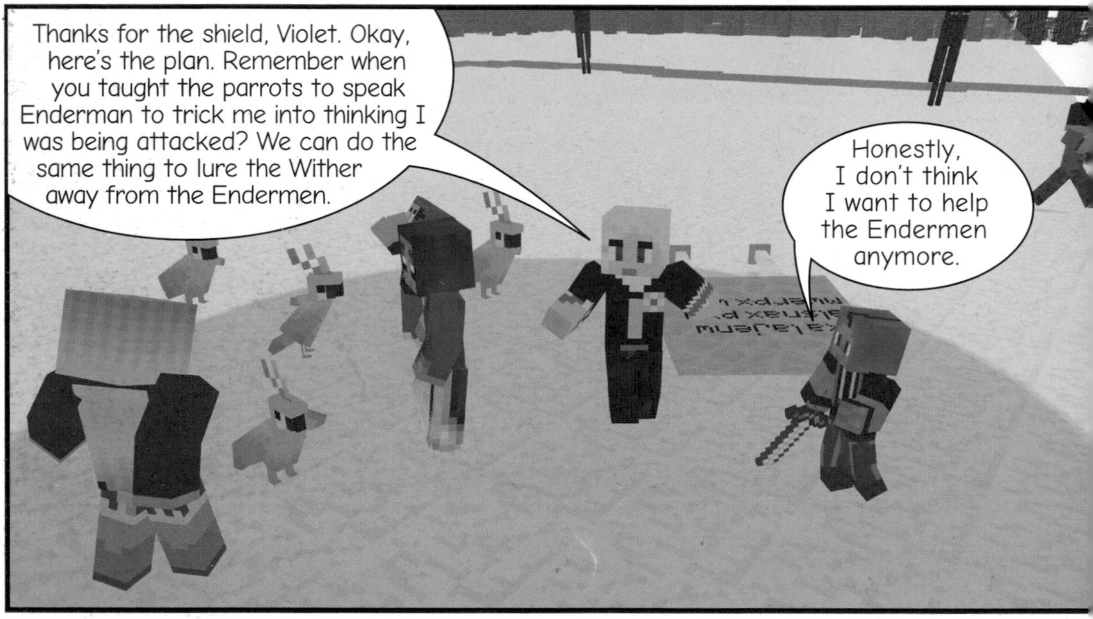
Thanks for the shield, Violet. Okay, here's the plan. Remember when you taught the parrots to speak Enderman to trick me into thinking I was being attacked? We can do the same thing to lure the Wither away from the Endermen.
Honestly, I don't think I want to help the Endermen anymore.

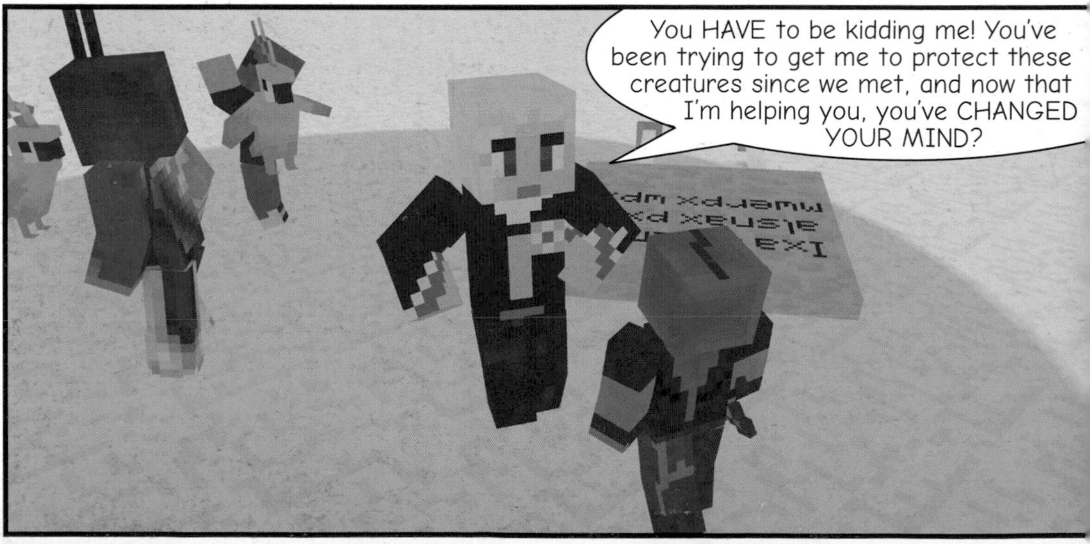
You HAVE to be kidding me! You've been trying to get me to protect these creatures since we met, and now that I'm helping you, you've CHANGED YOUR MIND?

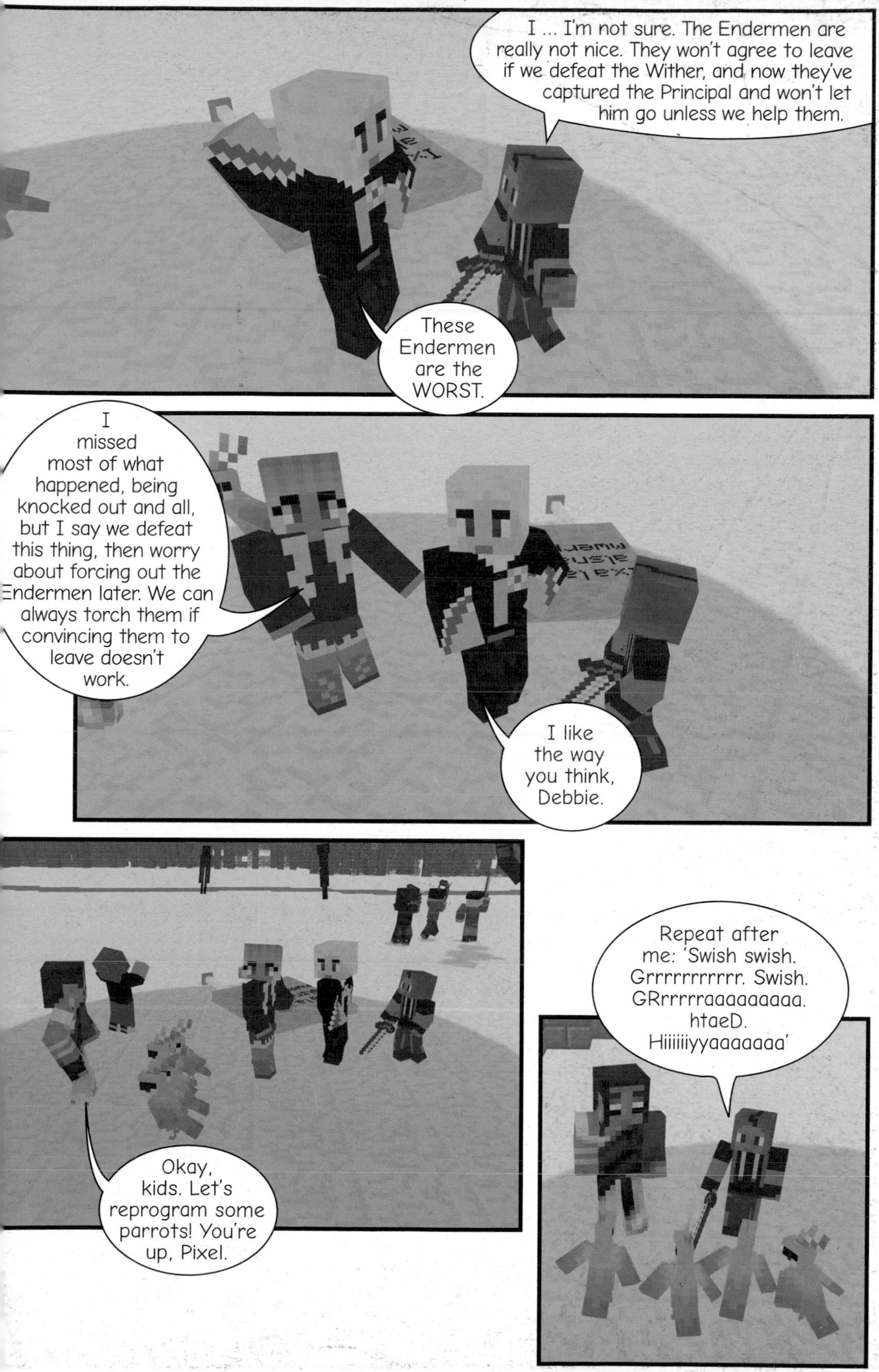
I ... I'm not sure. The Endermen are really not nice. They won't agree to leave if we defeat the Wither, and now they've captured the Principal and won't let him go unless we help them.
These Endermen are the WORST.
I missed most of what happened, being knocked out and all, but I say we defeat this thing, then worry about forcing out the Endermen later. We can always torch them if convincing them to leave doesn't work.
I like the way you think, Debbie.
Okay, kids. Let's reprogram some parrots! You're up, Pixel.
Repeat after me: 'Swish swish. Grrrrrrrrrr. Swish. GRrrrrraaaaaaaa. htaeD. Hiiiiiiyyaaaaaaa'

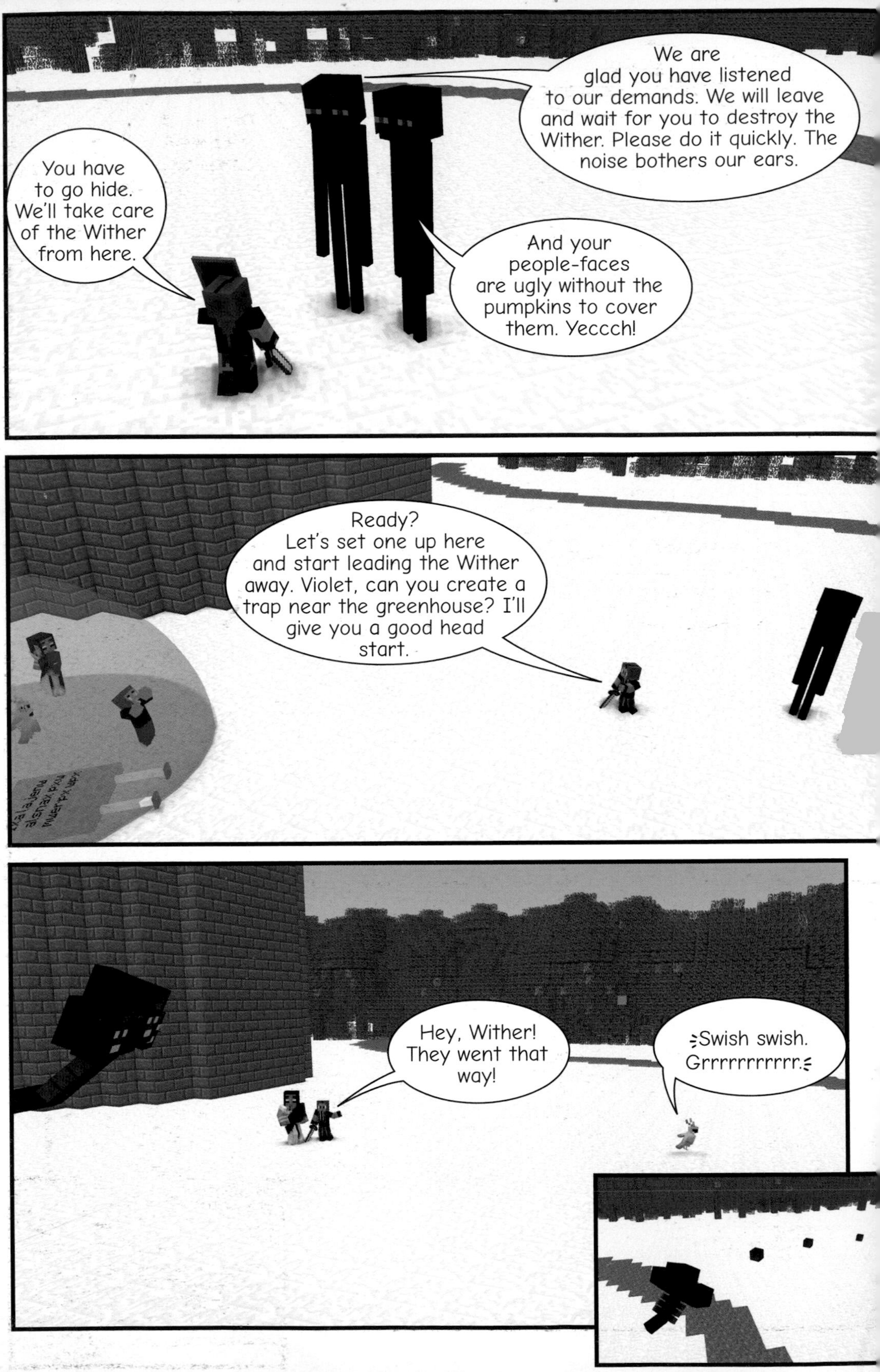
We are glad you have listened to our demands. We will leave and wait for you to destroy the Wither. Please do it quickly. The noise bothers our ears.
You have to go hide. We'll take care of the Wither from here.
And your people-faces are ugly without the pumpkins to cover them. Yeccch!
Ready? Let's set one up here and start leading the Wither away. Violet, can you create a trap near the greenhouse? I'll give you a good head start.
Hey, Wither! They went that way!
Swish swish. Grrrrrrrrrr.

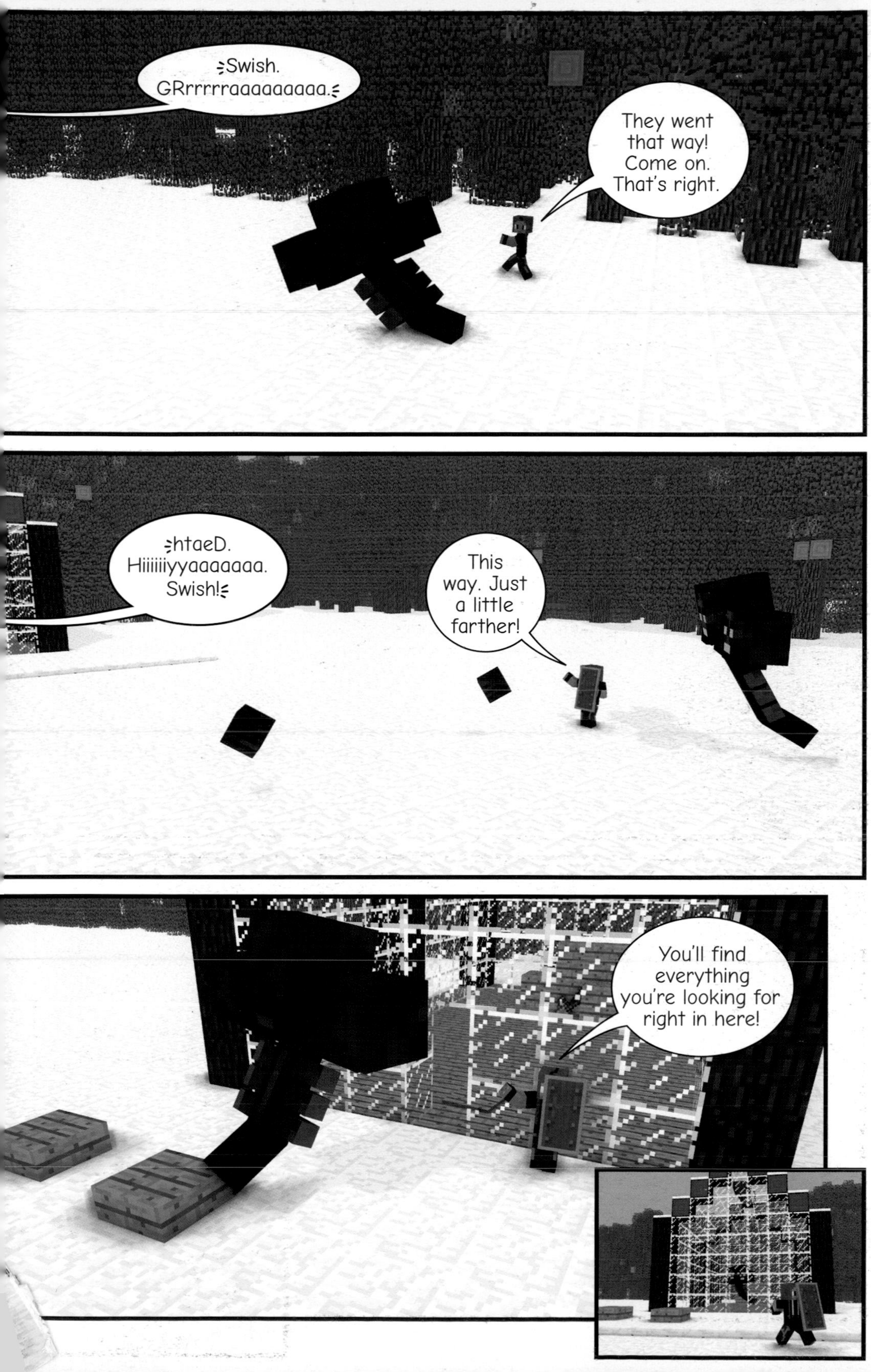
Swish. GRrrrrraaaaaaaaa.
They went that way! Come on. That's right.
htaeD. Hiiiiiiyyaaaaaaa. Swish!
This way. Just a little farther!
You'll find everything you're looking for right in here!

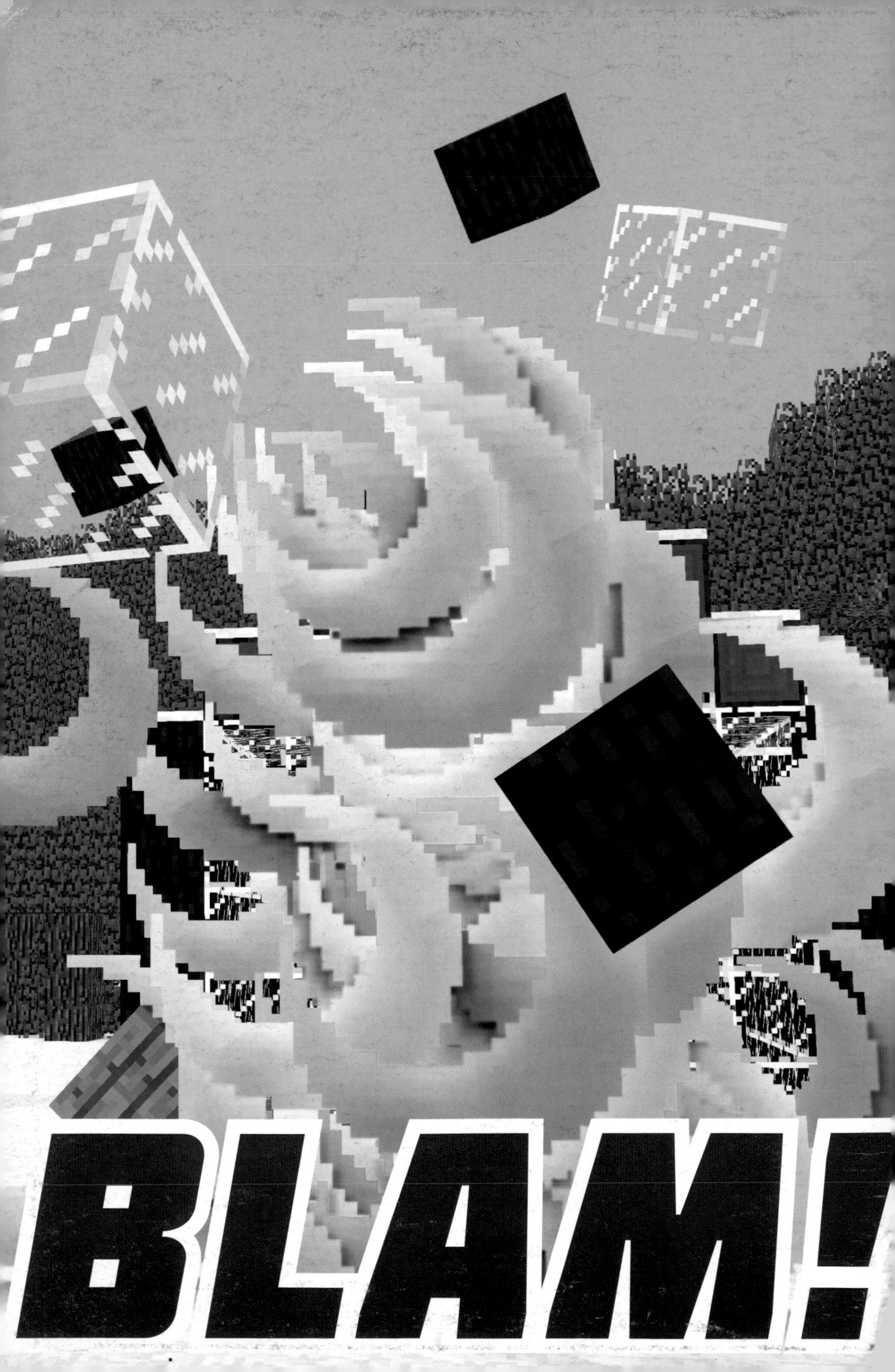
BLAM!

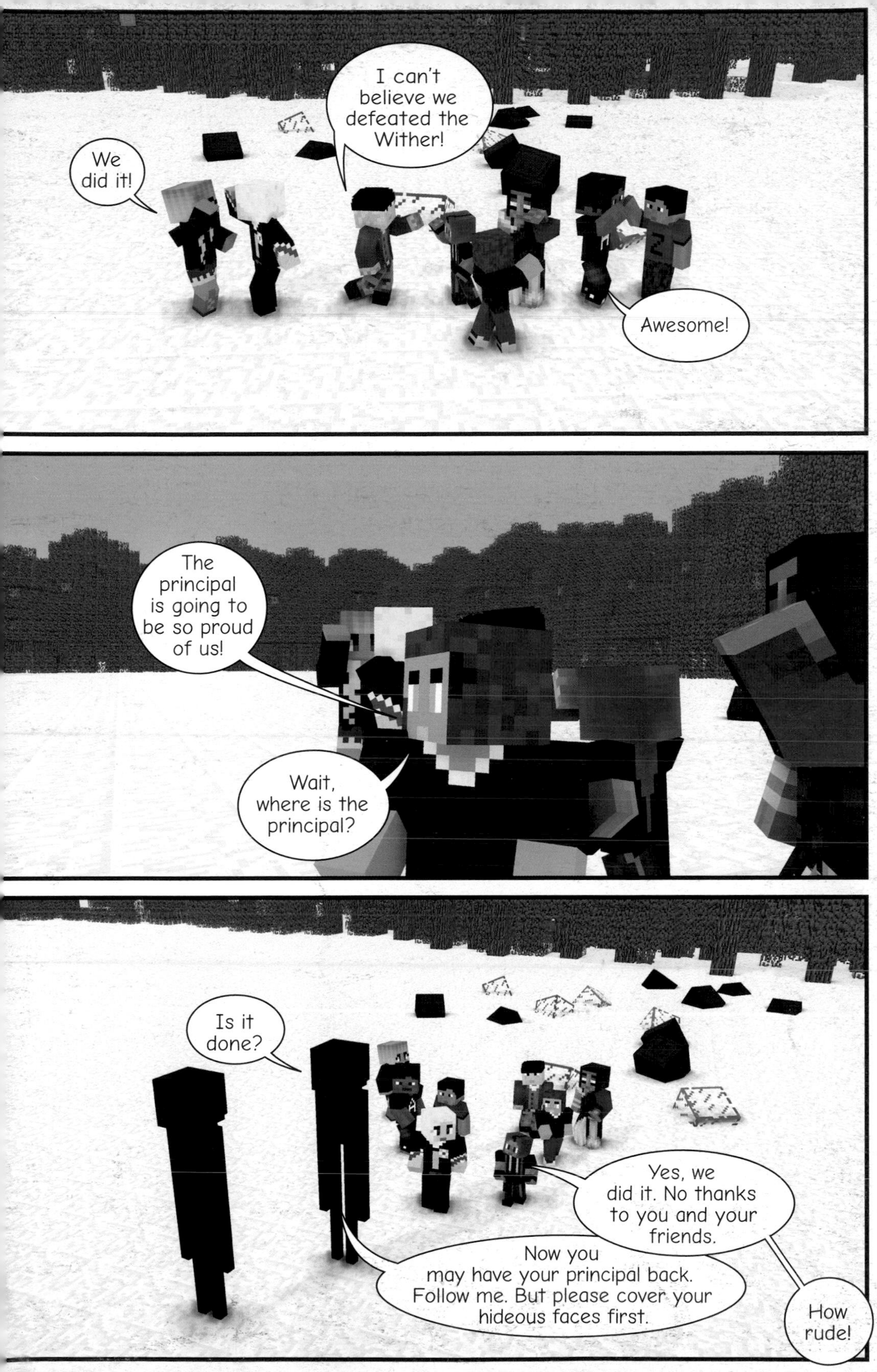
We did it!
I can't believe we defeated the Wither!
Awesome!
The principal is going to be so proud of us!
Wait, where is the principal?
Is it done?
Yes, we did it. No thanks to you and your friends.
Now you may have your principal back. Follow me. But please cover your hideous faces first.
How rude!

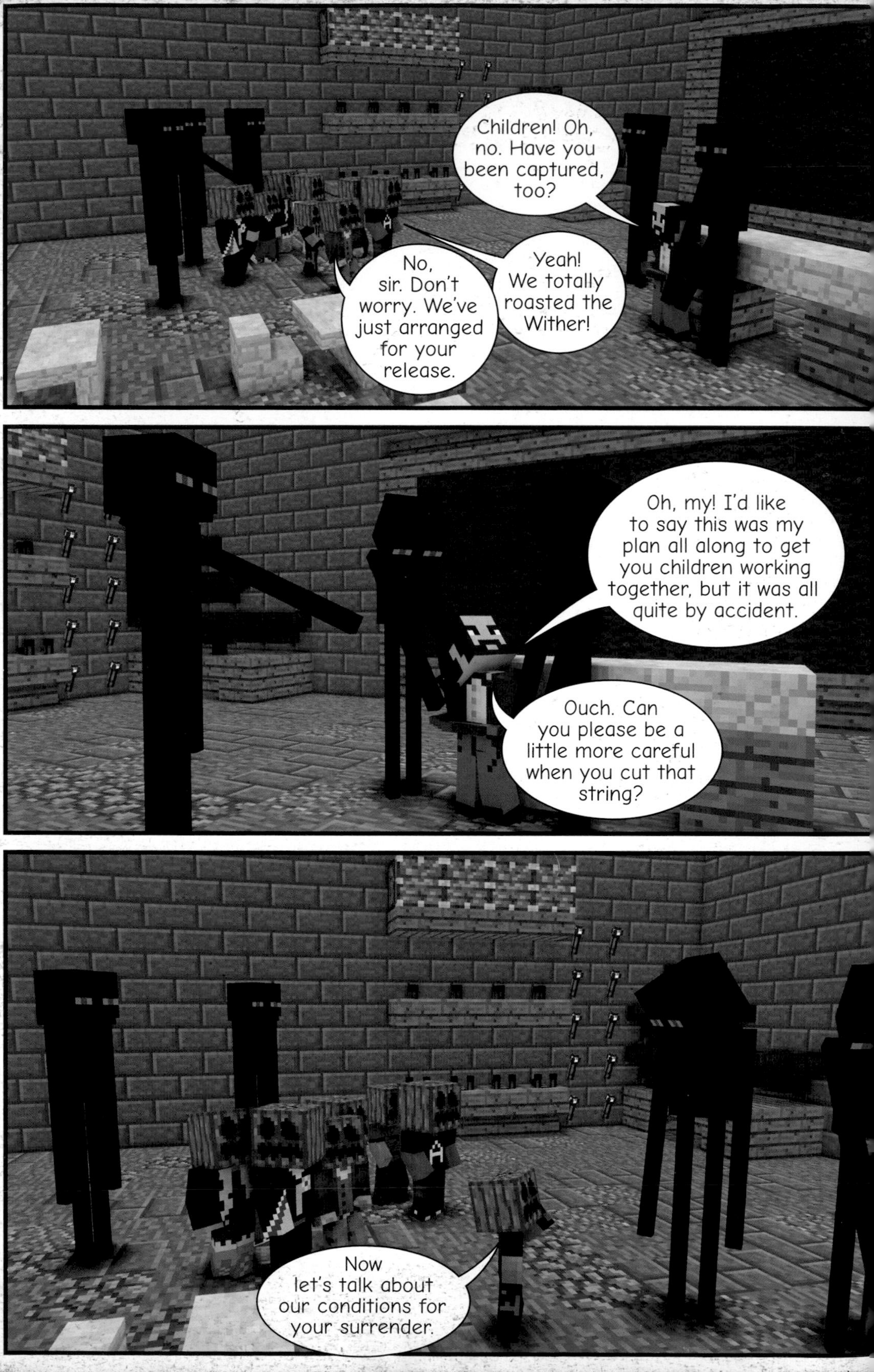

Children! Oh, no. Have you been captured, too?
Yeah! We totally roasted the Wither!
No, sir. Don't worry. We've just arranged for your release.
Oh, my! I'd like to say this was my plan all along to get you children working together, but it was all quite by accident.
Ouch. Can you please be a little more careful when you cut that string?
Now let's talk about our conditions for your surrender.

CHAPTER 13

THE FINAL
SHOWDOWN

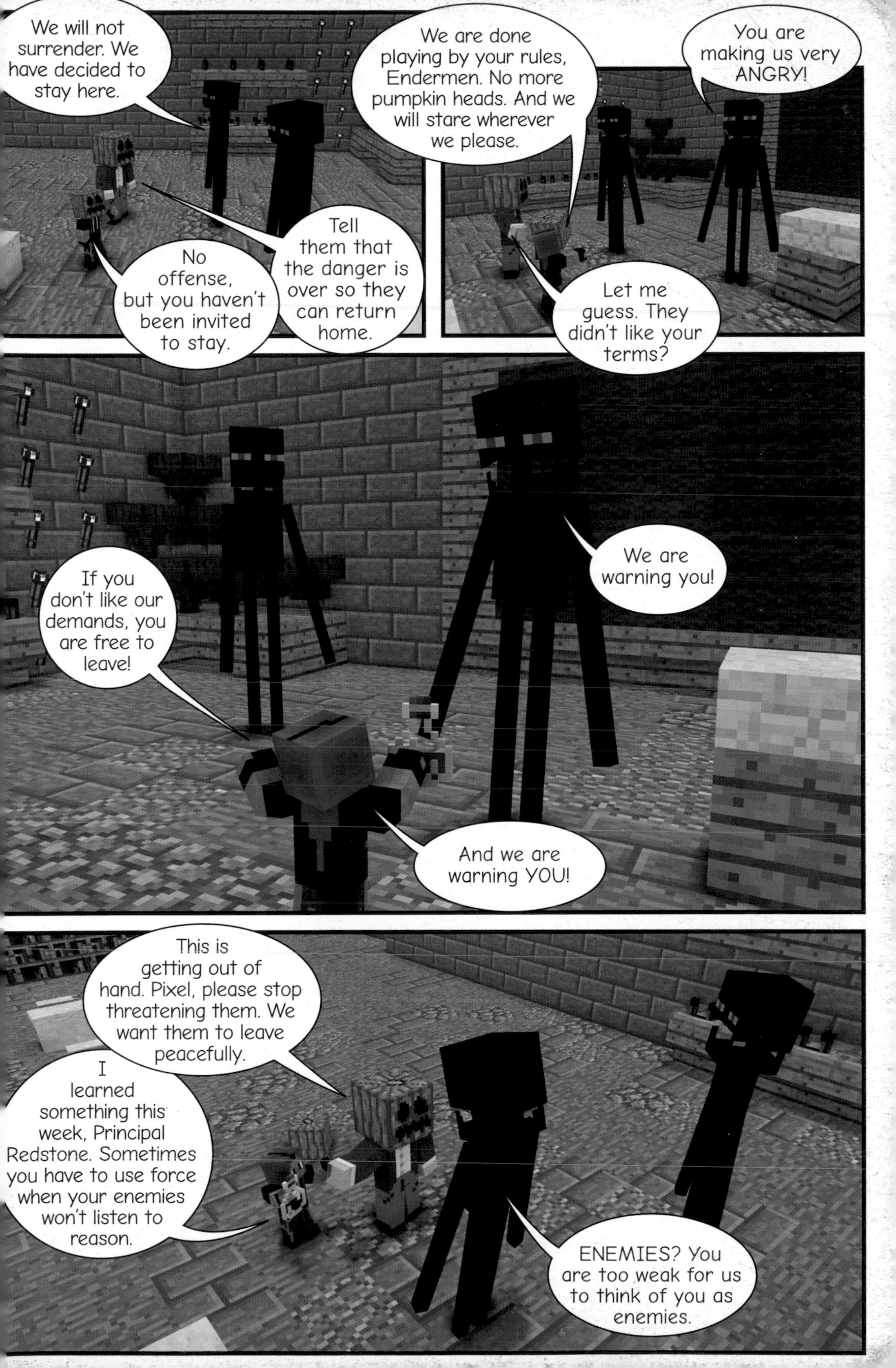
We will not surrender. We have decided to stay here.
We are done playing by your rules, Endermen. No more pumpkin heads. And we will stare wherever we please.
You are making us very ANGRY!
No offense, but you haven't been invited to stay.
Tell them that the danger is over so they can return home.
Let me guess. They didn't like your terms?
We are warning you!
If you don't like our demands, you are free to leave!
And we are warning YOU!
This is getting out of hand. Pixel, please stop threatening them. We want them to leave peacefully.
I learned something this week, Principal Redstone. Sometimes you have to use force when your enemies won't listen to reason.
ENEMIES? You are too weak for us to think of you as enemies.

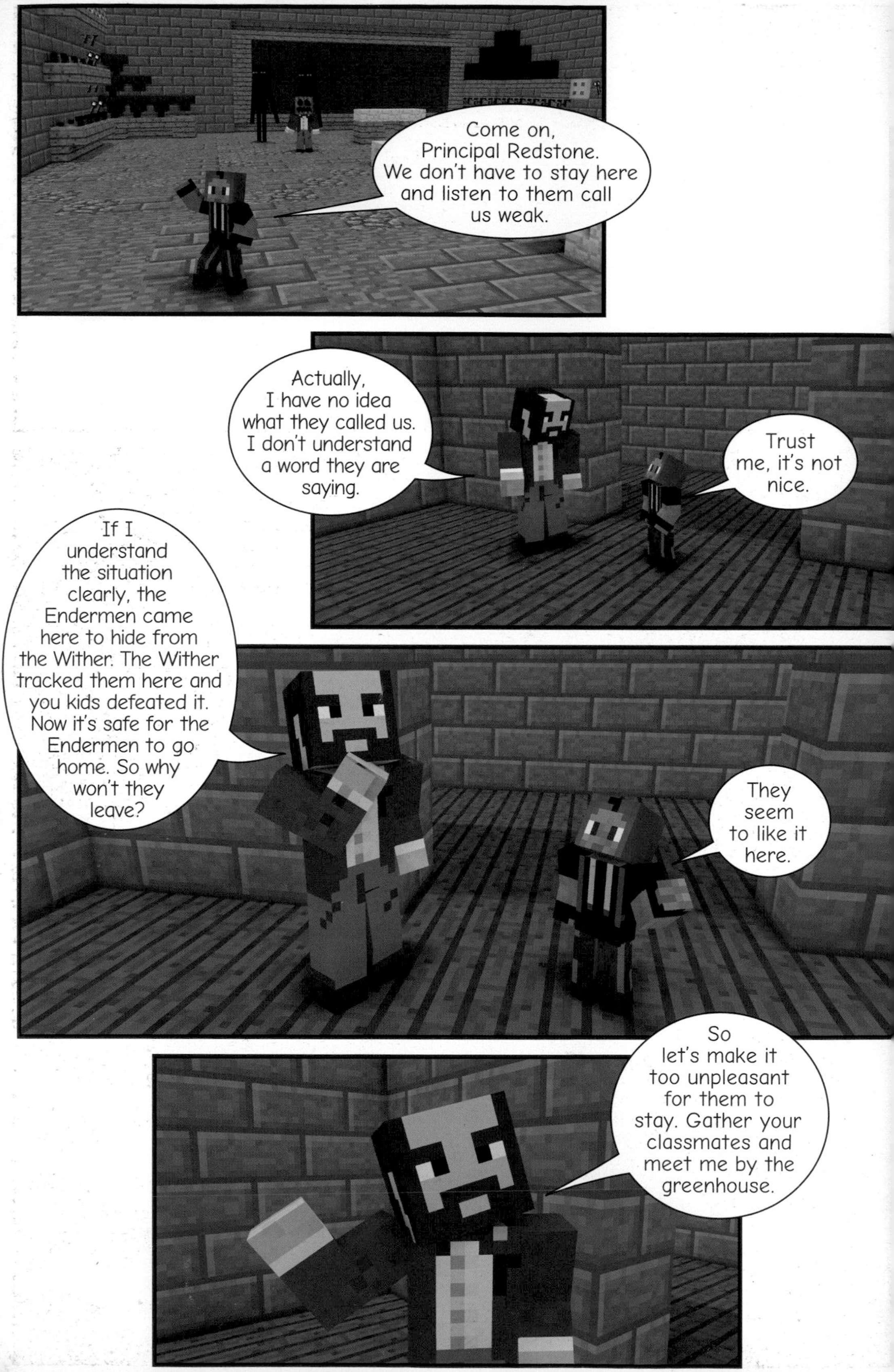
Come on, Principal Redstone. We don't have to stay here and listen to them call us weak.
Actually, I have no idea what they called us. I don't understand a word they are saying.
Trust me, it's not nice.
If I understand the situation clearly, the Endermen came here to hide from the Wither. The Wither tracked them here and you kids defeated it. Now it's safe for the Endermen to go home. So why won't they leave?
They seem to like it here.
So let's make it too unpleasant for them to stay. Gather your classmates and meet me by the greenhouse.

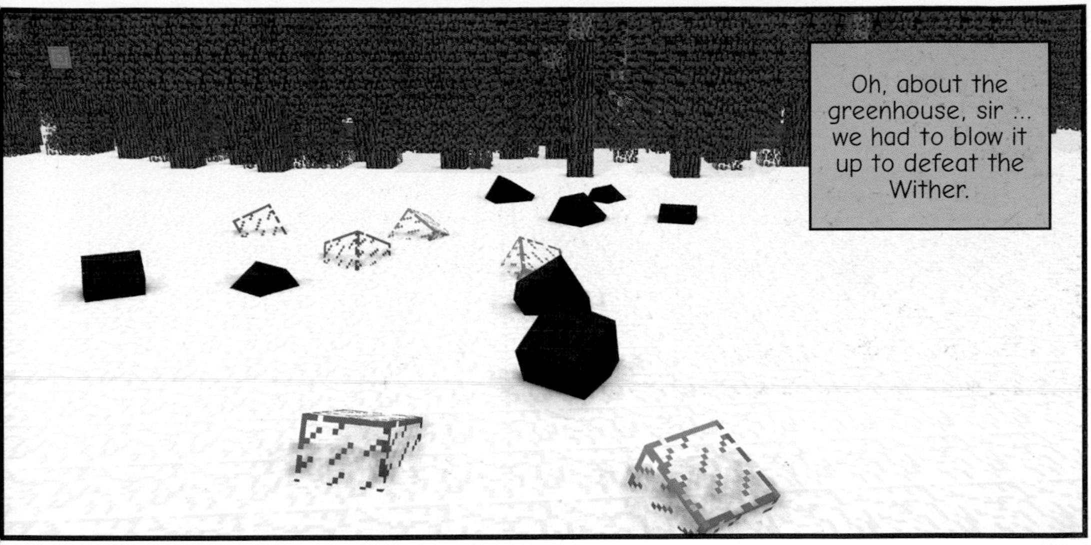
Oh, about the greenhouse, sir ... we had to blow it up to defeat the Wither.

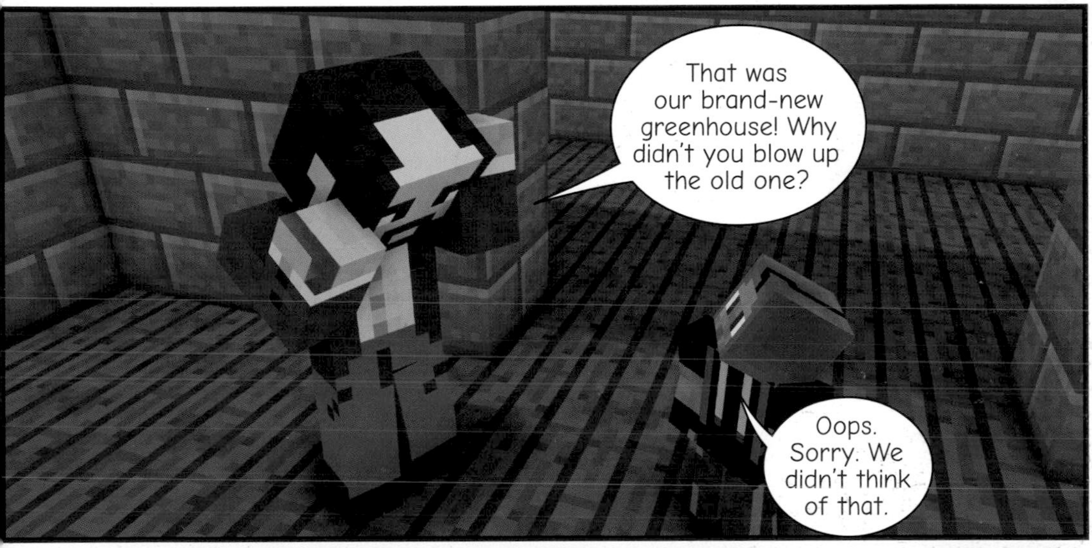
That was our brand-new greenhouse! Why didn't you blow up the old one?
Oops. Sorry. We didn't think of that.

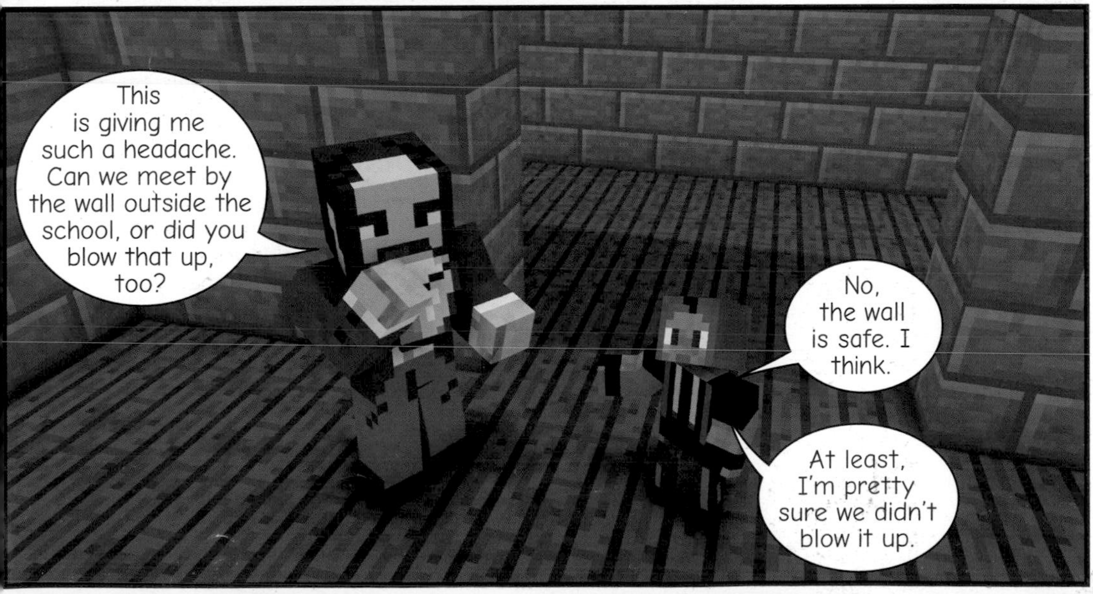
This is giving me such a headache. Can we meet by the wall outside the school, or did you blow that up, too?
No, the wall is safe. I think.
At least, I'm pretty sure we didn't blow it up.

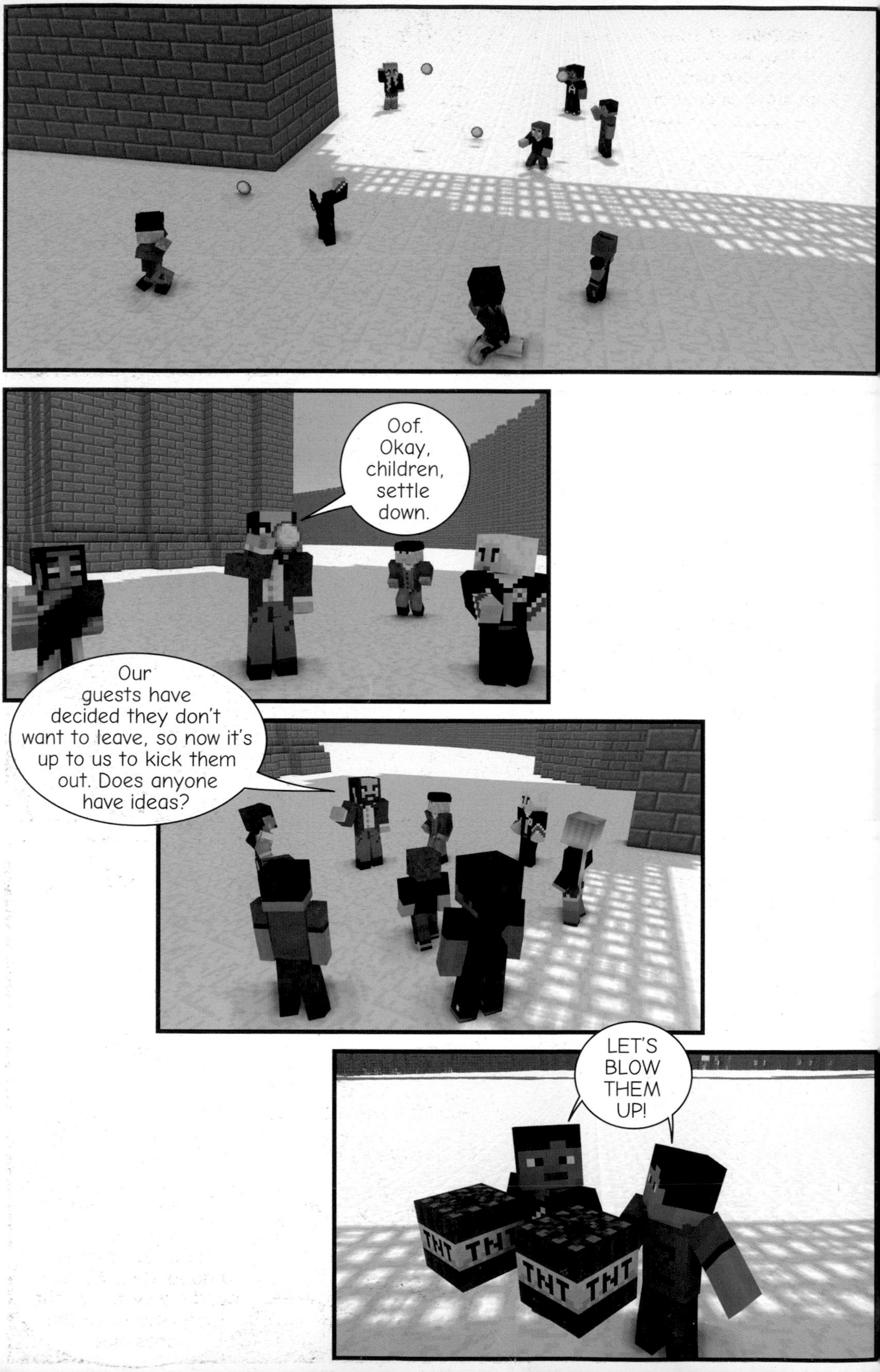
Oof. Okay, children, settle down.
Our guests have decided they don't want to leave, so now it's up to us to kick them out. Does anyone have ideas?
LET'S BLOW THEM UP!
TNT TNT
TNT TNT

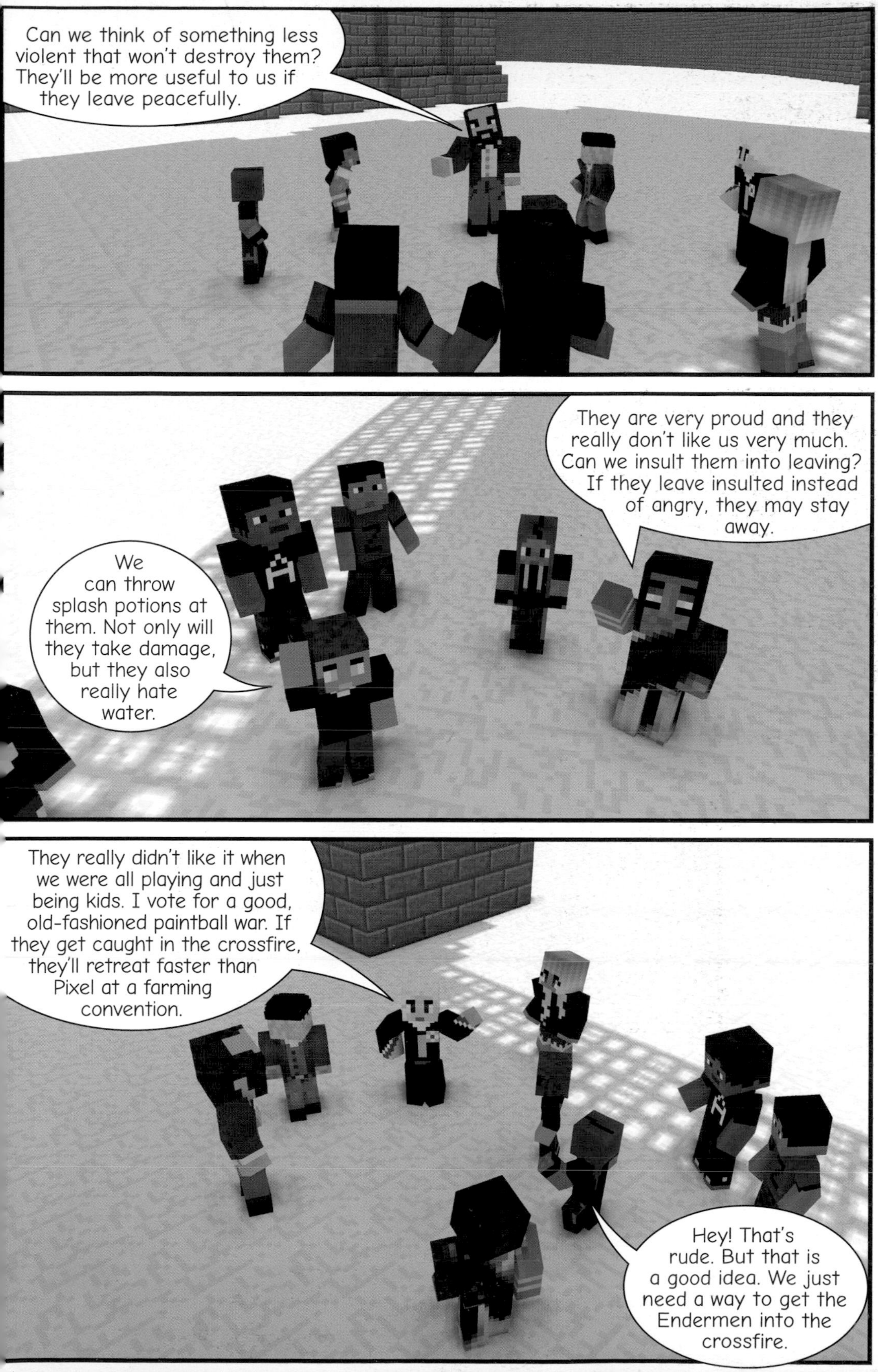
Can we think of something less violent that won't destroy them? They'll be more useful to us if they leave peacefully.
They are very proud and they really don't like us very much. Can we insult them into leaving? If they leave insulted instead of angry, they may stay away.
We can throw splash potions at them. Not only will they take damage, but they also really hate water.
They really didn't like it when we were all playing and just being kids. I vote for a good, old-fashioned paintball war. If they get caught in the crossfire, they'll retreat faster than Pixel at a farming convention.
Hey! That's rude. But that is a good idea. We just need a way to get the Endermen into the crossfire.

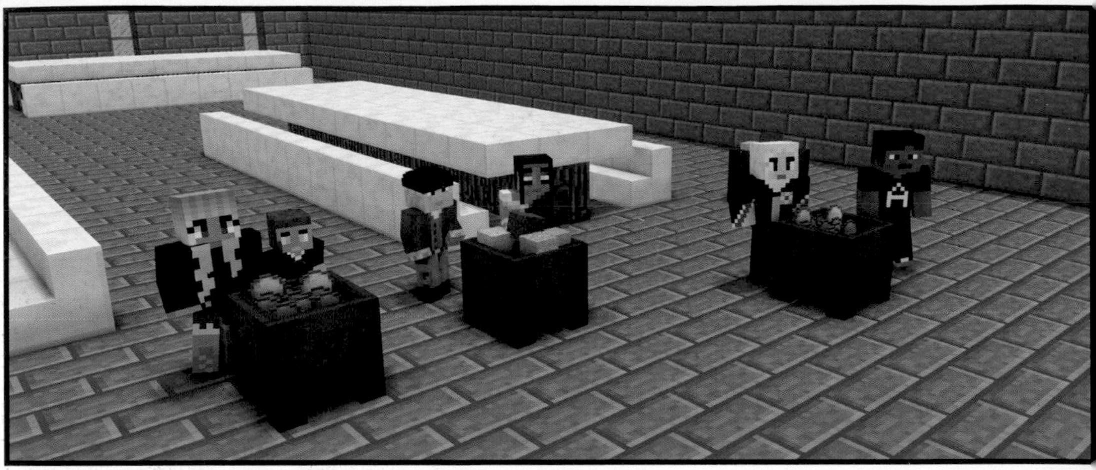

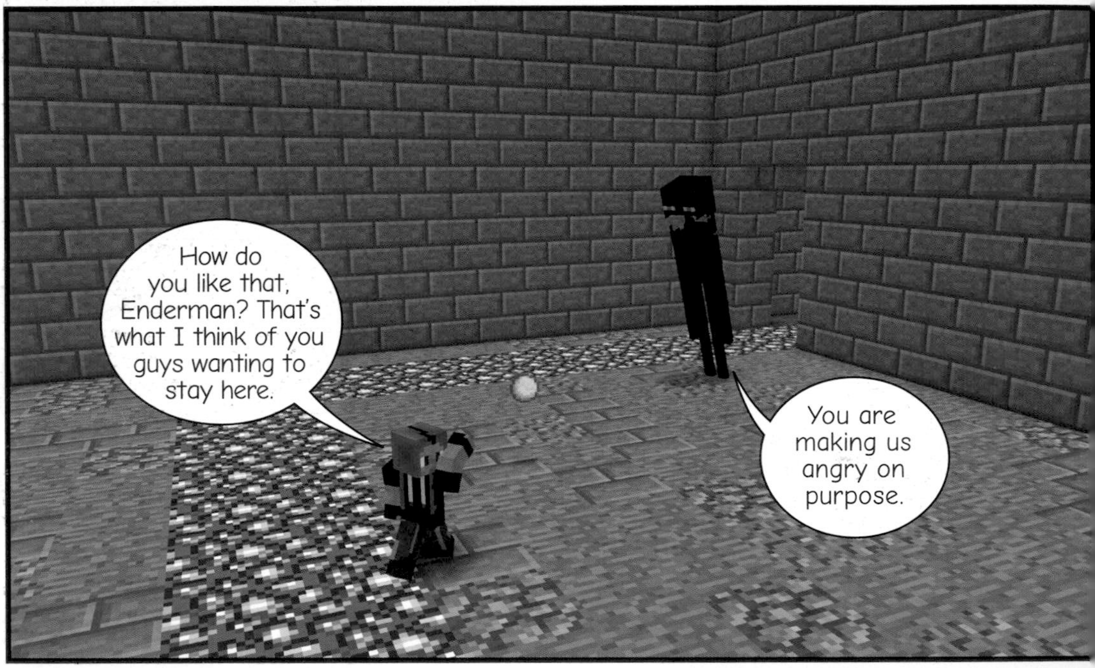

How do you like that, Enderman? That's what I think of you guys wanting to stay here.
You are making us angry on purpose.

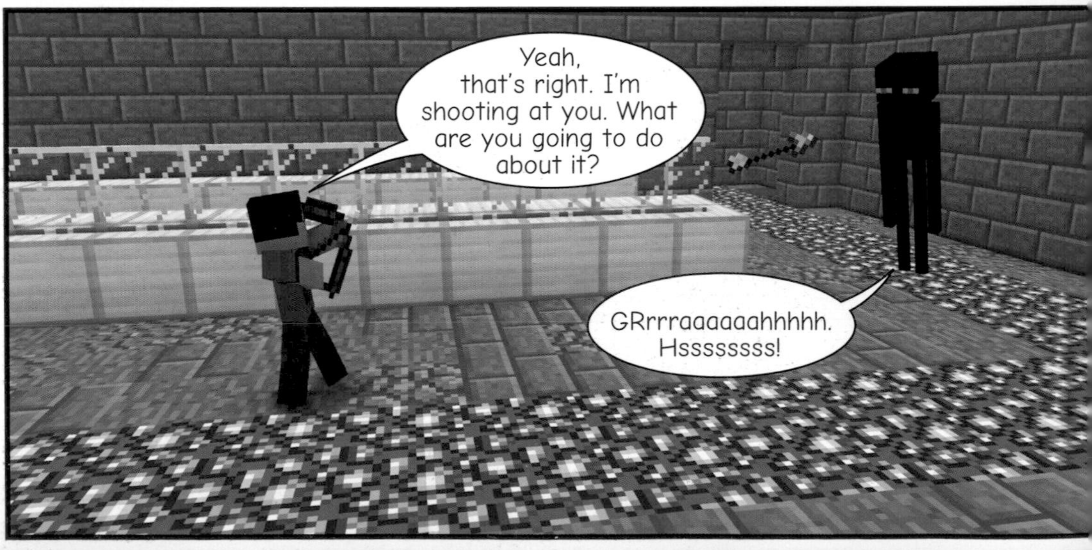

Yeah, that's right. I'm shooting at you. What are you going to do about it?
GRrrraaaaaahhhhh. Hsssssss!

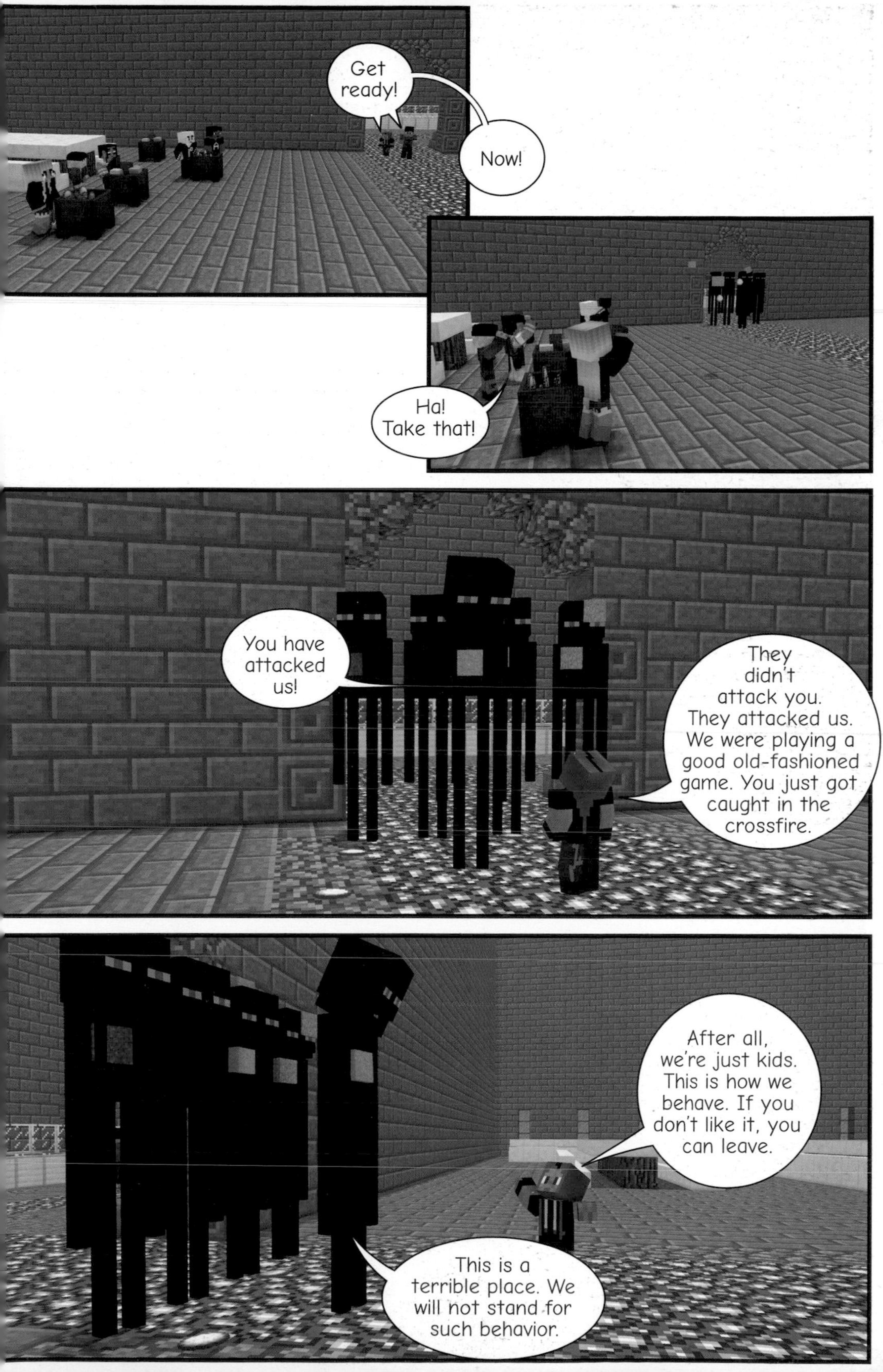

Get ready!
Now!
Ha! Take that!
You have attacked us!
They didn't attack you. They attacked us. We were playing a good old-fashioned game. You just got caught in the crossfire.
After all, we're just kids. This is how we behave. If you don't like it, you can leave.
This is a terrible place. We will not stand for such behavior.

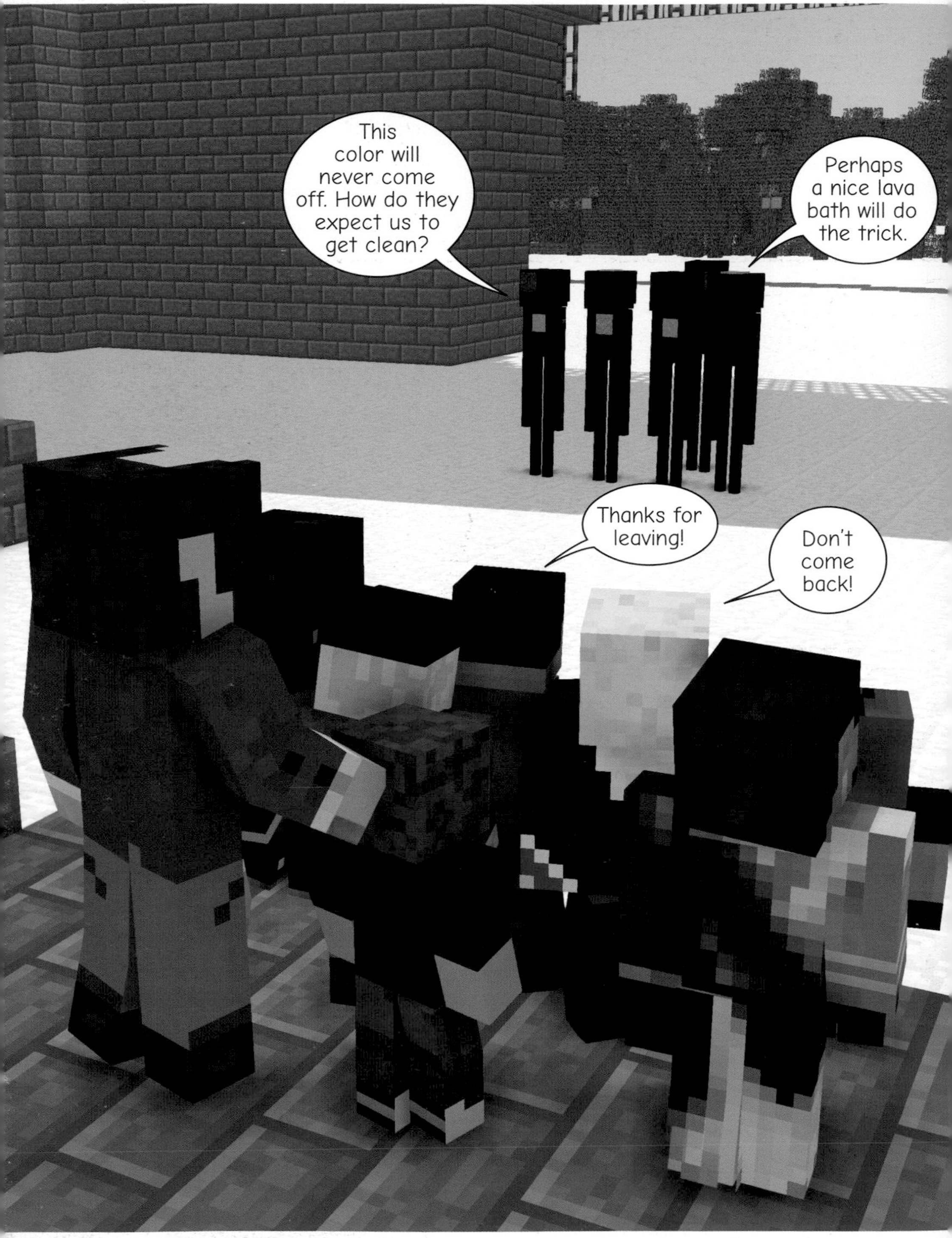
This color will never come off. How do they expect us to get clean?
Perhaps a nice lava bath will do the trick.
Thanks for leaving!
Don't come back!

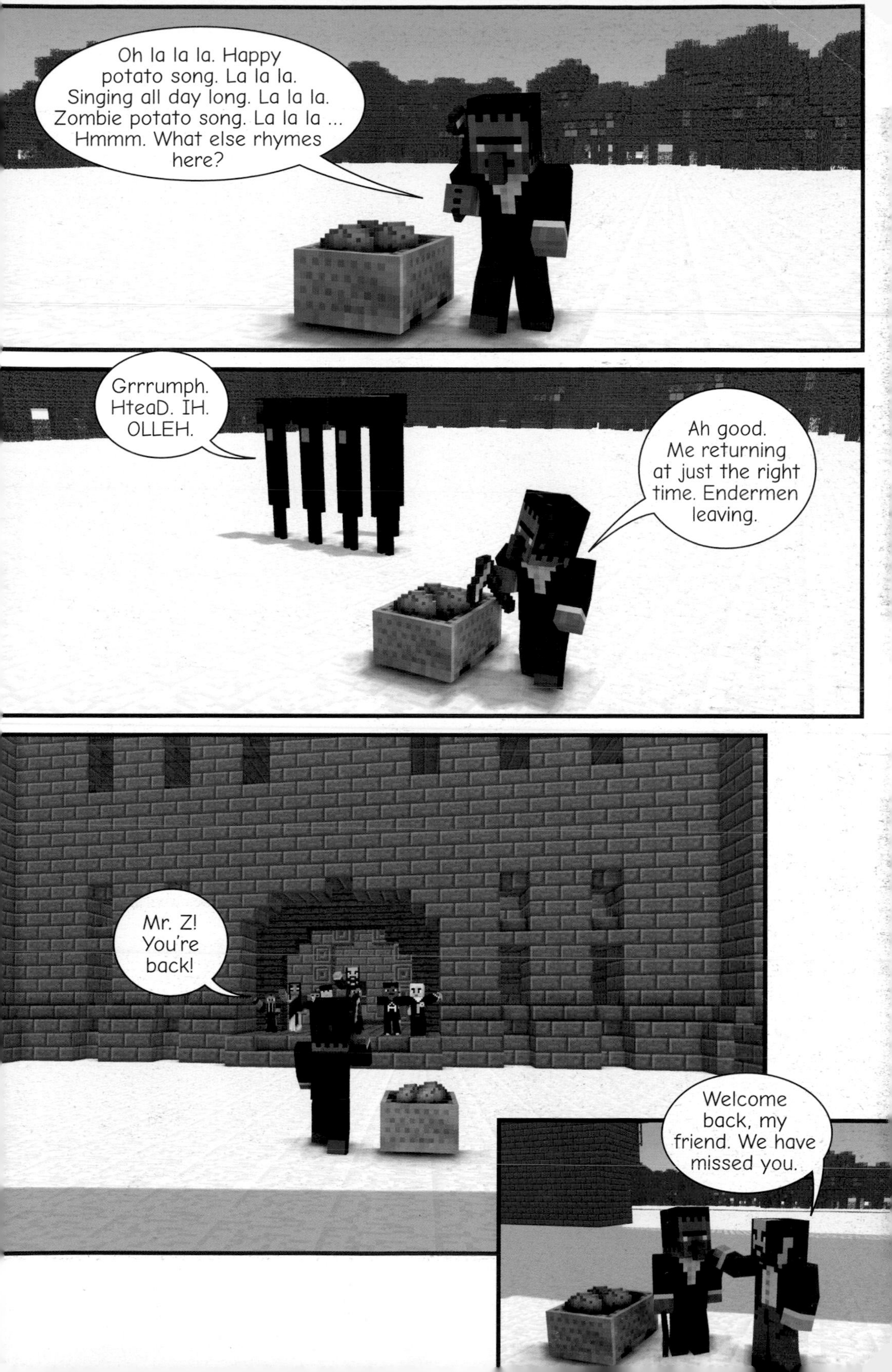

Oh la la la. Happy potato song. La la la. Singing all day long. La la la. Zombie potato song. La la la ... Hmmm. What else rhymes here?
Grrrumph. HteaD. IH. OLLEH.
Ah good. Me returning at just the right time. Endermen leaving.
Mr. Z! You're back!
Welcome back, my friend. We have missed you.

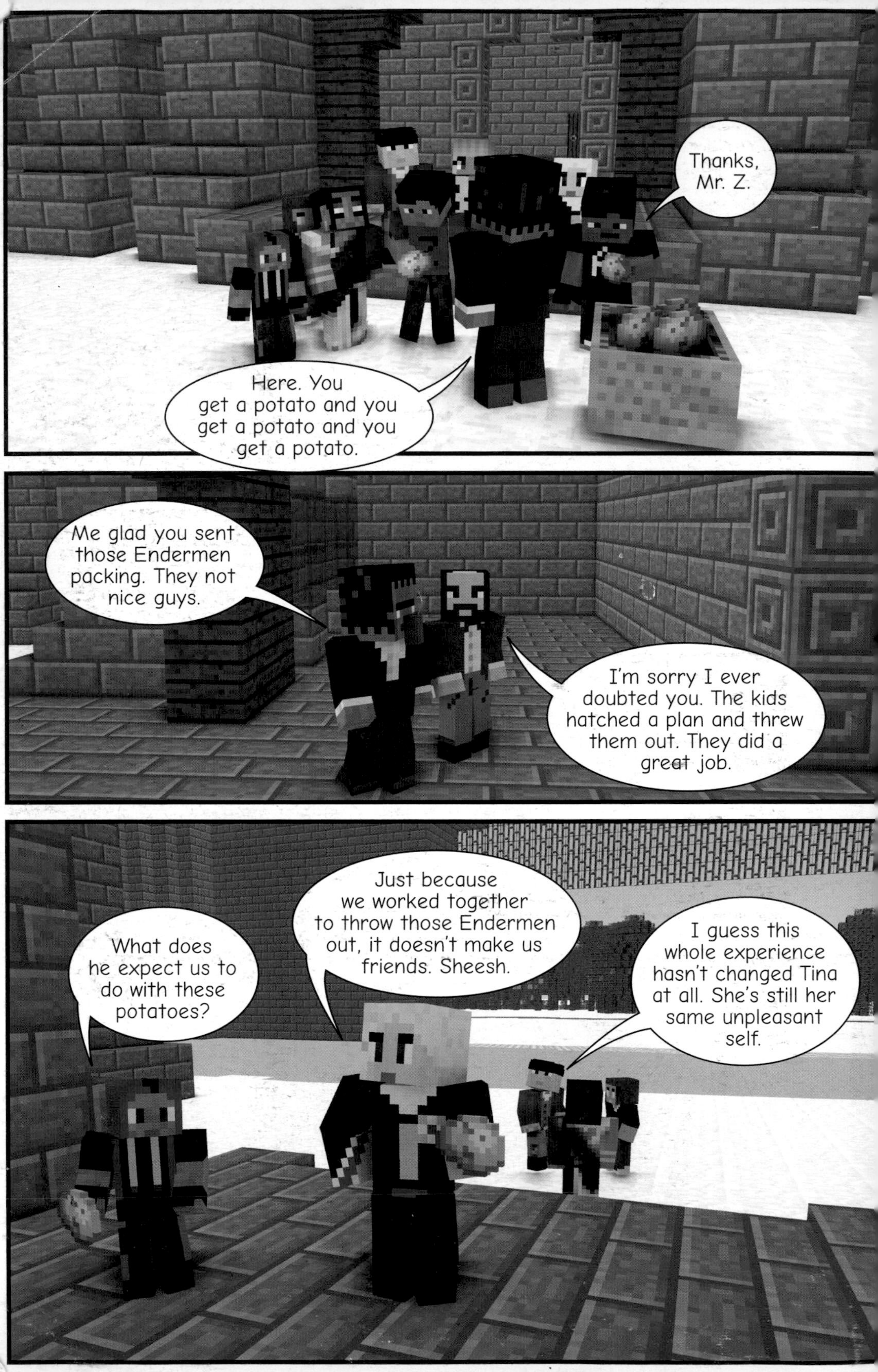
Thanks, Mr. Z.
Here. You get a potato and you get a potato and you get a potato.
Me glad you sent those Endermen packing. They not nice guys.
I'm sorry I ever doubted you. The kids hatched a plan and threw them out. They did a great job.
What does he expect us to do with these potatoes?
Just because we worked together to throw those Endermen out, it doesn't make us friends. Sheesh.
I guess this whole experience hasn't changed Tina at all. She's still her same unpleasant self.

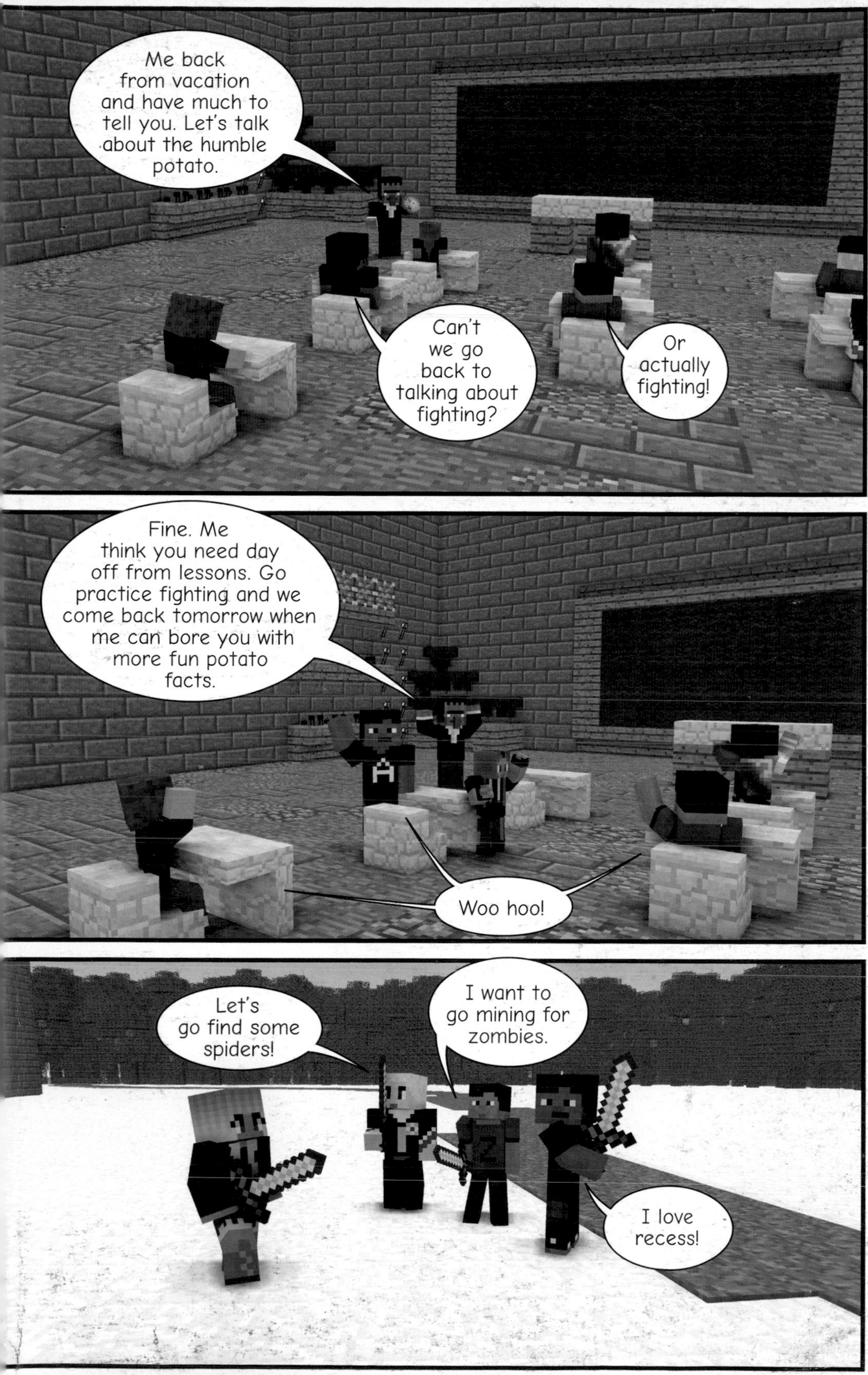
Me back from vacation and have much to tell you. Let's talk about the humble potato.
Can't we go back to talking about fighting?
Or actually fighting!
Fine. Me think you need day off from lessons. Go practice fighting and we come back tomorrow when me can bore you with more fun potato facts.
Woo hoo!
Let's go find some spiders!
I want to go mining for zombies.
I love recess!

JAN 2021

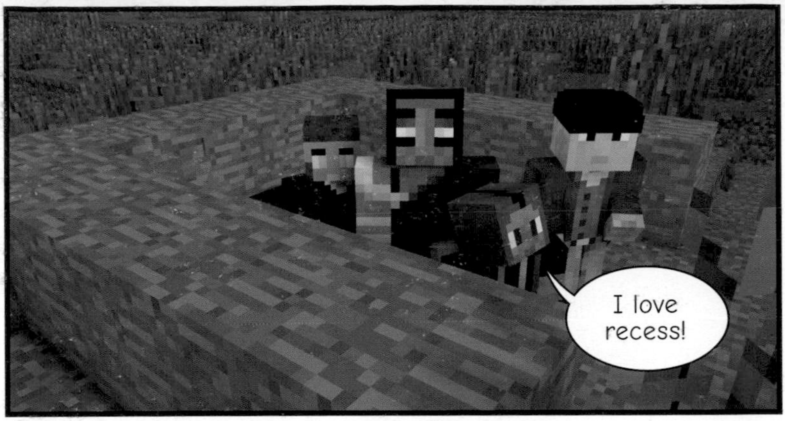
I love recess!

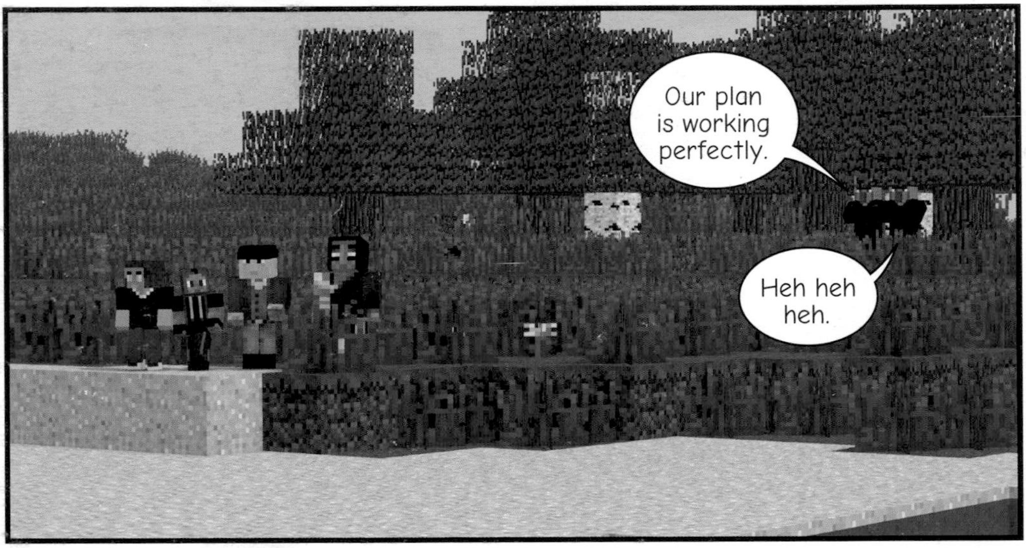
Our plan is working perfectly.
Heh heh heh.

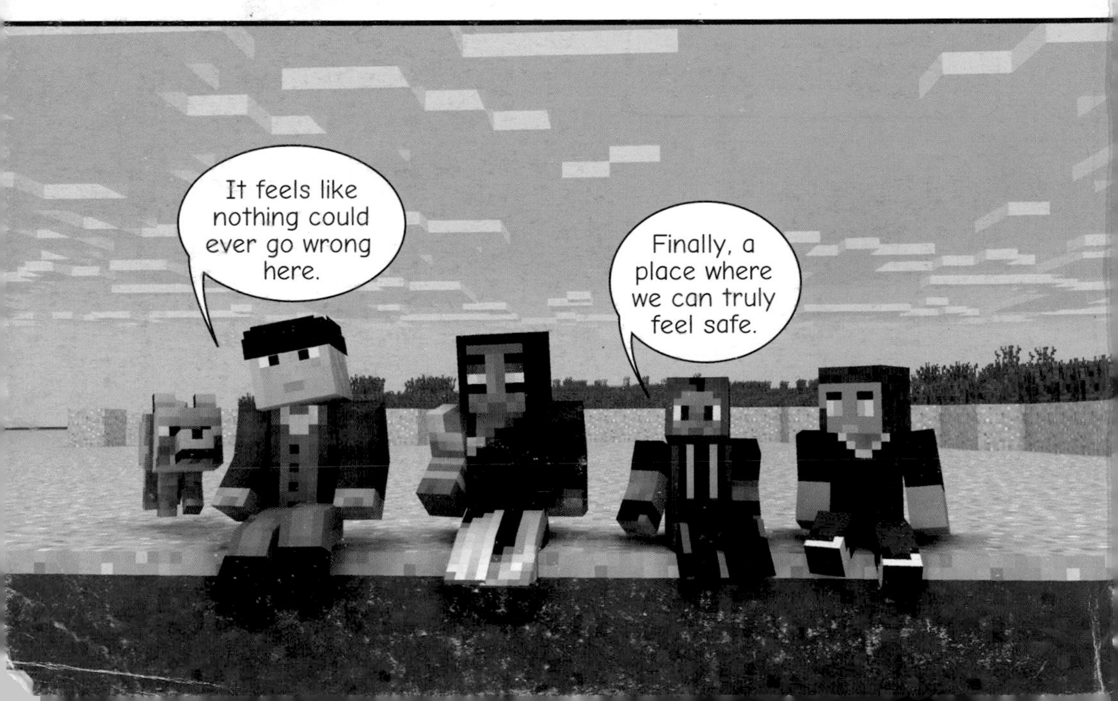
It feels like nothing could ever go wrong here.
Finally, a place where we can truly feel safe.